SIEGE TO THE THRONE

RELLMIRA DUOLOGY
BOOK TWO

LEAH MARA

PAPER HEART
PUBLISHING

Cover Design by Moonpress, www.moonpress.co
Map by Leah Mara
Ornamental Design by Alex

Ebook ISBN: 978-1-965527-03-0
Paperback ISBN: 978-1-965527-04-7
Hardcover ISBN: 978-1-965527-05-4

For anyone who's had their soft heart used as a tether—may you always find a way to fly.

KEYS TO THE CROWN
RECAP

After her mother's assassination, Kiera gave up being a princess to become a spy. The story starts with her first real mission after two years of training. It's mostly successful, and her mentor, Renwell, immediately gives her another mission—go undercover as a fellow prisoner to learn about a man who infiltrated a highly secure compound.

Kiera and Aiden meet in their shared prison cell and are quickly intrigued by each other. Aiden claims he needs a lot of gold, so Kiera offers the idea of stealing from the High Treasurer. They escape prison with the help of Aiden's best friend, Maz.

Together, they start planning the heist. Kiera trains as a dancer to go undercover at the High Treasurer's party while also trying to learn as much about Aiden as possible. She goes on a smuggling run with him and saves his friend Ruru from Shadow-Wolves—the elite night guard.

This ingratiates her with Aiden and his allies as she continues to slowly earn his trust while questioning the morality of her own actions. Her mentor, Renwell, increases the pressure on her to steal the gold and find out what Aiden needs it for.

They successfully pull off the heist—where Aiden and Kiera also give into their forbidden attraction by kissing. But just as their relationship heats up, Kiera finds out that Aiden is a secret heir in hiding who plans to assassinate her father, Weylin. He also reveals that Weylin killed his parents and stole the throne the night he was born.

Kiera convinces Aiden that she's still his ally. But then, Weylin demands that she find his stolen gold and betray the rebels or suffer punishment in their place. Instead of delivering Aiden, she helps rescue a family from Renwell's ire and leaves the city, breaking her mentor's rules.

Away from all their troubles, Aiden and Kiera share a romantic night in the woods. They talk of their pasts and futures, and Aiden reveals the planned date of his attack on Weylin.

When they arrive back in Aquinon, they discover that Maz is missing. Kiera is also grabbed and wakes up in a torture chamber next to him. She confronts a furious Renwell and, unwilling to give up any other secrets, she tells him the date of the attack to save Maz.

Renwell demands that she kill Aiden. Instead, she decides to reveal her true identity to him.

As she does, Aiden realizes that the knife she carries is the one he used to kill her mother, horrifying Kiera. Before she can attack Aiden, Nikella—Aiden's mentor—incapacitates Kiera.

Heartbroken at Kiera's lies, Aiden breaks into the palace to kill Weylin. But, having been freed by Ruru, Kiera interrupts the fight. Then she discovers that Aiden only killed her mother because she asked him to, so that Weylin couldn't.

Weylin orders Kiera to kill Aiden. When she doesn't, he commands Renwell to execute Kiera. Instead of obeying, Renwell beheads Weylin and takes his crown, revealing that this was his plan for many years.

Aiden forces Kiera to escape the palace with him, even

though she swears she will never forgive him for killing her mother.

They fight their way out of the city and flee on a ship, leaving Rellmira in more danger than ever, Renwell as the new tyrannical king, her brother and sister as his hostages, and war on the horizon.

AUTHOR NOTE

This is a high-stakes fantasy romance that contains content that might be triggering for some readers.

- Violence: death, battles, death of a loved one/relative, intense injuries
- Threat of sexual assault (not between main characters)
- Some graphic language
- A scene of consensual, explicit sex
- Verbal abuse

PRONUNCIATION GUIDE

- **Aiden:** ay-den
- **Kiera:** keeruh
- **Renwell:** ren-well
- **Weylin:** way-lin
- **Everett:** ev-rit
- **Delysia:** deh-liss-ee-uh
- **Korvin:** kor-vin
- **Mazkull:** maz-cuhl
- **Melaena:** muh-lay-nuh
- **Nikella:** ni-kel-luh
- **Ruru:** roo-roo
- **Sigrid:** sih-grid
- **Yarina:** yuh-ree-nuh
- **Davka:** dahv-kuh
- **Terraum, God of Earth and Architecture:** turawm
- **Arduen, God of Fire and Desire:** ar-dew-when
- **Viridana, Goddess of Life:** veer-i-dawn-uh
- **Mynastra, Goddess of Sea and Sky:** min-ass-truh
- **Rellmira (this story's kingdom):** rell-meer-uh

- **Aquinon** (the royal city of Rellmira): ah-qwi-non
- **Calimber** (the mining town north of Aquinon): cal-im-burr
- **Lancora** (name for the known world): lan-cor-uh
- **Pravara** (the southern Rellmiran province): pruh-var-uh
- **Winspere** (the northern Rellmiran province): win-speer
- **Niviath Sea:** ni-vee-ath see

DAG
KELDIKET
T
LANCORA

ARDUEN'S MOUNTAIN
URZOST VILLAGE
RIEL
YARGOTH CLAN
CALIMBER
MEDRIA RIVER
NORTH MEDRIA RIVER
SOUTH MEDRIA RIVER
WINSPERE
AQUINON
WARYN
RELLMIRA
PRAVARA
ELOREN ISLES

CHAPTER 1
KIERA

This ship was a cage. The sea, my prison.

Because once again, I'd locked myself in captivity with my enemy. But now he knew I was also his, and I had no key to release the shackles that grew heavier with every mile.

For the thousandth time on this gods-damned tiny ship, I rounded a stack of barrels, my hand instinctively twitching to the hilt of my mother's blade sheathed at my waist.

For there he was, standing at the railing, gazing out of the endless expanse of rolling waves.

Aiden Falcryn.

His black hair lifted in the cool breeze as he hung his head. He gripped the railing with long, strong fingers I knew too well.

But his father's falcon ring was now absent from them. I wanted to ask him why. My mind was drowning in a sea of *why, why, why.* But my voice refused to cross the hastily built wall between us.

Aiden hadn't spoken a word to me since we'd left the harbor.

He can't have you.

The words still induced a tiny shiver down my spine.

His dark clothes were still torn and stained from battle. Someone must've bandaged the knife wound on his side. I wondered if it pained him much. Or if he carried enough pain in his heart to numb the pain in his flesh—as I did.

Nikella had given me a salve for the many cuts I'd sustained trying to free myself from the ropes she'd bound me in.

Because of *him*. Because he'd finally learned the truth about me.

But I'd also learned the truth about him. Aiden was my father's would-be assassin. My mother's killer. And my . . . my . . . Nothing. Certainly not someone whose pain I should care about.

He was simply in my way, as he'd always been. But I refused to pick a fight with him on a ship full of his recovering allies.

So I did what I'd been doing the last two days we'd been sailing north—I turned on my boot heel and walked the other way.

Thank the gods, I'd gotten my "sea legs" as one of the bone-rattlers had informed me with a laugh when I could barely walk a straight line and kept staggering to the railing to puke my guts into the roiling waves.

They hadn't spoken to me much since then, but I felt their curious stares follow me as they clambered along the ropes and sails of *Mynastra's Wings*. I hadn't been with their original horde of fighters taking down the Den, yet I'd fled Aquinon on their ship, so who was I?

Nobody asked, and I didn't tell.

Silence had become my only weapon in a cage no one else could see.

A few of the Dags tried to congratulate me on my excellent use of fireseeds against the Wolves. But I withdrew from them as well.

They didn't know I was the reason those Wolves were there in the first place. They didn't know I was the reason they'd lost twenty-one members of their clan—eighteen to the Wolves and three on the ship due to their injuries. The bone-rattlers had lost fourteen of their own as well.

I'd demanded the exact numbers from Nikella instead of Aiden, who'd spent most of the last two days doing what he could for the injured and the dead.

From afar, I'd watched them slide the bodies into the sea. The Dags had sung while the sailors clasped their strings of bones and murmured prayers for Mynastra to treasure their dead brethren's bones in her bed.

I'd whispered my own prayers . . . and my apologies.

Afterward, I'd paced the deck a hundred times, guilt and rage pounding my heart like the cold waves that crashed over the railing.

But I preferred it over sleeping in my little hammock strung up in the ship's belly. Because, in my sleep, another man was there.

The architect of so much pain in my life. The reason I was fleeing Aquinon, abandoning my brother and sister to an unknown fate. The mentor who'd beheaded my father and taken his crown.

Renwell. As much as I battled him out of my thoughts during the day, he always found me in my dreams. Taunting me, hunting me, strapping me to Korvin's table and killing my family members one by one until I begged for mercy.

That look in his eyes—when he'd shot an arrow at me and missed as the sea pulled me away from him—I wouldn't be able to hide from him for long.

And I didn't plan to.

A large shadow blocked my path toward the other end of the ship. Reluctantly, I looked up into the bright blue eyes of Maz's youngest sister, Yarina. She'd been one of the Dag warriors to thank me for my resourcefulness, her bloodied scythes sheathed on her back, sweat dripping from her golden braids.

My heart twisted in my chest. Seeing her face reminded me of Maz. Fierce, lovable Maz, who was lying with the other injured warriors while he recovered from Korvin's flaying. Again, because of me.

Yarina folded her arms over her chest and stared me down. "Mazkull wants to see you."

I tried to sidestep her. "I can't."

She blocked me again, lifting one eyebrow with a smirk. "Got some other engagement planned? Another lap around the ship? I can tell you the scenery won't change."

"He needs to heal, not chase me down for conversation," I snapped.

Yarina's eyes narrowed. "Look, I don't know what happened to you back there or why you're here with us, but my brother has been asking for you since he found out you were on this ship." She grimaced. "He threatened to come get you himself and ruin the paste I just painstakingly applied to his sorry back. So if you care about his recovery, you'll come visit him."

Gods damn it, Maz, you don't want to see me. Unless . . .

My breathing hitched. Had Aiden finally told him what I'd done?

My only weapon was silence, but Aiden wielded the far sharper truth. I'd been waiting for him to use it.

Nikella was the only other one on board who knew who I was and what I'd done. But somehow, I knew she wouldn't say a word.

I studied Yarina's expression. Exasperated, sure. But not angry. Not disgusted.

She gestured toward the hatch. "After you, Kiera."

I grit my teeth. I couldn't hide forever, but I'd hoped I

wouldn't be on a ship in the middle of the Niviath Sea when I faced my reckoning.

Perhaps the truth would hurt me less if it came from my mouth. But the retaliation from dozens of betrayed Dags and bone-rattlers was sure to crush me just the same.

I slowly made my way to the hatch and stumbled down the stairs into darkness. "How is he?"

"Well enough, I suppose. Got him good and drunk after the funerals. He wishes he could've helped us kill more of those bastard Wolves. As do I." A snarl darkened her voice. "Especially that torturer, Korvin. My sisters and I had *plans* for that weasel."

The scars on my back itched as we tramped down the creaking corridor. I still wasn't entirely convinced a monster like that *could* be killed.

"What of your other sisters?" I asked. "Davka and Sigrid?" I'd learned their names from Nikella.

"Sigrid lost her left eye, but one of the bone-rattlers gave her a leather eye patch she loves." Bile rose in my throat, but Yarina continued as if such news were commonplace. "Davka has burns up and down her body from a burning Wolf that attacked her, but she said Aiden's salve soothed the pain."

An entirely unwelcome, unwarranted thought slammed into my mind— that of Aiden rubbing ointment into Davka's skin the same way he'd cared for the knife wound I'd gotten from a Wolf.

I crushed the image—and the squirm of jealousy that accompanied it.

You can't have feelings for a man who had his sword to your throat mere days ago. Who stabbed your mother in the heart. Regardless of what he says about why.

"I hope their injuries heal quickly," I murmured.

We halted in front of the infirmary door. I'd never been inside, avoiding it as though it had teeth and claws.

Gods damn your little weaknesses.

I clenched my trembling fingers and shoved the door open.

A gust of stale air tinged with salt and iron nearly made me retreat. But Yarina was crowding my back as she herded me toward her brother, who was lying facedown on a cot. I feared for the flimsy bed under Maz's massive bulk.

Several Dags and a few bone-rattlers occupied the other cots that littered the low-ceilinged room. Swinging lanterns bathed them in pools of yellow light.

Nikella sat in a corner with a Dag man, threading white bandages between each of his burned fingers. But her sharp eyes, so eerily like her brother's, speared me from across the room.

"As requested, you great oaf," Yarina announced. "Now you can stop threatening to ruin my excellent healing work."

Maz's head swiveled around, and he gave me a sideways grin. "Ah, lovely, there you are! I nearly didn't believe Nikella when she said you were on the ship. But I know our illustrious Teacher would never lie." He stretched out a massive hand. "Sit with me before I go mad with boredom."

My stomach churned. Aiden had kept the truth sheathed. But why? What was he waiting for?

I grasped Maz's rough hand and sank to the wooden floor beside him.

Yarina flopped onto an empty cot. "Aiden says you only need a few more days of treatment, Mazkull. Grandmother would put us on night-watch duty for a month if we let you run around re-opening your wounds."

"I'm fine," Maz muttered, the spark in his blue eyes dimming.

My gaze darted to his exposed back. The shiny pink skin where his mountain tattoo used to be was still raw in a few places. Shadows danced over my vision.

Maz's screams. Blood and skin discarded on the cave floor. Korvin's flaying knife and twisted grin.

"Kiera?"

I jerked my gaze back to Maz's concerned one.

"Are you all right? Nikella said you weren't gravely injured, but that's all she would say. And Aiden has been lost in his own head, barely speaking. What happened with you and Ruru? Did your side of the plan work?"

I swallowed hard. "Ruru . . . Ruru was alive and well the last I saw of him." Except now he was alone in a city controlled by Renwell. "He still has your whistler."

"You gave someone your whistler?" Yarina interjected. She slid one of her scythes from its harness and stroked it lovingly. "I could never part with Death Drinker here or her twin, Soul Stealer."

Maz rolled his eyes. "We're not all as in love with our weaponry as you are, little sister."

"Were you not going to get your lost axe inked on your skin?" I asked him.

Yarina snorted, and Maz chuckled—a sound that seemed out of place in this room. But Holy Four, it felt good to bring someone joy. For one moment, the shackles on my heart loosened.

But then the door opened, and Aiden stepped into the room.

Our gazes clashed in the shifting light. Those bright green eyes had captivated me from the first moment they found me in our shared cell in the Den. Right after he'd broken the jailer's nose for hurting me.

They had been filled with fury then. Now, they looked as haunted as I felt.

Maz squeezed my hand, drawing my attention back to him, and I realized I'd been crushing his fingers. I slackened my grip.

His teasing smile faded as he studied my expression. He glanced between me and Aiden, his brow creased.

"Kiera was just telling me of Ruru, Aiden," he said, holding me firmly in place as though he could feel my body tensing for flight.

I didn't dare look back at Aiden, but his deep voice pierced my heart all the same.

"And what did she say of him?"

"Our little brother is alive and well, still in possession of my whistler. Hopefully, he had the good sense to get out of Aquinon before Renwell looks for him."

"I told him to," I said quietly. I'd given him my gold from the heist as well, enough to buy food and lodging for a month.

"You're the very best of friends, Ruru."

"I wish you had been a better one."

"You spoke with him?" A subtle demand lurked beneath Aiden's question, tearing down the feeble wall that had separated us the last two days.

Anger sparked in my blood. Ruru had told me he wasn't supposed to free me. He'd disobeyed Aiden because he felt he owed me his life.

I lifted my gaze to glare at Aiden. "Yes."

Something flashed across his bronze face. Regret or disappointment, I couldn't tell which.

"Why wouldn't you have spoken with Ruru?" Maz asked. "Weren't you with him while he bombed the Old Quarter?"

All the air seemed to leave the room.

Aiden didn't break staring at me. And I couldn't look away from him. It was as if our eyes couldn't let go, now that they'd found each other again.

The last gaze Mother saw before she died.

Hot, bitter grief swelled in my throat.

His jaw clenched.

But then Maz's other sisters and a few Dag men burst through the door, talking loudly.

Aiden spun away to check a bone-rattler's bandages. I tried to escape, but Maz kept a firm grip on my hand.

"Not so fast, lovely. I want you to meet Davka and Sigrid."

Sweat beaded down my spine. Gods damn it, this was the last place in the world I wanted to be.

Davka and Sigrid approached, both taller than Yarina but with the same long, golden hair, half woven into braids. They wore leather vests and sturdy pants tucked into dirty boots.

Sigrid wore a gray woolen jacket embroidered with crimson thread and an eyepatch studded with glossy metal. Davka left her muscular arms bare, probably because of the shiny ointment covering the burn marks on her skin.

Both of them had broad swords and axes strapped to their hips and backs. And both of them regarded me with more suspicion than Yarina had.

Sigrid sat next to Yarina while Davka leaned against the wall behind them.

"This is my lovely Kiera," Maz announced, waving our joined hands. "She's the one I was telling you about. The knife-thrower."

Davka and Yarina leaned forward with interest, but Sigrid remained still.

"Did you really hustle a cattle herder from Winspere?" Yarina demanded, an eager smile growing on her lips. "And hit the target's center without looking?"

I tried to smile back, but my heart was pounding so loud I could barely hear her. "Yes. I . . . I've always enjoyed throwing knives best."

Yarina's eyes darted around my body, and she frowned. "Where are they now?"

Shattered on the royal bedchamber floor by Renwell's sunstone sword. Probably swept away with my father's blood.

Sigrid's remaining eye narrowed at me. "Maz said you were a

palace guard before he pulled you out of that gods-damned Den with Aiden. Perhaps you can tell us how our Rellmiran enemies knew we were coming that night."

My blood ran cold.

I felt more than saw Aiden pivot in our direction as the room went dead silent.

"Fucking Four, Sigrid," Maz huffed. "How would she know?"

But the fierceness in Sigrid's one-eyed gaze didn't flicker. Gods, what had she been like with two eyes?

"She might know, brother," she continued in the same steely calm voice, "because she didn't infiltrate the Den with us. She didn't join the fray until *after* we'd sealed it off and Aiden had blown up the tunnel to the palace."

Maz twisted to look up at me. "When I heard you joined the fight, I thought maybe you'd found them after you were done with Ruru. To have Aiden's back, like I asked, remember?"

The question almost sounded like a plea. As if he knew something was off and didn't want it to be true. Or he was reading the guilt in my expression and my silence.

But I owed him the truth. He deserved to know why he'd lost part of his clan.

"No," I whispered. "I came from the palace."

I ignored the murmurs that echoed through the room, focusing on the tightness in Maz's face.

"Why?"

"Because I was trying to stop Aiden from killing my father."

Maz recoiled, but still held my hand. "Your father? But who . . ."

Suddenly, I couldn't stand it any longer. The lies. The secrets. They murdered any peace of mind I'd once had.

I stared deeply into his eyes, wrapping my other hand around ours. "I was born Princess Emilia Torvaine. My father was King Weylin Torvaine. Renwell placed me in Aiden's cell to learn his secrets and betray you all."

CHAPTER 2
KIERA

For a moment, nothing. Nothing but suspended air and sound.

Then the room detonated like one of Nikella's bombs. Shouts rose from every corner. Maz's sisters shot forward as one, unsheathing their weapons. Twin blurs of movement darkened my periphery—Nikella and Aiden reaching for their own weapons.

But I couldn't look away from Maz's stricken expression. The strength bled from his grip, and I let his hand fall away from me.

Tears burned behind my eyes. "I'm sorry, Maz."

Outraged questions and accusations hurled around me like arrows shot from bows, but I was numb to them. Sharp blades waved around me, but I couldn't bring myself to grab my own.

Maz dragged his hand over his bearded face, then clenched it into a fist and slammed it on the floor. "SHUT UP!" he roared.

I flinched. Everyone else drew backward, falling silent.

He looked at me, his eyes swimming with pain and disappointment. "Why?" he croaked. "Gods damn it, why?"

The tears I'd held back for days suddenly spilled over.

"Because I thought you all were the enemy. I thought you were going to harm my family."

"So you decided to take out ours instead?" Sigrid hissed, still tapping her sword against her thigh as if she'd love nothing more than to plunge it into my gut. She gestured to Maz. "You handed our brother over to be *tortured* even after you came to know him?"

"No!" I blurted out, reaching out to reassure Maz before pulling back. "No, I would never give someone to Korvin. That's why I told Renwell when the attack was taking place. I was trying to save you."

I heard a sharp intake of breath. Aiden?

Something cleared in Maz's eyes. "You. You were the woman I heard screaming when . . . when Korvin had me."

I nodded, dashing away my tears. "I had to give Renwell a shred of what he wanted, or he would've never let me leave with you."

Maz's forehead dropped back to his cot. "You should've left me. My life is worth sacrificing for my kin and our allies."

"I'm sorry, Maz," I whispered again.

I shakily stood up, my gaze passing over the shadowed faces around me. Davka and Sigrid still looked murderous, but there was a flicker of understanding in Yarina's eyes. The expressions of the other Dags and bone-rattlers ranged from confused to contemptuous.

Nikella's face was unreadable, but Aiden . . . The intensity of his stare flayed me open like Korvin's knife. A muscle in his jaw pulsed, and his throat clenched as if he were barely containing the words he wanted to say.

But I couldn't handle any more. I rushed for the door, expecting someone to stop me, but no one did.

I hurtled through the dank passageways until I emerged topside. I stumbled to the back of the ship and gripped the railing, heaving in the briny air and looking south. Toward Aquinon. To the only family I had left, if they were still alive. But perhaps they hated me now, too. Just like everyone else I'd betrayed.

Maz's wounded expression and withdrawal from me battered at my bruised heart.

I bent over the railing and closed my eyes.

"Mind the draft if you're going to puke again."

I jerked sideways, staring wide-eyed at the red-haired man I hadn't noticed a moment ago.

Skelly, the captain of *Mynastra's Wings*, stood with his boots planted wide as he steered the ship.

I scowled. "Wasn't planning on it."

He shot me a smirk behind his bushy red beard. "All out, are ya?"

My scowl deepened, and he guffawed. "Ah, don't take it personally. Most of you land lovers take days to find your feet . . . and your stomach. Mighty Mynastra must have a soft spot for you."

"Or she was tired of me sullying her waves," I grumbled.

The weathered skin around his gray eyes crinkled. "My money's on that."

I slowly joined him at the wheel. "You have a daughter, right?" I asked, digging through my memories.

He nodded. "About your age."

"Where is she?"

"Home, at last, with her mother. I sent them back to Eloren after I paid off all the debts I owed there."

My lips parted. *All* of his debts? Ruru had mentioned Skelly liked to gamble. But where had he suddenly gotten enough money to—

Aiden. The gold from the heist. No doubt, payment for the risk Skelly was currently taking.

My heart twitched at discovering at least one answer it craved.

Skelly glanced at me out of the corner of his eye. "Of course, I left them with a large share as well. My girl will need something to take care of her mother when I perish in this foolish quest of Aiden's. Mynastra will, at last, have her wings," he added morosely, as he gazed at the billowing white sails of his ship.

I frowned. "Why help him then if you're so sure of your demise?"

Skelly looked at me as though I'd asked who Mynastra was. "Because he saved my family. He found medicine for my wife when she was ill, and he ensured they could return safely to the home they missed dearly. I don't care which Rellmiran rules. I owe Aiden a debt, and that is something an Eloren never forgets."

I pursed my lips and looked away. Aiden always seemed to get what he needed from other people. Whether they did in return was another story.

"What of the rest of your crew? Do they also have such debts with Aiden?"

Skelly shrugged, keeping his hands wrapped around the spokes of the wheel. "Their stories vary. But each includes the choice to stay on this ship and to obey their captain."

More blind loyalty. What inspired such a thing? Surely, they could see it only ended in early death.

Skelly nodded to where I was watching the sun sink beneath a mountain of pink and purple clouds. "That's a good omen. Means calm weather ahead. By my reckoning, we should draw abreast of Calimber soon. Then it'll be three more days to the Yargoth camp."

My thoughts stuttered to a halt. *Calimber.* The sunstone mine where Aiden and Maz had been imprisoned. I'd also overheard Lord Garyth mention it to Melaena.

I grimaced. Two more people whose fate I didn't know.

Garyth had wanted to know what my father was doing at the mine, hinting that it was something he didn't want the world to see.

But now my father was dead, and Renwell wore the crown. His sickening smirk filled my mind. He'd felt he deserved that victory. Gods only knew how he'd schemed in the shadows to tear my family down. And I'd been his willing puppet.

Vengeance burned in my gut. "Turn the ship," I commanded.

Skelly rasped a chuckle. "I don't know who you think you are, lass, but—"

"If you want to help Aiden, point this gods-damned ship toward Calimber."

The sea captain opened his mouth to snarl back at me when another voice cut him off.

"And why in the deep, dark, wandering hell should we believe you're trying to help me?"

My whole body stiffened, and I slowly rotated to find Aiden towering behind me. He must've slipped up the stairs like the silent shadow he was while I was busy staring at the western horizon.

Gods, he was close. So close I could feel his warmth. I could reach out and stroke his inky black hair or scratch the dark stubble on his taut jaw. Or I could shove him over the railing as I'd already been tempted to do.

We hadn't stood this close since I'd pressed my mother's blade to his chest.

"Go ahead. It's harder than it looks."

I glared at him, trying to cover for my brief distraction. "You know as well as I do that something's going on over there. What better time to find out than before Renwell gets there first?"

Aiden glared back at me, that same intensity from the infirmary burning in his eyes. I preferred his fury over his list-lessness.

His jaw worked, still reluctant.

Come on, fight me. Give me a reason to fight you back. Give me a reason to unleash my demons.

"You have no idea what we'll find," he ground out. "We could sail straight into another ambush. Unless, of course, that's what you want."

His words found their mark, cutting through bone and exposing my guilt. "I wouldn't be on this ship if it weren't for you," I hissed.

"Add it to the list of things you won't forgive me for, princess."

I inhaled sharply, my fingers curling into fists. "You think I shouldn't hate you for what you've done?"

Aiden's eyes narrowed to blades. "I saved you from the man you should hate the most."

"I never asked you to save me!"

"And you'll never have to," he snarled, his nose nearly brushing mine, his breath warm on my lips. "Now tell me why you want to see the mine."

My anger wavered. I wanted to keep shouting at him about every horrible thing I felt. But I also needed him to do my bidding. I *needed* to get the upper hand on Renwell.

Someone cleared their throat. We broke apart to find Nikella studying us with what looked like indifference, but I knew better. She'd been terribly quick to shoot me in the neck with that dart a few days ago.

"What's this about the mine?" she asked, her walking staff—which encased her spear—cradled in one arm. "I told you I haven't been able to get close to it in months."

"All the more reason to try by sea," I countered. "It'll be dark soon. They won't see us if we douse the lights."

"No," Aiden growled. "I'm not risking any more lives."

"That hasn't stopped you in the past," I snapped.

Pain flared in Aiden's eyes before he turned away, his face blank once more.

The scar on Nikella's face seemed to deepen in the setting sun as she stared at me. "Unless you have information we don't—"

"They're building something," I said, the memory popping into my head. "High General Dracles moved the newer army units from Calimber to Pravara, stationing his own elite soldiers at the mine instead. They're guarding something important."

"Where did you get this information?" Aiden asked stiffly, still facing the glowing horizon.

I swallowed. "My sister, Delysia. She . . . corresponds with one of the army captains, Henry."

Aiden shook his head. "Of course she does."

Fucking Four, he made me want to scream and commit violent murder.

I tried to breathe evenly through my nose. "It's the truth. If you don't believe me, there's a really easy way to find out." I stabbed my finger at the weakening sun.

Aiden was silent. Skelly waited for an order with white knuckles. Nikella simply stared at me as if she could divine the truth from each shift in my expression.

But every moment, the gentle breeze carried us farther north.

I threw one last blade at my target. "You underestimated Renwell in your attempt to assassinate my father. Do it again, and you might lose Rellmira forever."

Aiden twisted his head to look down at me, his eyes like glowing peridots. "It wasn't the first time I underestimated him." Before I could respond, he glanced at Skelly. "Turn west. Make for Calimber. Alert the crew to snuff the lights and remain silent when we get close."

My victory felt hollow as I watched Aiden stride off the back deck and disappear down the hatch.

Skelly grumbled curses under his breath, but slowly turned the wheel. Bone-rattlers' heads popped up around the ship to stare at Skelly.

"Sundown silence and shadow! We sail for Calimber, so shake your bones and pray to Myn!"

A chorus of "Aye!" with the clatter of bones filled the air as we chased the fleeing sun.

I pivoted to find Nikella still watching me. "You think it's a reckless plan?"

She shook her head, her long black braid swaying. "No. My brother thrives on secrets and having no weaknesses. I understand your need to find one."

I blinked, taken aback. She might be the only person in the world with such insight on Renwell. Other than me, perhaps. But I'd been just as duped as Aiden.

Never again.

Nikella rubbed her thumb over the smooth wood of her walking staff. "But be careful, Kiera. You will never make him understand the betrayal you suffered. You mustn't let vengeance steal your good sense."

I huffed. "Like it did with Aiden?"

To my shock, her mouth twitched, as if trying not to smile. "I think there was more than one thief at fault for that."

Then she also walked away, leaving me gaping at her back.

That was the *last* thing I expected Nikella to make light of. Let alone that she made light of anything. I'd thought perhaps whoever had carved up her face had also carved out her sense of humor.

"I hope you know what you're bloody doing, lass," Skelly griped at me from the wheel.

"Me too," I said grimly as we both glared toward Calimber.

CHAPTER 3
AIDEN

That woman would be the death of me.

"Fucking Four," I muttered to myself as I descended back into the belly of the ship.

I'd followed Kiera out of the infirmary to demand answers, desperate to know if she'd really given us up under duress, trying to save Maz.

But then I'd heard her ordering Skelly to bring us to Calimber. She knew nothing of what awaited us there, except perhaps Dracles's most elite soldiers.

It seems neither of us cares who we harm to achieve our goals, little traitor.

Yet here I was again, letting her lead me into danger on the chance we could discover *something* that would obliterate Renwell, Rellmira's newest false king.

I laid a palm on the infirmary door, glancing at the finger my father's falcon ring had encircled. The insignia of the last true king. I'd torn it off after we sailed into the open sea and shoved it into my pocket.

I had no right to wear it.

Taking a deep breath, I pushed open the infirmary door.

"Where is she?" Sigrid snarled the moment I stepped inside.

Nikella hadn't followed me back, leaving me alone to face the small, angry mob. But I supposed I deserved it. I'd been putting off these inquiries for days.

And now I was also going to tell them I was delaying our trip home to take yet another risk.

I leaned against the healer's table and folded my arms over my chest. The stab wound I'd sustained from that gods-damned coward, Weylin, twinged, but I ignored it. "Kiera's on deck with Skelly."

"Why did you bring her with us?" Sigrid demanded.

"How did one of Weylin's daughters end up in your company?" one of the injured bone-rattlers asked.

More and more questions hurtled from every corner of the room. Except from Maz, who stayed turned away.

"Did she know who you really were?"

"Is she still in league with Renwell?"

"What exactly happened in the palace two nights ago?"

"We should put her in chains and give her a taste of Dag justice." That last one was from Sigrid, of course.

"Enough!" I snapped. "You forget that she also helped us escape the Den. If it hadn't been for her quick thinking, we might have perished under that second wave of Wolves."

Sigrid twirled her blade in her hand. "There might not have been a second wave if she hadn't told Renwell what day we'd be attacking."

"She didn't tell him how many warriors we had or where we planned to attack. Only that I aimed to kill Weylin and what day I would do it."

"Why didn't she just kill you if she wanted to protect her family?" Yarina asked, her blue eyes thoughtful, as if this were the route she would've taken.

I scowled. "I don't know. Perhaps she was worried she wouldn't make it back to the palace alive if she tried."

"Or she didn't want to kill the man she loved," Maz mumbled into his pillow.

A shocked silence fell.

A memory flared of me bursting into Melaena's room at The Silk Dancer after I'd found out Kiera had been spying on us. My normally level-headed friend and business associate had shouted, *"She loves you!"*

My heart hardened. "She was never in love with me, Mazkull. Why are you making excuses for her?"

Before anyone could stop him, Maz rose from his cot, his head nearly brushing the roof. His blue eyes blazed. "Why aren't you? Have you asked her any of these questions, or did you immediately condemn her and cast her out of your heart?"

"Sit down, Mazkull," I ground out, taking a step toward him.

"No."

His sisters crowded closer. "Sit down, or we'll make you," Yarina threatened.

He glared down at her. "You would force me to tear my back in a fight you would lose? Your choice, little sister."

I pinched the bridge of my nose, a headache brewing behind my eyes. "What will it take, Maz?"

Maz interrupted his three-way scowling contest to glance at me. "Answers. Start from the beginning and tell us what you know."

I'd rather swim to Yargoth, but they deserved some truth. I nodded, and Maz sat on his cot. Everyone else settled in as well.

I told them of how I met Kiera and her offer of escape. I mentioned her saving Ruru from the Shadow-Wolves and her role in the heist. That seemed to garner some reluctant approval from my audience.

My story clearly had holes in it—gaps where I could only surmise what she'd done at the behest of Renwell . . . and why.

But then I reached the part of the story after the heist.

My voice roughened as I revealed how she'd been eavesdropping on me and Melaena, discovering my identity and purpose. How she'd convinced me she was on our side, that she hated her father as well.

I told them about the task I'd given her and Ruru and that I'd kept the bulk of our infiltration plans to myself.

"Only smart thing you did," Sigrid muttered.

I glared at her, continuing to when Kiera helped two fugitives, Helene and Isabel, escape Renwell's clutches.

More sympathetic murmurs echoed around the room.

"He took me that night," Maz jumped in. "Saying he learned about my involvement in the heist after interrogating the servants at Asher's mansion."

Yarina's eyes narrowed. "Not from Kiera? Er, Emilia? Or whatever her gods-damned name is."

Maz shook his head.

"Renwell could've been covering for her," Sigrid said.

"But then, why take Maz at all?" I asked. "It was a risky, desperate move. Something else was going on between Kiera and her master."

"Yes, that must be it," Maz said, relief heavy in his voice. "You didn't hear the way she was screaming at him. It was like Korvin took that gods-damned knife to her soul instead of . . . me." He swallowed hard and looked away.

We'd spoken little of it, but I'd given Maz dreamdew drops several times when the nightmares became too much. He'd torn his back yesterday, thrashing in his sleep.

Watching him suffer that way . . . I might've done the same thing Kiera had. Or I would've killed both Renwell and Korvin with my bare hands, regardless of the consequences.

I couldn't imagine what that must've been like to watch. Especially since Korvin was the one who'd scarred Kiera's back so deeply years ago.

For a moment, I was back in that warm, steamy bathhouse, holding Kiera's trembling body in my arms as she relived the terrible memory. Her fingers had dug into my bare skin as if I were a rock in a stormy sea.

I'd surrendered another small piece of myself to her then. Had she even wanted it? Or was it all part of her ploy to gain my trust?

"When did you find out who she was?" Maz asked.

Inwardly, I winced. "After you left for the ship. She . . . she revealed herself. Then Nikella shot her with a sleeping dart, and we tied her up in a room."

Gods, I would never shake the absolute horror I'd felt when she'd drawn that gold-hilted sunstone knife from her boot. Everything it meant had slammed into me all at once. I'd barely registered the fact that she was trying to tell me what she'd done before I revealed my own crime.

Then she'd leaped at me with that wretched knife, murder in her beautiful eyes.

Maz's eyes narrowed as if he knew there was more I wasn't telling. "Why did she reveal herself, I wonder?"

"Probably trying to save her precious father," Sigrid muttered.

I pressed my lips together. Kiera had stood between me and Weylin, more out of rage than loyalty. But then she'd learned his part in Brielle's death.

Yarina gestured impatiently. "Get to the part where Weylin dies. How did Kiera get inside the palace? And why didn't she stay with Renwell?"

"The first, I'm guessing she had help from Ruru."

Maz nodded, his face softening with fondness.

I continued, "She was also Weylin's daughter and Renwell's apprentice, so I'm sure that counted for something. As for your second question . . ." I ran my hands through my hair, reliving each heart-pounding moment. "After Renwell beheaded Weylin and took his crown, Kiera discovered the depth of his betrayal and tried to kill him."

A murmur of surprise and approval rippled through the room.

I couldn't help but agree.

My jaw had unhinged with the speed and accuracy of Kiera's flying knives. I'd hoped that at least one would find its mark, but that hope shattered along with her blades under Renwell's sunstone sword.

"So she took her chances with you instead of him," Sigrid summed up flatly.

"I didn't give her a choice." *And she hates me for it.*

Her rage on deck had felt like a wildfire that wanted to consume me, turn me to ash. But she was alive and away from Renwell. I refused to apologize for that. It was more than I'd been able to do for her mother.

I cleared my throat. "She wanted to stay for her brother and sister, but there was no way to free them."

"Ah, poor lovely," Maz murmured, stroking his beard.

"If she'd told the truth sooner, we might've been able to get them out," I snapped.

He shook his head. "You're trying so hard to justify the pain you feel that you're smothering hers. There's enough pain to go around, brother."

My chest tightened, darkness clawing from within.

I didn't want to hear about her pain. I didn't want to think of how I'd caused a large portion of it. I didn't want everything to be my fault, as it usually was.

Fucking Four.

Moments like this, I felt as though I were still imprisoned in the bowels of the mine with nothing but my guilt for company.

Gods-damned Calimber. Had I ever really escaped?

I cleared my throat. "I've ordered Skelly to change course." The Dags in the room tensed. "Not far out of the way. Just to Calimber."

Maz rose to his feet once more, but no one lifted a finger to stop him. "What in the deep, dark, wandering hell do you want with that place?"

I told them what Kiera had told me to very mixed reactions. Maz and Yarina were all for it until Maz declared he wanted to scout the place himself. Then he was shouted down by every Dag in the room.

Sigrid protested, citing every reason it was a terrible idea—many of which involved Kiera. Davka, as usual, said little, but her locked jaw conveyed her disapproval.

The bone-rattler whose bandaged head I'd just checked shrugged and told me to take Roark and Bardo for my rowers, as they were strongest.

Stavrik, the hulking Dag, glared at his heavily bandaged hands, then told me to take his bow and arrows. "That quiver had better be empty when you come back," he muttered.

I nodded. I didn't know what we were going to face on those cliffs, but a bow and arrows could only help.

"A moment, Aiden?" Maz asked, tipping his head toward the door.

We sidestepped Yarina arguing with her older sisters and slipped into the hallway.

Maz moved gingerly, but I didn't reach out to help him, as that would likely result in a hearty shove.

A flickering lantern swung into his head, and he swore. "Gods-damned ship is too small." He folded his arms over his chest, flinched, and let them fall to his sides. "I want to destroy

Renwell as much as you do. But don't go running into danger just because you hate to lose."

I sighed, rubbing my fingers over my unshaven jaw. "Sometimes I hate how well you know me, Mazkull."

His familiar grin flared briefly. "You shouldn't. It helps me keep you alive."

"You're only warning me away from Calimber now because your sisters refuse to let you scout it with me."

He smirked. "I guess we both understand each other, brother."

I shook my head. "Renwell's coup was too calculated, too well-planned, to be contained to just Aquinon. From what it sounds like, he already had Dracles and the army in hand before he killed Weylin. I want to know what else he's been working on in the shadows."

Maz quirked an eyebrow. "Planning a coup of your own, are you?"

A bitter laugh escaped me. "With my one-man army, yes."

"Two-man army." Maz thumped his chest. "Like I told you in that gods-damned mine, I'm with you to the bloody end."

Two men—and probably Nikella—against Renwell and an entire army.

They were the odds I'd grown used to over the years, but now they felt insurmountable.

After we'd returned what was left of the Dags to their clan and I'd sent Skelly back to Eloren to be with his family, my list of allies grew too short.

"So what weren't you saying in there about Kiera?" Maz asked abruptly, shaking me from my thoughts. "Does it have anything to do with why she looked ready to gut you earlier?"

"She found out what I did to Brielle. Her mother," I murmured.

Maz's face paled under his golden beard. "Holy Four, I hadn't pieced that together. I was so focused on what happened with her bastard father and Renwell . . . Gods help you, brother. You two have made quite the mess of things." He scratched at his hairy, tattooed chest. "But you told her what happened, right? She understands why you did it?"

I scuffed my boot at a cracked floorboard. "Not all of it, no."

"Well, what are you bloody waiting for, idiot?" He gave me a light shove toward the stairs. "Give the woman some peace."

I whirled on him, batting his arm away. "Peace?" I snarled. "And what peace do you think she wants from me, the man who stabbed her mother in the heart with the knife she still carries? What words will ease that pain, Mazkull? She can't even look at me without thinking I'm the reason her mother is dead, why she's left her brother and sister behind. She said she will never forgive me." I curled my fingers into fists. Gods, how I longed to smash them through something, preferably Renwell's smug face. "And how can I forgive her?" I breathed. "That little thief stole my vengeance, my purpose, my secrets, my trust, my—"

"Heart?" Maz interrupted.

My insides went cold. "Enough. We are never speaking of this again. Get some rest."

I turned on my boot heel and stormed away before he could respond.

Suddenly, a dark and dangerous boat ride to the most wretched place I knew sounded like just the escape I needed because it took me away from *her*.

CHAPTER 4

KIERA

NIGHT FELL CLEAR AND STARRY, BUT MOONLESS. YET SKELLY STILL declared any guards would see us from a mile away.

The sailors blew out all the lanterns and pulled in the white sails. They tucked away their bones, padding about the deck on bare feet.

The cliffs of Calimber towered in the distance. I strained my eyes to spot any watchman's torches. Nothing met my eyes but darkness. But perhaps they were using the cover of night as well.

Somewhere in those sheer, rocky faces was the sunstone mine . . . and an entrance. There had to be if Renwell was shipping prisoners to the mine. But Skelly said he'd seen no beach among these cliffs for miles in either direction. Aiden hadn't been able to provide a port location either, as he said no mine tunnel led to the sea when he and Maz were prisoners.

Thankfully, our small party didn't seem to mind the lack of information.

Aiden, with a bow and quiver of arrows slung over his back, helped Nikella lower a rowboat over the side of the ship. Trying not to shiver in my simple black clothing, I clutched the hilt of my mother's knife and joined them.

Yarina, who also carried a bow and arrows, and a few bone-rattlers waited to board the rowboat, scowling at me. No one had asked me to come along, but I intended to, even if I had to jump from the ship.

The boat landed with a soft splash, the oars rolling inside. It looked like a little wooden toy that would easily smash to bits on the cliffs ahead.

I swallowed hard. I hadn't done so well the last time I'd been on one of these, escaping the Den with Aiden, Maz, and Ruru. But I needed to see the mine for myself.

Before any of them had a chance to go first, I rushed forward, seized a dangling rope, and slid down to the rowboat.

I thanked the gods I'd thought to wear leather gloves over my tender palms, or the rope burn would've been unbearable.

I miscalculated the landing and ended up on my ass at the bottom of the rocking boat. A snicker came from above, and I glared up at the murky shadows gazing down at me.

I knew who would come flying down next before he even jumped.

Aiden landed with the silent grace of a cat, then seized my arm. "I didn't include you for a reason, Kiera. Get back on the ship."

I yanked my arm out of his grasp. "I'm not yours to command. This was my idea. I'm going."

His face was merely a shadow beneath his hood, but I could almost feel his jaw grinding. "The tide is rolling out, which means this will not be a pleasant trip. If you get sick, every guard on watch will hear you."

Gods damn it, was I never going to live that down?

"I can handle it," I snapped. "Let's just work together on this one thing, and then we can go back to hating each other."

"You think I hate you?" he breathed, his gloved fists clenched. "I don't even know you."

I jerked back as if he'd slapped me. My cheeks burned.

Gods, that shouldn't hurt. I didn't want it to hurt. Because he was right. He didn't know me. Just as I didn't truly know him. I hadn't thought he was capable of killing an innocent woman, or leaving me tied up in a room while he attempted to murder my father.

But then why did it feel as though he'd taken my knife and gutted me with it?

Aiden turned away and shoved the oars into their locks. Nikella, Yarina, and a few burly bone-rattlers slid into the boat. I scurried to the front, as far away from Aiden as I could get.

Yarina handed me a bucket. "I figure you'll need this, princess," she whispered.

"I'm not a princess," I hissed back at her.

"Whatever you say, princess."

"Silence," growled one of the bone-rattlers as he started heaving on his oar.

Yarina smirked at me, tapping one of her scythes ominously. I rolled my eyes and shoved her bucket to the bottom of the boat. She had too much in common with her brother. And oddly, she made me miss his company all the more. But I doubted I'd be welcome in it anytime soon.

The boat coasted over the waves, flying upward, then plunging downward. My stomach rolled with it.

I'd purposely not eaten any of the mushy porridge the ship's cook had passed around earlier. But that didn't stop me from clamping my lips together.

The cliffs loomed higher and higher. I searched for guards on top, but couldn't make any out.

Perhaps I'd been wrong to bring us here. Perhaps Renwell had already ordered everyone to abandon the mine.

"If we don't find that entrance soon, we'll be nothing but bones and kindling on those rocks," Yarina muttered.

A wave crashed over the boat, and I gasped under the spray of cold water. Wrapping my numb fingers over the edge of the boat, I leaned forward. But it was useless. I couldn't determine one cliff face from the next.

"There," Nikella said, the thunder of the waves nearly drowning out her voice.

We all looked to where she pointed. An irregularity in the cliff face. Two seams that nearly blended together but for the shadow in between. Where the waves didn't shatter but surged inward.

Aiden and the bone-rattler grunted as they pulled hard on the oars to direct us toward the inlet.

Our little boat shuddered against the sea's onslaught. We drew nearer and nearer the rocks.

"Bardo!" the bone-rattler who'd silenced us grunted at the other bone-rattler.

Bardo slid into place next to his fellow sailor, and they heaved on the same oar. Nikella abandoned her spear to seize Aiden's oar.

My heart pounded in my throat. If they weren't strong enough . . . If the oars snapped . . .

Another wave slapped me in the face. I swiped my hair out of my eyes, expecting to see sharp rocks.

Instead, calmer waters stretched out before us in a winding path. The boat ceased its wild tossing. The incessant drumbeat of the waves grew muffled as we slipped into the stone passageway.

Yarina sighed with relief. I lifted my face to the sky. Still clear and salted with stars.

Something glinted at the edge of the cliff. I stiffened.

But no shouts came. No torches burned.

Perhaps I'd imagined it. A trick of the slippery light.

I could warn the others, but we were so close. If we turned back now, all that would've been for nothing.

We drifted around one bend, then two. The oars hardly made a sound.

Then . . . a glow ahead. Just around the next curve.

The boat slowed.

My fingers shook as I reached out to anchor us against a mossy rock. There was nowhere to land the boat. We would have to hug the cliff to peek around the corner. The last thing I wanted was to drift out into the open in full view of whatever awaited us in the bay.

Yarina nudged my shoulder aside so she could crane her head around the rock wall.

"Fucking Four . . ." she breathed.

Gods, is it the whole army? Can she see the mine?

I practically toppled out of the boat trying to lean around her. My mouth fell open.

The inlet opened into a wide bay. Enormous torches and bonfires illuminated a rocky beach crawling with soldiers in shiny armor. They barked orders at prisoners in ragged clothing.

But they weren't hauling sunstone. No. They were building ships.

Two large ships, both twice the size of *Mynastru's Wings*, floated in the calm water. Each one bore catapults on swiveling platforms that branched out from the deck like wooden arms.

I thought no one had used catapults since the last great war between gods and humans. But somehow Renwell had made them smaller and more agile.

The ribs of a third ship poked up from a wooden platform on the beach.

Yarina suddenly disappeared from my side, replaced by a more familiar presence.

"Warships," Aiden murmured.

I tore my gaze away to stare up at him, the torches reflecting in his green eyes. "For what?"

"Renwell stole the throne. This is how he means to keep it. Or perhaps he wants more than Rellmira," he added quietly, almost to himself.

I shivered. How long had he been using the sunstone mine as a cover for building these monstrosities? Had my father known? If he did, then he'd been even more despicable than I thought.

The current shifted, pushing our boat into open water. I lost my footing and nearly tumbled in, but Aiden grabbed my arm and kept me upright.

Bardo tried to correct us, but his oar smacked against the hull, echoing into the bay.

A shout rose from the beach.

"Gods damn it." Aiden forced me to sit. "Get us out of here!" he barked at the bone-rattlers, who immediately complied.

I held on as the boat slowly swiveled to point back toward the passage. But I kept my gaze fixed on the closest ship.

A few guards clambered up onto a catapult platform while another loaded a barrel into the sling.

"Aiden . . ." I said through clattering teeth.

The catapult launched its barrel, a fuse sparking on one end.

"Aiden!" I screamed.

He turned around just as the barrel exploded behind us.

And set the sea on fire.

CHAPTER 5

AIDEN

KIERA SCREAMING MY NAME DESTROYED MY CALM, FASTER THAN the wave of heat and light racing toward the boat.

I shouted as the burning oil skimmed over the water. "Row faster! Get us out of range!"

Yarina and Nikella joined the bone-rattlers at the oars. The flames petered out inches from our stern. But the guards were already loading another barrel.

Fucking Four, I had nothing to fight back with except Stavrik's bow and arrows. Useless against oily fire. No doubt Renwell had known that when he mounted gods-damned catapults to his ships.

I had expected something nefarious, but not this. My failure in Aquinon went deeper than I thought.

"Incoming!" I shouted as another burning barrel arced toward us.

Yarina grunted out a string of curses behind me.

The barrel came much closer this time, exploding just to the left of our boat. Nikella hissed as a few drops of burning oil singed her cloak, but she kept rowing.

Kiera seized the bucket Yarina had given her in jest and hauled in sea water to toss at the flames trying to eat through the boat.

"Water won't work!" I shouted as I stamped out any drops that made it inside. "Suffocate it!"

Nikella and Roark tried to keep their oar from dipping into the burning oil while the other two worked double time.

We rounded the bend, leaving a smoke trail, and I breathed a sigh of relief. The catapults had looked short range, judging by the length of their arms. Even mounted on a swivel, they couldn't reach us around these stony bends unless they moved the ship from dry dock.

A shout rose above me. Gods damn it, there *were* guards up there. Torches flickered to life along the rim of the canyon.

I nocked an arrow into place and aimed upward. "Kiera, switch with Yarina."

I didn't shift my gaze, but I felt them scrambling to obey. At least Kiera could follow *one* of my orders.

An arrow slammed into the bottom of the boat, inches from Bardo.

"Fucking Myn!" he shouted, pulling harder on the oar.

I rotated, spotting a guard peeking over the edge. I fired just as a wave rocked the boat. My arrow went wide.

Swearing, I adjusted my footing and readied another arrow. Yarina's bow twanged as she fired. Someone shouted. A body tumbled down the cliff face and splashed into the sea.

"I count three more," she said. "I'll take—"

An arrow sprouted from her arm. She stared at it in shock. "Lucky bastards," she muttered and sagged to a bench.

Rage flooded my body like the oily fire we'd just left behind. With a roar, I fired again. Another body plummeted.

A flaming arrow bit into our hull, and I yanked it out.

I fired again and again, bringing down another body, but

more arrows fell around us. The sea grew rougher as we rounded the last bend. I stumbled, and my final arrow went wide.

A guard's arrow streaked past my ear, and someone gasped.

Kiera.

I whipped around, my eyes landing first on Kiera, then on Bardo, who'd slumped over, an arrow in his neck.

Roark bellowed in agony, reaching for his friend.

I slung my bow over my empty quiver and gently pulled Bardo's limp body from the rowing bench. After settling him in the stern, I took his place.

"Keep rowing," I murmured to Roark as he shook with pain, glancing back at his dead friend. "Get him home."

We pulled together in silence.

Yarina watched us from the bow, cradling her injured arm. "I'm sorry, Aiden," she croaked.

"It's not your fault," I grunted.

It's mine. Always mine.

Kiera was right. I led people right into danger. Why they kept following me into it, I didn't know. Perhaps they shouldn't. I'd been playing at being a leader for years now with nothing to show for it but imprisonment and death.

I'd even failed to kill the one man I'd set out to. Weylin had murdered my father, ordered Renwell to kill my mother, and stolen their kingdom.

He'd been at my mercy, my sword tip under his chin. But all I could think about was *her.* And how she'd hate me for it. Even though she already did for what I'd done to Brielle.

In the end, perhaps it'd been fitting that Weylin was murdered by someone he trusted.

The stab wound he'd given me throbbed in tandem with my breath. I'd probably pulled the stitches by rowing and using my bow. A dribble of warmth tracked down my side, but now wasn't the time to check it.

"We're taking on water, Aiden," Nikella announced.

I glanced down at my boots and hissed a curse between my teeth. Several inches of dark water sloshed inside the boat, like wine in a drunkard's cup.

"There's a hole in the side," Nikella continued. "The fire from the second barrel must have burned through the wood."

"We won't make it," Roark said dully, his huge hands sliding off the oar. "Mynastra will just have to take us all."

I glared at *Mynastra's Wings*, a hulking shadow that was anchored a very long swim away.

Could Kiera even swim? I'd never asked.

Her face looked paler than usual, her mouth a grim line as she stared at the large expanse of rolling sea like it was her executioner.

I hated to lose the boat, even more so to lose Bardo, but I had to save the others.

"Start shouting," I told them. "We're far enough from the cliffs that the guards can't reach us."

While Yarina and Kiera obeyed with enthusiasm—and Roark, halfheartedly so—I turned to Nikella. "Flint and steel?"

She retrieved the two items she'd carried with her since I could remember from one of her pockets. "I suggest we rip out a few planks and keep the oars for easier swimming."

"Agreed."

Yarina and Kiera kept shouting at the top of their lungs while Roark and I ripped out the benches and unlocked the oars.

I nodded to Nikella, who tore off a chunk of her cloak.

"Might still be some oil in it," she murmured as she laid it on the dry wood we'd just exposed by ripping off the bench.

"I can't swim," Kiera blurted out, as if she'd been holding back the confession. "Not well, anyway. And what of Yarina and her arm?"

"Don't worry about me, princess," Yarina said immediately. "I could swim there with no arms if I had to."

While boasting was a beloved pastime of the Dags, I knew she was telling the truth. She'd grown up by rivers and the sea, always trying to beat her brother and sisters in contests of strength and skill. And then she'd tried to outpace me when I'd lived with them for a few years.

But Kiera . . .

She shouldn't have come with us, but she was too gods-damned stubborn. Perhaps I never should've dragged her out of Aquinon.

"Keep hold of this plank, and you'll be fine," I said, handing her the chunk of wood.

"And Bardo?" Roark asked, staring at his friend's body.

"His bones will join Mynastra's sooner than intended," I said softly. "We'll drink to his honor on board tonight."

Roark nodded numbly, clutching his oar.

"May the gods find his soul," Nikella murmured, then struck her flint and steel together until the sparks caught on the oil-specked cloth. They danced over the dry wood, finding purchase like so many fireflies.

The memory of a firefly grove flickered in my mind.

"I'm yours."

"And I . . . am all yours. For us long as you wish to keep me, little thief."

I glanced at Kiera. Her eyes were closed in dread, her body turned toward the burgeoning flames as though soaking up what little heat she could before our cold plunge.

Gods, how I wanted you to keep me, Kiera.

I tore my gaze away and barked, "Stay in line with the burning boat so Skelly can find us easier. Go!"

Yarina dove overboard first, kicking through the dark sea while holding her piece of wood.

Roark followed, then Nikella.

Only Kiera and I remained at the prow, the fire burning steadily behind us.

Her profile was in shadow, but I'd memorized her features well. Not just the straightness of her nose or the curve of her cheek or the smoldering amber of her eyes. But the way her face lit up when she laughed. The way triumph made her look fiercely beautiful. And the way her face softened with desire when I'd made love to her in those stormy woods.

I hadn't lied when I said I didn't know her. I knew her expressions and her quirks, but I didn't know her heart. Not when it had deceived me so thoroughly.

She glanced up at me as if she could feel my thoughts. A battle raged behind her eyes. A battle with no end, as she leaped into the waves.

I followed a moment later, taking up the rear of our floating line as we kicked toward the ship.

The frigid waves heaved underneath me. In moments, my gloved fingers were so numb, I could hardly tell that I was grasping my plank. My jaw ached from clenching it. Better that than continuously gulping salty water that tasted of fish.

My stab wound burned, but the cold water would staunch the blood flow.

Small mercies.

I kept my eyes on Kiera's splashing boots. She hugged her plank like it might disappear.

I glanced back at the burning boat, the fire pitifully small amid the cavernous waves.

At least the tide was rolling out, or it would've thrown us back against Calimber's cliffs.

A shout rose ahead. I shoved my soggy hair aside and spotted Skelly's ship turning toward us. They must've seen our signal.

Relief seeped into my aching bones, but I kept kicking, kept watch on Kiera and the others to make sure they didn't drift.

What felt like hours later, we bobbed up against *Mynastra's Wings*.

Someone threw a rope ladder over. We clambered up, everyone else raining seawater over my head.

The next hour was a blur.

I explained what I could to Skelly. His expression went from dour to downright hopeless. After he set course for Yargoth once more, he called his crew together to commemorate Bardo. Roark disappeared into the midst of his bone-rattling brothers and sisters.

Still in a daze, I dried myself, then immediately set to work, removing the arrow from Yarina's arm and stuffing the bloody hole with cloudbird leaves. I also stuffed a few into my torn side. The soft, cotton-like coating soaked up the blood while the sticky leaf secreted infection-killing wax. But it did nothing for the pain. We would have to wait for Yargoth for that.

Yarina refused to go to the infirmary—probably to avoid Maz. I wasn't ready to face him, either. But her older sisters swarmed her with blankets, a mug of warm wine, and a plate of dry bread.

I ordered them to put a sling on her as well. Yarina immediately put up a fight, but Sigrid and Davka carried her off.

Belowdecks, I changed clothes and warmed my shivering body by the dining room fire. Nikella joined me. But she seemed in no mood to talk, and neither was I.

I glanced about until I found Kiera huddled under a pile of blankets in the corner, spooning hot broth between her bloodless lips.

For a moment, I imagined the last three days hadn't happened. I would stride over, pick her up, and hold her in my lap while I tried to infuse any warmth I had left into her skin. I would brush my lips over hers between feeding her spoonfuls of broth, licking any wayward drops from her mouth.

But it wasn't just the last three days I'd have to erase. She'd been lying to me from the moment she met me. I'd given her a handful of my trust, and she'd still betrayed me.

"She loves you!" Melaena's voice clamored through my skull again.

But no one had ever loved me in that way. I was starting to think it wasn't possible.

Kiera's gaze shot toward me, and she scowled. Setting her bowl down, she hobbled out of the dining room.

I faced the fire again and didn't look away for a long time.

CHAPTER 6
KIERA

I felt like I'd never be warm or dry again.

The sky had turned an endless gray, and the sea along with it. Bursts of rain and cold waves constantly soaked the ship over the next three days.

I rarely slept. Every time I closed my eyes, I saw those burning barrels flying toward us. I watched an arrow slam into Bardo's neck. I felt the cold, dark sea close around me as I swam like a drowning cat.

I remembered sitting in the ship's dining room after Calimber, trying to thaw my insides with warm soup, when I'd felt a gaze on me. Not a gaze, but a glare of bitterness and rage. I'd thought Aiden might be pleased with what we'd found. Or at least acknowledge that I'd been telling the truth.

But no. He still looked at me as if I were the source of all his problems. He was certainly the source of a lot of mine.

I stood at the front of the ship, facing northwest, where a dark smudge had appeared an hour ago. Loud celebrations had resounded throughout the ship, followed by feverish preparations for landfall at sunset.

But my mind was still in Calimber.

Warships. *Warships.* Three of them, nearly complete.

What are you doing, Renwell? What do you really want?

No doubt Aiden, Nikella, and the rest of them were already planning on how to destroy my old mentor. Without me. And why would they want me nearby? I was a traitor.

Which was why my time in Dagriel would be short. As soon as I'd rested, I'd beg for a horse and some supplies and make my way back to Rellmira.

Aiden could play at war. And I truly hoped he could defeat Renwell. But I hated to think of Everett and Delysia caught up in whatever Renwell was planning. Seeing his warships and nearly being killed by one was enough to give me the good sense Nikella had mentioned.

Revenge would have to wait.

I needed to sneak into Aquinon, disguised somehow. Perhaps I could use the tunnel to *The Silk Dancer*, where, if my luck held, Melaena would keep me hidden. Then it was just a simple matter of bribing my way through the bridge gate with money I didn't have and infiltrating a palace filled with Wolves.

I sneered at myself.

Even if I succeeded, the best way to reach my siblings would be through the many secret passageways in the palace, but Renwell surely knew about most of them.

Then we'd have to sneak back out.

My chest tightened with apprehension, and I rubbed it.

"You didn't come back to visit me."

I jolted as Maz joined me at the railing, his gaze fixed on the growing smudge that was his homeland.

He looked more like a Dag than I'd ever seen him. He wore a thick fur vest, flaunting his muscular, tattooed arms. His fur-trimmed pants were tucked into similar boots. His golden hair and full beard were longer now, giving him more of the wild look of the other Dags.

"I didn't think I was welcome to." I darted a glance behind him to see if one—or all—of his sisters were on his tail. "Should you be out of the infirmary?"

His lips twitched in a frown. "I refuse to arrive back home for the first time in years confined to a cot with my shame on display."

My forehead pinched. "Oh, Maz, I'm so s—"

"I don't need your apologies," he said brusquely. "We've all got things to atone for." He looked down at me, a slight quirk of his mouth belying the hardness in his eyes. "I'd prefer you tell me a story. A true one."

I nodded. "What would you like to hear about?"

"Tell me of your brother and sister—Everett and Delysia, was it?"

My eyes burned, and I faced Dagriel to hide the sudden emotion. No one else had asked me about them. No one else seemed to care about them. And for the first time, I could tell someone the truth as their sister, not their fake personal guard.

"Thank you," I whispered to the wind. Maz dipped his head in acknowledgment. "Delysia is my younger sister. She's beautiful, like our mother was. Everett is more serious and looks more like . . . well . . . he looks like himself. He loves our library and studying, but Delysia never cared for it much." I smiled. "One time, Delysia got me to play a trick on Everett . . ."

I talked and talked, the words coming easier than they had in days. Happy words. Hopeful words. No scheming or double talking. No agenda.

It struck me then that I was never cut out to be a spy. The waiting, the lies, the loneliness, the regrets. I never wanted it, and I was glad to strip that part of myself away and leave it behind.

I still wanted justice. I still sought the truth. But I no longer wanted to do so from the shadows.

Gods only knew if I'd ever get that chance.

Maz listened, leaning his forearms on the railing, chuckling during some parts, asking questions in others. All out of seemingly innocent curiosity.

Then he mentioned my mother.

"I met Brielle a few times," he said, staring at a place beyond the ship's bow I couldn't see. "She was lovely, a warrior in silk."

My throat caught.

Maz glanced at me, his eyes softening. "I'm sorry I wasn't there that night. A boy died in my place. Loss is never simple."

I couldn't breathe. I wanted to ask him everything he knew, every detail of his encounters with Mother. But fear and anger and a dozen nameless emotions clogged my throat.

Because he was right. Loss was never simple.

Sigrid called for Maz just then, slicing through the taut thread of regret between us.

But before he left, he briefly rested his hand on my shoulder. "Knowing the part I played in your sorrow—the reason you saw us as enemies—eases the pain of the part you played in mine. But we Dags are a proud lot. We fight as hard as we love, and we never surrender on either front. If someone turns their back on us . . ." He shook his head. "However, it brings me some comfort to know my gut"—he patted his flat stomach—"was always right."

On that cryptic note, he sauntered away.

I let loose a fractured breath, but the emotions remained, scratching at my insides.

My eyes caught on a dark figure leaning against the railing several feet away, his face angled toward Dagriel.

Aiden. Had he been listening?

I whirled away, fists clenched. Gods, I hated showing him any weakness, like I had when I admitted I couldn't swim.

He didn't deserve to learn about the family he'd torn apart and abandoned. He had enough weapons to use against me. All the more reason to go back to Aquinon as soon as possible.

Another day or two, and I'd never have to see him again.

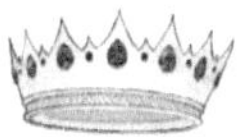

As we neared the shores of Dagriel, the sun broke through the gray blanket of sky.

My lips parted in wonder as I drank it all in. I'd never traveled anywhere. This was my first time outside Rellmira, or really Aquinon.

The land was so different here. A thick blanket of furry, pointed trees and others with white trunks and shockingly golden leaves covered the rocky shores.

In the distance, huge snow-capped mountains rose to the sky. I'd only ever seen them drawn in books, and no picture could do them justice.

The air was crisp and sweet as if it'd just rained, releasing all the scents of the earth.

A loud shout arose as we rounded a bend and came into view of a river mouth where a dozen large boats had lain along the black shore like dry fish.

What looked like a hundred Dags waved and called out. Children in fur capes shrieked with joy and chased each other around the rocks. Huge dogs barked and splashed in the surf, long pink tongues lolling.

The Dags on the ship shouted and waved back, Maz and his sisters loudest of all. Even the grieving bone-rattlers smiled at such a raucous welcome.

A strange sense of longing pinched my chest. So many people who were so happy to see each other. What must that be like?

Skelly commanded his crew to lower the anchor and prepare the remaining rowboats. The bone-rattlers hurried to do his bidding, but didn't climb into them. Perhaps they preferred their rollicking tub to solid ground.

Aiden and Nikella loaded the first boats with the wounded, taking great care not to jostle them. The rest of the Dags impatiently waited their turn.

This time, I didn't fight my way to a boat. Instead, I clambered down the rope ladder into the last one. A Dag woman wrenched the oar out of my pale hand and propelled us to shore.

The distance across the water was mercifully short. I practically flung myself onto dry land with a sigh of relief. But now it was the dark shore that pitched beneath my feet. I half-sank, half-fell to my knees, grasping the smooth, wet pebbles between my fingers.

The Dags were still making a world of noise, but now cries of sorrow and sobbed names reached my ears. Tears glistened on almost everyone's cheeks, of relief, of sadness—I couldn't tell. Perhaps all of it. The Dags seemed to be a people who felt everything out in the open with each other.

Delysia had hugged me at Mother's funeral, and Everett had held my hand. But we'd saved our tears for the privacy of our bedrooms. Away from Father's disapproving eyes.

"That bitch should've died on the executioner's stand like the traitor she was!"

Murdering bastard. I hoped he wandered the Longest Night even now, stalked by his demons.

A sharp stab of pain made me glance down. One of the rocks I clutched had sliced open my palm. Blood trickled onto the wet beach, disappearing quickly.

"That means you're one of us now," said a raspy voice.

I looked up and met the bright blue eyes of an old woman, her moon-white hair in several long braids and a life's worth of smile lines on her weathered cheeks.

She wore similar clothing to the others, but with a white fur cape around her shoulders and beribboned staff in her hand.

She extended her other hand to me. "My grandson, Mazkull, tells me you are Kiera, late of Aquinon. I am Frieda, head of the Yargoth Clan."

Maz's grandmother? The one who gave him romantic advice? I didn't know she was the *leader* of the clan.

Dazedly, I laid my bleeding palm on hers and stood up. "I'm happy to meet you," I fumbled out.

She smiled, and I saw Maz and his sisters in her eyes. Her attention fell to the knife sheathed at my waist. I tensed. Could she tell it was a sunstone knife? The Dags probably wouldn't like that I carried the weapon of their enemies. But I refused to part with it.

"Come," she said suddenly, beckoning. "There are stories to share, songs to sing, and food to eat."

That sounded gods-damned amazing. The last part, anyway. And hopefully, there was a warm, dry bed in the plans as well.

I followed Frieda like a lost bird who'd fallen from its nest.

Everyone piled into the Dag boats or rode ahead on a pack of horses. I spotted Aiden's dark head among the riders that galloped off.

That bothersome loneliness nipped at me once more.

Until Maz waved me over to his boat. Gratefully, I scurried in and tried to ignore the curious stares of the Dag strangers. Yarina, with her arm still in a sling, gave me a short nod. Sigrid and Davka ignored me, but that was better than outright hostility. Maz must've tamed their anger toward me somehow.

I settled onto a middle bench. The Dag boats were long and

narrow, with curved ends—larger than that of Skelly's rowboats. Frieda stood at the front and gave the order to row.

I braced myself for another wave of sickness, but none came. The Dags rowed in perfect unison. The boat glided up the river as though it were made of glass.

Maz tapped my shoulder, then pointed at our surroundings. "This is the Yargoth River, which leads to our camp, but also splits north toward Arduen's Mountain. The pine trees stay green in every season, but those white aspens burn gold close to Terraum's Harvest."

He continued speaking, and I soaked in every word. Not just the knowledge, but that he was talking to me at all. He'd said it would be hard to forgive me, but perhaps this was his way of moving toward that.

A few of the other Dags chipped in with their own facts and stories, eager to show off their home.

Thundering hooves caught my attention, and I glanced over to see Aiden on a black horse riding at breakneck speed. They wove on a path between the trees like they were one spirit. The other Dags raced to catch up with him, whooping and grinning. They shouted challenges to each other and waved to the boats.

But my eyes stayed on Aiden, my breath stuck in my chest. He rode as if his horse would sprout wings at any moment and fly.

"Ah," Maz said in my ear. "That's Wicked, Aiden's horse. I figured those two would be inseparable as soon as they saw each other."

Our paths bent away from each other, and Aiden disappeared among the trees.

I frowned. "Wicked?"

Maz nodded. "My father bought him just before he died, and the horse became very difficult to tame. Yarina named him Wicked because he remained ill-tempered until I brought Aiden home with me. Those two bonded over several weeks and became inseparable. I imagine Wicked was quite distraught about Aiden's absence over the last few years."

"He was," Yarina grumbled. "Cantankerous animal wasn't good for anything but carrying supplies. Even then, he'd try to take a bite out of you."

I licked my lips, knowing my next question could set back our tentative alliance. "What happened to your parents?"

Yarina turned away, but Maz's expression merely grew sad. "Our mother passed from a lung sickness when I was ten. Our father died at the hands of a Rellmiran border patrol."

"Raiding party is more like it," Yarina snarled, still not looking at me.

Maz nodded, his face grim. "Shortly after, I gathered some of our warriors to hunt the Rellmirans down, but we were captured and . . . and thrown into the sunstone mine."

"Oh," I whispered. "That's awful."

I'd known that Maz and Aiden had met in the sunstone mine and escaped together, but I hadn't known why Maz was imprisoned there.

Why were so many children doomed to lose their parents in such unjust ways? It bred nothing but resentment and revenge.

If only there was a better way. A better king or queen who protected their citizens instead of using them and who sought friendship with neighbors instead of trying to steal what wasn't theirs.

Aiden, the true Rellmiran heir, emerged in my thoughts. But I tossed him back out. He would never be my king. Rellmira needed someone without blood on his hands.

An argument broke out just then as Maz tried to take over one of the oars, and his uncle or cousin—I couldn't remember which—gently shoved him back to his seat. Yarina butted in, saying she could row one-handed, and they refused her as well.

I offered to row, but was met with quirked eyebrows and shaken heads. Which suited me fine. I didn't know if I could keep up with their perfect rhythm.

The last bit of light had bled from the sky when Maz suddenly grabbed my arm. "This is it, lovely. We're home."

CHAPTER 7
KIERA

WE ROUNDED ANOTHER BEND, AND A LARGE MEADOW CAME INTO view. Dense forest formed a protective ring around it, and the mountains rose much closer, their peaks blocking out part of the starry sky.

In the meadow, dozens of domed lodges and tents glowed by the light of a dozen fires. Shadowy figures dipped in and around the little village. Dogs barked and horses grazed in a wooden pen. The sweet smell of wood smoke and roasting meat made my mouth water.

The river met the meadow on a gently sloping beach where other boats rested. As soon as our boat slid to a stop on the gritty sand, a shout went up within the village.

Once more, it was mayhem as dozens of Dags rushed out to greet our party. I jumped from the boat and skirted the tangle of hugs and conversation.

I spotted Nikella doing the same from her boat, but so did a huge Dag who broke off from the chaos and rushed toward her.

I tensed, taking a step in their direction. But then my mouth dropped open as the man swept her into a bone-crushing hug that knocked her hood from her head. She seemed to have expected it, though, because she angled her staff away from him. She gave him a one-armed embrace, then shoved him off.

"Enough, Jek," she grumbled, pulling her long hood back up.

The handsome older Dag bowed, his silver grin matching his long hair and beard. "Of course, my beautiful Teacher. I just wasn't sure I'd ever see you again."

"And now you have." Nikella straightened and strode to the village, leaving Jek to stare at her with what I could only describe as a love-struck expression.

I swallowed the incredulous laugh that rose in my throat.

Nikella seemed at ease no matter the task at hand—building bombs in a secret room of the Temple, keeping me prisoner, killing enemies with her spear, healing wounds on a ship. Yet this was the first time I'd ever seen the enigmatic Teacher uncomfortable.

I hurried after her, tucking that bit of information away even though I had no idea who to ask about it.

Nikella wove through the village until she came to a huge, central bonfire. She moved to the other side of it and sat next to Aiden, who reclined on a fur blanket, talking to a gaggle of wild children. A few of the older children beamed at Nikella and surrounded her as well.

Discomfort fishtailed in my chest. I fruitlessly rubbed at it.

They had people here who knew them and—by the looks of it—loved them. They belonged.

It doesn't matter. You'll be leaving soon, anyway. These aren't your people. This isn't your family. Remember who's waiting for you.

I turned to leave, but immediately ran into Frieda, who gave me a gentle shove toward an unoccupied blanket.

"Stay, child. You must eat, and we must remember."

I dutifully sat and was soon pinned in by Maz and Yarina, who dropped to either side of me.

We passed wooden plates of juicy meat and mugs of something that smelled like mead around the fire. I didn't know what kind of meat it was, and I didn't care. I tore into it like I was starving.

For the first time, the Dags were relatively quiet as they also dug into the hot meal.

But soon enough, friends and family sought out Maz and Yarina, or called to them across the fire, congratulating Yarina on her war wound and offering a myriad of interesting ways to dismember Korvin for Maz. This considerably cheered up Maz. As did his constantly refilled mug.

A young boy offered to refill mine as well. I hesitated.

Yarina nudged me. "Too good for our mead, princess?"

I glared at her and held out my mug. The boy filled it with a grin and moved on.

"When in Dagriel, I suppose . . ." I muttered to myself and gulped half of it.

"That's the spirit!" Maz thumped me on the back, causing me to splutter. "It's no Sunshine, but don't tell Davka that."

Davka cuffed him on the back of his head.

"Did you make it?" I asked her. "It's lovely." A small burp escaped me, which seemed to please her. She dipped her head at me.

Drums started appearing around the fire, and suddenly I was grateful for the extra mead. If only I had some hot, buttered biscuits to go with it.

My gaze couldn't help wandering over to Aiden. The flames danced between us, but nothing could hide those green eyes when they met mine.

I felt warm inside and out. My ever-racing mind had slowed and centered.

Gods, he's beautiful.

His black eyebrows drew down as if wary of my attention.

But then a slow drumbeat echoed around the camp, tearing my gaze away.

Frieda rose from her fur-covered chair. She thumped her staff, and an immediate hush settled over the crowd. Even the dogs stopped barking and lay down.

"Tonight, we thank the Four for bringing our warriors home."

Cheers and whistles answered her. Maz lowered his head, staring into his mug. I tentatively squeezed his arm. His hand shot out and kept mine there. I squeezed harder, the memory of clutching his bloody, unconscious body in the Wolves' wagon still too vivid.

I slugged back the rest of my mead. Gods damn it, that was good.

Frieda thumped her staff again. "We also gather to remember those we lost. We may not have bodies to burn"—sad murmurs rippled around the fire—"but we have their names, their memories. We have the love we bore for them, and we will carry that in our hearts until we meet them across the Abyss."

Resounding agreement thundered. I found myself nodding along.

"Zolta, brother of Halka. Bronwyn, daughter of Dietra and Gamli..."

The drums continued their sorrowful beat as Frieda listed off the dead. Soft cries fell like rain, making me feel cold again.

What had become of their bodies in the Den? Perhaps Renwell had burned them where they lay. Or they'd been gifted...

Bile rose in my throat, and I swallowed hard.

Don't think about him. Don't think like that. The gods will find their souls. They will. Their loved ones will see them again.

A woman's singing lifted my blurry gaze. A short, round woman had replaced Frieda. She was wrapped in fur and a dark red skirt. Her graying braids coiled around her head like thick weaves of yarn. And her voice . . . was beautiful.

"Everything given
Must be returned
Every story
Must be earned.
Take their ash
and take their bones
take their souls
to your thrones.
See our tears
and hear our cries
when you take their souls
beyond the skies.
Remember our love
remember their fate
remember we lose
what we choose to hate.
We sew our souls together
And our stories to skin
To find each other
Again and again.
We remember . . .
We remember . . ."

Many voices joined hers in the last lines, tears glistening on cheeks, including mine. Several men and women clutched colorful, patched scarves to their chests, eyes closed.

Maz let go of my hand to stroke the tree tattoo on his arm. Across the fire, Aiden drained his mug.

"Are all Dag funerals like this?" I whispered to Maz.

He nodded. "That's why we fight so hard in life. So that when we mourn, we mourn only what we lost, not what we refused to give."

"No regrets," I murmured, glancing once more at Aiden.

He was already staring at me. His eyes burned and warmed at once. The intensity made me ache all over. For what, I didn't know.

His black hair was wild, as if he'd been running his hands through it. Or perhaps it was from his furious ride earlier.

I licked my lips, tasting mead and salt.

His jaw tightened, and his hand that had been dangling over his knee flexed and clenched. He looked angry now.

He beckoned the boy with the pitcher, who filled his mug again. As he drank, I tore my gaze away from his pulsing throat.

The man who had hugged Nikella—Jek—stood and told a story about one of the deceased. His deep, powerful voice had a very soothing effect, and I couldn't help smiling at the memories he shared.

After him, it was another storyteller, then another. I lost count. Just as I lost count of how many times that boy filled my mug. I felt warm and soft and good. Like the mead, the food, and the stories had created a thick blanket around my heart, keeping away the cold, dark feelings.

Soon, a cry rose, "Another song! Another song!"

I cheered, looking around for the next performer, when Aiden rose to his feet with a slight sway. The cheers grew louder, people stamping their feet and clapping.

"Aiden! Yes, Aiden! Sing! Sing!"

I hiccuped and shouted along with them. When in Dagriel, right?

Aiden stood in front of everyone, his cheeks flushed and his eyes bright. My heart beat faster. I'd only heard him sing once, through a door, at a horrible moment, and it'd made me sob. What would he do to me this time?

He opened his mouth, and instead of a sad song, he sang a bawdy drinking song. The crowd roared with approval and joined in. Maz stumbled to his feet and staggered up to Aiden. They slung arms around each other and swayed, singing.

I gaped.

Yarina leaned against me, her eyes wide as well. "Is Aiden drunk?" she asked in a slurred whisper.

"I think he is," I said in awe.

"He *never* gets drunk. Fucking Four, I'm going to enjoy this."

She clambered to her feet and joined her brother and Aiden, who kept singing. Even drunk and singing about a man who got drunk, couldn't find his own tent, then made love to an innkeeper, his voice plucked at my heart.

All around me, people were getting to their feet to dance and sing along. The drumbeat picked up, and the dogs started howling in harmony. Laughter bubbled out of me. Gods, when was the last time I'd laughed?

Aiden's gaze shot toward me as if he'd heard it, and his face lit up with a smile.

I had to catch my breath. My chest felt too tight.

Maz roared my name and beckoned me over. I went without hesitation, letting him tuck me under his sweaty arm. We swayed in a big group. I caught on to the chorus and belted it out with the rest of them.

My singing was awful, but nobody seemed to care as the mead continued to flow and the world grew ever brighter.

One song led to another. The swaying turned to dancing, where I found myself twirled and passed along between strangers who laughed and showed me the steps.

But then the crowd began to disperse. Couples snuck off to tents. Others cuddled and kissed in front of the fire. Some fell asleep right where they stopped dancing.

Nikella had long since disappeared. So had Jek. Together?

Aiden had vanished. Sigrid and Davka were also gone. A tall woman towed a flushed Maz into a lodge. Yarina was in the lap of a handsome Dag man, her lips fused to his. The sight awoke a strange fire in my belly.

Was Aiden also enjoying eager company somewhere in the village?

Suddenly, I needed coolness and air.

I lurched away from the fires. Away from the tents. One of which I hoped held a bed for me.

I breathed a sigh of relief as I stepped further into the meadow. The cold night air had a bite to it I wasn't used to. But it smelled of leaves and grass and . . . was that the pine Maz had mentioned? Gods, it was delicious. And so clean. I could cleanse my lungs with this mountain forest air.

The soft whicker of a horse drew my attention to the fenced-in part of the meadow.

A dozen horses flicked their tails and grazed in the darkness. A man leaned on the fence next to one of them. He was watching me.

My feet brought me to him of their own accord.

His words echoed in my mind from another night in the woods. *"Lately, it seems I can't run in any direction that does not lead me to you."*

I halted a few steps away. His expression gave away nothing. He merely waited.

"Aiden," I murmured.

"Princess."

We were back to that, were we? "Failed assassin," I snarled.

His smile was sharp and nothing like before. He straightened away from the fence, stepping closer to me. "Successful spy."

"Murderer."

His arm shot out and wrapped around my waist, crushing me against his hard body. "Liar," he growled.

My heart beat so hard it hurt. My fingertips dug into his chest, piercing his own rapid heartbeat. But I didn't push him away. His nose brushed mine. Almost a nuzzle. But no. He wouldn't.

"You lied to me too," I whispered.

His eyes searched mine. "And you stole everything from me, little thief. It's time I stole something back."

His lips crashed into mine, obliterating my senses. My heart was falling, flying, trying to survive. He kissed me like he was angry. Or desperate. His mouth demanded payment.

With a tight groan, I kissed him back. My fingers seized his shirt like they might rip it to shreds. My body melted into his, surrendering. Just for a moment.

He made a noise deep in his chest. Approval. His warm lips coaxed mine apart, and he tasted my tongue. Breathed me in. His hand wrapped around the back of my neck and clenched.

I shivered, and he kissed me harder. I shoved my hands in his hair and met every stroke of his tongue, every press of his lips with my own hunger.

The heat was nearly unbearable. My clothes felt scratchy and heavy. All our anger and sadness. The hurt. It was burning. Burning away. I wanted it to burn away our clothes, too.

Aiden's fingers wrapped around my braid and pulled my head back. I gasped as he trailed his lips and teeth down my throat.

"Fucking Four . . ." I hissed. "I can't . . . I can't even remember why I hate you."

Aiden stiffened. Slowly, painfully, his mouth left my skin. The air between us suddenly felt much cooler. He drew back to stare into my eyes.

His cheeks were still flushed. His pulse still beat rapidly in his throat. But his eyes were hard once more.

"Perhaps because you don't hate me at all, princess," he said.

I scowled and shoved away from him. His hold on me broke easily.

"Just as you don't know me at all," I spat.

His jaw clenched, and he rubbed his thumb over his lips as if he could still feel me there. "I'm starting to think the problem is I know too much."

What in the deep, dark, wandering hell did *that* mean?

My fists clenched. "Gods damn you, Aiden."

He gave me a bitter smile. "I'm sure they already have."

Snarling in frustration, I whirled around and stomped back to the camp. My head pounded, reminding me of all the mead I'd drunk.

We were both drunk. That was why we'd kissed. And my emotions had been running high because of the funeral. Otherwise, I never would have . . .

It didn't matter, anyway. It would never happen again.

CHAPTER 8
KIERA

The fires were burning low as I wandered back through the camp. My head ached and my stomach sloshed. Whatever meat I'd eaten was turning on me. I was also tired to my bones. I just wanted to sleep and forget this night had ever happened.

I considered wandering into random tents to find an empty one, but I doubted that would go over well with any occupants.

I wondered where Aiden would sleep.

Cursing my treacherous mind and wishing I couldn't still feel his hands and lips on my skin, I trudged back to the main fire.

The smell of charred meat and sour mead hit me like a sea wave, and my stomach heaved. I scrambled for a bucket just in time to vomit into it.

I groaned, thankful everyone was asleep. Well, almost everyone.

Yarina rolled over from where she'd been dozing next to the man she'd been kissing, her clothes askew.

She smirked. "Ah, so you do it on land, too, princess."

The title reminded me of Aiden, but exhaustion defeated the rise of anger. "Shut up, Yarina."

She chuckled. "Take my bed in the lodge over there." She jerked her chin to the round lodge behind her. "Davka snores, but Sigrid's on night watch, so you should be safe."

Comforting. But I was desperate for something that wasn't a hammock or the ground.

Besides, I had my sunstone knife if someone got hostile.

I patted my hip to make sure it was still there. Odd. I hadn't even thought to use it on Aiden. Nor had he taken it from me.

"Perhaps because you don't hate me at all, princess."

As if he could possibly understand how I felt.

I wiped my mouth with the back of my hand and set aside the bucket.

"I'll take it," I told Yarina. I gathered myself off the ground and walked past her. "Thank you."

"Wouldn't want you to hurt your royal backside."

I rolled my eyes and ducked around the heavy fur flap that served as the lodge's door. The lodge itself was basically a huge, very sturdy tent shaped like an upside-down bowl.

A small lantern illuminated the wooden skeleton frame that housed three beds and an assortment of chests. Clothes and weapons were strewn about the place. It was surprisingly cozy— the hides and furs covering the wooden frame kept out the cold wind.

And true enough, Davka was sprawled across one bed, snoring loudly. The other two beds sat empty. I did a thorough examination of both to guess which one was Yarina's, as the last thing I wanted was to wake up to Sigrid dragging me out of her bed at knifepoint.

Yarina's scythes lay next to the one with sky-blue and crimson bedding, so I collapsed into that one. I kicked off my boots and rolled under the blankets.

The bed smelled a little stale and unfamiliar, but it was soft, and I could fully stretch out in it.

I fell asleep in moments.

And then . . . I was kissing Aiden again. It should've shocked me how easily my mind fell back to him. But in my dream, I walked toward him without hesitation.

His familiar scent of salt and sunshine mixed with leather enveloped me. He smiled at me, tucking a strand of hair behind my ear. "My little thief."

My heart fluttered as it had before. His green eyes glowed before he kissed me. Soft and gentle at first, then deeper and harder, like he couldn't get enough. Happiness spread through my body. This was right. This was good.

But then something changed.

His rough stubble grew softer and longer under my fingers. His scent changed to that of a candle just blown out. And we weren't kissing. We were standing on the edge of a cliff, a canyon of impenetrable darkness stretching before us.

I took a step back, taking in his dark hair and beard. His deep brown, emotionless eyes.

Renwell had found me.

A shiver rattled between my shoulder blades. I reached for my mother's knife, but only grasped air.

"Where are we?" I demanded.

He smiled. "At the Abyss, my dear apprentice."

My heart stilled. I glanced away from him to the pit of blackness. The Longest Night. Legend said demons waited at the bottom for those who couldn't cross.

I peered at the other side of the Abyss, but it was empty. Barren.

"She's not waiting for you on the other side," Renwell said softly. "No one is."

I closed my eyes tightly. "You're lying. My mother would never leave me."

"But she did. She chose death over you."

Pain ripped through my heart, and I gasped, my eyes widening. I reached for my chest, but nothing had struck it. I felt only the thin scar from the Shadow-Wolf's sunstone knife.

Renwell watched me, his pale face devoid of emotion. He gestured to the Abyss with a gloved hand. "You can either jump and meet your father at the bottom. Or . . ." He extended his hand out to me. "You can come with me, and you'll never be alone again."

I ground my teeth together, my breath coming in short bursts. "The only way I'm going into the Abyss is if I take you with me."

A spark of excitement lit his eyes. He beckoned me. "Come try, then."

My sunstone knife suddenly appeared in my hand. I leaped at him, stabbing toward his chest. He blocked me easily. His sword swung at his hip, but he didn't reach for it.

Enraged, I swiped again and again, and met only air. He tripped me. My ankle gave way on the uneven, rocky surface, but I scrambled back to my feet, limping.

He grinned, his expression fully coming alive as it only ever seemed to in training.

I switched the knife to my other hand, the hilt growing slippery with sweat. I lunged, my movements slow and sluggish. He evaded.

On and on it went. For hours. Days. I didn't know. I was too weak, too slow. I could never defeat him.

Without warning, Renwell seized my throat and swept me over the edge of the Abyss. Immediately, screams and howls rose from the darkness. As if the demons within sensed their next victim.

I gasped and struggled, my legs flailing over nothing. Renwell didn't react, as though he were stronger than ten men.

He stared at me, contempt twisting his mouth. "You will never see them again."

Then he let go.

I fell with a scream.

Falling, falling into darkness.

Then somebody was shaking me, calling my name.

My eyes flew open with a gasp. Yarina's tired blue eyes stared back at me. She grasped one of my arms with her usable hand.

"Put the knife down, princess," she commanded.

Still panting, I glanced down. Mother's knife was clutched in my sweaty fist.

I swore and dropped it onto the rumpled blankets.

Yarina slowly released me, sitting next to me on her bed. Her braids were mussed, and she had a crease on one cheek as though she'd just woken up.

I rubbed my damp face. "Is it morning?"

"Yes. I came to change when you started thrashing like an eel." Her eyes narrowed, studying me. "Bad dream?"

I averted my eyes. "It's nothing."

"Grandmother always said bad dreams are like weeds. If you don't kill the source, they'll just keep coming back."

I grunted. If only it were that easy.

"You kept saying the name 'Renwell.' Same bastard that took over your kingdom?"

"Yes."

"He do that to you?"

She pointed at my chest where my shirt had drifted down to reveal my scar.

"No. One of his Wolves did."

Yarina's nostrils flared with disgust. "I hope you gave him a worse one."

"He's dead." *Aiden killed him to save me.*

"Excellent. How come you have one of their knives?" She pointed to where Mother's knife glittered on the bed between us.

"It's not theirs. It was my mother's." I sheathed it back at my waist.

She waited as if I would fill in more of the story, but I was in no mood to oblige. Besides, it wasn't just my story.

"Regardless," she continued, "I'd keep it hidden if I were you."

I frowned. "Why?"

Yarina stood up and started rooting through the mess on the floor. "People know it as the weapon of the enemy. You're already a Rellmiran princess and spy. Folks won't take any more kindly to you if you're wielding a blade made from the gods-damned stone our friends and relatives are mining in captivity."

Fucking Four, I wished I could destroy that whole damn mine and Renwell's plans along with it. If I'd become High Enforcer, that would've been my first stop. That and cleaning out the Den of any prisoners who shouldn't be there.

But I was powerless. Just like I'd been in my dream.

"I'll keep it hidden," I told Yarina. "Unless Renwell happens to wander by. Then I'll shove it in his heart where it belongs."

Yarina's golden eyebrows shot up. She grinned. "Now you're talking. You know, I think I'm starting to like you, princess."

"Not if you're still calling me princess," I grumbled, swinging my legs over the side of the bed and reaching for my boots.

She laughed and plucked a shirt from the mess.

"Do you need help?" I asked, gesturing to her arm in its sling.

"Absolutely not. But you can go rinse your mouth for me. Your breath stinks."

I blew her a breathy kiss, and she pretended to gag, then elbowed me in the ribs on my way out.

Her teasing reminded me of Everett and Delysia. How we used to be with each other before we got older and slotted into our predetermined roles. Things were so much simpler back then. And now ...

My smile dimmed.

"You will never see them again."

Had Dream Renwell been referring to my siblings? All the more reason to get to them sooner. Kill the nightmare, as Frieda had said.

I shoved open the fur flap. Sunlight pierced my skull like a spear, and I groaned. Gods-damned Dags and their mead and their wild funerals.

The day seemed closer to noon than dawn. Yet a few Dags still laid about on blankets. Others sat and smoked pipes and chatted with neighbors.

Steaming pots hung over the ever-present fires tended by men and women alike. I recognized a tall, willowy figure and made my way over to Nikella.

Her scarred arms were bare over the heat of the fire. She expertly stirred whatever was in the pot, her focused expression aligning the deep scar that bisected her face. Without her usual long-hooded robe, she looked more like a warrior than a Teacher. But I supposed all Rellmiran Teachers used to be warriors before Father had outlawed fighting instruction.

I wondered if Nikella had obeyed that particular law.

She glanced up at me, and for a moment, her stern look reminded me of her brother.

"Hungry?" she asked.

I nodded. "And thirsty."

She pointed to a bucket of water. Hopefully not the same bucket I'd vomited in the night before.

I ladled myself a sip.

Cold, clean water washed over my bitter tongue. I gulped more and more. It tasted amazing. Like the freshness of the air, but in water.

"There's tooth powder if you need some of that, too," Nikella said, ladling what looked like porridge into two bowls. "I mixed it up this morning."

I picked up the satchel of glittery pale green powder. I rubbed a pinch over my teeth, appreciating the hard flecks that scraped away the grime. A minty taste bloomed in my mouth.

I spat and rinsed, then joined Nikella on a worn log. She handed me a bowl and spoon, and we ate in silence. The porridge was good. Thick and creamy, with a hint of cinnamon and apple. It helped settle my stomach.

A few Yargoths passed and greeted Nikella, who offered each one some of her porridge. They took it gladly and went on their way.

I wanted to ask her about Aiden and where he was. About Renwell and what they planned to do concerning the ships at Calimber. But really, I only needed to ask her one thing.

"Will you draw me a map?" I asked as we watched the Dags go about their day. "Of a path from here to Aquinon by foot."

She scraped her bowl clean and ate her final bite without changing expression. "What are you going to do in Aquinon?"

I bit my lip. At least she hadn't outright dismissed me. "Find my brother and sister and get them out."

"Alone?"

I twirled my spoon in my porridge. "Yes."

She tilted her head to stare at me. I'd seen her giving the same look to Aiden and Maz. As if she could read their minds and souls through their eyes.

I tried not to fidget as I held her gaze.

She finally nodded. "I will draw the map for you."

I blinked in surprise. "You aren't going to stop me?"

"You are aware of the danger that awaits you. You know the likelihood of your success." She lifted her eyes to the cloudless sky. "I've only ever asked the gods for one favor: to choose how I die. I would not begrudge someone else's desire to choose their own fate." Her eyes pierced me once more. "You have your reasons, after all."

"I do," I murmured, my grip tightening on my bowl. Why had she asked the Four for such a thing? And was she so sure that I would die in my attempt to free Everett and Delysia?

"Renwell won't kill me," I said, almost desperately. As if I could convince her that my goal wasn't completely foolish. "You knew he wouldn't kill you because you're his sister. Well, he had a chance to kill me when we escaped, and he didn't. He might—"

"Care for you?" Nikella's voice sharpened. "It's not affection that keeps him from killing us. It's his need to control, his need to play a game with our lives. He never removes a piece from the board unless it's no longer of use to him. There's no telling when that thread of control will snap."

I remembered how quickly Renwell had beheaded Father. He'd claimed it was to prevent my execution, but none of the Wolves would've obeyed Father, anyway. They only listened to Renwell because he'd planned it that way.

Just like he'd probably planned to kill Father in that exact moment, regardless if I was there or not.

"I have to try," I said.

"I know. I'll have the map ready in a few days." With that, Nikella stood and left me alone.

I finished my porridge slowly. I should feel grateful that Nikella had agreed to draw a map and hadn't argued against my leaving. But I simply felt hollow.

Perhaps all of my goodbyes would be this easy.

CHAPTER 9
KIERA

Five days passed and still no map.

I traded Yarina's bed for one of my own in a smaller lodge shared with Nikella, who was always asleep when I came to bed and gone by the time I woke.

Frieda agreed to lend me a horse and some supplies for my journey. In return, she put me to work around the camp, patching lodges, cooking meals, drawing water, cleaning dishes, and caring for the horses.

She'd asked me if I hunted, and I said no. Instead, I'd watched Aiden and Maz go out with a small hunting party every day.

Frieda tried to show me how to clean their kills and preserve the hides and meat from the various animals. But all I could see was Korvin carving Maz's back. When Frieda noticed my pale, shaking hands, she kindly gave me another job tending their small gardens. I was so grateful I hugged her.

I found that I truly enjoyed kneeling in the dirt among the tangle of stems and colorful vegetables. It reminded me of Mother with her flowers.

Even though Frieda kept me busy from dawn until dusk, I still took meals with Maz, Yarina, and Nikella. Jek usually joined as well, entertaining us with wild stories and even earning a few smiles from Nikella.

Nikella also told stories, but they were of the Four and their time. When she spoke, I finally saw her as the other Teachers I'd known growing up. But this time, I listened more closely.

Children of all ages would follow her, asking her questions. She answered every single one and even taught reading, writing, and counting to the interested ones.

I shared time with nearly every person in camp, except Aiden. I hadn't spoken to him since the night of the funerals.

Maz always gave excuses for his absence, even when I didn't ask for any. He said Aiden had already eaten, or he was on watch duty, or a dozen other things. But Maz's sad smile said he knew Aiden was simply avoiding any space with me in it.

Just as well. If we weren't talking to each other, then I wouldn't have to say goodbye.

The idea of saying goodbye to the others pained me more each day. Especially Maz. He was smiling and joking more. He threw himself into tasks to regain his strength. But there was still a shadow of pain in his eyes that I felt responsible for.

I kept asking Nikella if the map was ready, and she'd shake her head and say, "Not yet." I didn't know if she was holding off on purpose, or if it was truly taking that long.

A small, cowardly part of my mind was relieved that she was taking her time. I was enjoying this pocket of peace I'd found in the mountain meadow.

Maz said they'd soon paddle north on the Yargoth River for the fireseed harvest on Arduen's Mountain. It sounded beautiful and exciting, but would also be the perfect moment for me to slip away south. Back home.

The day before we all planned to leave, Frieda asked me to

harvest any ripe vegetables so the frost wouldn't take them while the Yargoths were gone.

I took my basket to the sunny patch of dirt where colorful squash and rows of corn were ready for picking. A few children and older men and women also meandered the rows, filling their baskets.

They chattered among themselves about the upcoming harvest festival. Frieda said they usually celebrated at the foot of Arduen's Mountain with other clans while several Teachers and appointed Dags collected the fireseeds from the glowing flowers.

In Aquinon, we'd celebrated Terraum—god of the harvest— by dressing up and having grand feasts. All for a bounty from the fields of Pravara that we didn't grow or harvest.

But here in the warm sunshine and cool air with my fingers plucking each vegetable, I truly felt connected to the earth. I sent up a prayer to Father Terraum that the food I gathered would get the Yargoths through the winter.

A long shadow fell over me. I startled, wondering if I'd accidentally summoned Terraum. But when I looked up, it was no god. Just an angry man who looked like one.

"When were you going to tell me you're leaving?" Aiden demanded, his arms folded over his chest. His black shirt was untied at the top, the laces swaying in the breeze.

He glared down at me as if he could intimidate me. Or provoke me. I refused to give in to either desire.

I turned back to my yellow squash. "I don't need to tell you anything. I assumed Nikella would inform you if you realized I was gone."

Perhaps I shouldn't have added that last part. I didn't want him to think I missed his presence. But I supposed he could take my words however he gods-damn wished.

He growled in frustration, and I could almost hear him running his fingers through his hair.

"Were you planning to run out on Maz and his family as well? The people who gave you food and shelter? Or was it just me?"

I scowled and yanked on the stubborn squash until the stem snapped. "I'm not *running out* on anyone. I asked Frieda for a horse and supplies, and Nikella for a map. I was going to say goodbye to Maz and Yarina tomorrow."

I placed the squash in my basket with the others, but didn't pick it up as I stood to face him.

"I'm not letting you go," he said.

Despite my best intentions, fury rose like a storm inside me. "*Let* me go? I wasn't aware that I was your prisoner."

"You're not. But I can't let you go on some foolish quest—"

"I am not asking your permission," I hissed in his face. "Foolish or not, I need to make sure my brother and sister are alive because I'm the only one who cares if they are."

"I am just as responsible for their lives as I am for yours," he snarled back. "I swore to your mother—"

"Don't you *dare* invoke my mother." I stabbed my finger into his chest. "If it weren't for you, she'd still be alive. *You* got her into a mess that forced *you* to kill her to clean it up."

Aiden seized the finger that was trying to puncture his chest, his green eyes blazing. "And I will *never* forgive myself for it. But I wasn't the first one she went to for help in getting rid of your father."

I froze, my heart slamming against my chest. "You're lying."

"Why would I lie? I have nothing left to lose. I'm trying to help you find some gods-damned peace."

"By telling me my mother—my sweet, innocent mother— was soliciting assassins in her spare time because she wanted the throne that damn much? You're insane."

He growled, tightening his grip on my finger. "She wasn't soliciting assassins, princess. She was only allowed out of the palace on festival days to go to the Temple. She *quietly* asked the Teachers for help. Do you remember Librius? He knew Nikella and knew I was in Aquinon. He arranged for me to meet Brielle at the Temple. She was my mother's best friend. She recognized me instantly."

Some of the rage left my body like a dying wind. I swallowed hard. Queen Rhea had died giving birth to Aiden after my father had murdered King Tristan and Renwell had shot her with an arrow as she fled.

But my mother and his mother . . . had been friends?

Aiden's voice softened. "Brielle said she was pregnant with Everett when my parents died. She was distraught and vowed that one day she would make it right, however she could."

"And you used that vow for your own revenge plan," I whispered, my voice in jagged pieces.

His eyes searched mine, my pain reflecting in his. "She wanted me to be king. To restore my father's house. But I refused. I merely wanted Weylin gone. She agreed to take the throne and clear a path for Everett one day."

"That's why you wanted Everett to be king."

Aiden nodded. "It was what she wanted. Now tell me, am I lying?"

My instincts said no, but he'd bested me in Death and Four, so I was no great judge. Which reminded me of something else. "You lied to me before," I said. "When we were playing Death and Four at *The Weary Traveler*. You said you knew nothing about my mother's death."

He scoffed. "Should I have told the whole tavern that I killed the queen? That I aimed to kill the king as well? I survive by not sharing all my secrets with every person who asks. Though you did try your damnedest. Tell me, how much did your old mentor know by the end?"

I tried to jerk away from him, but he held me fast. He leaned closer, his scent and warmth muddling my senses. I desperately tried not to think about kissing him last night.

Aiden continued, seemingly unaffected. "Clearly, Renwell knew about the heist and the date of our attack, but what else did you tell him? Maz insists that you had nothing to do with him being captured and tortured. I'm inclined to believe him, but it doesn't make sense. Why would a spy only divulge information under the duress of losing her supposed enemy?"

Hope sparked in my chest. "He doesn't blame me for what happened?"

Aiden's jaw clenched. "He still thinks it would've been better if you'd let Korvin torture him instead of giving up the date."

"You would've done the same thing in my position."

"I would've lied my way out."

I barked out a bitter laugh. "Renwell always knows when someone is lying."

"He's not a god, princess."

My lip curled. "You forget who put me in your cell. Why would he do that if he didn't think I was just the right key to unlock your secrets? You even said it yourself."

"Yes, I did," Aiden said softly. "I thought it was much too convenient that such a beautiful, intriguing woman ended up in my cell. I thought perhaps he *did* recognize me in his torture room, and he knew what my weakness would be when his fists didn't find one."

My heart shrank in on itself like a flower hiding from the night. Renwell had admitted to figuring out Aiden's identity before I did. Another secret I'd kept from my mentor. But Aiden didn't need to know that. Why defend myself when I'd still done the unforgivable in his eyes? Yet, he continued to defend his own unforgivable crime.

"You didn't recognize me, even though you knew my mother," I blurted out, then immediately wished I could call the words back. They made me sound weak and desperate. I knew I didn't look like her, but it still hurt.

Something flickered in Aiden's eyes. Moments drifted by as I became acutely aware of how his fist wrapped around my finger. How his dark hair fluttered over his drawn brow. How my knee brushed his.

My stomach quivered.

I was casting about for something else to yell at him for when he murmured, "You're more like your mother than you think." He glanced down at my captured finger. "She always had dirt under her fingernails, too. I never asked her why."

Tears burned suddenly in my throat. Grief was strange. Days would pass without a single tear shed, then a little reminder of her, of who she'd been, would hit me so hard it felt like she'd left me yesterday.

"She loved to garden," I whispered. "Flowers. Her favorites were lilies. She was always trying to grow different colors."

Why was I telling him this? He didn't need to know. He hadn't cared to ask back then, so why would he care now?

Suddenly, Aiden dipped his head and placed a featherlight kiss on my fingertip.

CHAPTER 10
KIERA

My heart tripped over itself. My lips parted, but no sound came out.

Aiden frowned, as if surprised he'd done such a thing, and released my hand.

We couldn't keep doing this. Hating each other one minute, sharing kisses and painful memories the next.

"I am truly sorry," he said in that deep voice that reminded me of his singing. "I wish I could've saved her."

I peered into his deep green eyes and saw only sincerity. It shook the shields around my heart like a battering ram.

Why didn't you save her then? What really happened that night? What were her last words? Did she regret what she'd done? Did she want us to know the truth? Why, why, did she do it?

The questions piled up at the tip of my tongue, but my voice refused to release them.

Aiden shook his head at me. "Is it truly easier to hate me than to ask me for the truth? Because it's there, waiting for you to want it. I wish it were the same for the truth I seek."

The walls around my heart shuddered again. But I ordered

them to hold. I couldn't do this again. The last time I'd tried to tell the truth, my whole world had crumbled around me.

He might paint a portrait of my mother that I could never unsee. And that was if I trusted him to tell me everything accurately.

One breath, two breaths, three.

My walls held. My heart was safe. It would be even safer tomorrow when I left.

I took a step back. "It doesn't matter," I said in a hollow voice. "We will probably never see each other again. Nothing we say can save a trust so broken."

A myriad of emotions burned through Aiden's gaze. For a moment, I thought he might reach for me. For a moment, I wanted him to. In the space between one breath and the next, I wanted him to fight for me, to never let me go, to tell me we'd find a way back to where we'd been.

But that would've been a lie as well.

He opened his mouth to say something when a shout rose from the village. A horn blew, dogs barked, and people ran toward the sound from all directions.

Aiden followed at a sprint, with me on his heels.

Were we being attacked? Had Renwell found us?

My breath grew sharp in my lungs.

Chaos reigned in the village until a bellow from Jek silenced everyone.

Standing in the middle of the crowd, Frieda cleared her throat and announced, "A fisherman spotted a large Rellmiran ship sailing north a few hours ago." Her gaze narrowed in on me and Aiden. "A heavily armed ship with catapults."

My heart sank to my toes as Aiden swore between his teeth.

At least one ship from Calimber must have been seaworthy to follow us so quickly. But they weren't coming for us.

"They must be headed to Arduen's Mountain," Jek proclaimed. "We need to get there first!"

A chorus of shouted agreement rose. The Yargoth warriors lifted their axes and bows and spears in the air, shaking them and yelling.

My chest heaved, trying to find enough breath. They were racing into a battle they couldn't win. Even if they arrived at the mountain first, they couldn't defeat one of those ships.

Barrels of fire and Bardo's limp body flashed through my mind.

More people would die. Would there be any Yargoths left after this?

Frieda seemed to share my grim thoughts, her wrinkled face stern and devoid of its usual brightness. She held up her arms for quiet.

Everyone hushed.

"We will send every able warrior to assist the Urzost Clan in defending our sacred mountain. Any warrior too injured to lift an axe will remain here."

Every warrior? I immediately glanced at Aiden, whose jaw was set. Fear oozed into my veins. He was leaving with them. Of course, he was going to fight.

I turned away.

I didn't care. He seemed to love a plan with a high risk of his death. Why should I try to stop him anymore? I wouldn't let him hold me back, either.

It doesn't matter. It doesn't matter. I tried chanting the mantra that I'd been repeating over the last few days. But it rang false in my head.

"I *can* lift a bloody axe!" I heard Yarina shout from a distance. "I can best both of you with one arm, and you know it!"

I craned my head until I saw her facing off with Sigrid. Maz stood between them, his arms folded across his chest. He met my gaze with one of fierce determination. He was going, too.

I bit my lip. Gods damn it. I was going to lose them all.

Jek shouted orders, and the chaos shifted into well-practiced movements.

Something brushed the back of my hand. I glanced down to see Aiden's hand retreating.

"May the gods go with you," he said softly. "If anyone can rescue Everett and Delysia, it's you."

I blinked up at him. The finality in his eyes stole my voice.

"Goodbye . . . Kiera." Then he was gone. Swallowed up by the other warriors preparing to depart.

My hands curled into fists, my dirty fingernails biting into my palms. I wanted to scream, to cry, to order them all to stay. But I couldn't. These weren't my people. They would never listen to me.

That feeling of powerlessness swept over me again, like shards of glass tearing through my skin.

My vision blurred as I watched Maz and Yarina strap axes, scythes, and huge knives to their bodies.

Maz took a step toward me, his blue eyes tight. But I couldn't handle another goodbye. I made a strangled noise and bolted.

I was supposed to have time. Just one more day. It seemed so little, but in the face of forever, that day was suddenly invaluable.

I'd just made it to the treeline when I heard hoofbeats behind me.

"Kiera Torvaine!" someone shouted.

Shock at hearing my full name slowed my escape. I dashed the tears from my eyes before I whipped around. Nikella galloped up to me on a gray horse, her staff in one hand.

"Enough running," she said sharply, jerking her horse to a snorting halt.

My jaw slackened. I expected a stoic goodbye or possibly

even the map she owed me, not a rebuke. My mouth snapped shut.

"I'm not running," I ground out. "I'm still going back home to rescue my siblings, as I said before."

Nikella looked every inch the warrior Teacher as she stared down at me. "You *are* running. You know as well as I that Renwell won't harm your brother and sister if they are still pieces he can play. And right now, they are serving as bait to draw you back to him. Don't give him what he wants, Kiera."

I growled in frustration. Fucking Four, how did she do that? Take the fears that had been lurking in my mind and spin them with logic. Draining me of the last hope I had.

The horn sounded again, and I glimpsed warriors on horseback heading north—a familiar rider on a wild black horse in their midst.

"What would you have me do?" I snapped at Nikella, tearing my gaze away. "Stay here? Either way, Renwell wins."

Her horse pranced sideways, shaking his head as if he knew they were supposed to be galloping with the others.

"Fight with us," Nikella said. As if it were that simple.

My eyebrows arched in disbelief. "Fight with you?" I snorted. "No one wants me to fight with them. I'm a traitor, remember?"

"You've made mistakes. You chose honor when you admitted them. It's time to move on."

"To what?" Desperation edged into my voice. "A war we can't win? You saw those ships. What can a few dozen warriors do against catapults?"

Nikella nodded. "There's a chance we might not win." Her dark eyes softened. "But that doesn't mean the battle shouldn't still be fought. Sometimes the victory is in the fight itself, regardless of the outcome. Giving up guarantees defeat."

Her words singed my soul like sparks of truth. I wanted to

keep fighting. I wanted to win. I wanted to defeat Renwell and make my mother proud. I wanted to keep my friends safe.

"But I'd be giving up on Everett and Delysia," I rasped.

"We will find a way to them, Kiera. But right now, there are other brothers and sisters who will be fighting for their lives and the lives of their families. Their homes. Their sacred mountain." She sighed, her head bowed. "I learned a long time ago that my place is between monsters and the souls they try to steal." She offered me a scarred hand. "I think your heart is also already in that fight. You just need to follow it."

Hope and fear clashed like thunder in my chest, shaking my body. Those sparks ignited and burned. My heart beat faster as if I were back on the Temple roof, reaching for one of the bells suspended between earth and sky.

Because yes, *yes,* this was what I always wanted. To fight the monsters who preyed on others. To render justice where it was due.

I wasn't the High Enforcer. I was hardly even a warrior. But I *was* a gods-damned fighter.

I took a deep breath and grasped Nikella's hand.

CHAPTER II
AIDEN

The steady drum of Wicked's hoofbeats usually calmed me. But not this time.

This time, they echoed the fear and pain that bled from my heart with each beat.

From confronting Kiera to telling her a rushed goodbye and now riding into an unforeseen battle, I was rattled. At least she would be safe from this fight. But if she was headed to Aquinon...

I swore and squeezed Wicked's sides. He snorted and galloped faster.

The path through the woods was well-worn and as yet unburdened with snow. But here in the mountains, that could change overnight.

It would take a day and a half of hard riding to reach Arduen's Mountain if we slept little.

Eventually, the path grew too narrow and twisted to race along. Clouds of steam puffed from Wicked's nostrils as he restrained himself to a fast trot.

Maz pulled up next to me on his golden horse, Valiant. He adjusted the axes strapped to his back, grimacing.

"Pain?" I asked.

He shot me a glare. "No. Just a bit too tight. It's been a while."

I patted the bag I'd secured to Wicked's rump. "I brought what healing supplies I could for you and your sisters. And anyone else who might need it."

Maz clenched his jaw. "Do you think the ship will beat us there?"

"We have the shorter route, but if the wind favors them, or we run into trouble . . ." The potential consequences played like a grisly memory in my mind.

"Who do you think's on the ship?" Maz asked, glaring at the dense woods ahead. "Sailors? Soldiers? Wolves?"

I'd been trying to figure that out from the moment I heard the news. "We know that Dracles and some of his men were stationed at Calimber. Could be that Renwell ordered them to take one of the ships here."

"Or your little jaunt to see the ships scared them, and they're looking for us."

My spine stiffened, even though I'd wondered the same. "They sailed right past *Mynastra's Wings* and the river entrance. Perhaps they didn't see Skelly's ship hidden in the bay, but the route to the Yargoth camp isn't exactly a secret."

"I suppose," Maz grunted, stroking his beard. It'd grown long enough that he'd started braiding it again. "I suppose there's no way a ship that gods-damned big would make it up our river. Perhaps they aim to send boats down the river from the north. In which case, we could ambush them on their way down."

A rabbit ran across the path, causing Wicked to dance sideways. I stroked his mane to calm him. He wasn't a war horse, but he'd been through a few skirmishes. Riding into battle would hopefully give us an advantage. And we'd need every one against that ship.

"The fireseed harvest is too close to be coincidental," I said. "Renwell either wants to steal the fireseeds, or he wants many Dags gathered in one place where he can use catapults on them all."

"Fucking Four, Aiden," Maz grumbled. "You're like a mirror in a sewer. All you see is shit."

A weak chuckle rumbled in my chest. "Give me something else to look at, then."

Maz pondered for a moment, then snuck a glance at me. "Did you say goodbye to her?"

My fingers tightened on the reins. "Who?"

Maz rolled his eyes. "We may be riding to our deaths. Spare me the idiotic denial."

Kiera's worried amber eyes filled my mind. A small, desperate piece of my crumbled heart hoped some of that worry had been for me. But she'd made her feelings clear.

Nothing we say can repair a trust so broken.

"I said what I could," I replied.

"She ran away from me. You should've seen her lovely face." Maz sighed. "I hope she'll at least stay the winter with us. If we're still alive."

She won't. She's probably far beyond our reach by now.

Regret prickled in my chest, but I ignored it. There was nothing I could do about it now.

I twisted around to check on the rest of our party. Jek and a few other warriors rode ahead while Sigrid, Davka, and Yarina kept close behind us.

Farther back in the line, I spotted Nikella's gray horse and her long-hooded cloak through the golden foliage. Good. I wasn't sure why she was riding so far back. But she'd been a little skittish around Jek, so perhaps that was why.

Nikella had joined forces with the Yargoths much the same way I had with Maz in the sunstone mine. For almost two years, she'd worked with Jek to help us escape. I lived with the Yargoths for a while after that, but Nikella returned to her nomadic ways.

She and Jek had always seemed close, but perhaps something else had strained their friendship.

Maz and I talked little as we continued to ride for hours. Any time the path straightened out, Jek urged our party to ride faster. But soon, the sun had disappeared, and the sweat on Wicked's coat grew cold.

Just as Maz started to grumble, Jek gave the order to make camp.

He'd chosen an area close to the river with some roughage for the horses. A few rocky outcroppings provided a buffer from the bitter wind that kicked up in the darkness.

Our thirty-seven warriors broke into groups. I helped manage the horses while others built fires and retrieved water. By the time I finished unsaddling and watering the horses, a few fires crackled near the river. Someone had set a pot of water to boiling on a few propped branches.

Most of us had brought nothing but weapons and what was already packed in our saddlebags. I'd had the forethought to toss my father's ring to Frieda for safekeeping before galloping away.

Thankfully, Nikella had a pouch of dry meat and vegetables to add to the water, so no one had to hunt. The tantalizing scent of stew made my stomach growl, reminding me I hadn't eaten all day. But first, I needed to ease my thirst.

I slipped down to the riverbank. A shadowy figure hunched over the rushing water. A woman, judging by her slight frame. But she wore a cloak instead of the usual Dag furs and capes.

She turned, brushing her cloak aside to scoop water from the river with her hands. A gold hilt glinted in the faint light.

My heart jerked in my chest. No. It couldn't be. I was never meant to see her again. She would never . . .

"*Kiera?*" I rasped.

She spun around, water dripping from her lips and fingers. Was it only five nights ago I'd stolen a kiss from that mouth? In my drunken state, I'd thought to take something back from her, but she'd stolen my thoughts and dreams in the following days and nights, anyway.

And here she was, armed with only her mother's gods-damned sunstone knife and staring at me with that defiant tilt of her chin.

"Don't bother telling me to go back," she said, her voice harsh. "I'm not doing this for you."

My eyebrows tightened. "I didn't think you were."

Her gaze shifted, as if my agreement surprised her. Her fingers danced around her waist the way they used to when searching for her usual throwing knives. Instead, her hand settled on her mother's knife hilt.

I remembered her expression when she'd threatened me with that knife in Renwell's office. Her grip had held little conviction, but her words and her eyes had contained plenty.

"*I will never forgive you.*"

I'd told her to try and stab me then because I knew she wouldn't. When really I wanted to say that her gods-damned knife had already harmed me more than it ever could in her hands.

"Nikella said she would teach me the sword," Kiera blurted out, misreading my intense gaze on her knife.

I scowled. "And you think you can be proficient enough for battle tomorrow?"

Her cheeks flushed. "Perhaps. But I intend to do as Nikella advised and simply make sure any villagers, especially children, are out of harm's way."

I blew out a breath. That was something, at least. I didn't doubt Kiera's skills as a lone street fighter or a tavern hustler. But to fight as a unit with weapons she'd never used against a ship with catapults? I wanted her as far from that as possible.

And what was all this about Nikella? My mentor must have interfered for reasons known only to herself.

"What of Aquinon?" I asked.

Worry flickered in those soft amber eyes. She bit her lip as she seemed to decide what to tell me. "Aquinon can wait." She gestured toward the makeshift camp and beyond. "They can't."

She moved to walk past me. My hand stretched out to grasp her arm before I yanked it back to my side. I didn't even know why I wanted to stop her. To express my relief that I hadn't seen her face for the last time? To assure her of my protection?

She had lied to me. Used me. Chosen her bastard father and her manipulative mentor over me.

I couldn't fathom why I struggled to harden my heart this time. It'd been easy after the horrors of the Pravaran rebellion and in the dark hell that was the sunstone prison mine. And after losing Brielle.

But now? Perhaps I couldn't harden my heart with pieces of it still missing.

Still clutched in a thief's scarred fingers.

I kneeled at the river's edge and splashed water on my face. The iciness of it set my teeth on edge and sliced through the haze in my mind.

I had a battle to fight that had nothing to do with Kiera. Just as her choices excluded me. As it should be.

When I returned to camp, the stew was ready. Nikella handed me a full bowl with a spoon. A silent argument passed within our gazes.

Why didn't you tell me?

I didn't need to.

I don't like it.

You don't have to.

My glare softened, and I gestured with my bowl. *Thank you for the soup.*

She dipped her head, a small smile interrupting her scar. *You're welcome.*

I sat with her while Maz happily took a spot next to Kiera, throwing an easy arm around her shoulders.

Even Yarina seemed pleased by her unexpected arrival. "You can't win a battle with that piddly knife. I'll teach you how to wield any weapon you wish."

"Including a scythe?" Kiera asked lightly.

Yarina shoved her shoulder, nearly spilling Kiera's soup into her lap. "Never, princess. Like I said, no one touches my scythes but me. Even if I only have one hand to wield them."

Jek sat next to Nikella with a sly grin. "I hear Vorkahn is an expert at one-handing his weapon. Perhaps you should ask him for advice."

Chuckles rumbled around the fire, the loudest from Vorkahn —a Dag as tall as a tree with skin like bark and a laugh like thunder.

A corner of Kiera's mouth lifted. Distracted, I tilted my bowl, and hot soup dripped onto my hand. I subtly licked it off.

I looked up to see Maz watching me with a knowing grin. I scowled at him and took my soup elsewhere while the Dags continued to rib each other.

I ate quietly in the dark next to Wicked, who kept nipping at my pockets for carrots. Jek wandered past on his way to take a piss and asked me to stand first watch. I agreed.

The night turned even chillier. I'd forgotten what it was like in the mountains. Especially as winter neared. I'd actually grown somewhat fond of Aquinon's storms and heat.

After an hour of shivering under my cloak, I unsheathed my

sword and ran through several mock fights. I'd had little opportunity to practice my swordsmanship the last few years, despite the training room beneath the Temple.

I needed to be ready for whatever awaited us.

I wondered what Kiera would have said if I'd offered to train with her.

My body felt loose and warm by the time Maz stumbled away from camp to relieve me.

The fires had burned low, their embers rippling with heat. I quietly picked my way around the sleeping bodies to where I'd left my sleeping roll propped against a rocky ledge.

I froze when I saw Kiera curled into a ball next to my roll. Even though her blanket was tightly tucked around her body, she was shivering in her sleep.

I stepped closer. Not just shivering. Her face contorted as if in pain, and little whimpers escaped her lips.

Gods damn it. I rubbed my hands over my face. I sincerely doubted she realized she'd curled up next to my bedroll, but I couldn't just leave her like this.

However, my face might be the last thing she'd want to see if I woke her up.

What did she dream of? Was it moments she regretted or moments she feared would happen?

My mind liked to frequent both in my sleep. The last time it hadn't was in that tent in The Hollow. With her.

I glanced around the camp, but no one stirred.

Resolute, I unrolled my thick blanket. My fingers worked swiftly and quietly, unbuckling my sword and knives. I laid them in a heap at my back. I balled up my cloak for a pillow, then carefully stretched out behind Kiera, dragging my blanket over both of us.

She continued to fret and tremble, so I slid closer until her back nestled into my chest. She seemed to sense my body heat and pressed herself more firmly against me.

Warmth flickered in my chest. I slowly draped an arm over her side. She released a soft sigh, and I relaxed.

"Aiden," she murmured.

I tensed again, waiting for her to shove me off. Instead, her breathing deepened.

My body hummed with contentment. Perhaps even hope. If I could vanquish her nightmares, perhaps I could defeat whatever awaited us at the mountain.

But when I awoke a few hours later, Kiera was gone.

CHAPTER 12
KIERA

The distress horns were faint at first.

We'd been riding all day when Nikella stiffened in front of me. I'd been dozing against her back despite the constant jostling.

I hadn't slept well last night. At least at first. I'd been having nightmares where I seemed caught between awake and asleep, not knowing what was real. But then I dreamed Aiden had lain down behind me and held me close. And I'd faded into blissful darkness.

When I'd awakened in his arms, I realized it hadn't been a dream. My cheeks had burned, wondering what had happened that caused him to take pity on me. Had I called out for him in my sleep?

The last time we'd lain together like that had been in The Hollow.

Unbidden, the memory of his deep voice whispering into my ear had floated through my waking mind.

"For the first time, I have hope. Hope that my heart might not be

too scarred for a certain beautiful thief to consider stealing the rest of the pieces she hasn't already taken."

A warm ache had stirred in my belly that I escaped as hastily as his unconscious embrace.

Yarina and Nikella had shown me a few sword maneuvers by firelight as the others packed up the camp.

I'd borrowed a sword from Vorkahn, who was a walking armory. He'd handed it to me with a hard glint in his eyes, saying it'd belonged to his niece, Bronwyn. I recognized the name from Frieda's funeral speech as one of the dead. It felt clunky and unwieldy in my unpracticed hands, but I didn't dare turn down such an offering.

Renwell had never seen fit to teach me much of the sword since my father had banned them from Aquinon.

My lip had curled in disgust when I told Nikella such. And of the deadly sunstone sword with which Renwell had beheaded my father.

She'd nodded as if she expected this and corrected my sword grip.

We spoke little as we continued north. When Aiden rode past us, I turned my face away.

Dawn came and went. The air grew colder, stabbing at my nose. The golden trees faded away, leaving only a blanket of fuzzy pines.

Nikella passed me dried meat and apples for lunch, but we never left the saddle. As the sun set again, I was beginning to think I'd never be able to fight if I couldn't regain feeling in my ass.

But I forgot all about my aching body when we heard the horns. Faint, but blowing fast and frantic. Fear rippled through our party with grim expressions and stamping hooves.

Jek shouted, "Onward, faster!"

Everyone galloped down the path. I clung to Nikella's cloak.

Please, Holy Four, help us get there in time.

We burst from the tree cover onto a ridge that rolled down into a valley. A wide river snaked through the bottom. And on the other side, a behemoth mountain pierced the sky. The setting sun bathed the valley in bloody light.

Arduen's Mountain sparkled with snow and flecks of light like fireflies. A beautiful, dream-like scene. But the valley below was a nightmare. Waves of fire engulfed the large Urzost village spread out before us. A ship floated on the wide river, its catapults flinging balls of fire into the village.

I gaped, unable to take it all in. Unable to comprehend.

The distress horns had fallen silent.

Nikella kicked her horse, and I nearly flew off the back.

We roared down the ridge in a flurry of hooves and furious shouts. My heart felt as though it would jolt straight up my throat.

Terrible screams filled the air as we neared. I squeezed my eyes shut, hiding for just one more moment.

But then Nikella yanked her horse to a stop and leaped to the ground. She tore off her cloak and unsheathed her spear, then looked up at me with a fierce calm. "Get them out."

She charged into the burning village on foot while Maz and his sisters galloped after her. They shouted a one-word war cry I couldn't make out.

A black horse reared amid the cluster of stampeding Dag warriors. I locked eyes with Aiden. Fury lined his face. He lifted his sword in a salute, then rushed after Nikella and Maz.

Gods, what if they didn't—

A flaming barrel hit a lodge, tearing a hole in the roof and showering the air with oily fire.

High-pitched screams sounded within. I slid from the horse's back and raced toward the lodge. My boots slipped in the icy mud, but I didn't slow down.

The heat from the burning lodge seared my skin. Black smoke billowed out, and I coughed. Ripping off a chunk of my borrowed cloak, I tied it around my mouth. I tried to open the wooden door, but it wouldn't budge.

Fucking Four, come on!

I shoved harder, grunting, my eyes tearing. A child's voice cried out from within, shredding my heart.

With a roar, I kicked the door, and it finally gave way the tiniest bit. I peered inside, but all I could see was a piece of wooden furniture that blocked the door.

I seized a smoking board nearby and wedged it in the gap. I threw my body against it. The door shrieked open another few inches. Enough for me to stick my head inside.

Smoke blasted my face, blurring my vision and raking down my throat. I coughed and blinked rapidly. "Hello? If you're still in there, come out this way!"

A child's sob reached my ears. I craned my neck further and saw a small girl huddled next to a larger body crushed under a burning timber.

"Please," I choked, sticking my arm through the gap. "Come here, I'll get you out!"

The girl looked at me, her blond curls a tangled, sooty mess, her cheeks streaked with tears. "Mama," she cried.

"I know," I rasped, tears burning my eyes. "I'm sorry. But your mama wants you to be safe." An ominous groaning filled the lodge, and I looked up to see the rest of the roof caving under the vicious flames.

I waved my hand desperately. "Please, please, hurry!"

Much too slowly, the girl crawled away from her mother.

"Yes, that's good, so good," I coaxed her, even as the roof groaned louder. "Now, shove this table a bit."

She screwed up her face and pushed on the table blocking

the door. Flaming embers rained down, one striking her arm, and she cried out.

"Fucking Four!" I shouted, grabbing my board and jamming it against the table.

Just a few more inches. Just a few more *gods-damned inches.*

Sweat poured down my skin. Then the table shifted backward. I tossed away the board and held the door open.

"Hurry!" I beckoned for the girl.

She crawled out just as the rest of the ceiling collapsed with a roar. I swept her little body into my arms and sprinted away from the burning rubble.

"Camilla? Camilla!"

The girl pulled her face away from my neck and waved wildly at someone over my shoulder. "Brodney!"

I twisted around to see a young boy chasing after us, his clothing singed and torn. She wriggled out of my arms and into the boy's. He pressed a kiss to her matted hair. He couldn't have been more than twelve years old, but he had the grim expression of a warrior who'd seen too much.

"Who are you?" he demanded. "Are you with the Rellmirans?"

I shook my head. "I'm just here to help. My name's Kiera."

"She saved me," Camilla announced.

Brodney subjected me to another moment of suspicion before relenting. "I'm her cousin. I'll take care of her," he said.

I nodded, relieved. There would be others, and I couldn't search for them with Camilla wrapped around me.

I pointed to where Nikella's horse had trotted to a patch of grass to graze, as if the world weren't burning down. "Can you ride?"

Brodney gave me a look that reminded me so much of Ruru, I couldn't catch my breath. "I've been riding since I could walk."

"Good. Go as far as you can. Don't come back until the ship is gone."

He nodded and hurried toward the gray horse, tugging Camilla with him.

Swallowing hard, I turned back to the burning lodges. They were much larger than the Yargoths' and more permanently built, with thick wooden beams and stone. But that didn't stop them from succumbing to the barrel bombs.

I checked each structure, working from the outside in. Most were empty or already ash. Families fled through the muddy streets, heading for the safety of the treeline while shouting for their friends and relatives.

In a healer's shop, I found an old man with his leg crushed under a bookshelf. Torn books littered the floor around him, and liquid from crushed bottles flavored the smoke in the air with heavy herbal notes.

I held up the bookshelf long enough for the man to crawl out. Then I helped him hobble partway up the ridge. He said nothing, just stared at the destroyed village with hollow eyes.

At some point, I lost my face covering, but I didn't stop searching for survivors.

The closer I moved to the center of the village, the more bodies I stumbled over. I tried not to look, but I still saw too much. Burned and broken bodies. Some large, some much too small.

Then there were the others. The ones with missing limbs and bloodied clothes. Warriors with shattered weapons and Teachers with torn robes.

Fire didn't do that.

With shaking fingers, I unsheathed my borrowed sword and edged closer to the center of the village. A small square that must have been a market, judging from the destroyed carts and spilled goods, opened before me.

War raged within.

Dags clashed with figures dressed all in black with metal masks covering their faces. Figures that haunted me like gods-damned demons. *Shadow-Wolves.*

Holy Four, save us.

The Wolves stole life all around me. Young. Old. Men. Women. They didn't care. Their glittering black swords and knives carved death with every strike. And carved away my sanity with it. Leaving wounds that would never heal.

A young woman in a bloody dress tripped and fell in front of me. A Wolf noticed and swung his sword high above her head.

Rage flooded my body, and I charged forward. I shoved my sword through the Wolf's side with every ounce of strength I possessed. His body jerked. His sunstone sword fell behind him. He collapsed over the woman, twitching on the end of my sword.

Gasping, I yanked it from his body.

The woman stared up at me with wide blue eyes. "Thank you," she whispered. Then she slid out from under the body and kept running.

My arms shook. My fingers were sticky with blood. But I didn't care. I wanted more. I wanted *revenge* for every life they dared take. I wanted them to feel some sliver of the pain they were wreaking.

More barrels exploded around the square, but I hardly noticed as another Wolf sprinted at me with a sunstone knife in each fist.

He slid to one knee and swiped at my ankle. I dodged and swung my sword at his neck. Too slow. He blocked. Sunstone sliced through steel. My sword split in half.

Hissing through my teeth, I jabbed at his chest with the broken sword. The metal fractured, vibrating my arms.

Fucking Four! Sunstone armor!

He came at me in a flurry of blows. I tossed the useless hilt and focused all my energy on evading. He cut me a few times. But I felt no pain. As I ducked, I felt the press of a familiar knife I'd forgotten at my hip.

The Wolf swung again, and I whipped out my mother's knife, meeting his sunstone blade with mine.

He faltered for a split second. I knocked his blade aside and sank my knife into his stomach. He stumbled backward.

But then a fist crashed into my temple. I fell to the ground, close to the first Wolf. My knife flew away.

I flipped over and scuttled backward, away from a huge Wolf that stalked toward me, a sunstone-tipped spear in his hands.

Suddenly, Davka barreled into him, knocking him back a few steps.

She growled, wielding two swords. The Wolf threw his spear at her, and she twisted away with a grin. He produced a small sunstone knife and attacked.

While they fought, I scrambled for a weapon of my own. I didn't see my knife. But there had to be another—

A victorious cry rose. I whipped my head up to see Davka with her two swords buried in the Wolf's stomach.

But then another Wolf snuck up from behind.

"DAVKA!" I screamed.

She turned just as the Wolf shoved his sword through her chest.

CHAPTER 13
KIERA

Davka gasped, her face pale.

"N-No. *No!*" I cried.

The Wolf kicked her body off his sword and turned to me.

White-hot wrath poured into my veins like lightning. *"You bastard!"*

My fingers seized the hilt they'd been searching for. The Wolf stabbed for my heart. I sidestepped and whipped the sunstone sword through his neck like it was a twig.

Just as Renwell had done to my father.

It was easy. So very easy.

The head tumbled away, and the body collapsed at my feet. Blood and gore dripped from the long, glittering black blade. But I felt nothing. Death came for my rage as it'd come for the Wolf.

A harsh gasp tore my attention away. Davka had rolled over, a crimson puddle blooming around her.

I hurried over and fell to my knees at her side, dropping my sword. Blood soaked her chest and my fingers as I tried to cover the wound.

"It'll be all right. I can stop the bleeding. I'll—I'll get some bandages. Some herbs. Nikella probably has some. There's also a healer's shop nearby," I babbled.

Davka shook her head, grasping my fingers. More blood trickled from her lips as she opened her mouth.

"P . . . protect," she said in a garbled whisper.

I nodded rapidly, my tears dripping onto her chest. One breath. Two breaths. Then she was gone.

Protect. Protect what? Whom?

It was the only gods-damned word she'd ever spoken to me, and I didn't know what she wanted me to do.

Throwing my head back, I howled at the burning night sky.

She'd died protecting me because I couldn't fucking fight. The burn marks on her arms from the Den battle weren't even healed yet.

A shout drew my attention to a distant corner of the square where Aiden fought three different Wolves. His sword was soaked with blood, and several other Wolf bodies lay in a mangled heap.

I watched in awe as he attacked like a feral animal without hesitation. Like he knew every one of their moves before they made it.

But he was outnumbered.

I seized my sunstone sword and raced toward him. I swung at the legs of the nearest Wolf. His body fell. Legless.

Blood coated my boots. My mind.

The sword was so light in my grip. So deadly. Having it in my hand made me feel powerful. It was intoxicating.

My eyes landed on the dead gaze of a Teacher next to one of the severed legs. My mother's eyes had looked like that. My father's. Now Davka's. And so many others.

I gripped the sword harder. Whatever blood I shed, it wasn't enough. Never enough.

"Kiera!" Aiden shouted.

I glanced up in time to see a Wolf lunging for me with a knife. I swung for his arm but missed. The force of my swing spun my back to him. Fiery pain exploded across my shoulders as he sliced me.

Aiden roared with fury, taking a step toward me. But his distraction cost him. The Wolf who'd been on his knees in front of Aiden flung a knife, which burrowed into Aiden's thigh.

I cried out as he stumbled.

Gods, no. Not Aiden, too. I can't—

With a growl, he ripped the knife from his leg and whipped it toward me. I gasped. It whirred past me and sank into the neck of the Wolf who'd been about to strike me again.

But the remaining Wolf had seized Aiden by the throat, knocking the sword from his hand. Aiden kicked backward, but the Wolf held on.

Hefting my stolen blade, I stumbled forward.

Seeing my intent, Aiden used his whole body weight to spin the Wolf toward me. I lunged and stabbed the Wolf's armpit.

He released Aiden. Aiden snatched up his sword and whirled in a flash of silver to slit the Wolf's throat.

Then, it was just the two of us, standing ankle-deep in bloodied bodies. We stared at each other, panting.

Something warm trickled down my back. My shoulders burned every time I shifted. But I shoved the pain to the back of my mind. I was still alive. I could still fight.

Aiden's eyes raked over me. I waited for him to tell me to go back, to stay behind.

Instead, he murmured, "Stay close to me."

I nodded. We picked our way across the square. I couldn't help glancing back at Davka, her unseeing eyes fixed on the glowing sky.

My throat tightened. Gods, what was I going to tell her family? And Maz . . . I was going to break his heart. Again.

Someone shouted from the north end of the square. Yarina waved to us. "Our warriors broke through to the shore, but we need to help them!"

Aiden strode faster, blood trickling from his thigh. I hurried after him.

Yarina was splattered with blood, but otherwise looked unharmed. She gave me a tight grin, waving a gory scythe in her good hand. "And they thought I couldn't beat everyone one-handed."

I hesitated, wondering if I should tell her about Davka. But then something whooshed overhead.

A burning barrel careened into the tall wooden building next to us and exploded.

Aiden, who'd pulled ahead, jerked around and locked eyes with me, just as the building buckled.

I grabbed Yarina's arm and flung us backward. The building crumbled at our feet, pouring rubble between us and Aiden.

"Kiera! Yarina!" he shouted.

Perhaps I was imagining the panic threaded in his voice. But it warmed my weak heart, anyway.

"We're here!" I tried to shout back, but immediately coughed on the cloud of dust and smoke that billowed over us. Yarina groaned.

"Gods damn it," I muttered.

Her foot was stuck under a burning timber. "Go on, get out of here, princess," she said through clenched teeth, trying to tug her foot out. "Or we'll both be easy kills."

Protect.

Davka would never leave her sister. But there was no way I could lift that log. Even with leverage.

"Hold still," I ordered.

I lifted my sunstone sword and brought it down on the thick wood.

Yarina shouted in surprise. Aiden yelled again from his side of the wreckage.

The sword had bit nearly halfway through. I just had to make sure the next strike didn't go too far.

Yarina and Aiden continued their ruckus while I focused. Sweat dripped into my eyes, and I wiped it away. I raised the sword again.

Breathe in. Breathe out. One, two—

I swung. Splinters flew. Yarina cried out in pain. I yanked the sword out of the cracked wood. Yarina dragged herself away, swearing up a storm. Her ankle was bent at a bad angle, and her boot had a gash in it from my sword.

"Gods-damned lunatic," she growled.

I collapsed next to her. "You still have your foot."

She squinted at me with a smile twisted with pain. "Pure fucking luck. Remind me to take your training more seriously after this."

Aiden bellowed, "Kiera, if you don't answer me in the next gods-damned second—"

"We're fine!" I shouted back. "I'm taking Yarina up the ridge."

Immediately, Yarina protested. "I can still—"

"I will knock you out and *drag* your stubborn ass all the way back to Yargoth if you don't cooperate," I snarled.

She blinked twice at me, then grinned. "Spoken like one of my sisters. Fine then. Help me up."

My heart stumbled over the word "sisters." She didn't know she had one less of those.

"Keep your guard up," Aiden called out. "We'll rout the ship and meet you on the ridge."

Be safe, my heart murmured. Words I didn't have the courage to speak.

Instead, I focused on Yarina. I wrapped her arm around my shoulders, biting hard on my lip at the sudden pain.

"What's wrong?" she asked as we hobbled upright.

"Nothing."

We traipsed back through the square. I avoided the spot where Davka lay. We would have to collect our dead later.

Footsteps pounded.

"Left!" Yarina shouted and dove to the side.

I raised my sword and turned just as a Shadow-Wolf's sword arced toward my neck. I blocked. The sunstone blades shrieked against their jagged edges. My arms throbbed.

I stared at the Wolf's snarling metal mask, wishing him and all of his brethren to the Abyss.

He came at me again and again. I kept blocking. But my movements grew more sluggish. Yarina crawled through the spilled vegetables she'd fallen into, screeching curses and threats at him and swiping at his ankles with her scythe.

The Wolf bellowed in pain when she nicked one. He delivered a swift kick to her head. She dropped like a stone.

Fucking Four, don't do this to me.

I attacked him again, but I wouldn't last like this. I had failed Davka as I would fail Yarina and so many others. It was like I was back in that alley in Aquinon. That same desperation and hopelessness swimming in my veins.

Perhaps death hadn't liked that I'd gotten away that night. But Aiden couldn't save me this time.

Gritting my teeth, I ducked another swing and stabbed for his gut with all the strength I had left. He shifted. But I still caught his side, slicing through skin and ribs.

He howled and swung for my head. I pulled back. The black tip grazed my nose. Then—

An odd whistle. And a black arrow slammed through his neck. The Wolf wavered, then crashed to the ground.

I looked up, gasping.

A cloaked figure stepped from the shadows between burning

buildings with an empty bow. My heart beat slower and slower. Then stopped.

Dark eyes and an even darker smile. Renwell had found me.

CHAPTER 14
KIERA

WHAT IN THE DEEP, DARK, WANDERING HELL WAS *RENWELL* DOING here? Had my mind broken under the weight of all the horror it'd experienced tonight?

I wanted to check on Yarina, but couldn't take my eyes off him.

He looked the way I was used to—plain black cloak, gloves, and boots, his dark hair and beard shadowing his pale, gaunt face. No Rellmiran crown or royal clothes in sight.

Then again, he never enjoyed drawing attention to himself until his bloody schemes were successful.

The only thing that had changed was the handful of silver scars that crisscrossed over his face.

I felt a grim satisfaction knowing that he hadn't left our last encounter unscathed.

"Look at you," he murmured, stepping closer. His eyes glowed with a rare pride that sickened me. "Just how I always pictured you."

"Fighting for my life against your Wolves?" I spat, trying to hide the way my body shook.

"Wielding my blade." He nodded to the sunstone sword in my clenched fists. "Feels good, doesn't it?"

"It feels like death. Something I've seen too much of lately. Because of you."

The furrows in his cheeks deepened. "You seem to have no trouble dealing death to my Wolves."

"Neither do you," I retorted, gesturing at the body by my feet. I remembered what Nikella had said back at camp. *He doesn't remove a piece from the board unless it's no longer of use to him.* "Why did you kill him?"

Renwell tilted his head to the side. "I think you know the answer to that."

I scowled. "You want something from me."

"You betrayed me. Tried to kill me. Ran off with my enemies. What could I possibly want from you?"

"Then *why* did you save me just now? Why spare my life when I escaped?" I ground out.

He stayed silent. His dark gaze slowly scraped over me, leaving me feeling raw and vulnerable.

My heart beat faster with every passing moment. I'd never admit it, but I desperately wanted to know if Nikella was wrong. I hated him, yes. But that hatred was rooted in pain. Pain that all the time he spent training and protecting me had everything to do with his plotting and nothing to do with care for me.

Shouts echoed from afar. The square still smoldered around us. Renwell ignored it all, acting as if we were back in his study playing a simple game of Death and Four.

He stepped closer to me, his gaze unblinking. "You're still trying to find a weakness where there is none."

"Everyone has a weakness," I breathed, my grip tightening on the sword. "You just hide yours better than most."

"And you display yours for all to see. Speaking of which, I'm surprised you haven't asked about your brother and sister. Or do you no longer care for them now that you have a new family?" He pointedly glanced at the square full of bodies. "Although you do seem to keep losing any family you have."

Fury streaked through my veins. The sword twitched in my hands. Renwell's smirk curved into something predatory.

"What did you do with Everett and Delysia?" I growled.

He held out a gloved hand and beckoned to me like a dog. "Come with me and find out."

I wanted to slice off his hand with the sword he loved so much.

"I'm not your apprentice anymore, Renwell," I snarled. "I will never follow your orders again."

"Not even to save your siblings?"

My breath snagged. "They're alive?"

"Perhaps." Renwell shrugged, lowering his hand. "Perhaps not."

I pointed my sword at his chest, still several feet away. "Tell me the gods-damned truth."

Renwell tossed his bow aside and pulled his sunstone sword from its sheath in one smooth motion. "Make me."

The taunt echoed from years of training together, but I was too angry to care.

I lunged for him, and he quickly sidestepped, tapping my shoulder with his hilt.

Snarling, I swung again, but he disappeared. Again and again. I struck, and he evaded like we were back in my gods-damned nightmare.

I stabbed air again. "Fight back," I rasped, my body on fire with pain and exhaustion.

He tapped the tip of his sword on a bloody patch of dirt. "As you wish."

He lunged before I drew breath and knocked my sword out

of my hands with a bone-rattling hit. Then he kicked me in the stomach.

I sprawled on my back. The stars shifted and blurred above me while I gasped for air.

One moment. Defeat could happen in one moment, and I'd let it.

Renwell's face filled my vision as he leaned over me. The sharp point of his sword nipped at the soft skin of my throat.

"That's for ever thinking you could beat me at my own game," he whispered. "And this . . . this is for the marks you left on me."

Horrible, stinging pain sliced across my cheek.

I screamed, jerking my face away from his blade.

"Now we match, little monster," he snarled in my ear.

"Renwell!" shouted a hard female voice.

His head snapped up. He straightened away from me, sword at the ready.

"Nikella," he murmured. "Ever the survivor, I see."

Nikella? Thank the gods. If anyone could defeat Renwell, it'd be his sister. I'd seen her take down a dozen of his Wolves.

I lifted my fingers to my burning cheek. I felt blood, then a searing pain, and drew them back with a hiss.

I tried to drag myself away, but Renwell slammed his boot on my chest, pinning me like a bird with broken wings on the cracked cobblestones.

My chest heaved under his muddy boot, trying to draw in enough smoky air. My torn shoulders screamed. But the humiliation that filled my soul was a different kind of agony.

"Let her go, Renwell."

I couldn't see Nikella, but I clung to the steady command in her voice.

"I'm not quite done with her, sister."

"Yes, you are. Just as you are done here. Order your ship to cease firing."

Renwell smirked. "They won't until I'm back on board."

"And what if I kill you here and now?"

I twisted my head to see Nikella a few yards away, her bloodied spear held firmly in her hands.

Renwell let out a coarse chuckle. "You're welcome to try, Nik. But I have a feeling that even with all your warrior training, you still can't defeat me." He twirled his glittering black sword for emphasis. "I have conquered everything I set out to. Just as I said I would, all those years ago."

"That proves nothing. Having more power doesn't make you right. It makes you more responsible for defeating the evil in this world. Which you have not." Nikella's voice softened, as if she were instructing a young one. "You will lose that power, same as those you took it from."

An ugly expression twisted Renwell's face, and his boot pressed harder into my chest. I swallowed a whimper of pain and tried to shove him off. To no avail.

"I will lose nothing," he hissed, his gaze fixed on Nikella. "I have taken over an entire kingdom. I have built ships that can defeat any that sail." He spread his arms wide. "I have stolen power from the gods themselves by taking control of their precious fireseeds and sunstone. Their power is now *mine*."

My mouth fell open. His normally pale face was flushed. Spit flecked his beard from his harsh words. I'd never seen him so impassioned. Nor so careless.

Silver streaked over my body. Renwell twisted away with a snarl, lifting his boot. I scuttled backward. Nikella's spear clattered to the ground behind him.

Renwell grunted, putting a hand to his side. His leather glove came away wet.

Nikella gripped my arm and hauled me to my feet. She held a short dagger in her free hand.

Renwell's eyes burned with malevolence. "Naughty little Nik."

Nikella stiffened as if she'd been struck. Her scarred face blanched.

"You shouldn't have done that," he continued in the same vicious voice. "Now you'll finally get what's been coming to you all these years."

My eyes darted about, frantically searching for a weapon nearby. But instead of attacking, Renwell slowly retreated to the shadows he'd emerged from.

"I'll see you soon, Kiera," he called out, then disappeared.

Nikella and I remained stone-still for several moments. He didn't return. Slowly, my wounds started announcing themselves all over my body.

I groaned softly, then realized Nikella was still clutching my arm. Her body hadn't shifted out of its fighting stance, as if she were locked in a battle I couldn't see.

"You can let go now, Nikella," I told her softly.

Her chin jerked toward me, and her eyes cleared. She released me immediately. "Are you harmed?"

I gestured to my bloody cheek with a grimace. "Other than my pride, not mortally."

Suddenly, I remembered. "Yarina!" I gasped and rushed over to where she lay amid an overturned crate of pumpkins.

Her chest rose and fell steadily. I breathed a sigh of relief, then pressed my finger to her neck. A strong, steady beat met my touch.

"Thank the Four," I murmured.

I smoothed away her disheveled braids and folded a discarded cape under her head.

"More coming." Nikella's terse voice came from behind me.

I twisted around to see she'd retrieved her spear and was now guarding us against a storm of hoofbeats coming from the south. I seized the nearest weapon—one of Yarina's scythes.

A group of a dozen Dag warriors rushed into the square, axes and swords flashing molten orange in the firelight. Their clothing was like the Yargoths and Urzosts but stitched in whites and grays.

"The Berengar Clan," Nikella murmured to me, lowering her spear.

Their leader, a woman with a longer braid than Nikella, rode up to us. "Good to see you again, Teacher. We were out hunting when we heard the distress horns. Where is the enemy?"

"We've routed them from the village back to their ship. Our warriors fight on the riverbank." Nikella pointed toward the street that ran east out of the square, as yet free of rubble. "That way should be clear."

The woman nodded and rode forward, her warriors on her heels. Perhaps they would cut down a fleeing Renwell on their way.

I prayed they didn't. He had too much to answer for.

"You're not going with them?" I asked Nikella.

She shook her head. "Renwell most likely went back to the ship. He'll leave now that he got what he came for. We need to gather the dead and the injured and start treating—"

"Princess," a voice croaked from the ground.

I dropped to my knees next to Yarina. Her eyes were open, but still unfocused. Until they narrowed in on my hand.

"What in the bloody Abyss are you doing with my Soul Stealer?" she growled.

A painful smile pinched my cheeks. "Protecting your ungrateful ass. You can yell at me later. We need to get out of here first."

"In a moment." Nikella nudged me aside and examined Yarina's head and eyes. "Pupils look normal. If you feel nauseous at all, lie back down."

Yarina huffed. "I'm fine."

I threaded my arm under her shoulders and helped her sit up.

"What happened to your face?" she grumbled. "It looks like you were—"

Her words cut off. I followed her gaze to where Davka's body rested.

Yarina let out a blood-curdling scream and pitched herself forward. She fell on her hands and knees and crawled to her sister, sobbing her name.

My body shook and my eyes burned at her wild grief.

Nikella gripped my shoulder. "Stay with her," she whispered.

I stumbled forward. Nikella didn't know why Davka died. Neither did Yarina. I slowly stepped closer to her. She'd curled over Davka's chest, hugging her tightly.

I could simply comfort her. Tell her how sorry I was. That I'd lost my parents and my siblings' fate was uncertain. I could lie and say I had no idea how Davka had died. I could tell a partial truth and say she'd died a true warrior. But not because of me.

Not my fault. I don't want it to be my fault.

My thoughts—the lies and truths—tangled with each other until they were a knot of fear in my mind.

I sank to my knees next to Yarina. I hesitated, then placed my hand on her shoulder as she wept.

"Sh-she can't be dead. She's the strongest. The best. How did she die? Those fucking Wolves! I'll send their souls to the Abyss and tear their bodies to pieces for this." Yarina gasped for air, tears mixing with dirt and blood on her pale cheeks. "Fucking Four, was she alone? Why wasn't I there? I could've saved her and I didn't. *Why wasn't I there, Kiera?*"

I closed my eyes at the onslaught of her grief. I remembered staring down at Mother's body and demanding the same thing of myself.

Why didn't you go with her? Why didn't you see the danger she was in? Her last moments were filled with fear because you weren't there to save her. To love her. She was stolen from you, and you'll never get her back.

My eyes flew open, and the truth spilled out. "Davka died saving my life."

Yarina jerked away from my touch. "You . . . She . . ."

I swallowed hard and forced myself to continue. "She was the better warrior, which was why the Wolf tried to stab her in the back. I . . . I was with her in her final moments."

Yarina's bloodshot eyes filled with more tears. "Did she suffer? Did she ask for us?"

Gods, this hurt more than any battle wound.

"She didn't suffer long," I murmured. "I tried to stop the bleeding, to tell her we could heal her. But she shook her head and . . . and . . ."

Yarina curled her fingers over my clasped hands.

That one simple touch released a flood of relief. Tears fell down my cheeks. My cut stung anew, but I ignored it and took a deep breath.

"She only said one word to me, 'Protect.'"

Yarina's face crumpled, and her grip tightened. "Are you sure?"

I nodded, my throat too tight to speak.

Yarina let out a sob and pressed a gentle kiss to her sister's forehead. Turning back to me, she wiped her eyes and her nose on the back of her sleeve.

"It was the last thing our mother, and then our father, said to us before death took them. It's the word we always say to each other before we part ways. It encompasses what my parents used to say to us: 'Protect your clan. Protect each other. And our souls will be together forever.'"

My heart pounded. Davka had told me her family's parting word. Suddenly, I was overwhelmed with gratitude that I'd been there to hear it. To pass it along to her remaining family. Even if they hated me for why she died, I was glad I could do that one small thing.

I'm trying to help you find some gods-damned peace.

Aiden's words echoed in my skull. Is this what he meant when he wanted to tell me of the night Mother died?

Yarina squeezed my hands, bringing me out of my thoughts. "Thank you for being with her," she whispered. She withdrew her hand to place it on Davka's still chest. "You protected us all to the end, Davka. You kept your honor. May the gods find your soul and bring it to Mother's and Father's."

I bowed my head, sending up my own silent prayer for Davka.

A loud cry rose from the north. I fixed my gaze on the glowing mountain.

Holy Four, I hope the reinforcements find Aiden before Renwell does.

CHAPTER 15
AIDEN

It was too far out in the river, and a swarm of Shadow-Wolves stood on the pebbled beach between us.

Our force—a mix of Yargoths, Urzosts, and Teachers—had half the numbers but double the fury. We were holding our own with splintered weapons and bloodied fists. But the Wolves wouldn't break. And the ship never ceased flinging those gods-damned burning barrels. We frequently had to scatter to avoid catching fire.

The screams of the dying, human and animal alike, frayed the edges of my sanity.

Most riders had abandoned their horses by choice or by force. During the village fight, I'd slapped Wicked's rump and sent him charging away from the bloodshed. I only hoped he stayed out of sight.

Jek shouted at the few archers we had left to aim for the ship's sails and the sailors loading the catapults.

"How many of these fucking bastards did Renwell buy?" Maz shouted as he cut down a Wolf with his axe.

Blood flowed from a wound on Maz's arm, and his teeth were crimson as he bared them at his next target.

I grunted, favoring my left leg as I dodged another barrel. I wasn't losing too much blood, but I hated fighting on a weak leg.

Because you got distracted. Because of Kiera.

I growled, tearing my thoughts away from her. I clashed with a Wolf carrying a sunstone sword and knocked him into Maz's waiting arms. Maz snapped his neck, and we moved on to another.

There was always another.

"Barrel!" Maz shouted and shoved me hard to the right while he dove left.

Heat seared the backs of my legs as I stumbled away from the small, fiery crater.

A shadow teased the corner of my eye. I glanced up to see a hooded man in a long black cloak striding for the ship. Not a Wolf, but certainly an enemy.

As if he could feel my gaze on his back, he turned.

I sucked in a harsh breath. Renwell. Of course that gods-damned murderer was here. He loved to get his hands dirty.

My gut tightened with sudden fear. He'd come from the direction of the village.

Kiera.

I stalked toward him without thinking. His pale face hardened with recognition. He ripped his black sword from its sheath.

A few Wolves tried to get in my way, but he shouted, "Leave him! Kill the others."

Rage whitened the edges of my vision as I charged, my remaining sword and knife in each hand.

I raised my sword as if I'd be stupid enough to let him see my strike coming. He lifted his sword, no doubt eager to slice mine in half with his gods-damned sunstone.

At the last moment, I changed direction, ducked under his sword, and sliced for his knees. He whirled out of the way and struck for the back of my neck. I rolled on the rough ground and vaulted back onto my feet.

"After I kill you, I'm going to shred you into so many pieces, there will be nothing to burn or bury," Renwell snarled, his eyes glittering with hatred, as we circled each other.

I'd seen him pissed, but always in control. This Renwell was not in control. He looked unhinged. Perhaps because of the blood coating his side. Or perhaps because he hadn't been expecting this much of a fight.

Either way, I could use it to my advantage.

Sweat poured down my face and back as I tried to hide my limp. "This is, what, the fifth time you've tried to kill me, Renwell?" I taunted him. "Perhaps you should learn your lesson and crawl back into the dirty hole you came from."

Renwell sneered. "I never thought my little apprentice would kill you. I just wanted her to see the murderer she was stupidly coming to care for."

I almost stumbled on the uneven beach. "I would never kill Kiera."

"I knew that, too. But you've killed others, and I wanted her to see that. To understand." His face twisted with a grimace, part pain, part fury. "But it doesn't matter now. She'll come back to me willingly. Once you're dead."

She's still alive.

I barely had time to register that thought before Renwell attacked. He moved like a warrior half his age. I evaded his strikes the best I could while preserving my blades from his sunstone and slicing any part of him I could reach. Which wasn't much.

Pebbles flew beneath our boots. Our breaths grew shorter and harsher. I could see nothing but this battle.

Him or me.

He swung wide, and I stabbed for his chest. He recovered just in time to sweep upward and sever my knife at the hilt.

Roaring, I threw the hilt at his face. He ducked with a savage smile and came at me harder.

I called on every bit of training I'd received over the years. Sadly, none of my mentors had taught me how to avoid ever touching my enemy's sword with my own.

But this man had murdered my mother. He'd orchestrated Brielle's demise. He'd hunted down and killed Rellmirans during the People's Council rebellion. He was responsible for so many deaths in the mine and now here.

He should not survive this night. Or me.

I set my teeth and fought back harder and faster, using every trick I could. I jabbed my elbow into his jaw. I kicked his wounded side. When he knocked me to the ground, I grabbed a rock and smashed it into his knee.

But then he swung his sword so fast, I had no choice but to block it. My sword broke into jagged slivers.

I shot up and rammed my shoulder into his chest. We crashed to the ground, rolling. I seized his sword hand and slammed it on a rock, over and over.

He grunted and dug his free hand into my leg wound. Blinding pain made me rear back with a bellow. He kicked me in the chest, sending me sprawling.

My leg shook. My chest felt as though it were caving in.

Renwell heaved himself upright and poised his sword over my chest. "This was always your end, Falcryn. It just took a little longer than I planned."

I stared into his dark, venomous eyes. I had nothing left.

Someone shouted, drawing Renwell's attention. Hoofbeats neared. My fingers swept the dirt around me.

He hissed under his breath and pointed his sword at my heart. But his distraction had cost him.

I shoved a piece of my sword into his wrist. He howled, dropping his sword. I kicked him off me and glanced over my shoulder to see a party of Berengar warriors riding up to us. During our fight, we must've drifted closer to the village.

I turned back around to see Renwell, with his sword in his other hand, racing for his ship and remaining Wolves.

I couldn't let him get away. He didn't deserve to live after everything he'd done. I could end Rellmira's suffering with one death. Just one more.

"Bow!" I shouted at the oncoming Berengars.

Their leader halted next to me and handed me her bow and an arrow without question.

I nocked the arrow and aimed at Renwell's fleeing back. But I wanted to see his face. As he'd looked into my mother's. And shot her anyway.

"RENWELL!" I roared.

He whipped around. I fired.

I didn't hear its whistle. I barely saw its streaking shadow. But I would always remember the way it struck his body. The bloodthirsty triumph that filled my heart. And the cold disappointment that followed when I realized I hadn't struck his heart. Merely his shoulder.

Renwell would survive. At least it would be with a scar to match the one Nikella bore from him.

He staggered into the swarm of his Wolves, and they retreated onto their ship.

"Bow," the Berengar leader ordered in a clipped voice.

I handed it to her. She led her warriors to join the others as they tried to pick off any enemies they could. But the impenetrable ship pulled up anchor and started sailing back toward the Niviath Sea.

There were no victory shouts. The beach was silent apart from the crackling fires left by the oil barrels and the soft moans of the injured.

We had lost, and I didn't even know how badly yet.

"Brother!" Maz burst out of the knot of Dag warriors still left and wrapped me in a bone-cracking hug. "I lost track of you. Those mongrels were coming from every bloody direction. What happened?"

"Renwell," I gritted out.

Maz's pale eyes widened. "Here?" His gaze darted around as if searching for him. "You'd better have killed that piece of dog shit—"

Regret was like an arrow to my stomach. "I did my best, but he escaped."

Maz sheathed his stained axe and clutched my shoulder. "You'll get him next time." As if Renwell were a deer or a rabbit who'd evaded the hunt.

But he wasn't. He was smarter than Weylin. He had more power and more plans. My gut told me I'd never get so close to Renwell again. Not without starting a war first.

I clenched my weaponless hands into fists. *Then a war is what it'll be. Even if I have to fight it alone.*

Sigrid appeared at Maz's side, her eye patch askew and her right arm dripping with blood from a deep gash. She clasped forearms with Maz. "Davka? Yarina?"

"Haven't seen them yet," Maz said tersely.

My stomach twisted. And so began the grisly search for friends land family in answer to the worst question. *Alive or dead?*

"The last I know is that Kiera was taking Yarina up the ridge," I said. "Nikella went back to the village to save the wounded. I haven't seen Davka since the battle in the village square."

Maz's gaze filled with dread, but Sigrid clenched her jaw and fixed her eye patch. "Let's start in the square then."

"I'll help you look," I said quietly.

The warriors still standing were already picking through the fallen on the beach. Jek and Vorkahn carried bodies a safe distance from the fires. And slit the throats of any Wolves still twitching.

I turned from the grisly scene, memories of an even worse massacre pecking at my mind like crows.

There had been so much noise at first in that Pravaran field. The thundering hoofbeats of a thousand war horses. The metallic clanging of the soldiers' armor and weapons. The screams of the rebels—farmers and fishers, really—as Dracles's men cut them down by the hundreds.

But the silence afterward had been worse. The stacks of silent bodies. No voices left to mourn the dead because they were among them.

And instead of joining their number, I was cast into a pit of darkness with the worst parts of myself for company.

But here, the cries had already begun. I steeled myself as I followed Maz and Sigrid back into the smoldering village.

A few buildings still stood, scorched but strong. Others had collapsed into piles of embers—like the one that had cut me off from Kiera. I rubbed my chest. The fear that had filled me, knowing I'd never reach her in time, had frozen me in place.

I heard her voice. Renwell all but confirmed it. She's still alive. She has to be.

But the village—like its people—would continue to die through the night. Such was the aftermath of battle.

Our footsteps quickened as we reached the square. My throat tightened at the carnage that filled it.

Maz gave a hoarse shout and sprinted toward Yarina, who was curled over a body on the ground.

My heart jerked, and I stumbled. My vision darkened and narrowed.

Fucking Four, not Kiera. Please, not Kiera.

But she was with Yarina last. Which meant she was . . . she was . . .

A thousand memories raced through my mind. Kiera unchaining me, then stealing the key from me. Kiera fighting off a Shadow-Wolf for Ruru. Kiera eating biscuits at *The Weary Traveler.* Kiera laughing. Playing Death and Four. Bathing. Dancing like a golden goddess. Kissing me. Wrapping around me in the woods and whispering such beautiful things I forgot every bit of darkness that'd haunted me my whole life.

My vision blurred. A storm raged in my ears.

It's not time. We weren't finished yet. I need—

A single whisper calmed the storm. "Aiden?"

I twisted around to see Kiera standing in a charred doorway, clutching an armful of bottles. Blood and soot streaked her clothes and skin, but she was still here.

"You're alive," she breathed. Her lower lip trembled, and she bit it, as if to hide it.

Without a word, I strode over to her and swept her up in my arms, bottles and all. I buried my face in her smoky hair. Her body trembled against mine. She didn't let go of the bottles, but she tucked her face into my neck with a sigh I probably wasn't meant to hear.

We stayed like that for a few moments. Just a few breaths of peace were all we could have.

She pressed out of my arms and stepped back. Her amber eyes were lined with tears, but she didn't let them fall. Even though her cheeks were streaked with their trails.

I frowned and gently cupped her cheek where a wicked cut dripped blood.

She stepped further out of reach. Pain rippled through my chest, but I let her go.

"Davka's dead," she said in a gritty voice, like charred wood scraping over stone.

I grimaced and glanced to where Maz was huddled with his sisters, weeping.

I bowed my head. *May the gods find your soul, Davka.*

"I should go to them," I murmured. But my feet wouldn't move.

Kiera stared at me, her face a battlefield of emotions. Something must have happened in this square. I could almost feel her mind racing.

I wanted to demand the words she bit back. I wanted to be free of this agonizing pull toward the woman who'd lied to me and used me.

I wanted *her.*

But that was never going to happen. So, I turned my back on her and walked away.

CHAPTER 16
KIERA

I DIDN'T REMEMBER HOW I'D GOTTEN HERE.

One minute I'd been handing out bottles of medicine and mead and bandaging wounds, the next I was here—curled up next to a discarded basket of clothes. Staring at Arduen's Mountain. The beautiful white snow. The many pinpricks of light that someone told me were the fireflowers glowing before they died tomorrow night.

It all looked so pure and untouched. So unlike the charred, broken village behind me.

I'd busied myself the moment Aiden had walked away. The relief I'd felt to see him alive and standing had nearly shattered me in a way I was too exhausted to understand. We stood on a narrow precipice, him and me. One small push and we would lose each other forever.

I'd watched him comfort Maz and his sisters from afar. My heart ached for them, but I felt like an intruder. Davka had spoken one word to me in the few weeks we'd known each other, and she'd protected me in a battle I wouldn't have survived without better warriors like herself.

But Maz had sought me out, anyway. He came up behind me while I was sponging blood from an old woman's forehead and wrapped his huge, sweaty arms around me.

"Thank you, lovely," he'd murmured. "I know you did everything you could for her. And Yarina as well. Like you did for me."

I'd turned and buried my face in his chest and finally released the sob I'd been holding back.

"I wish it'd been enough," I whispered raggedly.

"If you gave it your all, then you gave enough." He hugged me tighter as a few of his tears dripped into my gnarled hair.

After a few moments, we'd parted ways.

Soon after, little Camilla and her cousin Brodney found me. Camilla had raced forward and wrapped her skinny arms around my legs. My small smile cracked the dried blood on my cheek, but it was worth it.

Brodney informed me they'd tied Nikella's horse with the others so it wouldn't wander off. I thanked him and directed the pair to where they could find a bowl of soup and a blanket.

And now I was here, an ant before the mountain. Alone under the cold stars. Nothing but pain for company.

Except the footsteps headed toward me. I didn't look over as Nikella settled down next to me.

"How'd you find me?" I asked hoarsely. Gods, when was the last time I had a sip of water?

"Aiden." Of course. He always knew, didn't he.

Nikella set a few things on the grass. "He said you haven't taken care of your wounds."

"Others had worse."

"They're taken care of. Now it's your turn."

I didn't bother answering. Just kept staring at the strangely luminous mountain.

Nikella washed my cheek and spread a thick paste on the cut. It made my eyes sting, but I didn't flinch.

"Any broken bones?" she asked crisply.

"Not that I know of."

"Aiden said you had a bad wound across your shoulders. May I see?"

His concern for me reached into that hidden, bleeding part of my heart.

"Yes," I whispered.

Nikella carefully helped me out of my dirty shirt, the cloth sticking painfully to my shoulders.

The cold breeze swept over my exposed skin and pierced the open wound on my back.

I sucked in a breath the same moment Nikella did.

She slowly washed the crusted blood from my shoulders, but then hesitated.

"Is it that bad?" I grunted, my hands clenched around my knees.

"It's hard to tell in the moonlight," she murmured. Her cool fingers traced my skin. Not my wound, but the scars around it. "My brother did this to you."

I stiffened. I would've jerked away if I hadn't been so gods-damned tired.

"No," I said harshly. "It wasn't Renwell."

"I meant my other brother. Korvin."

My stomach plummeted as my thoughts shuddered to a halt —uncomprehending of the shadowy obstacle in their path.

Brother. Korvin is her brother. Which means, he and Renwell are also brothers.

I squeezed my eyes shut, realizations falling into place and more questions rising.

"He never told you," Nikella surmised.

"No, he never told me about you *or* Korvin." A bitter laugh broke past my teeth. "What Renwell didn't tell me could fill the Abyss."

Nikella hummed in agreement. I couldn't see her face, but I felt her eyes on my shoulders.

Dread stilled my heart like a bird who'd caught sight of a hunter. "How did you know Korvin gave me these scars?"

Nikella didn't answer me. Instead, she spread paste on my wound. The cold stripe on my skin puckered. She gently eased my shirt back over my head.

As I gingerly pushed my arms back into the sleeves, she slid forward to sit next to me. Her shadowed gaze rested on the glittering mountain.

"The whip he used on you," she said quietly, "he invented for me."

Holy Four. I ground my teeth together to keep any sound from escaping.

She unfastened her cloak and pulled up the back of her shirt, turning to reveal a wide swath of her muscled back.

I gaped, thankful she couldn't see me.

The firelight glimmered over a patchwork of scars. They told a story of hatred, of monstrosity. Her skin was gouged and stripped, probably from the sunstone bits Korvin had threaded into his special whip.

Was this how my back looked? I'd never seen it in a mirror. Had Aiden noticed the similarities in our scars? Or had he never seen his mentor's?

Nikella's looked . . . old. Layered. Carved into more tender skin that hardened over time.

"How could a brother do that to his sister?" I murmured, thinking of how Everett hadn't even wanted to pick up a wooden sword to duel with me.

She dropped her shirt and faced me again. "Our shared blood never stopped him from spilling mine. He's always been that way. I was simply the easiest target."

I winced, then studied her more carefully, seeing a new facet to this enigmatic woman. She was every inch the fierce warrior. Beautiful under her scars. But that strength had been born from a desperate need to survive.

No wonder she spoke about defending people from the monsters that roamed the world. She'd been raised with them.

My gaze halted on the deep scar that bisected her face.

Nikella pursed her lips. "Korvin gave it to me the night before I escaped. With what was perhaps the first sunstone blade ever created." She noticed my wide eyes and sighed. "We were born and raised in the village of Calimber. Our father worked in the sunstone mine back when it was a voluntary job. But that didn't make it less of a miserable one. Just gave him the money to get drunk every night."

I curled in tighter on myself, resting my uninjured cheek on my knees. Every word out of her mouth was like a drop of light that illuminated the mystery surrounding her and her brothers.

I wanted to know everything. But something told me not to push.

Nikella looked back at Arduen's Mountain, her voice soft with memory. "Our mother died when I was little. I never knew her. Some said she was kind and quiet. Others—mainly my father—said she was arrogant and ungrateful, too good for our little town. But, of course, if a woman aims for more or better, it's presumptuous. When a man does, it's ambition."

Which is probably why Father was so furious when he found out what Mother was planning. His vanity demanded her death.

My brow furrowed. That was the first time my thoughts hadn't blamed Aiden. I shoved that revelation aside as Nikella continued speaking.

"Our father beat us. All of us. Drunk or sober. Good day or bad. It didn't matter. My brothers inherited his spite in different ways. Perhaps I did, too," she added thoughtfully. "But in those days, I only ever dreamed of running."

"How did you escape?" I asked.

"An old Teacher came to Calimber when I was about fourteen. Father was dead, and Renwell had left for Aquinon. It was just me and Korvin. But I was desperate for an education, like the other children received. I snuck out to meet the Teacher—a kind man named Hadrian. He taught me to read and write, to understand history and religion, even a few defensive maneuvers. He was the first person to show me true kindness."

Nikella ceased talking as a Dag warrior rode past. He startled at seeing the two of us sitting on the ground, but he gave Nikella a deep nod, which she returned. He continued riding to the river.

Something deep inside me craved that same respect. But I didn't begrudge her for it. She'd earned it. Despite shooting me in the neck with a dart. But she'd done it to save someone she loved, which I understood completely.

"Hadrian told me I could become a Teacher," she continued. "One of my dearest dreams. But I knew Korvin would never allow it."

My stomach curdled, guessing what would happen next.

Nikella's voice turned hollow. "Korvin found us training one night. I'd never seen him so enraged. He tied me up and . . . and tore Hadrian to shreds in front of me. No matter how much I begged, he wouldn't stop. He said it was my fault."

Nikella swallowed hard and turned her face away.

My own throat tightened. I'd never heard her stumble over words. What she was describing was truly awful, but her evident pain surprised me. That even a warrior like her would still feel pain over a death that had happened decades ago.

But love was a trickster like that. It couldn't be caged by time or distance. Or even death. Not when it was true.

Mother's face filled my mind. *I'll never forget you either, Mother.*

Nikella cleared her throat. "After Hadrian was dead, Korvin

took his knife and did this"—she gestured to her face—"to me. He wanted to make sure I'd be too ashamed to ever leave. Too afraid."

She turned abruptly to face me, her eyes burning. "Have you ever been the weakest one in the room, Kiera?"

Dozens of memories played behind my eyes. Moments with Father, Renwell, Korvin, Wolves, guards, men from taverns . . . And tonight. In battle.

"Yes," I whispered, hating the truth.

"I was, too. For many years. Until that night. As I lay bleeding in the dark, I realized he would kill me eventually when he'd wrung every bit of pain and humanity from my being. But then something else occurred to me. All of my scars—the new and the old, the ones in my skin and my soul—weren't evidence of his strength, but of *mine*. I was still alive. I still had hope. I could be better than the monster the world kept trying to make me.

"That strength gave me the courage to take the first step out the door. Then another. And another. I took nothing with me. I never looked back. I ran all the way to Aquinon and chased the dream that had always seemed so impossible. Then my fate merged with Aiden's, and I've never stopped fighting."

Gods, I couldn't even comprehend the darkness she'd been through. She probably hadn't even told me the half of it. But it was the most she'd ever spoken to me and never about such deeply personal details.

"Why did you tell me all of this?" I asked softly.

Nikella sighed again, her breath clouding in the cool air. "We share some of the same scars. I thought it might ease your mind to know you're not alone. To understand that what happened to you was their fault, not yours. Something I wish someone would've told me all those years ago."

My eyes burned, and I bit my lip, staring hard at my clenched knees. "I know it's not. Or at least, that I'm supposed to know it's not my fault. But sometimes it doesn't stop me thinking, if only I'd been more obedient or more loyal . . ." *Father might not have used Korvin to punish me. Or Renwell might have actually cared for me the way he'd seemed to.*

Nikella squeezed my shoulder. "Desiring love is not a weakness. Knowing you deserve love and recognizing it when you see it—*that* is strength."

Her words hung in the air like the smoke from the village. It was so strange to be sitting with a Teacher—Renwell and Korvin's *sister*—in the shadow of Arduen's Mountain after a bloody battle and having this conversation.

But it felt like exactly what I needed, more than any rest or medicine. Sharp, painful longing sang through my blood.

"Teach me," I said harshly. I licked my lips and tried to soften my voice. "Please. Teach me how to be strong. How to fight." Davka's dead stare needled my mind. "How to protect others better. Teach me how to win."

Nikella studied me in the shifting light. Her dark eyes were unfathomable. And for a moment, it was two years ago, and I'd just found out my mother had been killed and I was demanding that Renwell teach me to be him. To make sure no one ever harmed my family again.

Now I was here. Asking to be his sister's student. Becoming reluctant allies with my mother's killer. All to take Renwell down. To make sure I never fell beneath his boot again.

I was as desperate now as I had been back then. The guilt and humiliation still burned in my gut. But I wasn't as ignorant. I knew what needed to be done.

"I will train your mind, heart, and body," Nikella said. "Alignment of the three will give you the strength you seek."

I wasn't sure what that meant, or why she said it like a warning, but I didn't care. This was what I needed.

I nodded.

She quirked an eyebrow. "Does that mean you plan to stay with us for the foreseeable future?"

"Yes." I gently touched my stiff cheek. "I refuse to let Renwell bait me. The next time I see him, it will be on my own terms."

Nikella stood, offering me her hand. "Then I suggest you get some rest. The clash of swords and fists is only the first half of a battle."

I grabbed her hand and rose, my bones creaking and my muscles aching. She gathered her supplies, and we walked back through the village of embers.

Most of the injured now rested in large tents that huddled on the outskirts of the village. Warriors stood on watch at the perimeter, red-eyed but alert. They nodded at us as we passed through their ranks.

Someone called out for Nikella, and she followed the voice.

I picked my way through the camp, not seeing Maz or his sisters. Perhaps they stayed with Davka. My body sagged with exhaustion and grief. Gods, I hoped sleep offered some respite.

I didn't realize what I was searching for until I saw his tall form lying out on a bedroll, his arms folded under his black hair and his gaze wandering the starry sky. A thick bandage encircled his thigh.

My chest tightened. *You were never really my enemy, were you, Aiden Falcryn. But why can't I forgive you?*

His green eyes flicked to me and held, as if he'd finally found what he'd been looking for.

My chest prickled with heat.

We'd saved each other's lives on the battlefield, but these quiet moments felt the most dangerous.

I'd put distance between us after he hugged me because it was too much. My feelings had been too sharp and painful, like burrs coating my heart. Any more pressure and they would've clawed deeper.

But I was too tired to avoid what I needed in this moment. Like warriors bedding down between the living and the dead when the fight grew too exhausting.

I grabbed a blanket from a pile and laid it out next to his.

CHAPTER 17
AIDEN

I didn't tell her I couldn't sleep. That I planned to search for her if she didn't come back soon.

Instead, I tugged her blanket until it overlapped mine.

She sank down with a sigh. Her cheek was painted with hornleaf paste, so Nikella must have found her. I hoped her wounds didn't pain her as mine did. I still didn't know how she'd gotten the one on her cheek, but I prayed to the Four that he was as dead as the Wolf I'd killed for cutting her back.

Kiera curled onto her side and tucked herself against me like she had on the road here.

My arm twitched as if to pull her closer, but I resisted. She hadn't wanted my embrace earlier. She might not now.

But even just sharing her warmth and having her next to me, to know she was safe, eased my mind.

And hers as well, it seemed, because she drifted off before I did.

I dreamed of fire and arrows, then nothing.

When I woke, the first rays of dawn were piercing the valley.

Something tickled my chin. I glanced down—and smiled. Kiera had rolled over in her sleep and nestled her face into my neck. Her hair—tugged from its braid—caught on my unshaven jaw.

Her beautiful, scarred fingers curled into my shirt collar as if seeking more heat. One of her legs lay atop mine, just below my throbbing stab wound.

My traitorous arm had gotten what it wanted in my sleep by curving around her waist.

I wished we could stay like this for hours more. This was simple and easy. I could almost trick myself into believing she hadn't spent the last few months lying to me. Our bodies sought the comfort they'd shared in Aquinon. But our hearts? Shielded as ever.

Around us, the camp was waking up. A few Dags stirred the bonfire coals and added fresh wood.

Maz, still covered in blood, stepped around the sleeping warriors and cooking fires. He spotted Kiera in my arms and gave me a tired grin, which didn't quite reach his sad eyes.

"Figured that'd happen sooner rather than later," he said. Thank the gods he spoke quietly enough not to rouse her.

"It's not what you think," I murmured, slowly rolling Kiera back onto her blanket.

"Sure it isn't," he muttered, combing his fingers through his dirty beard. "I need a fucking bath."

"You and me both, brother."

Bereft of Kiera's sleepy limbs, I rose unsteadily from my bedroll. Blood rushed back into numb places. My wounds throbbed, but I ignored them.

"Is it time? I asked.

Maz swallowed hard and nodded. My gaze lingered on Kiera for another moment before I followed Maz.

A chilly mountain breeze that smelled of snow nipped at my

cheeks and tried to burrow under my torn clothes. But I'd be covered in sweat soon enough.

We walked past the ashen village to the riverbank. Last night, we'd moved as many of the dead as we could to the shore and wrapped them in shrouds. The bodies laid on the pebbles like odd pieces of cargo, ready for loading.

Jek, along with other Dags, including Sigrid and Yarina, beached the longboats we'd salvaged.

Silently, we placed the bodies into the boats.

I tried to steel my heart against the sensation, but carrying bodies was something I would never grow used to. Despite the number of times I'd done it.

When I scooped up a young boy who couldn't have been much older than Ruru, something cracked in my chest, filling it with pain.

Fucking Four, watch over Ruru, because I can't.

My arms trembled as I nestled the boy in the boat with the other bodies. But I went back for another. And another. Until the boats were full.

We had more bodies than boats, so we would have to make multiple trips.

Maz held Davka's body in his arms as his sisters and I rowed our boat across the river to Arduen's shore.

It was a short trip, but fatigue already crawled through my bones. Made worse when we began carrying the bodies up the mountain.

Teachers from centuries ago had carved a winding set of stone stairs into the mountain. They were still clear of snow from when the Teachers had harvested the fireseeds before the attack.

As I carried body after body up the stairs to lay them among the dimly glowing fireflowers, I thought about what the Teacher from Keldiket had told me last night.

He'd approached Nikella as she stuffed my stab wound with

cloudbird leaves. She'd offered me the last of her hornleaf paste for the pain, but I told her to save it for Kiera. I was gritting my teeth and trying not to pass out when he spoke.

"T-Teacher Nikella?" He looked younger than my twenty-five years, only the first hint of dark stubble appearing on his small chin.

"Yes?" she grunted without looking up from her work.

"I'm Teacher Silas," he said, his fists clenched in his torn, long-hooded robes. "I'm . . . I'm the last Teacher alive here. Other than you now," he added hastily.

"You were here for the fireseed harvest?" I rasped, sweat pouring down my face.

He nodded. "My mentor, Teacher Vera, brought me here to aid the other Teachers for this holy event. We traveled from the Keldiket Temple in Hibraxos."

My eyebrows pinched at the mention of Keldiket's royal city. "That's a long journey through some hostile territory."

Silas dipped his head and ran a hand through his short, dark curls. "Yes, the desert can be unforgiving, and the hostile Dag clans of the west even more so, but Teacher Vera, she . . . she was a legend. She kept us safe."

"May the gods find her soul," I murmured the same time as Nikella did. Her eyes flicked to mine for a moment, a wordless emotion in their depths.

She'd been by my side since birth, but one day, I would lose her, too.

"Tell us what happened, Teacher Silas," Nikella commanded through pinched lips as she started wrapping my leg.

As though he'd been itching to do just that, Silas launched into his story. "We've been here several weeks. The Urzost Clan was very welcoming. We each had our own room at the inn. Can you believe it? After months of sleeping in tents and caves, it felt like such a luxury. I shared a room with three others at the Temple, but we had the softest—"

"The attack, Teacher," I interrupted, more gruffly than I meant to.

He flushed and shifted on his feet. "Right. Of course. Well, the Teachers here were more than happy to have help with the harvest. They were expecting delegates from all the clans to show up for their bounty over the next few days. And you know how things can get when these clans intermingle. Having Teachers to keep the peace was essential. But few had arrived yet. Which was just fine, as the Urzosts were quite fond of throwing parties every night with so much food and mead as I haven't seen in years—"

"Why not?" I interrupted again. But, gods, the man didn't seem to draw breath when he spoke. "Were they starving you in your Temple?"

Nikella gave me a sharp look, but I was curious. I hadn't been to Keldiket in over a decade.

Silas's eyes widened. "There's been a terrible famine the last two years. The waters refused to rise, keeping the crops from growing. The emperor wishes to keep it a secret and hasn't let many leave our borders. But Teacher Vera convinced him to let us come here so that we might observe the next few holy days here in this sacred place. That way, maybe the Holy Four would see fit to aid us."

I'd heard nothing of a famine. Nor had Nikella from the way she frowned at him, her fingers absentmindedly tying the knot on my bandage.

I stored that scrap of information away and returned to the matter at hand.

"The attack, Teacher Silas," I said, leveling my sternest glare at him. "When did it start? Why was no one prepared?"

The young Teacher's eyes widened. "Only an hour before

you arrived. They must've killed the watchmen along the river who usually blow their horns when something is amiss. At least that's what Teacher Vera said before . . . before one of those barrels hit her."

I grimaced. Renwell had probably scouted the distress horn locations in advance. The village never stood a chance.

"It was awful," Silas continued in a distant voice, staring at the destroyed square behind me. "There was fire everywhere. People screaming and trampling each other, trying to get out of the way. Then those . . . those *demons* invaded the village."

"Shadow-Wolves," I said grimly.

Silas nodded. "Ah, yes, I've heard that name. King Weylin's guard, correct?"

My jaw clenched. Of course, the news hadn't traveled this far north yet.

"King Weylin is dead," Nikella said in the silence. "His High Enforcer has declared himself king now. He's the one who attacked here."

Silas's mouth fell open. "Holy Four, I had no idea. Why would the Rellmirans want to kill so many innocent Dags and *Teachers*?"

I leaned forward with a snarl, my patience snapping. "That's what we're asking you."

Silas looked taken aback, then his face cleared as if remembering something. "They did take all the fireseeds we'd harvested. Every last one."

CHAPTER 18
AIDEN

I stared at the Teacher, unsure if I'd heard him correctly. "They took all the fireseeds? Nothing else?"

Silas shook his head. Nikella, however, looked disappointed, but unsurprised.

"You knew," I told her.

"I guessed. From what Renwell said to me."

My eyebrows shot up. "You spoke with him? Did he harm you?"

"Of course not," she said sharply. "It was I who wounded him."

His bleeding side.

"You may have saved my life by weakening him," I murmured.

"I was aiming for his heart," Nikella snapped, as if I shouldn't be grateful.

I narrowed my eyes at her. Something else had happened, but she wouldn't like me prying in front of a stranger. Even if he was a Teacher.

"What does he need with a mountain's worth of fireseeds?" I wondered aloud.

Neither of them answered me.

Soon Silas moved on to help a few crying children—undoubtedly, he was excellent at telling them stories.

Nikella stood to leave, but I caught her wrist. "What did he say to you?"

She pulled out of my grasp and leaned against the somewhat whole house we'd sheltered by.

"He bragged about all he's done," she said. "Claimed to have the power of the gods themselves with his fireseeds and sunstone. That he could rule the whole world if he wanted to."

I frowned. That seemed rather grandiose for a man who'd just stepped out of the shadows to take over one throne.

Nikella fixed her dark stare on me, the way she always did when she was about to tell me something I didn't want to hear. "He also warned me. In a way. He's sending Korvin to hunt us down."

Unease rippled over my skin. I didn't bother asking her if she was certain. Nikella would never bring up her oldest brother's name unless it was absolutely vital.

"I'm sorry, Nikella," I said softly.

I'd give my life to save her from him, but I knew that wasn't what she wanted. She'd taught me how to face my monsters since they were mere shadows in my childhood nightmares. She expected nothing less of herself.

"It changes nothing. Only that we must never drop our guard. I will deal with Korvin when it's time."

Renwell. Korvin. The Wolves. Our list of enemies continued to grow. Where did it end?

I grimaced and shifted my feet to the ground. Gingerly putting weight on my leg, I stood next to Nikella as she gazed into a small fire that was still stubbornly burning amid the rubble.

"I keep telling myself one more death," I said softly. "Just one more death and it'll all be over. I told myself that with Weylin and now with Renwell. But it's never true."

"Of course not. There will always be another enemy to defeat. But you could at least prevent more powerful enemies from controlling Rellmira."

I frowned. I'd been fighting for a better Rellmira since I could carry a sword. Nothing I'd done seemed to make a difference. By trying to eliminate Rellmira's most powerful enemies, I'd only caused more innocent deaths.

"How?" I asked.

"As king," she said, as if it were the most obvious answer.

I sighed. "We've been over this, Nikella. I—"

"Don't want to be king. I know. But I swore to your mother—"

"She's dead. My father, too. And no one needs their son to take the crown."

Nikella faced me and cupped my cheek in her hand as if I were still a young boy. "Your birthright is your obligation to Rellmira. Who you are, Aiden Falcryn, the man who protects others and fights for justice—that is why you *need* to be king. The more you hide, the more it allows men like Weylin and Renwell to step in and destroy everything."

I flinched away from her touch. "You've taught me to hide who I am since I was old enough to understand."

Her eyes hardened. "To protect you until it was time. It's time, Aiden."

A familiar fear wriggled loose in my chest, something that had grown and festered while I was a prisoner in the mine. Each of my failures since the Pravaran rebellion had only multiplied that fear like worms in fertile soil.

"I don't deserve that kind of power," I whispered, my jaw tight.

"Power isn't inherently good or evil. It only becomes so in the hands of who wields it. Your heart is good, Aiden. Don't squander it by locking it in a cage."

No good has ever come from sharing my heart, either. Even when a certain beautiful thief steals the key.

"I saw Kiera head west out of the village just before you found me," I said, my voice tight. "Her face was still bloody, which means the wound on her back is likely the same. Take care of her, would you?"

Nikella pursed her lips. "Why don't you?"

I shrugged, already walking away. "Like I said, I know when I'm not wanted."

Perhaps it'd been petty, but I'd been too gods-damned tired to disguise the edge of hurt in my voice.

But Kiera had come to me later that night. Slept by my side. So perhaps I wasn't the only one with contrary feelings.

After two more mind-numbing trips up the base of the mountain, we ferried the mourners across. They filled the stone steps, a safe distance from the glowing fireflowers.

Kiera came with them, her hair re-braided and her face clean apart from the paste on her cheek. Her amber eyes glowed golden in the setting sun. She hugged Maz and gripped Yarina's hand. Whether to ease the weight off Yarina's injured foot or because she needed the support, I couldn't say.

Sigrid flanked Maz, dark circles under her eyes. I stood on Kiera's other side. She darted a glance up at me. Her mouth seemed to soften for a moment, but then she faced forward again.

Either someone had told her what to expect or she was too exhausted to question the strangeness of seeing shrouded bodies lying amid the fireflowers.

There were no drums this time. No mead. No party would follow. Most of these souls had been lost in a massacre, not a battle between warriors. It was murder. There was no honor to celebrate in that.

Yarina swayed a little, like the fireflowers that bowed over Davka's body. Maz looked paler than I'd ever seen him. Even after Korvin. Sigrid's hands were clenched into fists.

Jek, Nikella, Vorkahn, and most of our war party lined the steps below them. The Berengar woman whose bow I'd used to shoot Renwell, and her warriors, stood on the steps below.

What was left of the Urzost villagers and their warriors huddled on the steps above me, their eyes glassy. A woman about Nikella's age stepped into the snow by a small body and sang the funeral song.

Her body trembled with anguish, and her voice sagged with unshed tears and buried cries, yet still she sang on.

I opened my mouth and added my voice to hers, comforting her the only way I could think.

You're not alone, I tried to say beneath my words. *You're not alone.*

More voices joined in. Including one right next to me. I tore my gaze away from the bodies to stare at Kiera. She fumbled a few of the words, but she kept singing with me.

A kernel of warmth wedged itself in my chest. It stayed there as the last rays of sun disappeared from the valley, along with the final notes of our song.

We waited in hushed silence. Then, one by one, the fireflowers burst into flame. They caught the shrouded bodies on fire, and within moments, the entire mountainside burned.

Usually, only dead Teachers were allowed to burn with the fireflowers, but Nikella had agreed to an exception. She stood with Silas higher on the steps, their long hoods shadowing their faces.

Thank the Four that Renwell hadn't destroyed the flowers when he stole the fireseeds. He must've known when the harvest would be complete and timed his attack perfectly.

The fireflowers would grow back and produce more seeds next year. If they'd been plucked, they would be dead forever. Hence, why the god Arduen had named Teachers as the gatherers—to prevent destruction.

But Renwell had stolen them all. Many Dags would go without the ease and warmth of the long-lasting fires that the small seeds provided. Not to mention the money they earned by selling off a portion.

Was that what Renwell wanted? To drive up the price? It was what Weylin would've done. Or perhaps he'd wanted to destroy as many Dags as he could—announce his newfound power to the world.

Whatever his plans, a man who murdered innocent villagers and Teachers should never be king.

The fireflower blaze melted the snow, which ran down the mountain like gushing tears.

But my eye caught on something else that gleamed in the light. A black gauntlet encircled Yarina's wrist like a stretch of night sky. Sunstone. She must've taken it from one of the dead Wolves.

We'd noticed a fair bit of sunstone armor, along with their usual weapons, when we'd stacked their bodies away from the others. We had yet to decide what to do with it all.

But now my brain pieced together the information it'd been too tired to understand last night.

Renwell had built warships. He'd added more men to his army. Those men had an increasing amount of sunstone armor and weapons. He mentioned having the power of the gods and using it to take whatever he wanted.

Long ago, Nikella had told me that Korvin created the

sunstone knives by melding the chunks of raw stone over a fire fed by the god-given seeds.

"Renwell is preparing for war," I breathed.

Kiera shifted closer to me. "War?"

I gazed down at her, the realization galloping through my mind. "That's why he stole all the fireseeds. He's building a sunstone-clad army. Rellmira isn't enough for him. He wants *Lancora*."

Kiera's eyes widened, but I saw the same threads weave together for her as they had for me.

"What are you whispering about?" Yarina griped, craning her tear-stained face to look at both of us. "War for Lancora?"

While Kiera relayed what I'd said to Yarina, and then Maz, who poked his head into our huddle, my mind raced with possibilities.

Who would he attack first? Obviously, he'd already attacked the Dags. But was that just to steal the fireseeds, or was it also to weaken them for further invasion? Perhaps that was why he'd left the fireflowers alive. He was going to come back when they bloomed again.

If he were to attack the Elorens, he would need many more ships and a damn good reason. They were sailing experts and controlled much of Lancora's trade.

He could target Keldiket since it boasted the wealthiest cities. Unless the famine Silas had mentioned had lowered their worth—or provided the perfect opportunity for invasion.

We'd already seen what *one* of his warships was capable of. Gods help the rest of Lancora if he built a fleet and aimed it at bigger cities.

Maz gripped my shoulder, his eyes fierce in the flickering light. "Let's ride to Aquinon and finish killing the bastard before he can strike again."

Yarina and Sigrid nodded. Kiera bit her lip, her eyes fixed on the burning bodies.

Remembering what I'd said to Nikella about one more death not being enough, I shook my head. "We've tried assassination. It doesn't work, and it'd take weeks, if not months, of preparation. Renwell probably has Aquinon locked up tight, expecting something like that."

Maz scowled.

"I could go," Kiera said quietly. "He wants me to come to him. I could—"

Red seared across my vision. "Give him exactly what he wants? Let him manipulate you into being his little soldier again? Over my gods-damned body."

Kiera jerked back, a look of shock and hurt crossing her face before her jaw clenched. She whipped around and hurried down the stone steps, weaving around mourners.

My rage departed as swiftly as it'd appeared. But it wasn't a lie. I knew the devastation that snake could wreak. As did she. So why was she volunteering to run back into his arms?

"Gods, you're an ass." Yarina folded her arms and turned back to the funeral pyres.

I gritted my teeth. Not too long ago, Yarina wanted to kill Kiera for her betrayal. Now she defended her.

I met Maz's gaze over her head. He said nothing. Just jerked his head to where Kiera was disappearing down the mountain.

I frowned. I strongly doubted that Kiera wanted me to follow her. But I needed to get off this scorched mountain. The other mourners were staring at me with narrowed eyes and tight lips.

I needed somewhere I could fucking think.

As I stalked past Sigrid, she grabbed my arm. Her one eye burned with hatred, but not for me. "Wherever the battle is, we will be there, too. All of us."

I dipped my head, and she released me. I descended the

mountain and came to a stop where the boats were waiting. A lone figure that haunted me awake and asleep stood in front of them, her back to me.

Bitterness still coated my insides like ash.

"Don't want to row, princess?" I couldn't resist jabbing at her. Perhaps because I'd rather see her angry than hurt.

I got my wish.

Her body stiffened, and she shot a glare at me over her shoulder like an arrow. "I didn't want to strand the others without a boat."

I hummed. "There's more than one way across a river."

She scowled at me as I backed away from her. When the shadows folded around me, I turned and strode upriver and out of sight.

I needed a bath, after all.

I stripped off my dirty clothes and gathered them up with my boots. The rocky beach didn't pierce my bare feet, but the cold water would likely be excruciating. Perfect.

Chills rippled over my skin as I let the river lap at my feet. Arduen's River was wide but shallow here. The current wasn't as strong either, from what I remembered.

The wind blew softly, carrying not the scent of smoke, but of snowy pine. I filled my lungs with it. Yes, this was exactly what I needed.

Footsteps crunched behind me.

"Oh gods, are you *naked*?"

CHAPTER 19

KIERA

I never thought I'd see Aiden naked again.

And—Holy Four, help me—I wasn't entirely upset that I was wrong.

His broad shoulders, swirled with scars and ink, beckoned me. The muscles that rippled down his back and thighs taunted me. And gods, his *ass*. I remembered how it felt in my hands as he—

I tore my gaze away, swallowing hard, just as Aiden turned. Thankfully, he held his discarded clothes and boots over his manhood. But every other bit of sculpted perfection was on display. No amount of dirt or blood or bandages could disguise his beauty.

However, his smirk certainly made it easier to ignore.

"Nothing you haven't seen—and touched—already, princess."

My hands balled into fists. His humiliation of me on the steps wasn't enough? "Stop calling me that."

"Why? Isn't that what you are?"

"No," I bit out. "My father disinherited me the moment I

became Renwell's apprentice. I have no lawful claim to the throne anymore. Not that he did, either," I added bitterly.

Aiden's dark eyebrows drew together. "You gave up your crown . . . to train under Renwell."

Did he think Renwell had manipulated me into being his apprentice? That I still wanted that? He must think me weak. *Little soldier.*

"I trained under Renwell because I wanted to keep my family safe," I snapped. "Giving up the throne was an added gift."

Surprise smoothed Aiden's expression.

I stepped closer, remembering why I'd stomped after him. Before his nakedness and name-calling had gotten under my skin.

"I only offered to go back to Renwell, to *give him what he wants,* because that would be the quickest way to get what *we* want. Renwell dead."

Aiden's voice grew softer. "That's exactly what he'll expect, and there's no telling what he'd do to keep that from happening."

He brushed a stray hair away from my sticky, aching cheek. His warmth and scent of leather and sweat embraced me.

So much bare skin. So near.

My heart pounded.

"He did that to you, didn't he?" Aiden murmured.

I nodded, unable to speak.

"Every moment, I wish my arrow had gone through his gods-damned heart, not his shoulder. Then we would both be free."

Free of him? Or each other?

"You don't trust me, do you?" I tilted my face to gaze directly into his eyes. "That's why you don't want me to go to Renwell. You think I'll betray you again."

His gaze roamed from my cheek to my mouth to my eyes. "Maybe not at first. But he's convinced you to do it before."

When he'd let Korvin torture Maz until I admitted when Aiden's attack would happen. But I'd fed Renwell much more information than that.

"I thought you were my enemy," I whispered. "By the time I realized you weren't, it was too late."

Aiden bent closer. Gods, his mouth was nearly on top of mine. My body betrayed me, my lips parting.

"Was it all a lie?" he whispered, brushing each word over my lips. "Was it all to maintain your cover? To make me trust you?"

A shiver rattled down my spine. My skin felt too warm, but not warm enough. An ache trembled in the pit of my stomach.

He wanted to know a truth I was scared to give. It was something he could use against me. Just like Renwell used all of my little weaknesses to bend me to his will.

But I didn't want to be afraid anymore.

"No," I said, the word quiet but as unyielding as sunstone. "I lied about who I was and what I wanted. But I defended Ruru and tried to save Maz because my heart needed to. As for you . . ." My voice shook. I licked my lips—making Aiden's eyes flare—and continued. "Our time in The Hollow . . . that was the most truthful I'd been in years."

Aiden closed his eyes as if my words had struck him. A slow, heavy breath eased from his lips.

Sadness pierced my heart. Not for the first time today, but differently.

I had told him I would be a light for him. Someone he could trust. And I'd betrayed him so thoroughly, he believed the most intimate moment of my life had been an act on my part.

Gods damn it, I was right. We didn't just break each other's trust. We shattered it. Nothing can fix this.

"Swim with me."

I blinked at him. "Excuse me?"

A playfulness I hadn't seen in weeks teased his shadowed

mouth. "I find myself in desperate need of a swim in icy water. Join me. Or go back and wait for a boat."

My jaw dropped as he turned and sauntered into the water, his clothes thrown over one shoulder.

He flashed a grin at me when the water reached his waist.

"You know I don't swim very well!" I called out to him.

"You won't have to," he called back. He waded across the river and tossed his clothes on the other bank. Then he dove underwater, headed for me.

I glanced around nervously. No one in sight. And I really didn't want to wait for the mourners. Perhaps that was selfish of me, but I wanted a respite from the heavy grief.

Trying not to think too much about it, I slid off my boots and socks.

Aiden resurfaced close to me. He raked back his wet hair, water cascading over his muscled torso.

"Don't look," I commanded.

He pressed his lips together, no doubt thinking of how I'd already gotten a few eyefuls of him. And he knew my body, perhaps even more intimately than I knew his. But he turned around without complaint.

My fingers trembled as I undid my pants and shirt. I'd found Mother's knife before the funeral and tucked it in Nikella's saddlebag for safekeeping.

I was unarmed for the first time in a long time.

I hesitated before also removing my breast band and underwear. I'd hate to hunt down dry ones after this.

Clutching everything to my chest, I slowly tiptoed into the water that seemed to attack my skin with a thousand icy needles.

"F-Fucking Four, that's cold," I squealed.

"You'll warm up," Aiden said, his back still turned, his eyes on the stars.

"L-Liar."

His deep chuckle actually did warm me a bit, but in a place the water didn't reach.

My skin tightened as I waded deeper and deeper. The frigid river took my breath away. I tried to keep my clothes out of the water, but it was now up to my chest.

The heavy paste Nikella had put on the cut across my back softened and loosened, but I didn't care. The cold water dulled any pain the paste uncovered.

I drew even with Aiden, who glanced down at me. Then farther down.

His jaw tightened. "Allow me." He stole my clothes and waded to the other side.

I frowned and looked down. *Oh.*

Even though the water covered them, my breasts were still visible, like little moons in the river. And my nipples were as hard as arrow tips.

Biting my lip, I sank into the water.

Aiden tossed my clothes next to his and swam back to me.

I wrapped my arms around my body, trying to ease my shivering. "This is n-nothing like the bathhouse in Aquinon."

Aiden drifted closer, small waves splashing against the seam of his smile. "I didn't think I'd miss many things about Aquinon, but a heated bath is one of them."

I dipped my head back and unbraided my hair. The river teased it apart. If only I had soap. At least the river would make it smell better than ash and sweat.

The stars glistened above me. The dark pine trees crowding the shore reached for them like furry fingers.

"The view is quite spectacular, though," I murmured.

"The one I had in the bathhouse was just as beautiful."

I lowered my chin to find him staring at me in a way that made my toes curl around the slippery rocks on the river bottom.

He'd looked at me the same way in The Hollow. Just before we ran for our tent.

But I couldn't let him get to me. Or I might do something stupid like wrap my naked body around his and create a warmth of our own. But this time, I wouldn't have the mead to blame for my recklessness.

Just loneliness. And desire.

He reached for me under the rippling water, his fingers brushing mine. Stroking my palm in a soft invitation. The river's gentle current pushed me toward him as if it, too, wanted to give him what he wanted.

I slipped out of his reach, kicking my feet to give us some distance. "Is this the cold river Maz boasted about swimming in?"

"We've gone swimming in this river many times. But I'm sure he was talking about the times when the rivers of Dagriel freeze into ice so thick, many people can walk on them."

My eyebrows arched. "That sounds incredible. And dangerous. And much too cold for me."

Aiden chuckled. "It is. But of course, the Dags make a game out of it. They cut holes in the ice to fish but also to jump into, to see who can stay in the longest."

I snorted. "That sounds like outright torture."

"It's not so bad if you get out, wrap yourself in furs, and run for the bonfire."

"You've done it?"

"Of course." Aiden shook his head with a smile. "But not after Maz stole my clothes and all the blankets, and I had to run back to camp naked."

I laughed outright this time, my face tipped to the sky. "Oh gods, I would've kicked his ass off a mountain."

"It wasn't so bad after the icicles melted off my skin. Although I paid him back in kind." Aiden swam up next to me and mimicked my position. "Late one night, after he passed out from much more mead than usual, I—along with his three lovely sisters—dragged him out of his lodge and threw him in an ice hole. He woke up with a roar so loud, Jek came running with his sword, thinking we were being attacked by a bear."

My shoulders shook with laughter and shivers. I could picture everything in my mind. Their mischievous looks, Maz's snoring, then his shouting.

A pang of sadness hit me at the thought that Davka wouldn't be in their future stories.

That was one of the hardest parts about losing Mother—she wouldn't be in my stories anymore. She wouldn't get to share the rest of my life. All I had left were old memories that would continue to fade.

I rolled over and paddled through the water, trying to thaw the blood in my veins and the ice in my heart.

"You seem to swim just fine," Aiden remarked, watching me with hooded eyes.

Cheeks burning, I stopped, wondering how much of my naked body he could see.

"The pool at the palace was large enough for me to get the idea," I said. "And this river is much calmer than the sea outside Calimber." I shuddered at the memory of those huge waves and that bottomless feeling beneath me.

Aiden stilled. I did, too, glancing over my shoulder in case he'd spotted someone. But no one was there.

"What's wrong?" I asked.

"Calimber," he said in a strangled voice. "I'd bet all the gold in Rellmira that Renwell's forging his sunstone weapons and armor in Calimber."

I swallowed, tasting river water and salt.

It made sense. There were no forges in the Den or the palace. The only forges in Aquinon churned out steel or bronze armor and weapons. Sometimes Father had imported what he needed for his soldiers from Keldiket.

Besides, if Renwell had been hiding his new sunstone armor and weapons from Father, Calimber would've been the perfect place to do it. He'd hidden warships there, after all.

"Your sister didn't mention a forge or anything else about the mine?" Aiden asked, his voice urgent.

I shook my head. "Just that her soldier lover had been moved away from there. And that there was a lot of secrecy around it, much like Nikella and Lord Garyth found when they sniffed around Calimber."

Aiden frowned. "I thought that was because of the warships, but perhaps there was more."

"Logs!" I blurted out. "Nikella told Lord Garyth that my father was excessively logging out of Twaryn and sending it to Calimber. For what, they didn't know. But perhaps Renwell needed the extra wood to feed a forge, as well as to build warships."

Something like admiration flickered in Aiden's eyes. "It's possible. I won't know for certain unless I see for myself."

My body grew impossibly colder. "You want to spy on Calimber? Where the High General is camped? Where those terrible ships are?"

Aiden's face hardened with grim determination. He looked like he had when he'd spoken of his plans to assassinate Father. Like a man who had to do the impossible, and he was the only one who could do it.

"Renwell needs to be stopped before something like this"—he gestured at the distant village—"happens again. And if he's using Calimber to create indestructible weapons and armor and more of those warships, then that's where I need to go."

"I'm coming with you," I announced, trying to hide the tremble in my jaw.

I expected him to forbid me, as he had with my suggestion to go to Renwell. But I hadn't asked. I was merely letting him know.

He clearly wasn't pleased, judging by his tightened brow. "Why?"

I glanced toward the trees that hid the burning part of the mountain from view. Maz's words from last night came back to me. "I haven't given my all yet. Therefore, I haven't given enough. Renwell was able to commit so many crimes partially because I couldn't see him for what he was." I peeked at Aiden from under my eyelashes. He was still scowling. "I set out to protect my family, but also Rellmira, and I haven't done either. So I'm trying to do what I should've done from the beginning."

Aiden tilted his head to the side, studying me. "It's strange sometimes to see my thoughts reflected in someone else's mind."

I took a step back.

He spoke of his regrets, his guilt. I remembered what he'd said about Mother vowing to help him in whatever way she could. And those plans had taken her away from us.

"I'm not doing this for you," I said, more harshly than I meant to. "Not because of my mother's vow, and not because I owe you. I'm doing this for *me*. For Everett and Delysia. For Rellmira."

The words floated between us like the flecks of snow that had started to fall, kissing the river.

"I understand," Aiden said softly. His drying hair curled over his brow, and he looked almost . . . sad. Defeated.

My body was shivering uncontrollably, and my teeth chattered, despite my attempt to look stern.

He jerked his chin to the shore. "Get your clothes, Kiera. Wrap your hair in a blanket if you can, or you'll catch a fever." He turned his back to me without waiting for a reply.

I hesitated, part of me wanting to take back what I said, to assure him I would ally with him against Renwell. That he didn't need to worry about my loyalty on that front. But I had no assurances on my loyalty to *him.*

We would just have to trust each other enough to win a war.

Impossible, I thought as I sloshed toward my clothes, snow prickling against my skin.

Yet I knew with my whole heart that Aiden wouldn't turn around until I was gone.

CHAPTER 20
KIERA

The snow followed us to Yargoth. It was beautiful the way it coated the forest's branches and muffled the horses' hooves.

I had my own horse now. A dark brown one with a black mane and tail named Ozlow.

The day before we left the village, Nikella and a Teacher named Silas had divided up the possessions of the dead. I'd learned it was customary as the Dags were not a wasteful people.

Nikella handed me Ozlow's reins, saying she'd chosen him for me because of his gentle temperament and small, but hearty size. He'd belonged to an Urzost warrior woman. He'd stared at me with his big brown eyes, and I swore I saw sadness in them. I kissed his nose and promised I would take care of him.

Nikella also gave me a set of steel throwing knives with leather grips and a brace, as well as a sword and a bow with arrows. She said I would need it all for our journey ahead.

The rest of our warriors were similarly re-outfitted.

Then came the matter of the dead Wolves and their gear. After much shouting between clans, the Yargoths and the

Urzosts won out, and the Berengars—the clan who'd ridden to their aid—left in a huff.

The Dags stripped the Wolves of their clothes and weapons and burned the bodies in an unceremonious heap. They carted the unbreakable weapons and armor to the sea and threw them in.

They wanted no part of anything mined by their captive brethren. Something the Berengars—who lived much deeper in the north—wouldn't understand.

Nikella asked them to spread the word to the other clans about what had happened. Perhaps she hoped they would rally behind the Yargoths and the Urzosts and fight against Renwell. But I doubted they would.

Most people didn't act until the enemy was on their doorstep.

But the Berengars had stopped hunting to aid the village without question, so perhaps there was hope yet.

We'd left the next day at a silent, unhurried pace. So much different from the one we'd kept on the way here.

We'd lost ten of our party, plus a few too severely injured to travel. We rode a fair distance apart, as if keeping gaps open for the missing riders.

I hadn't spoken to Aiden since our river swim. I hadn't slept next to him either. I'd laid my mat next to Nikella the last few nights, even though sleep was difficult to come by.

Especially after she told me that Aiden was putting together a plan for Calimber. She'd seemed pleased that I insisted on joining.

She hadn't started training me yet. But she rode next to me, instructing me on my form.

I'd griped, asking if there was a technique to make my ass hurt less.

"Practice," she said.

The only bright spot of our snowy journey back to Yargoth

was holding throwing knives again. I practiced with them every time we stopped, using a tree for a target.

It also seemed to cheer the Dags up a bit because they appreciated my skill and enjoyed a good-natured competition with me.

I only wished I weren't shit at every other weapon.

My fingers had itched with desire as I'd watched the Dags cart away the sunstone weapons. That sword had been so easy to wield. So deadly. It would've been child's play to steal one from the cart.

But keeping it hidden would've been much harder, so I let it go. Yarina had given up her stolen sunstone gauntlet much more unwillingly.

As we neared the Yargoth camp, I smelled smoke once more. But this time it was just from a campfire. Yet, memories of the burning village persisted.

Children on fuzzy ponies alongside barking dogs raced out to greet us.

I urged Ozlow to hurry through them, unwilling to watch the joy and grief about to spill forth. But their cries still pierced my back like a dozen arrows.

I took my time putting Ozlow in the paddock and caring for him as Nikella had taught me. I'd discovered that my horse loved to be brushed, especially along his strong neck.

The others tended to their horses as well, but hurried toward the bonfires, where the smell of cooked meat beckoned.

When I felt I couldn't delay any longer, Nikella joined me by the fence.

She tapped me on the shoulder with a wooden practice sword, a second one gripped at her side. She also had her staff tucked under her arm as if she couldn't bear to part with it, even in the serene Yargoth meadow.

"Time to practice."

I frowned. "Now? It's almost dark, and I haven't eaten all day." And my whole body ached from riding Ozlow.

"Doesn't matter," Nikella said, her eyes gleaming in the sunset. She tossed the sword, and I instinctively caught it. "Your enemy will not wait for daylight or a full stomach. They will want to attack you when you're at your weakest."

I swung the wooden sword in a few test arcs. It was heavier than the sunstone sword, but so was the steel one at my hip. My movements tugged on the tight scab across my shoulders. I prayed it wouldn't start bleeding again.

"We aren't going to war just yet," I reminded her.

Nikella strode a few feet away, her boots leaving faint prints in the dusting of snow. "When we go to Calimber, we'll likely run into the Rellmiran border patrols that stand between us and the mine. They will not hesitate to attack a group of armed Dags."

I pulled up short. I hadn't thought of border patrols. Rellmirans. Fighting and killing Shadow-Wolves didn't prick at my conscience because they were murderous mercenaries. But Rellmiran soldiers? They were usually young men enlisted from farms in Pravara, ranches in Winspere, and the streets of Aquinon.

My empty stomach rolled when I remembered Shayn and the other guards Father had banished on my account. Gods, that seemed like a lifetime ago, but they might still patrol Rellmira's borders. Which borders, I didn't know.

"I don't want to kill Rellmirans," I said stiffly.

Nikella gently laid her staff aside, then twirled her practice sword in graceful circles. "You can try not to. But you will have to fight if you want to defend yourself and others."

That was my goal. But I'd been picturing a fight between me and Renwell, not me and dozens of my people.

"I don't want to be like him," I whispered. "Killing anyone who gets in my way."

I didn't have to say his name. Understanding flickered in Nikella's eyes.

"Who we are is a choice," she said. "Renwell chose to be who he is. I chose to be the opposite of who my family wanted me to be. You can do the same. You already have."

She stepped closer to me and tapped two fingers on my chest. "Remember, what grows from your heart"—she tapped my forehead—"feeds your mind and strengthens your hand." She gripped my sword hand and angled my sword up.

I nodded, silently repeating the words and storing them away. "Did the Teachers at the Temple tell you that?"

A rare smile flashed under Nikella's hood as she backed away. "No. A gladiator from Keldiket did."

My eyebrows shot up, and I opened my mouth to ask the dozen questions that flooded it.

But Nikella barked, "Attack!"

I obeyed, lunging forward and clumsily swinging my sword. Nikella twisted out of the way.

"Again," she commanded. "Until you strike me."

Gritting my teeth and trying to ignore my stiff muscles, I tried again and again. Sweat trickled down my hairline and stuck my skin to my clothes.

But Nikella was faster than the Wolves. As fast as her brother.

She blocked my strikes a few times, but didn't taunt me. Didn't use her strength against me.

Our boots kicked up a bald spot in the snowy meadow at the edge of the woods. The silver and indigo of the night played tricks with my eyes. But Nikella always seemed to sense my next move, anyway.

"Enough," she said.

I immediately bent double, trying to catch my breath.

"You're fast and agile," she continued over my panting. "Your footwork is decent, and I know from watching you throw knives that you have a good eye and quick fingers."

I stared up at her in disbelief. My only other fighting instructor had been Renwell, and compliments were certainly not his way.

"But your arms need to be stronger to compensate for the weight of the sword." She tossed her sword from hand to hand, spinning it and whipping it around her body as if it weighed nothing. "It should feel as dexterous as another limb."

"Right. Another limb. Understood." Gods, I hoped there was some food left. Maybe I could eat it in bed so I could fall asleep immediately after.

"You're also hesitating. You don't want to hit me, which I appreciate, but I'm not the one you need to be ready for."

I slowly straightened, the wound across my shoulders itchy. "I won't hesitate fighting Renwell."

"With him, it will be the opposite problem. You will be emotional. Emotions make you messy. He will taunt you until you wear yourself out."

"And how do you plan to prepare me for that?" I asked. I couldn't imagine her being as nasty as Renwell.

She shrugged. "I have an idea we'll try out later."

Well, that sounded ominous.

"It's too dark for bow training." Nikella dropped her sword in the wet grass. "But I would like to test your skills without a weapon. As that often happens in battle."

I bit my lip, then tossed my sword aside. "Renwell taught me a few tricks, but he thought it was a waste to teach me more. He told me I wouldn't win against a stronger person. Therefore, I should always strike from a distance, like with my knives."

"He lied to you," Nikella said simply. "He wanted to keep you weaker than him. A good teacher wants you to be stronger."

I'd surmised as much for myself after he put my throat under his boot heel. Twice. I couldn't imagine being stronger than Nikella.

But I'd do everything she said if it meant I got close.

"Now, I'm going to grab you, and you have to free yourself."

I swallowed hard and bent my knees, hands at the ready.

A twig snapped in the forest.

Both Nikella and I whirled to peer between the shadowy trunks. The snow that had fallen through the foliage gleamed. But I didn't see anyone or anything.

"Perhaps it was an animal," I whispered.

Nikella shook her head. She slowly bent to pick up her staff. In one smooth, silent movement, she unsheathed her spear. Had she been expecting an intruder?

I picked up my sword, the wooden grip clammy in my hand.

Another twig cracked, followed by a soft whinny.

My breath caught. A horse. With a rider? How many?

"Alert the others," Nikella said out of the corner of her mouth. "We—"

A horse burst out of the forest, a rider slumped on its back.

We sprang out of the way as the horse snorted and pranced in the snow. With a tangled mane and muddy coat, the poor creature looked like he'd been traveling for weeks.

I peered into the woods, but no one else came through.

The rider started slipping sideways toward me. Dropping my wooden sword, I caught the person about the shoulders, and Nikella helped me slide the body to the ground.

The rider's hood fell back. My heartbeat came to a crashing halt.

"Oh, gods!" I cried out. "Ruru!"

CHAPTER 21
KIERA

"Kiera?" Ruru mumbled, stirring in my arms.

His dark brown hair had grown past his ears and over his eyes. He felt thinner than I remembered. His cheekbones sharper. Gods, how did he make it all the way here by himself?

"I'm here, Ruru. You made it," I said soothingly.

He grunted and fell unconscious.

"What's wrong with him?" I asked Nikella, my voice cracking.

She pressed the back of her hand to his forehead and cheeks. "He's exhausted. Underfed. No fever, but I'll need to check him for injuries. Foolish boy," she muttered affectionately under her breath.

We cradled Ruru between us and settled him back onto his horse, who was surprisingly calm after all his prancing around.

"I'll walk with him," Nikella said. "Run ahead and get blankets, food, and water."

I was already sprinting by the time she finished speaking. Questions raced through my mind faster than my feet.

How did he find us? What happened after we left Aquinon? Did he know the fates of Everett and Delysia?

I burst into camp, drawing the eyes of everyone I raced past. I skidded to a halt before the main bonfire. Aiden, Maz, his sisters, and a dozen others stared at me. Most of them reached for a blade.

But I locked eyes with Aiden. "Ruru. He's here."

Aiden's eyes widened, and Maz dropped the piece of bread he was holding.

I took a deep breath. "He's unconscious and—"

Aiden rushed back the way I'd come. Maz shouted and charged after him.

"I—I need blankets. Food. Water."

"Is this the boy from Aquinon Maz told us about?" Yarina said.

I nodded.

Without another word, she spooned soup into a bowl while Sigrid grabbed a whole loaf of bread.

"Water and mead," Frieda commanded a young boy from her chair.

Jek appeared at my side with an armful of blankets.

By the time Ruru's small procession arrived, we had everything laid out for him by the fire.

Aiden eased Ruru off the horse and carried him to the nest of blankets I'd made. Maz followed close behind, wiping his eyes. Nikella unbuckled the horse's saddlebags and handed the reins over to a young girl with quiet instructions.

Aiden laid Ruru next to me. We removed his mud-caked cloak and boots. I frowned at his thin clothes. They were better suited to the sun and warm storms of Aquinon. Not the snowy forests of Dagriel.

I hung back while Nikella examined him.

Please, please—

"He's fine," Nikella announced. "A few cuts and bruises, but nothing serious."

Several sighs, including mine, echoed around the group.

Nikella looked at me. "Get him to eat and drink, then let him rest."

I nodded vigorously. I would do as she said, but Ruru had answers I needed.

Nikella left, and Jek followed her.

Aiden propped Ruru up on a pile of furs. Yarina handed me the warm soup, and I nudged a spoonful between Ruru's chapped lips.

It took a moment, but then he sipped it. Slowly, he chewed a few of the meat chunks and soft vegetables.

His eyes opened. He looked startled until he saw Maz, Aiden, and me among the others. Aiden gave him a tight smile and squeezed his narrow shoulder.

Ruru stared at me. "I thought you were dead. When I didn't hear from you . . . When Aiden sailed away . . . I thought—"

"I was on the ship, too." I set down the soup and gently hugged him. "I wish I could've gone back for you."

Ruru threw his arms around my neck. "I'm just glad you're alive."

I let out a muffled laugh. "Does that mean you forgive me?"

"Of course I forgive you, Kiera. You're my friend."

I scrunched my eyes shut and soaked that in. Forgiveness. Friendship. Two rays of light in the darkness that had chased me since that dreadful night.

Someone cleared their throat, and we broke apart.

"I can't believe I made it," Ruru said hoarsely, looking at everyone gathered around him.

Maz beamed and reached around Aiden to slap Ruru on the back. "You did, little brother. You're a gods-damned warrior to make it here all by yourself."

Ruru smiled a little, and the sight made my eyes prickle again.

"Eat more," I said gruffly, shoving another spoonful at his mouth.

His brown eyes crinkled at me, but he gulped the soup down. He licked his lips. "I'll take the bowl, if you don't mind."

I smiled and handed it over. He devoured it while we watched. Sigrid tore off chunks of bread for him, which he took with a nod of thanks. She was much more welcoming to him than she had been with me. But then again, Ruru wasn't a traitor.

"Gods, that's good," he groaned between mouthfuls. The light was coming back to his eyes, but the shadows beneath them remained. He glanced between Yarina and Sigrid. "Are you Maz's sisters? I've heard so many stories."

They both nodded and introduced themselves.

Ruru frowned. "Where's the third sister you mentioned, Maz?"

A shadow fell over Maz's face, and he swallowed hard. He opened his mouth, but the words wouldn't emerge.

Sigrid answered for him. "Davka died in battle."

"Oh, I'm sorry . . . What battle?"

"Later," I murmured in his ear.

He nodded. "Is my horse all right?"

"He's taken care of," Aiden said.

Maz seized on the new topic with enthusiasm, his grin a little too bright. "When did you learn to ride?"

"On that horse." Ruru took the water I gave him and downed it in a few gulps. "I think my ass is shaped like his back by now."

A chuckle rippled through the group.

I waited for the laughter to die, twisting my hands in my lap. "Ruru, before you left Aquinon, did you hear anything of my brother and sister?"

Ruru's grin softened. "I saw them."

I blinked, not sure I heard him right. "You saw them? They're alive? Where? Are they safe?" Each question tumbled over the next like water over sharp rocks.

Ruru grimaced. "They're alive and unharmed, as far as I could tell. But they were with Renwell in the prison square."

"What?" I gasped.

"Not as prisoners," Ruru said quickly. "But as part of his coronation."

My face crumpled, and I buried it in my hands.

They're alive. They're alive. They're alive.

That one simple truth echoed through my mind, roaring louder and louder. It drowned out the incessant worry.

But then other fears appeared, stacking on my shoulders like stones.

How long would he keep them alive? What was he doing with them? By going with Aiden to Calimber, I could be condemning them.

But they'd been alive and well this whole time. Nikella had been right. Renwell had dangled my brother's and sister's fates to get me to follow him home, like raw meat in front of a dog.

Gods damn that man to the deep, dark, wandering hell. I hope I get to send him there one day.

Someone wrapped an arm around me. I lowered my hands to see Yarina half-hugging me, tears in her blue eyes. But I knew those tears weren't for me.

"You'll see them again soon, I'm sure," she whispered.

She would never get her sister back, but I still had a chance to save Everett and Delysia. If Renwell was keeping them alive to lure me home, then I needed to make sure I had more than my knives when I faced him again.

I returned Yarina's half-hug, then clasped Ruru's hand. His thumbless grip was so familiar and comforting. "Thank you for telling me. You don't know how much that means to me."

He squeezed my hand. "I do know. I would've given anything for someone to tell me of Daire's fate."

Shadow-Wolves had taken his older brother years ago, before Ruru resorted to stealing food and Aiden had helped him evade capture.

I met Aiden's eyes over Ruru's head. They blazed with a fierce emotion I couldn't name. Deeper than happiness. More grim than worry.

"Start from the beginning, Ruru," Aiden said quietly. "What happened after we left?"

Everyone sat in a crescent around Ruru, ready for a story.

"After you sailed away, I hid out for a few days, hoping for news," Ruru began. "I never stayed in one place very long, but when nobody came after me, I figured I was safe."

"What has Renwell done to the city?" I interrupted. Sigrid shot me a glare. Interrupting stories was tantamount to a crime around a Dag fire.

"He's got it locked up pretty tight," Ruru said. "Curfews and such. Shadow-Wolves prowling at all times of the day. It's awful." He glanced at Aiden. "I went to check on Melaena using the tunnel, but Renwell must've found it. Filled it with rubble."

Aiden grimaced. "Is Melaena safe?"

Ruru nodded, and I nearly melted with relief again. I'd never told Renwell about that tunnel, but he'd guessed what I was hiding from him.

"Renwell's keeping a close eye on her club, though," Ruru continued. "Probably hoping the three of you will show up. I sent her a coded message, and she sent—" Ruru jerked upright with a wild look. "Fucking Four, my bags! Did you grab—"

"Calm down," I said, dragging his saddlebags forward. "Nikella took them off your horse."

Ruru sagged with relief. "Thank the Four. After what I went through to keep these safe . . ."

"What's in them?" Maz pawed through one. "Letters?" He held up a wrinkled piece of paper with an air of disappointment.

Ruru snatched it out of his hand. "Yes, letters Melaena gave me. What were you hoping for?"

Maz shrugged. "I don't know. A Wolf's head. Renwell's battle plans. Gold."

"I'd already taken my coins from the chest in the Temple," Ruru said. His cheeks pinked as he glanced between me and Aiden. "Kiera's too."

Aiden frowned at me. "You don't have any coins with you."

I opened my mouth to answer, but Ruru beat me to it. "That's because she gave hers to me. To get me settled outside of Aquinon."

Everyone stared at me, different levels of begrudging respect on their faces.

Heat crawled up my neck, and I dropped my gaze to my boots. "It was the least I could do."

"Did this conversation happen when you freed Kiera?" Aiden's deep voice made me look up again.

Ruru clutched his remaining bread like he'd been caught stealing. "Yes. But I had to, Aiden. I owed her."

"I would expect nothing less from you, Ruru," Aiden said softly. His eyes met mine. "In the end, I'm glad you did."

I blinked. He was glad? Even though I'd interrupted his assassination of my father?

"Good," Ruru said with a sigh of relief. "And it's lucky I grabbed the money when I did because, two days after you sailed away, Renwell invaded the Temple."

"He did what?"

We spun around to see Nikella towering behind us in her Teacher robes, her eyes blazing, her fist clenched around her spear. I'd never seen her so furious.

Jek stood behind her, holding our wooden swords and gazing at her like she was a goddess he'd gladly kill for.

Ruru's voice trembled. "He went into the Temple with a dozen Shadow-Wolves. When they came out, they had Librius in chains. They ripped apart the bookshelves and collapsed the entrance to the secret room."

Aiden paled, and Maz swore loudly.

"How did Renwell know we were using that room?" I wondered.

"Any Teacher, including the High Teacher, could've spied on us," Aiden said darkly. "He could've—"

"It doesn't matter," Nikella barked. "He's an elite spy with informants. The point is, he destroyed the entrance and arrested Librius. He must've figured out that Librius was helping us."

I remembered the Teacher who'd been nothing but kind to me the few times I'd seen him. Was Renwell punishing him for being our ally? If so, then why had he spared Melaena?

My stomach growled as my head pounded. In all the turmoil, I'd forgotten about my empty stomach.

Wordlessly, Ruru tore his bread and handed half to me. It reminded me of when we'd share sticky bread from the market. A market that now had Wolves stalking through it, day and night.

I shoved the bread into my mouth.

"Tell us about the prison square and the letters," Aiden said.

Ruru swallowed his last bite of bread. "Renwell dragged Weylin's body to the square and burned it in front of hundreds of people." He glanced at my wide eyes and winced. "Sorry, I know he was your father—"

"Don't be," I rasped. "The man was a murderer and a usurper who tried to execute half his family, including me. I'm glad he's dead."

Surprise flickered in the eyes of everyone listening.

Did they really think I cherished the man who was only a father by blood? He'd destroyed so much of my life—my first love, my friends, my future, Mother.

I avoided Aiden's gaze, even though I could feel it burning a hole in my wounded cheek.

Ruru cleared his throat. "All right, then. So, Renwell made a big speech about how he was king now, that Weylin had stolen the throne in the first place, and that there were no heirs. He pointed at Everett and Delysia and said they had no legal right to the throne and that the Falcryn line had died. He never mentioned Kiera or Aiden by name." He glanced at me. "Which is also why I thought you were dead."

Gods, that was a lot to take in.

Renwell had revealed the truth about Father's claim to the throne. He'd effectively cut off any support Everett and Delysia might have garnered. And he'd stricken me and Aiden from the story altogether.

No one to miss us. No one to look for us. No allies. Just enemies.

And we had no way to tell anyone otherwise.

CHAPTER 22
AIDEN

It was a good plan.

Make Rellmira think they had no other option for a ruler than the High Enforcer who held their royal city in the palm of his hand.

Weylin had stolen the throne via a quiet assassination and well-told lies, making him look like the rightful heir.

Renwell simply removed any arguments in the matter. Not that anyone would want to argue with a man who controlled an army of Shadow-Wolves.

Kiera looked troubled, no doubt many of the same thoughts racing through her head.

Maz was scowling. Yarina and Sigrid looked indifferent. After all, Rellmira's politics didn't concern them. Instead, they hounded me about Calimber every chance they got.

Nikella . . . Nikella was furious. Which was rare for her. I remembered it happening only a handful of times. But her brother arresting a Teacher and destroying part of a sacred Temple had pressed a nerve.

Gods, I hated to think about what they were doing with Librius. Or what they'd already done.

He would probably meet the same fate as Garyth.

A memory of Garyth's mutilated body covered in leeches flashed behind my eyes.

My chest tightened. Everyone who helped me received terrible deaths. Perhaps I should stop fighting. Let Rellmira go. Let the Falcryn line truly die out, as Renwell proclaimed.

I glanced at Kiera, her scarred cheek, her damp hair.

The memory of swimming naked in the river together surfaced in my mind. An heir who wanted to remain hidden and a false princess who gave up her crown. We made quite a pair, avoiding the same throne as best we could.

But despite the truths that still needed to be told, I clung to the one she'd given me that night.

"Our time in The Hollow . . . that was the most truthful I'd been in years."

Those words had healed a part of my heart that had lost hope. But now that troublesome emotion was back. Nothing brought more heartbreak than hope.

Ruru suddenly let out a snore. The poor boy had dozed off in the silence.

"The letters," I reminded him, gently shaking his shoulder.

His eyes snapped open. "Right, right. Er, in my bag. Melaena said you'd know what to do with them."

I gave them a cursory glance and left them in the bag. "Excellent. Thank you, Ruru," I said. "Now let's get you to bed. We can finish catching up tomorrow."

He nodded, his chin already dropping toward his chest again. My heart warmed with fondness. Ruru's loyalty and dedication to his friends were truly unmatched. I'd hated leaving him behind in Aquinon, but I'd also hoped he would escape sooner and find a new, quiet life for himself.

But of course, he'd traveled through dangerous territory just to bring me this stack of scribbles. He probably didn't even know what they were.

I did. And while I was relieved Melaena had gotten rid of the incriminating letters, they would do little good out here. Ruru's presence was far more valuable. Tomorrow, I would ask him how he survived on his own, having never been outside of Aquinon before.

"He can take the extra bed in our lodge," Maz said.

I nodded and helped Ruru get to his feet.

"Maz. Whistler," he mumbled, pointing in the general direction of his bags. Then he slumped against me.

Kiera shored up Ruru's other side, his boots in her other hand, while Maz dove for the unopened saddlebag.

He dug out his shiny whistler and a handful of darts, beaming. "Fucking Four, Ruru, how did you get all this out of Aquinon?"

Ruru's head simply lolled in answer.

"Tomorrow," I told Maz.

Kiera and I half-carried Ruru to the lodge I shared with Maz. I hesitated at the threshold, wary of bringing Kiera into our sleeping quarters. Neither Maz nor I had taken the time to do anything other than dump our gear.

But then I remembered she used to share a tiny apartment with us in Aquinon.

I pushed through the heavy fur curtain that served as a door and kicked aside boots, clothes, and weapons to clear us a path to the small bed against the far wall.

We draped Ruru across it, laying his head on the thin pillow. I covered him with blankets while Kiera tucked his boots next to the bed.

Then we stood and stared at him as if neither of us could truly believe he was here.

"He must've suffered so much," Kiera whispered. "There was no food or water left in those bags."

I glanced down at her. Her shoulder brushed mine, and I missed her with a sudden, fierce ache that rushed through my veins.

"Perhaps he only made it this far because of the extra coins you gave him," I whispered.

Her sad amber eyes were like a fist to my chest. "They were never mine to begin with. I sacrificed nothing to give him those coins."

"But you did it because you loved him, and that may have kept him on this side of the Abyss."

"Why are you trying to defend me against myself? Why do you care after everything else I've done?"

Unable to resist, I cupped her jaw in my hand. Her eyes fluttered closed.

"I don't know," I said, my voice low and rough. "Perhaps because when I get a glimpse of the woman I . . . admired, it makes me feel like I wasn't completely wrong about her. That maybe her other life was a lie, and her real one was in that apartment with the three of us. With me."

"Aiden," she whispered, swaying closer to me.

I swallowed hard, grazing my thumb on her cheek. "Like when you said you were glad your father was dead. I didn't realize—"

Kiera jerked out of my grasp. "My father? Did you think I was ignorant enough to still care for that murderer? Just like you think I'll happily become Renwell's puppet again?"

"*No,* gods damn it." I shoved my empty hands through my hair. How did we get into a fight every time we spoke to each other? "The way you talked about my attempt on Weylin's life made me think you hated me for it. Even if I couldn't finish the job in the end."

She froze, her eyebrows pinching together. "What do you mean? If I hadn't interrupted, you wouldn't have killed him?"

"I wanted to. But then I saw your eyes in his and realized I didn't want to be the man who took both your parents from you."

Kiera inhaled sharply. Her eyes bounced back and forth between mine. I wanted to know what she saw. An enemy? An ally? Someone she wished she'd never met?

I'd seen her as all three. And more.

"Tell me what happened that night," she whispered.

My hands clenched into fists at my sides. I knew by her tone which night she meant. "Are you sure?"

She nodded, her eyes already rimmed with silver. "I want to know the truth once and for all. I want to know why she had to die."

I yearned to reach for her again, but that never seemed to end well anymore. I rubbed my hand over my bristly jaw. "I've never told anyone else the details before."

"Not even Nikella?"

I shook my head. She knew the general information, as did Maz. But some bits and pieces I'd kept for myself, unable to bare such ugly pain to someone else. Until I found out who Kiera was.

Striding over to my bed, I cleared it of my bags. I sat down and gestured for Kiera to join me. She sat next to me, an arm's length away. Her fingertips danced over her thigh. I almost smiled at the familiar gesture.

I clasped my hands in front of me. Words eluded me. How did I start such a story?

Ruru's snores filled the lodge, like a creaky door that kept swinging in the wind.

"You said she was best friends with your mother?" Kiera asked, her voice strange and unsure, as if she didn't know where to start either.

My shoulders relaxed an inch, something Brielle had said

that night coming back to me. "Yes. Strange, isn't it? That we could've grown up together. We might've even been friends—you, me, Everett, and Delysia."

A smile peeked around the corners of Kiera's mouth. "I can hardly imagine it. You would've been like another older brother . . . or my first crush."

"Definitely the latter," I growled.

Her smile quirked higher, then disappeared. "I'm sorry for what my father did. I know it's not my fault, but I am sorry for all the pain he caused. None of you deserved that."

Something burned deep inside my chest. An old wound that never received much attention, but was grateful for the soothing balm of kind words, anyway.

"Thank you, Kiera. But as Maz told me, there's enough pain to go around. My family wasn't the only one to suffer."

"No." Kiera bit her lip. "Tell me what happened that night."

I dragged in a long breath. I didn't have to dig deep for the memories. They were my constant companions, a chronic pain I couldn't ease.

"Two years ago, on Viridana's Day . . ."

CHAPTER 23

AIDEN

Two years ago . . .

One more hour. One last meeting. One final death. And then Rellmira would be safe.

I paced the dirt floor of the abandoned warehouse. The stale air still smelled like the barrels of wine Melaena's merchant friend used to store. Now the floor-to-ceiling shelves stood like skeletons against the wall. Nothing else inhabited this building, save for the lone torch I lit while I waited.

I'd burned all of Brielle's maps of the palace and her scribbled notes about her husband's routines and guard rotations the moment I memorized them. I never wanted to leave any evidence of a meeting in case someone searched the building.

The thick wooden door swung open, and a hooded figure slipped inside.

I breathed a sigh of relief, my feet finally able to stand still.

She latched the door and slid the heavy crossbar over it before facing me. "Aiden."

I dipped my head. "Brielle." From our very first meeting, she'd refused to hear me call her by a queenly title.

"I didn't see Maz on lookout," she said, tucking some of her golden hair into her hood.

"Late shipment for Melaena. I insisted he go. The dock master has been skittish lately. I paid a stable boy to keep watch. He'll whistle if he sees anything."

She nodded, her blue eyes troubled as they darted from my face to the barred door.

I tensed again. "Problem?"

It'd been several months since we'd last met, but that wasn't unusual since we could only meet on the Four's feast days.

Brielle shook her head quickly, almost as if to shake off whatever thought nagged her rather than assure me.

"A position opened up, at last," she said, limping a little as she moved toward me.

I scowled, sweeping my gaze from her covered head to her simple white dress—a nod to Viridana—and her dainty silk slippers. She was favoring her left ankle.

"What happened?" I demanded. "Did he hurt you again?"

Her pale cheeks flushed. "No. When I climbed out the Temple window, I landed badly." She gestured to her slippers. "I couldn't find my boots. Weylin had already started dinner, and I didn't want to keep you waiting."

My conscience twitched for the thousandth time. The risks she was taking. My mother probably wouldn't approve of what I was asking her best friend to do. I hated it, too . . . but it was the only way.

"Did you hear what I said about the position?" She slid a bag out from under her cloak. "A gardener. I managed to get the uniform as well."

Hope rekindled in my chest as I reached for the violet uniform she handed me. I rubbed my thumb over the Rellmiran crest stitched over the chest—a half sun rising over a shadowed moon.

"It's not too late, Aiden," she whispered.

I jerked my gaze up.

"After Weylin's gone, you could still be king," she continued in a rush. "It's what your mother would've wanted. Your father, too."

My fingers curled into the stiff uniform. "I doubt my parents —or anyone else in Rellmira—would want an assassin for their king."

Her mouth formed a grim line. "It's no worse than what Weylin did to them."

"Perhaps not. But then I would be no better than him, stabbing my way to the throne. I'm here to right a wrong and put the crown on your head. That's what we decided, Brielle."

She clasped her hands in front of her, the dirt under her fingernails at odds with her status.

"I feel as though nothing I do can atone for what happened to Rhea and Tristan," she said. "And to you."

I squeezed one of her small shoulders. "It's not your crime to pay for."

She closed her eyes. "I wish things had been different. I wish you had grown up alongside my son as Rhea and I always dreamed our children would." Her shoulders trembled. "I miss her."

My heart grew cold. I couldn't miss someone I'd never known. That life had been stolen from me by Renwell's arrow and the knife that Brielle always carried in her belt.

"Courage, Brielle," I murmured. "It's almost over. Remember the plan."

She nodded, stiffening her spine. My hand fell away. When she looked at me, I glimpsed the queen I'd first met at the Temple.

She'd agreed wholeheartedly with my plan to kill her husband. She knew, better than most, what sort of monster sat on the throne. What he had done to get it and what he had done to keep it.

My parents' murders and the subsequent lies of succession. The massacre in Pravara and the executions in Aquinon during the rebellion. The mistreated—and often innocent—prisoners in the sunstone mine.

All for a throne he'd stolen.

It needed to end. And Brielle and I had come up with the perfect way to smuggle me into the heart of the palace. I was going to kill him and escape, leaving Brielle to take up the crown and piece Rellmira back together.

"The head housekeeper, Gilda, is expecting you," Brielle said. "She knows how particular I am about the gardens, so she didn't question me too much when I told her I'd found someone to replace the old gardener."

"Excellent. I'll report for work tomorrow and use her name to get across the bridge."

Brielle nodded, her gaze darting once more to the door.

Dread curdled in my gut. "What aren't you telling me? Do you think someone followed you?"

"No. I always adhere to the routine you gave me. Walk at different speeds. Take extra turns. Loop back. I . . . I just . . ." Her throat bobbed. "I think Renwell is getting suspicious."

My dread flared into fear. Renwell—the man who'd hunted down People's Council sympathizers and whose Shadow-Wolves I'd been dodging since I'd arrived in Aquinon.

"Why do you think that?" I bit out. "Has he said anything to you?"

"No. But . . . he caught me in his study a month ago."

I crushed the uniform in my fist. "Gods damn it, Brielle. What were you doing in there?"

She lifted her chin, a steely glint in her eyes. "I wanted to find more evidence of the horrors he and Weylin are carrying out in the Calimber mine. I heard there were children working in that gods-forsaken hole. *Children*, Aiden."

"I know," I growled. I hadn't told her much of my time in the sunstone prison, but I'd seen those horrors with my own eyes. I still saw them in my nightmares. "But what did he do when he discovered you?"

"I played the simple, dutiful woman and claimed I was looking for a piece of paper and ink to leave him a note, asking whether he would join us for our special Viridana's dinner tonight."

I winced. "Did he believe you?"

Contempt hardened Brielle's face. "I never know with Renwell. That man could lie to the gods themselves and get away with it. He also refused my invitation, so I don't know where he is right now."

This time it was me who glanced at the door, then around the empty warehouse. Nothing stirred. I also hadn't heard a whistle from outside.

Brielle said she hadn't been followed, and yet . . . I felt it, too. A wrongness. A prickle at the back of my neck.

Gods damn it, I shouldn't have made Maz go to the docks.

"You should leave," I said. "Get back to the Temple before your guards question the Teachers. I'll follow to make sure no one else is."

Brielle nodded, then hesitated before resting her palm against my unshaven cheek. "If we don't speak again, I want to thank you, Aiden. For letting me know my husband didn't kill my best friend's son. And for helping me fight for my family's— and our kingdom's—freedom. Thank you," she whispered.

I swallowed hard against the knot of guilt in my throat. I didn't deserve her gratitude. I'd done nothing but lose more lives since I'd started fighting back.

But I only needed one more. Weylin's.

Brielle led me to the door. Just as the latch started rising.

We both froze.

The latch continued to glide upward. The door creaked as someone pushed it from the other side. But the crossbar held firm.

Slowly, I grasped Brielle's arm and dragged her behind me. She shook like a leaf in a storm, her mouth clamped shut.

"Brielle," said a deep, deadly cold voice.

Brielle let out a low moan of terror, her nails digging into my arm. "It's Renwell," she gasped. "Holy Four, he found me."

Gods damn it, why didn't the stable boy warn us? Unless Renwell had found him first.

My heart beat frantically as I hauled her away from the door. The *only* door.

Something crashed against it, making Brielle jump.

"I know you're in there, Brielle," came Renwell's voice again. "I know what you've been doing. Is your new gardener in there as well?"

Fucking Four. His words were like matches that set fire to our plans. Years. Gone.

Rage filled me. I tossed aside the useless uniform and unsheathed one of my blades. "Stay here, Brielle. Don't come out until he's dead."

"Aiden, no, he'll—"

"Don't try to escape," Renwell commanded. "I have a dozen of my Wolves surrounding this building. Things will get a lot bloodier if we have to chase you."

Shit. If he was telling the truth, I wouldn't be able to fight my way out. And he was blocking the only exit. Unless . . .

I glared at the hatch in the roof. It was little more than a window to let in light, but we could fit if I made the hole bigger. I had my knives, a few fireseeds, and the torch. I could make that work.

I sheathed my knife and dragged Brielle over to the towering shelves. I laced my fingers together, forming a foothold. "I'll boost you up as high as I can, then—"

She stepped away from me, shaking her head.

Something dark and frantic sank its claws into my chest. "Brielle, don't—"

Another crash echoed, making her wince. "I can't run, Aiden."

"Yes, you can," I growled. "Even if I have to strap you to my back."

She took another step backward, closer to the groaning door. "He knows about me. Which means Weylin knows. It's over."

"No, it's not. I'll hide you where he'll never find you. I'll get you out of Aquinon."

She smiled sadly. "You can't save me, Aiden, but I can still save you, as I should've done all those years ago." She withdrew the gold-hilt sunstone knife Weylin had sunk into my father's back. "Go. Before he sees you."

Understanding sliced through my mind like lightning. I seized her knife hand, keeping the blade well away from her.

"Don't do this, *please*." My voice shook. "Don't give up. If not for me, then for your children."

All the color leached from her face, and she sagged in my grip. "I'm doing this *for* them. Weylin warned me, years ago, what he would do to them if I betrayed him. He . . . he had my daughter beaten in front of me just to prove his point. I can't . . . I *won't* be the reason he hurts them."

Another crash and the sound of wood splintering reverberated through the room. But my gaze never wavered from hers.

I was failing. Again. Someone else was going to die because of me. Again.

I gripped her hand tighter. "I'm not letting you go."

Tears trembled in her blue eyes and tumbled down her

cheeks. "They'll torture me, Aiden. Then they'll hurt my children. And I'll tell them everything I know about you to keep that from happening."

I drew in a ragged breath. "I'll kill him. I'll kill them all for this."

"I always told you it would be Weylin's death or mine. I just never thought . . ." She closed her eyes as more tears fell between us. For a moment, her face crumpled with pain. "I should've said goodbye. My son. My daughters. I'll miss the rest of their lives. I had so many things I wanted to do with them. So many words I'll never get to say. Yet this is how it ends."

The world felt muffled and hollow. As did my chest. My fingers grew numb around hers.

She slowly aimed the knife at her heart. The tip wavered, scraping her skin. Whether from my trembling or hers, I couldn't tell.

"Please, Aiden," she whispered. "Please. Help me."

Her words clapped against my eardrums like thunder. I immediately resisted. The darkest request. An act that would stain my soul. Make my heart a stranger. I would never be free of this moment.

"It's mercy, Aiden. Please. I can't do it myself."

Somewhere, in another world, glittering black knives, like the one I held with Brielle, stabbed through the door.

But I wouldn't let them have her.

"May the gods find your soul."

Brielle smiled tremulously, cupping my cheek once more. "Tell my children I love them."

I wanted to close my eyes. But I couldn't dishonor her by hiding. I tried to ignore the sensation of piercing her delicate flesh, of the quick drive home.

But my hand would not forget. My ears would forever ring

with her last desperate breath. My heart would never forgive me for stabbing hers.

Her hand fell away from my cheek. Her blood flowed over my hands. Shaking in pure agony, I threw my head back and roared.

For a moment, the world grew still. The crashes stopped.

I gently laid her on the dirt floor. She deserved so much better than this. I brushed her eyes closed over her final tears.

I whispered my last promise to her and rose to my feet. I stared at the splintered door as if from a great distance as Renwell and his dogs attacked it anew.

Clutching the thin torch in my teeth, I hauled myself up shelf after shelf. Away from her, but still covered in her blood.

With numb fingers, I plucked a fireseed from my pocket and nestled it in the wooden frame of the window.

I shielded my face as I held the torch to it. Heat exploded around my hand, but I didn't let go. I hacked at the weakened wood with my knife until I'd made a jagged hole large enough for my shoulders.

A loud crash echoed below as the door crumbled to bits and shadows poured in. Against all my instincts, I hesitated. I needed to see him—the man who'd already stolen so much.

Renwell's dark eyes and pale face gazed up at me.

Without thinking, I released the rest of my precious fireseeds, and as they bounced down the dusty shelves, I threw down the torch.

Flames howled to life, devouring the connection between us.

I dragged my body through the hole, ignoring the tears in my clothes and flesh, and climbed onto the roof. My body remembered how to slide over the warm tiles and hurtle itself over gaps between buildings.

But inside, I stitched every moment, every feeling, into the fabric of my mind so I would never forget this either.

Because one day . . .

CHAPTER 24

KIERA

"ONE DAY, I WOULD TELL HER SON AND HER DAUGHTERS THAT SHE loved them to the very end," Aiden finished his story, his voice raw.

Tears poured down my cheeks and splashed against my hands. The pain was nearly unbearable. It tore through my body over and over.

Gods, the terror Mother must have felt. The horror she had to face.

I let out a quiet sob.

I didn't know how long I sat there on Aiden's bed, mired in pain so deep, I couldn't move. But slowly, the icy waves slowed, and I could look at Aiden.

His eyes were red, and a tear clung to his lower lashes.

I finally understood. I knew Mother had already been fighting her own quiet battles before Aiden arrived. I understood her reasoning for why she didn't run.

"That bitch should've died on the executioner stand like the gods-damned traitor she was!"

"She was right," I said hoarsely. "My father would've killed her. Or used us against her. He made her watch when he ordered Korvin to whip me. I was the daughter she was talking about."

Aiden nodded slowly. "I thought your scars were because of a misdeed you committed as a palace guard."

I curled my hands into fists. "No, it was because he caught me sneaking out of the palace. I didn't know he threatened her because of it."

"She eventually realized the only way to keep herself and her children safe was to get rid of Weylin. Then, when our plan failed, she did the last thing she could to protect you."

I stared into Aiden's haunted eyes and tried to find my rage or my hatred. But they were gone. Instead, my heart echoed the guilt and pain he'd felt for the same two years.

He'd stayed and tried to kill Father and make Everett king, like Mother wanted. But I'd gotten in his way.

"You said you decided not to kill my father at the last moment because of me," I said. "But Mother wanted him dead."

"I would've taken him prisoner and let Everett decide what to do with him," Aiden said in response to my unspoken question. "That way I could've honored my word, in part, to her, but also the promise I made to protect you. Even from myself."

I remembered how he'd held his sword to my neck, pretending that he would kill me, but Renwell had seen through it before I did.

"Ah, you've fallen for my little spy as well, Falcryn. You won't kill her."

"No, I won't."

But was it because he felt he had a duty to my mother or because he'd fallen for me, as Renwell suspected? He might've had feelings for me before he found out who I was. But my betrayal had thoroughly doused them.

A realization that hurt worse now that the truth had peeled away the layers of anger hiding it.

Still, he'd kept me safe even after he discovered my lies. He'd also honored Mother's last words.

I carefully took Aiden's hands in mine, trying not to think of them shoving a knife into Mother's heart. I knew why, now, but the image lingered like a festering sore.

"I said I would never forgive you, and I never will," I said. He flinched and tried to escape my grasp, but I held firm. "Because there's nothing to forgive, Aiden Falcryn. You saved my mother from terrible pain and an even worse death." I remembered Yarina's words about Davka. "I'm . . . I'm grateful you were with her in the end."

Aiden gripped my hands tighter and slowly drew me closer to him. He leaned his forehead against mine, his eyes closed. "I never thought it possible that a few words could pierce the darkness in my soul. But you, Kiera, have always been a light worth fighting for."

Tears burned in my eyes once more.

I'd never realized what a difference that could make—having someone believe in me, despite the mistakes I'd made.

Mother hadn't just died a senseless death. She hadn't just been pruned out of my life like a dead branch, no longer worth keeping alive.

I'd thought Aiden had persuaded her to enact his plans, that she'd been a tool of his revenge. But she'd known the risks. She'd chosen to confront the danger again and again.

A warrior in silk, Maz had called her.

I dishonored her by thinking anything less.

Mother had fought for me. For Everett and Delysia. And gods help me, I was going to make sure they knew that someday.

Aiden's breath feathered against my lips. He still held me as if he never wanted to let go. "Kiera, I—"

The fur curtain bowed inward, and Maz burst inside. His

eyes widened at the sight of us. "Oh, shit, sorry, wrong lodge!" He fumbled his way back outside.

"Idiot," Aiden grumbled.

I drew away from him with a little laugh, rubbing my gritty eyes. Truthfully, I was thankful for the interruption. Whatever Aiden had been about to say, I wasn't ready for it. I wasn't ready for much of anything after such an emotionally exhausting evening.

I glanced at Ruru, who hadn't so much as twitched in his deep sleep. "What are we going to do with him? We can't send him back to Aquinon. I doubt he'd stay here while we go to Calimber."

Aiden frowned. "You still want to go?"

I hopped to my feet and paced the small room, trying to relieve my tight muscles. "Of course. Especially knowing it's what my mother would've wanted." I pulled her sunstone knife from my belt and examined its glittering black ridges in the low lamplight.

My gaze flicked to Aiden, who was staring at the knife warily. I sheathed it again.

"I know you want to find the forge and the ships," I said. "But I also want to free every single prisoner and crush that mine into rock and stardust."

Aiden's green eyes warmed, and a smile curved through his dark beard. "Now, *that* is the best idea I've heard in years."

After a surprisingly dreamless sleep, Nikella woke me for training.

My eyes still burned after all the crying. I drained several cups of water and shoved some dried deer meat into my mouth before running after Nikella.

The sun had crested over the wet trees, their needles glistening with frost like crystals. Several older children tended the horses in their paddock.

Nikella faced me in the middle of the damp meadow, her expression impassive. She didn't mention my appearance or the events of last night. But her jaw was tight. Probably because of what Ruru said about Renwell arresting Librius.

After an hour of making me stretch my muscles and run circles around the busy clearing, she handed me a wooden staff, similar in length to her steel spear.

I lifted my eyebrows. "I thought you wanted to teach me physical combat."

"Not today."

She whipped her double-ended spear in a set of dizzying movements. The metal whistled in the cold air. She ended with a lunging strike that would've impaled three men.

Fucking Four, who was she imagining on the other end of her spear?

"That's what you're aiming for," she said, barely out of breath. "Here's where you start."

She slowed the movements down and led me through each one at a snail's pace.

I'd nearly memorized the pattern when a happy shout reached us.

I smiled as Ruru jogged over to us, looking much better than he had last night.

"Aiden said you were out here." His eyes widened, and he pointed at my shoulders. "Did you know you're steaming like a cooked fish?"

I shrugged, feeling the layer of sweat under my long-sleeved shirt. "Keeps me warm."

Ruru grinned. "Can I join you?" He looked at Nikella for approval.

She jerked her chin toward camp. "Get a staff from Frieda."

Ruru raced off, then joined us again, carrying a staff like mine. Nikella led him through the same movements while I practiced nearby.

We didn't speak much, but gods, it felt good to be with Ruru again. After the emotional turmoil of last night, his sweet, uncomplicated friendship was what I needed.

After my arms began to feel like warm dough, Nikella declared that was enough for today.

She strode off without another word, her spear gleaming like a streak of lightning.

I collapsed into the wet grass, not caring if the bits of snow still clinging to the blades soaked through my pants.

Ruru dropped next to me with a huff. "Fucking Four, I always wanted to train to be a warrior, but that's brutal."

I laughed. "Now you just need to do it a thousand more times, and you'll be a true warrior."

"We both will," he declared. "Although, I guess you had years of training before this."

I ducked my head, staring at my scarred hands. Renwell's voice rattled around in the back of my mind, taunting me, insulting me, telling me not to be weak.

"I had some training, yes," I said quietly. "But not the kind I'd want to continue."

Ruru nodded, then elbowed me in the side. "Think you could keep teaching me how to throw knives? I was getting pretty good before . . . before everything happened."

I smiled weakly at him. "Sure. I just got some new ones we could trade off practicing with."

"What happened to your old ones?"

I told him of Father's death and Renwell's betrayal.

Ruru scowled. "I'm glad you scarred up his face. Maybe he'll think twice before trying to hurt you again."

I gestured at my cheek wryly. "A little late for that."

"You fought him again? Where? This battle at the mountain no one wants to talk about?"

With a sigh, I told him about that battle as well. "That's how I got my new knives," I finished. "And a horse that I can barely ride. Him." I pointed at Ozlow rubbing his shaggy coat against a fence post.

"He looks like a good horse. I bought mine off a Pravaran farmer who came to Aquinon and couldn't afford to keep him anymore."

I propped my chin on my hand. "Your turn to tell a story. How in the deep, dark, wandering hell did you get out of there?"

"You remember Sophie? Well, she does laundry for a family whose son is a courier. He delivers mail all over Rellmira. I paid him with some of your gold to take his place on his next job. I hid the whistler and Melaena's letters in the lining of my bags, so when the guards at the main gate stopped me, all they found were the identification papers of the other boy and his legitimate letters."

"Holy Four, who's the spy now?" I teased him, tossing a bit of snow at him.

He shook the snow out of his hair, his cheeks red. "Yeah, well, not everyone bought it."

I frowned.

"Everything was going fine for a while," he continued. "I headed north, trying to steer clear of Calimber and offering to do odd jobs, like round up a stray cow, for the Winspere ranchers in exchange for food. But eventually that food ran out, and the only people I met were border patrols."

I grimaced. "One of them figured out you were lying?"

Ruru nodded, his face tight. "The first just sort of shrugged me off after looking in my bags. The second took the rest of the coins I'd been saving to buy more food. The third . . . the third patrol was ruthless. They stopped me and dug through my bags, trampling over the mail I meant to leave at a courier post on the border. They strapped me and my bags to my horse's back and whipped him, so he'd run in circles while they shot arrows at us. 'Target practice,' they said."

My blood roared in my ears at the shameful look on Ruru's face.

I'd told Nikella I didn't want to kill Rellmirans, but if we ran into that border patrol, I had a knife for each of those gods-damned cowards.

"How did you get away?" I ground out.

"My horse," Ruru said with a sad smile. "He kicked one of them in the face and bolted. They chased us for a while, then gave up. I took Maz's whistler out of its hiding spot in case they came back, but they didn't. I also took off my messenger's outfit, so I wouldn't get recognized.

"I must've wandered into Dagriel eventually, because I kept going north until I saw mountains. Some days, I just seemed to go in circles in the woods, especially when clouds and trees hid the sun. I thought I'd be lost forever. That's when I took out Melaena's letters and tried to read them, hoping to feel less alone. But I couldn't make sense of them."

I stilled. "Did one of them have the People's Council seal on it?"

"Yes. How did you know?"

I bit my lip, remembering my first mission and my desperate flight with Garyth's wife and daughter. Melaena must've wanted Aiden to have the letters Garyth had been desperate to hide. Thank the Four that Helene, Isabel, and the letters were far out of Renwell's grasp now.

"I saw them once," I said vaguely.

Ruru shrugged. "Aiden left them in my bag, so I tucked them into his. He must've forgotten."

Probably because he was too distracted by the pain I forced him to dig up. "I know he's grateful you found us, Ruru. We all are."

He nudged me with his shoulder. "I found more than I hoped for."

"You certainly do have a knack for that."

He grinned. "As do you, it seems. I'm surprised to find you getting along so well with the warriors you betrayed, the Teacher who shot you in the neck with a dart, and the man who . . . who, you know," he finished awkwardly.

I grimaced. At least he hadn't heard us talking near him last night while he slept. But all of it put together made my situation sound implausible and ridiculous. None of us should work well together, and yet . . .

"I suppose fighting a common enemy makes for a quick friendship," I said.

"Is that why you're training so hard? For another battle?"

I nodded. "Of a sort. We're leaving for Calimber soon. We're going to spy on it, then hopefully destroy it. You can—"

"I'm coming with," he said firmly.

"Ruru—"

"No. I can rest, eat, and train on the way, same as you. I go where my friends go."

I gripped his shoulder, hoping to all four gods that being my friend didn't kill him. "Then we'd be honored to have you, Ruru."

CHAPTER 25
KIERA

The next two days were a blur of training and preparations for the journey to Calimber.

Any time I wasn't gathering food or stocking the camp with fresh wood and water, I was training with Nikella and Ruru. She had shifted to yet another tactic—fighting on horseback. She said that was likely how we'd face the border patrol, and we needed to have absolute control of our horses.

Ozlow and I were . . . doing our best. My palms still sweat every time I had to jerk him to a halt and wheel him in the opposite direction or urge him into a gallop. I'd only fallen off once, but it'd been enough to make me nervous.

I rarely saw Aiden as he helped with other preparations. He hunted with the others to supply the Yargoths with enough food to make up for their warriors' absence. He also rode to where Skelly was anchored off the coast and told him where we were going and to wait for word from us.

But unlike the last time we were in the camp, Aiden always sought me out when he was passing through. Even if it was just a glance or standing by to watch me train for a few moments.

We'd only spoken a few words in passing. But those words had been polite. Awkward. Like gentle fingers tapping around a sore spot to see if it still hurt.

What was I supposed to say to the man I'd half fallen in love with, only to realize he'd killed my mother . . . but for a good reason?

I was a mess of impatience. I wanted to mount Ozlow and gallop to Calimber. Hunt down our enemies like Renwell had hunted down my mother. I wanted to rain fire down on his camp in retribution.

It still wouldn't be enough. It never would be.

When Aiden told me to join everyone after dinner in Frieda's lodge, I wolfed down my rabbit stew and dry biscuit so fast I barely chewed.

I handed off my dirty dishes and hurried to Frieda's lodge. It was no larger than the rest, painted with a dozen Dag symbols, including the Yargoth mountain one. The same that Korvin had sliced off Maz's back.

Aiden and Nikella had already beaten me there and were sitting on two of the cushions strewn about the fur-covered floor.

Aiden was in a tense discussion with Frieda, who sat hunched in a chair of twisted branches.

"—more runners. They might send—"

"No," Frieda cut off Aiden. "We have sent enough. We have lost enough. I can barely afford to let you take the four I promised."

I shuffled in the doorway, not sure if they'd noticed me.

Aiden's jaw clenched. "They'll be back before Arduen's Night."

Frieda sighed, rubbing her wrinkled forehead as if she could erase the worry inside. "I trust your word, Aiden. I know you are simply trying to save your people. But I have my own people to protect. A winter to survive. Do you understand?"

"Yes," Aiden murmured, but his shoulders remained taut.

"Good. Come in, Kiera. Take a seat."

I hurried forward and sat near Aiden on a green cushion stitched with an image of wolves chasing a deer. I heard the dog-like creatures howling most nights.

"How's training coming along?" Frieda asked with a strained smile.

I answered her, hardly knowing what words I used. I kept glancing at Aiden. Why did he want to send out runners? To ask the other clans for help?

Frieda kept up a steady stream of polite questions about training, chores, and the weather until everyone else had arrived. Ruru darted to the purple cushion next to me.

Nikella lit a few more lanterns until the whole lodge was bathed in a sleepy glow.

"Let's hear the plan, Aiden," Frieda said.

Aiden cleared his throat. "Before I begin, I want to make something very clear." His sharp gaze pierced each of us. "Renwell is not just my enemy. Or even our enemy. He is Lancora's enemy. He's a murderous madman who will stop at nothing to get what he wants, as we have all experienced."

The scar on my cheek throbbed in time with my racing heartbeat.

He will not have me.

"I don't know his plans," Aiden continued. "And I doubt he wrote them down and left them lying around Calimber for us to snatch up. But if Renwell is building more of those warships and forging more indestructible weapons and armor to clad his Wolves and blood-thirsty army, then we must destroy him before we *can't* stop him."

The horror that filled me was swift and vivid. Burning villages. Massacred rebels. Executions in the square. Shadow-Wolves devouring the world.

"Destroy his resources," I whispered. "Then destroy him."

Aiden nodded, his face grim.

"I thought that's what we all bloody signed up for?" Maz growled, his muscular arms folded over his chest.

Jek dipped his head, his silver hair gleaming like snow at night. "We know the risks, Aiden."

Aiden shared a glance with Frieda. Her brow was still puckered with worry, but she nodded once.

"You've made your point," she said. "Now state your plan."

Aiden relaxed infinitesimally. "It takes five days to reach Calimber. We'll likely run into border patrols before then, which may add time to our journey. We'll scout ahead and avoid them the best we can, but—"

"Sometimes the quickest way is through them," Sigrid declared. She wore a dark brown fur cowl, the creature's claws still attached and draped over her shoulders like it was caressing her.

I hadn't been thrilled when Maz told me she was coming, too, but I supposed it made sense. Yarina was joining as well.

Aiden's lips thinned. "Yes, but we want to avoid that, as I said. I want everyone getting in and out in one piece."

Sigrid snorted as if there wasn't an alternative.

"We'll have to keep moving camps," Jek spoke up. "Those patrols are always on the move, even if they stick to designated patterns."

Aiden nodded. "Yes. It will be difficult, but we'll only be in Calimber long enough to assess what Renwell is doing there. Then we'll regroup somewhere safe."

"Regroup? Are we splitting up?" Yarina called out. She'd brought her dinner with her, balancing soup and bread in her lap.

Aiden took a deep breath, as if gathering strength. His gaze flicked to me for a heartbeat. My stomach sank. I wasn't going to like this answer.

"Maz and I will infiltrate the mine," he said finally.

"Absolutely not," Sigrid growled.

Yarina nearly upended her soup, shifting forward to glare at Aiden. "I'm coming, too."

Maz shook his head. "Not happening, little sisters."

They instantly argued back, talking over each other.

"Enough, you three!" Frieda clapped her hands once. "By the Four, you all still act like a pack of wolf pups. Listen before you howl."

The siblings faded to grumpy silence.

"Why you two?" I asked Aiden. "If they find your prisoner scars and that you covered them with tattoos—"

"We're already lost if it comes to that," Aiden interrupted gently. "But we know the layout as no one else does."

I shook my head stubbornly. "You really think you can just walk in? That they won't question you? Let me go. I could pose as a messenger or a servant. Someone no one would notice."

"They notice everyone," Nikella said, speaking for the first time. "It took me over a year to communicate with Aiden in that prison. My messengers—water carriers from the town—kept dying due to discovery or the dangers of the mine." She and Jek shared an intense glance across the room. I supposed he understood more than most what she went through during that time, as I'd heard he helped her.

"And besides, we won't look like ourselves," Maz added, nudging Aiden with his elbow. "Show them."

A muscle in Aiden's jaw twitched, but he slowly reached behind him and pulled out a bulging sack.

He dumped out a wad of familiar black cloth, glittering sunstone weapons and armor, and with a decisive *clunk*, two black metal Wolf masks.

Sigrid recoiled as if they were on fire, her one blue eye flaring with hatred.

Yarina picked up a sunstone cuff. "I can't believe you stole this shit after you forced me to return mine." She tossed it back on the pile.

Maz smirked. "It was Aiden's idea."

I quirked an eyebrow at Aiden. "Who's the dirty little thief now? You've used this trick before."

A glint of humor appeared in his eyes. "Let's hope it works better this time."

It gods-damned better. Last time he'd stolen a Shadow-Wolf uniform and infiltrated a dangerous place, he'd wound up captured in the Den.

Now I realized how lucky it was that Renwell had put me in that cell with him. If he hadn't, Aiden would've been tortured and executed, or perhaps even sent to the one place I knew he still feared—the mine.

I wanted to ask him if he'd considered this carefully. If being back in the mine would be too difficult for him.

But those were questions to ask in private.

Instead, Ruru voiced a possibility I didn't want to think about. "What should we do if you don't come back out?"

Tension cloaked the room like a burial shroud.

"That won't happen," Aiden said firmly, but I noticed the way his knuckles whitened as he clenched a Wolf mask. "This will be the perfect disguise. No one questions Shadow-Wolves."

"What if there are no Shadow-Wolves?" I asked. "Ruru said they're crawling Aquinon day and night. Why not disguise yourself as a soldier?"

"The longer we can hide our faces, the better," Aiden replied. "And even if it's just soldiers living in Calimber, they're at least used to seeing Wolves venture in and out with prisoners and weapon shipments."

"I still think I should be a Wolf," Yarina announced.

"As should I," Sigrid said quickly.

"Yes, that way, if we get discovered, at least we'll be with our imprisoned brothers and sisters and can stir up a rebellion from the inside, and Rellmira won't lose its true prince . . . king . . . whatever," she added, gesturing to Aiden.

He scowled at her. "They won't lose me. They don't even know they have me. And there's a much better chance of the infiltrators getting out of the mine if they know where they're going."

"And if they're men," Maz pointed out.

Immediately, Sigrid and Yarina raised a ruckus, and he held up his hands. "Fucking Four, I didn't make the gods-damned rules! Bring it up with the bastard who's in charge of hiring!"

I sighed, slumping on my cushion as they bickered.

"I don't like waiting off to the side," Ruru grumbled.

"Me either."

For some reason, I'd pictured me and Aiden sneaking into the mine. I'd thought of disguises and lies to tell. But all along, he had the Shadow-Wolf gear and the plan.

I conceded his plan made sense. But I wished he'd told me before this meeting. Perhaps he just hadn't had the time. Or he was worried that I would argue.

He'd been this way in Aquinon, too. Always secretive. Always wanting to be a step ahead.

It wasn't like I'd proven very trustworthy.

I pushed aside the sinking feeling just as Frieda intervened between the siblings again.

Aiden ignored them, focusing on me. "In the unlikely event that we don't return, you are all to leave immediately and come back here. No rescues."

This time Nikella and Jek added their voices to the loud

dissent. I merely folded my arms across my chest and shook my head.

Aiden's eyes narrowed, and he leaned closer so his next words were only for me. "What would it take for you to obey that command?"

A delicate shiver trickled down my spine. From the moment I'd heard his deep, alluring voice in the darkness of our cell, I'd felt a tug at the very center of my being. Inexorably drawing me to him.

Then. Now. And every moment in between, his pull on me never faded.

I tried to steady my breathing. "You once said I was stronger for the commands I didn't follow. This is one of them. If you and Maz get captured, then we'll liberate you when we free the other prisoners."

His jaw clenched, his gaze turning molten. "So I've become a dirty little thief, and you've transformed into a reckless rebel. How does it feel to swap roles with me?"

"Dangerous." My lips quirked. "But even if you add 'king' to that list of roles, I would still refuse to follow your command."

"Pity. That was the only perk of being your king."

My cheeks burned. I lifted my chin. "Rebels don't follow a king's orders. It's the most crucial part of the job."

His smile was slow and dangerous and full of things I didn't understand that my body seemed to understand all too well.

I squirmed as he whispered in my ear, "And the most crucial part of mine is fighting my way back to you."

CHAPTER 26

KIERA

Warmth invaded my heart.

His words were like sharp rays of sunlight. Pure honesty. Gone were the murky clouds lined with vague niceties of the last few days. And I wished them never to come back.

"If you two are done flirting, can we get back to planning our deadly mission?" Maz's drawl was like a bucket of cold water.

I jerked away from Aiden, my cheeks heating further when I realized everyone was staring at us.

"We were arguing, same as you," I fired back, my voice not nearly as strong as I'd hoped.

Maz smirked. "No siblings argue like that, lovely."

"Definitely not," Yarina said, wrinkling her nose at me.

I glanced at Aiden for assistance, but he merely leaned back with a smile.

Sigrid sighed loudly. "So the consensus is we will *not* just let the two of you rot in the mine, but—"

"Because we won't get caught," Maz interrupted.

"Sure," she ground out. "Then tell me why we're bringing two untrained warriors with us." She pinned me and Ruru with a one-eyed glare.

At least she hadn't said untrustworthy, but it was still an insult.

I narrowed my eyes. "I may not know how to wield every weapon in existence, but I know how to fight. I throw a knife better than anyone here. Most importantly, this is *my* kingdom, these are *my* people, and this is my gods-damned fight."

Sigrid quirked an eyebrow, looking the mildest bit appeased.

Ruru straightened next to me. "I'll tell you what I told Kiera —I go where my friends go. Even if that's all the way to the Abyss."

"Good enough for me," Jek said.

Yarina nodded. "And me."

"Fine," Sigrid grunted. "Are we done here?"

"Not quite," Nikella said.

Aiden frowned and tossed the Wolf mask back into the pile.

Nikella continued in the same steady voice. "Renwell will send Korvin to hunt us."

I reeled back, deaf to everyone else's reactions. How did she know that? Was he hunting us right now?

My skin crawled as if a dozen spiders had landed on me.

I glanced at Maz, whose face was white beneath his shaggy golden hair.

Frieda scowled. "Is that monster coming here?"

Nikella shook her head. Her scar seemed more prominent than ever now that I knew her brother had carved it into her face. "He's hunting me. I won't come back here until after he's dead."

"He will be," Jek promised with a guttural growl.

The others chimed in with their murderous threats, which brought a small smile to Maz's face.

Naughty little Nik, you'll finally get what's been coming to you for years.

What Renwell had said to Nikella in parting—that was about Korvin? I remembered Nikella's stiff body, her expression. It'd been fear. She'd known what he meant.

My gaze fell to Aiden, who almost looked angry.

"We leave at dawn tomorrow," he said abruptly. "Be ready."

Everyone gathered themselves to leave. Maz stuffed all the Shadow-Wolf gear back into the bag while his sisters hovered near him like guards, as if Korvin were waiting outside in the shadows.

The foreboding in my gut thickened.

"A moment, Kiera," Aiden murmured, brushing past me.

Immediately apprehensive, I followed him out of Frieda's lodge to the barren garden.

It took my eyes a moment to adjust to the darkness, and even then, his features were blurred. Perhaps he wanted it that way.

"I'm sorry I didn't tell you my plan beforehand."

I blinked, surprised. "Oh. Was it because you were worried I'd argue?"

"No, I wanted you and the others to argue with me. I didn't want to hide my reasons."

My eyebrows rose. "You were that confident you'd win?"

A deep chuckle rumbled in his chest. "Yes." He paused. "But I'm not so sure we can win Calimber. We are eight warriors against Dracles, his army, and the guards in the mine. And I won't let the prisoners become collateral."

I laid my palm on his warm chest. He immediately pressed his hand on top.

"We'll find a way," I whispered. "Because we have to. That's why we're spying on it first. Perhaps there's a weakness we can exploit."

"Perhaps. But we will need more allies, eventually. For this battle. Or the next."

I swallowed hard. "Is that why you wanted Frieda to send more runners? To rally more of the clans behind us?"

Aiden rubbed his jaw. "I thought perhaps Renwell destroying the Urzost village would be enough to unite the clans, but bad blood runs deep. Frieda is not hopeful and would rather preserve her clan than fight a battle that may swallow the Yargoths whole." He turned his face away from me. "It's what a good leader would do."

I bit my lip, remembering the comment I'd made on *Mynastra's Wings*. And the guilt that I knew weighed on him for Mother. "You don't needlessly sacrifice lives either, Aiden. Unless it's your own."

"You think my plan is foolish?"

I hesitated. An idea had taken root in my mind since learning that Renwell had told Aquinon there were no other heirs to claim the throne. The idea had only strengthened after I decided we should find a way to destroy Calimber.

"I think you're desperate to win," I said softly. "But it doesn't have to be alone or with a distant alliance. What if . . . what if we sent word to my sister's soldier, Henry? He's a captain in the army, in charge of hundreds of Rellmiran soldiers—"

"And you think they would join us so easily? Betray their oaths to serve the king? Destroy a mine they might benefit from? I wanted the Dag warriors because I trust them to see Renwell as an enemy who's killed and imprisoned their people."

"He's a *false* king who probably intends to use Henry and his men in battles they don't wish to fight. Their fellow Rellmirans are imprisoned in that mine, too. They'd be freeing their people."

Aiden shook his head. "Even if we got a message to Henry, neither of us actually knows him. We could give up our plan to someone who would then feed it to Renwell for a pat on the back."

"My sister is in love with him. They've carried on a secret affair even when he would've been thrown in prison for such a thing. I don't think he'd betray us."

"Have we not been betrayed enough to avoid such a risk?" he asked gently.

The words pierced my heart like a well-aimed knife. My eyes prickled. "Have we not lost enough to risk everything?"

He brushed his fingers over my brow and slid them down to rest against my throat. "There are some things I refuse to risk," he said roughly. "There are other battles I need to win."

Was he speaking of me? Us?

I closed my eyes for a moment, breathing in his nearness, his words. My pulse raced beneath his fingertips.

"I will not be the reason you fail again," I whispered.

His fingers slipped around my neck, pulling me closer. "I didn't fail completely. You were the only reason I won at all."

Oh, gods. There was no air. In my lungs, in the world, in the space between our lips. Some illogical, wild part of my mind insisted I would find it if I pressed my mouth to his.

Suffocating seemed easier.

"Breathe, Kiera," Aiden murmured, as if he'd read my thoughts, caressing my throat. "You don't need to worry. I won't be stealing anything else tonight. Even if I am a dirty little thief," he added with a teasing note.

Air rushed into my lungs, and I swallowed hard, my throat rubbing like a rock against sand.

"You like that name a bit too much," I rasped. My heart still beat erratically as he kept hold of me.

His smile flickered in the dim light. "Now I understand why it made your eyes flare every time I said it to you."

"It did no such thing."

"Liar." But there was no heat in the word this time. Only a softness that felt safe. "Get some sleep . . . my little thief."

I jerked away from his grasp, heat rising up my neck. His chuckle followed me out of the shadows.

We left the Yargoth camp under a blanket of fog.

Children ran alongside our horses, waving and shouting goodbye until we reached the edge of the woods. Then the trees swallowed everything behind us and what lay ahead.

Jek led the way once more, and Sigrid took up the rear. But everyone's gaze roamed the forest, looking for any threats that might've trespassed across the border.

I peered into every shadow, looking for Korvin's greasy black hair and evil eyes.

When the trail became wide enough for two horses, I eased Ozlow up next to Maz and his golden horse.

He smiled at me, but there were telltale shadows under his blue eyes.

"Did you know?" I asked quietly. "About Korvin?"

Maz shook his head. "Aiden told me later that he wanted to spare me and my sisters the added worry, but Nikella insisted. I told him we didn't need protecting."

I stared at the back of Aiden's head as he rode behind Jek. Of course, he'd wanted to protect Maz. But more and more I'd found that secrets were a sort of slow death. Of trust. Of honesty. Of relationships.

What had Delysia said to me when I visited her the night of Asher's death?

Keeping me in the dark doesn't keep me safe.

I frowned. *Oh, Lys, how much better I understand that now.*

"You look sad, lovely," Maz said, watching me carefully. "If you're worried about me, I'm fine. This plan was always going to be dangerous. I expected to encounter Korvin in the mine when I told Aiden I wanted to go with him."

"You volunteered? Why?"

Maz ducked his head under a low-hanging branch. "We'd both been there, and I didn't want him to be alone. Or with someone who didn't understand. He refused at first, but I won him over." He winked at me, and I saw a flash of the old Maz beneath the tired, worried one.

Korvin's torture and Davka's death had dulled his usual shine. Perhaps a victory would restore him. Or perhaps those shadows would cling to him forever.

I knew a thing or two about shadows of the mind.

I rubbed Ozlow's warm neck for comfort before I spoke again. "Aiden told me of the night my mother died."

Maz's eyebrows rose. "Did he now? Is that what I walked in on the night Ruru arrived?"

"Yes," I said, my throat thick.

"Good. I've wanted him to do that since we were onboard *Mynastra's Wings*."

I shifted uncomfortably in my saddle. "I was still so angry, so hurt . . . I don't think I would've listened then."

Maz grunted.

"I didn't answer you on the ship, but I want you to know I don't blame you for not being there that night. They would've killed you, like they did that poor boy."

"Perhaps." Maz dipped his head. "But I appreciate the sentiment."

I studied him closely. He didn't seem to carry guilt the way Aiden and I did. I doubted it was because he didn't mourn the deaths of my mother and the boy. Maz just seemed to under-stand his heart better than most.

He met my stare with a lifted eyebrow. "Speak your mind, lovely."

"What was Aiden like? After?" I blurted out. "I don't want you to betray his trust or anything, but—"

Maz reached over and laid a heavy hand on my arm, cutting me off. "He was devastated, Kiera. I've never seen him like that before or since. When I met him in the mine, he was bitter, angry, calculating. But after your mother . . . he was lost. After we brought the stable boy's body to the pyrist, Aiden withdrew into such a dark place that I worried I'd lose him. I sent a message to Nikella, and she came to stay with us for a while. Eventually, Aiden hammered that darkness into determination. Undeterred, until he met you."

I nodded slowly, my chest too tight, my heart too pained.

It was as I'd thought. I hadn't doubted Aiden's sincerity. But hearing that he'd suffered as I did in the aftermath of Mother's death soothed more of the hurt that sprang up like a cantankerous weed.

Perhaps I'd be cutting that weed with the truth over and over for years until it finally died.

Holy Four, I hope it doesn't take that long.

"Thank you, Maz," I whispered.

"You're always welcome," he said, squeezing my arm before letting it go. "I'm grateful that the Four wove you into my life story."

Tears blurred my vision as I smiled. "As am I." I sniffed and wiped my eyes on the back of my cold hand. "Does that mean you'll get a tattoo of me one day?" I teased.

He guffawed. "Tell you what. You take down that bloody bastard, Renwell, and I'll let you pick whatever tattoo you want me to get."

"*And* the placement?"

"Throw in a bottle of Sunshine, and you've got a deal." He stuck out his callused hand.

I grinned and shook it. "I can't *wait* to see what a giant heart on your ass will look like."

Maz threw back his head and roared with laughter. Several birds took flight from the trees, cawing loudly.

"What's so funny?" Yarina called out from behind us.

Aiden turned in his saddle to glance over his shoulder. When he saw me and Maz laughing, he flashed me a grin.

Warmth suffused my body. Gods, even just a moment of pure joy was strong enough to banish the darkness from my mind.

The next three days left little room for talking as the trail grew narrow and rocky. The chilly dampness of the air made the rocks slippery and every inch of my skin cold.

Every night, long after the last light had seeped from the canopy of trees, Jek called for a halt. Then we'd hurry to build a fire to catch whatever dryness and warmth we could. Any wood we found was wet, but a single fireseed from Nikella's pouch set the logs ablaze, anyway. Frieda had given her a handful from their store for this trip.

Nikella never gave me long to sit by the fire, though. She insisted on training every night and every morning before we began riding.

The exercises she put me through eased some of the soreness from riding Ozlow, but added to the burn of new muscles. I relished that ache. It meant progress. I wanted to burn and burn until I forged my body into a weapon as unbreakable as sunstone.

I was preparing for battle. I wanted to be a warrior who never fell. Who was never a burden. Who was *victorious*.

Ruru usually joined us at night and occasionally in the morning—if I could rouse him. The boy loved his sleep.

By the fourth day of riding, no one spoke at all. Every eye

searched the thinning forest. Every ear listened for an indication that we weren't alone.

Jek and Aiden took turns riding ahead to scout. I held my breath every time they came back, then let it loose with relief when they shook their heads.

We made camp that night with no fire, eating stale cornbread and salty deer jerky. We huddled under our blankets. A chilly mist that was equal parts rain and snow clung to my hair.

I could barely see the others, but I knew the distinctive shape of each of them by now.

"Gods, what I wouldn't give for a hot meal at *The Weary Traveler*," Ruru said mournfully after devouring his small portion.

I groaned. "Don't even talk about it. I could eat ten of those biscuits right now."

"Slathered with butter," Ruru said with a sigh.

"And endless pitchers of Sunshine," Maz chimed in.

"Shut up, or I'll eat whatever's left in your saddlebags," Yarina snapped. She became very testy when hungry.

My stomach growled. I tried not to think about food, but rather everything else I missed—the sun, hot baths, hot meals, a bed.

I missed the comfortable lodge I'd shared with Nikella. I missed the little apartment I shared with Aiden, Maz, and Ruru in Aquinon.

I even missed my palace room. Not the one Renwell had moved me to, next to his office. But my princess one, where Mother would come in to braid my hair in front of the gilded mirror or to eat breakfast with me, Delysia, and Everett on my little stone terrace.

We'd tell funny stories and stuff ourselves with fresh fruit while the rising sun banished the long shadows from my western view. A pocket of happiness in a palace of misery.

I'd been glad when Renwell moved me after she died.

She'd haunted me in my old room. I'd find her out of the corner of my eye, on the edge of reality and hopeful dream. Just a shadow, a trick of the light, and I'd see her still sitting there, soaking up the afternoon sunshine or arranging flowers in a vase she'd painted for me. A glimmer, and my heart would stop, desperate to clutch at that moment in time where she could still be with me. As I always wanted her to be.

But it was never real, and I couldn't keep torturing myself. So I'd let Renwell do it instead.

A hand landed on my shoulder, jolting me from my memories. "Your watch, Kiera," Nikella murmured. "No training tonight."

I nodded, then realized she probably couldn't see me. "Understood."

Peeling off my blanket, I rolled it up and stored it next to my pack. Then I belted my sword around my hips, nestled under my knife brace. The sword was cumbersome, a weight I was still getting used to, but the knives were a familiar, comforting presence.

Mother's knife took up residence in my boot once more.

I stepped around Jek, Maz, and Sigrid, who were sitting and staring in opposite directions. Aiden's familiar shadow leaned against a tree, guarding the horses.

"Be careful," he whispered as I passed by.

Was he as familiar with my shadow as I was with his?

I'd taken watch several times, so I began my route. Walking ahead on the trail. Walking behind. Then short forays into the creaking woods.

Mirrored eyes flashed at me before blinking away. We had yet to encounter a bear or a mountain lion, like the ones Maz told stories about. But my heart beat faster all the same.

Carefully, I slipped through the woods to the west, stepping around rocks and logs like I was sneaking around someone's house. But out here, I always had to keep track of where our camp was. Which was much harder without a fire to guide me.

Another gleam caught my eye, and I grasped the hilt of my sword. But this time, it didn't move or blink away. It flickered.

Holding my breath, I crept closer.

Fucking Four, it's a fire. Armored men. Horses. Saddle blankets with the Rellmiran crest.

A border patrol.

CHAPTER 27
KIERA

My grip trembled around my sword hilt as I tried to burrow into the tree I leaned against.

I counted eight of them. They were still unsaddling their horses and stoking their fire as if they'd just stopped patrolling.

Why weren't they using the trail?

Either they were hiding . . . or they were searching for someone.

Ruru? He'd said the border patrol he'd escaped had stopped looking for him, but what if they hadn't?

I needed to get closer.

Dropping to a crouch, I inched forward, breathing in the moss and pine needles that coated the forest floor. They muffled my slow footsteps.

Each soldier carried a huge sword and a bow with a case of arrows. They looked dirty, with rough skin and hair. One had a mashed nose ringed with fading bruises.

The one Ruru's horse had kicked?

My fingers twitched toward my knives. I could throw one, just one, and sneak away in the chaos. He deserved it after what he'd done to Ruru. What he might've done.

But then they'd know an armed enemy stalked them in the woods.

Gritting my teeth, I watched as they took turns pissing against trees while another skinned a rabbit and strung it to a spit.

They weren't worried about others seeing them. They probably assumed there was no one out here who would dare ambush them.

We could. We just don't have the time, I silently promised them.

I eased backward, pushing down on my sword hilt to keep the sheathed tip from colliding with anything.

But then my boot landed on a twig. *Crack.*

I froze.

Gods damn it. Maybe it was quiet enough. Maybe they won't see me. Hold still. Blend with the shadows. Don't move. Don't breathe.

"See anything, Mormont?"

Shit.

I sank closer to the ground, ducking my face under my hood.

Footsteps crashed through the brush, wandering left and right. Searching.

My heart hammered. Running was the wrong thing to do. They'd hear me immediately, spot me a moment later. Then I'd learn how good their aim was with a bow. I'd be no better than the rabbit that was now serving as their dinner.

But the impulse still flooded my veins.

Someone sighed loudly, only a few feet from where I was curled against some rocks.

"I don't see anything," Mormont called back. "And I'm fucking starving," he muttered under his breath. "Waste of fucking time . . ."

His footsteps slowly receded, back to camp.

I shuddered, slowly sipping cool air. I waited long enough that I could smell their meat cooking. Then I slithered back. And back. Once I could no longer see the light of their fire, I rose to my feet and hurried as fast as I dared.

East. East. Up the hill a bit. A horse snorted, and I nearly whimpered with relief.

Aiden darted out the moment he saw me. "What happened?" He grabbed my arms. "You're shaking. What did you see?"

"Border patrol. West. Eight of them."

Aiden swore and released me. "Tell the others. I'll ready the horses."

We were packed and mounted within minutes. Ozlow wasn't thrilled at being ridden again so soon, his extra grunts and huffs voicing his displeasure.

I rubbed his damp coat and whispered promises of carrots and apples. The Four only knew when I'd be able to make good on them.

I twisted in my saddle, keeping a steady watch on the western woods. I kept waiting for a shout, a blaze of torches, the thunder of hooves, but none came. They must've been as desperate for a fire and a hot meal as we were.

But they didn't mind the risk.

We rode for hours. It was nearly dawn by the time we stopped again. Peach and lavender light filtered through the misty trees, making them look less threatening.

Jek angled us off the trail to the east and found a clearing to stop in.

"We're an arrow-shot from Rellmira," he said, his red-rimmed eyes still darting around us. "Another day's ride to Calimber. There will be more patrols. We'll have to keep moving to avoid them. But for now, rest, water, sleep a wink."

Everyone nodded, too weary to speak.

I gave Ozlow a rubdown and some water before turning him toward a few clumps of spiky grass for grazing. I'd hardly slumped against a tree and closed my eyes before Yarina shook me awake.

"Up you get, princess," she said gruffly.

I didn't bother correcting her anymore. It didn't sound like so much of an insult lately.

As I saddled Ozlow, I noticed Aiden was missing, yet Wicked was still here.

"Where's Aiden?" I asked Nikella, who had already saddled her gray horse and sat atop him, holding tight to her staff—her steel spear safely inside.

"He's scouting the gap," she said without looking at me, her gaze to the south. "The Rellmirans built a stone wall along the border from the cliffs to the trail, and a bit farther west. The stone wall is too high for a horse to jump, and the trail leads to the only gap in the wall. Aiden is checking for patrols."

I swung on top of Ozlow. "Perhaps the patrol we evaded last night was in charge of the gap, but they decided to wander into Dag territory."

Nikella didn't answer.

We waited a few more moments before Aiden strode back with a grim look on his face.

"Six guards," he said. "Not very alert, but well-armed."

Maz swore.

"We could leave the horses and climb the wall farther down," Yarina suggested.

"Someone would have to stay behind, then we'd be short a warrior and our horses," Jek said.

Sigrid shrugged, her fur cape ruffling in the breeze. "Leave the boy behind. Our horses will be easily spotted on the plains near Calimber, anyway."

Ruru sat up straighter on his horse, his hair sticking out in all directions. He opened his mouth, most likely to protest, but Aiden cut him off.

"No one's staying behind. We may need the horses for a fast escape. We'll just have to cut back west, hugging the wall until it ends near the Winspere estates."

"What if we run into the patrol from last night?" I asked.

Aiden's green gaze flicked to me. "That's a risk we'll have to take. I'd rather face a possible danger than a certain one."

"Agreed," Nikella said. "But—"

An arrow slammed into the tree next to her. Her horse jerked sideways, stumbling into Ozlow.

Jek roared something I didn't hear. I was too focused on the lone horseman wearing the Rellmiran colors nocking another arrow into his bow.

He aimed for Jek this time.

"Down, Jek!" Nikella shouted.

He flattened himself on his horse's back just as the arrow shot through the space his body had been.

Gasping, I unsheathed my sword, exhaustion and adrenaline at war in my veins.

But then the rider tumbled from his horse, an arrow sticking out of his chest.

I glanced around wildly. Sigrid slowly lowered her empty bow, her expression cold.

Everyone else exhaled in relief.

But then the rider staggered to his feet and screamed, "ENEMIES TO THE NORTH!"

"Shit," Ruru muttered, grasping his sword like I was.

Aiden leaped on top of Wicked. "Charge them," he said in a hard voice.

My stomach bottomed out, but I rode after him as he led us to the gap.

The rider must've been a scout, or the rest of his patrol would've followed him.

When we galloped up to the gap, the other soldiers were scrambling for their horses and weapons.

I tried to remember Nikella's training, everything a blur as we came close enough to see their faces.

One soldier rode toward Aiden, swinging a sword. Aiden clashed with him and knocked him off his horse. But another rode out, his teeth bared in a snarl. He roared toward me.

My body instinctively curved away from his sword strike, and I stabbed at his torso. He wheeled his horse away. Jek crashed into him, and the two tumbled.

More horsemen stampeded the gap. Yarina, Sigrid, and Nikella surged forward to meet them.

Ozlow pranced and tossed his head, likely feeling the fear coursing through my body. I twisted in my saddle, looking for Ruru. I didn't see him in the chaos.

An arrow whirred past the tip of my nose.

An archer stood farther back, on the Rellmiran side of the gap, shooting at us. Clearly not caring if he hit his own men.

I kicked Ozlow's sides and raced for him. I held my sword steady as Nikella taught me.

The archer loaded another arrow, his helmet shining like a beacon. He paled as I galloped toward him. Fervent desperation twisted his face in a way that wrenched my heart.

But he was trying to murder my people.

He settled the arrow and swung it toward me. Time seemed to slow. Ozlow's hoofbeats matched my heart.

Breath. Sweat. Wind. Tears.

How would death feel?

He let go of the bow string.

No pain. Ozlow didn't falter.

I swung wildly and missed. I whipped Ozlow around,

keeping my seat. I felt a burst of pride a moment before the archer grasped my ankle and yanked me from my saddle.

I collapsed on the ground with a strangled cry. My sword flew out of my hand.

"Stupid bitch!" the archer snarled, seizing my braid and jerking me upright. He reached for a knife in his belt.

I grabbed two of mine. Jabbed one in his arm, the other in his neck.

Warm blood sprayed over my hand and face. He released me with a gargle, his eyes wide, and fell back.

I stood over him, gasping, heaving.

Holy Four, this was worse than killing a Shadow-Wolf. The mask hid so much. But now, I watched the imminence of his death sink into his expression. His hatred. His fear. Fleeting moments until his eyes rolled up into his skull.

I staggered backward, bile rising in my throat.

Someone shouted my name. *Aiden.* I stumbled toward the gap, just as he rushed through on foot, his expression wild. Blood coated his sword.

He grabbed my shoulder roughly. "Are you hurt?"

I shook my head. "The others?"

"Alive, give or take a few scratches and bruises. These soldiers were more like street brawlers than Wolves." He looked over my shoulder at the dead archer. He gently pushed me through the gap. "Go. I'll grab Ozlow. We need to be prepared if another patrol happens by."

My feet felt too heavy as I walked through the mud to join the others. Yarina and Sigrid gathered weapons while Maz and Ruru chased down the horses. Nikella and Jek dragged the bodies into the woods.

Nikella spotted me first. Her eyes widened, and she hurried forward.

"Injuries?" she asked tersely.

I shook my head again.

"Then clean those and sheathe them," she said, nodding to the knives still clutched in my hands, as if the blood had sealed them there.

I nodded, feeling like a puppet, unable to speak. I dragged my sleeve over my face, trying to clean off some of the blood. Then I wiped my knives on my damp boots. Good enough for now. I slid them back into my brace.

Gods, that archer was just the first. There would be more before this new war was over.

Ruru gave me a swift hug, easing some of the tension from my shoulders. Maz patted me on the back, and Yarina gave me an approving nod.

Aiden returned with Ozlow, who was munching on some grass he'd found.

"What do you want to do with the horses?" Ruru asked him, holding the soldiers' horses by the reins.

"Remove their gear and turn them loose," Aiden said. "They'll be happy in this field."

"We should take their uniforms," Maz said, watching Jek drag the archer's body through the gap. I turned away.

Aiden nodded. "They could be useful if our Wolf disguises aren't enough. Let's gather them up, along with some armor, and use one of their horses to carry it."

He seemed so calm, so in control.

I wanted to cry and sleep for two days.

Perhaps becoming a warrior would get easier. But not today.

We cleaned up our mess and rode out within the hour. The soldiers' morning cook fire was still smoldering when we left.

The terrain immediately opened up into the wide, open plains Winspere was known for. It felt strange to be a speck in so much space after crawling through the forest for days.

I felt exposed. But so were any threats that hunted us. I tried to take comfort in that.

We rode south, the milky sun arcing overhead. We halted at a small stream shrouded on both sides with scraggly bushes and short pines.

"This is the last bit of cover before we reach Calimber," Aiden said. "We'll rest here until dark, then scout the mine by foot."

I tumbled off Ozlow, my body more sore than usual. The moment I'd unclasped his bridle and saddle, Ozlow raced for the water. I followed him, stripping off my cloak and weapons.

Kneeling in the spiky grass, I plunged my hands into the cold water and scrubbed them clean of blood. Then I splashed some on my face, drinking a bit as I did.

My mind still felt every bit as bloody, but I couldn't fix that.

The others washed and drank as well. I kept to myself, curling into a ball under a tree and falling asleep in moments.

My weariness must've been too deep for dreams, because all I found was darkness.

Then Aiden was squeezing my shoulder. "Kiera. We're back."

I sat up groggily. Night had fallen. The stream bubbled cheerfully next to me.

"Back?" I croaked. Gods, how long had I slept?

"Jek and I scouted Calimber."

Something in his voice blew away the fog clouding my mind.

"And?" I asked. "Is it bad?"

"It's not good. It's as your sister's lover said—there's a whole army encampment surrounding the mine entrance. Guards on horseback run a perimeter around the camp. I assume the town, which lies even further south, is also overrun."

I bit my lip. "So, how are you going to get in?"

"We need a distraction."

CHAPTER 28
KIERA

Two Shadow-Wolves stepped out from behind the bushes.

My heart climbed into my throat, even though I knew it was just Aiden and Maz in disguise. But the snarling metal masks still sent a bolt of fear through me.

"Fucking Four, that's eerie," Ruru muttered.

The slimmer one—Aiden—stopped in front of me. Even though the mask had eye holes, I couldn't see his eyes.

I fought the urge to run.

His gloved hand clasped mine. "Be careful," he said, his voice distorted behind the metal. "Remember, if we're not out by dawn, go back to Yargoth."

Before I could question myself, I threw my arms around his shoulders and hugged him tightly, the silky cloth cool on my cheek. Aiden embraced me as if he'd been waiting for this very moment. His masked chin nestled into my neck, sending tiny shivers across my skin.

Gods, this was strange. But I might never get another chance.

"Don't get caught, my little thief," he whispered before pulling away.

"Never," I said with a brave smile.

He moved to Nikella, who grasped his arms and whispered something to him.

I hurried over to hug Maz, my worry nearly choking me.

"Protect, lovely," he rumbled in my ear.

I blinked back tears. "Protect, Maz. Make sure you both come back."

He dipped his head, his mask flashing in the bare moonlight.

Yarina grasped his arm. "Remember, don't say a word. No swearing. No threats. Just wave your sunstone shit around, and people will do what you want."

"I'll try my best," he said dryly, rolling his shoulders, as if nervous.

"Mazkull," Sigrid said, her voice thick and scratchy. She held her arms tightly around her body. "If you . . . if you see Bruna or Tarza or Zekrill or . . . any of the others, you can't say anything to them. Don't give yourself away."

Maz hesitated, then nodded.

Sigrid rarely let her emotions out, so she must care deeply about the captured Dags she'd mentioned. I wondered if any of them were still alive.

Like two shadows, Aiden and Maz melted into the night. Ruru stood shoulder to shoulder with me. Jek grabbed Nikella's hand, and I was surprised when she didn't remove it.

"We worked so hard to get those boys out of that gods-damned cave," Jek muttered.

"We'll get them back again," Nikella said. "But we need to do our part."

An hour later, I caught my first glimpse of Calimber. The encampment gleamed like an ember in the plain. Hundreds of tents in neat rows formed a barrier on every side.

Of course, I couldn't see the mine from here. It'd be underground. A network of tunnels in the cliffs facing the Niviath Sea.

Ozlow shifted under me as if he could feel my trepidation. There were so many soldiers. Eight of us against an army. And deep beneath a canopy of sunstone, dozens, maybe hundreds, of prisoners.

My jaw tightened.

"Fucking Four, this helmet stinks."

"Quiet," Jek growled at Yarina.

I couldn't blame her. I wanted to claw this dead soldier's clothes from my body. They reeked of blood and body odor. I supposed the scent would help sell the disguise.

"Make it fast. Make it loud," Jek said.

Yarina nudged me with her armored elbow. "Just the way I like it."

A laugh burst out of me before I could stop it.

Jek glared at both of us. Clearly, this wasn't the time for lewd jokes. But the humor calmed me the tiniest bit.

We watched the perimeter guards circle east, away from the large horse pen we'd marked as our target.

"Let's go," Nikella barked.

We rode toward the pen. A few guards leaned against the fence, smoking pipes. They straightened when we approached, their hands going to their sword hilts.

The first test.

The Dags had shoved their braided hair up into their helmets, and we women had smeared dirt on our faces. The bulky uniforms would hopefully give the impression of broad shoulders and no breasts.

Ruru, who'd been uncharacteristically quiet since we'd finalized our plan, had also smudged mud on his chin to look older.

"A little early for patrol change, aren't you?" asked one guard, squinting at us in the torchlight.

"Two of our men got drunk and wandered off a cliff last night," Jek said with a shrug. "Figured I'd report it now and wait for replacements where there's better food. Any meat tonight?"

The guards relaxed a bit, not seeming to care that two soldiers were dead.

"Rabbit again," spat the second guard. "Get it from the cook near the High General's tent. He burns it the least."

Jek dipped his head. "Much obliged."

He dismounted, and we imitated him.

"You two," he barked at me and Ruru, "go find us some meat while we take care of the horses."

Heart in my throat, I nodded with a grunt while Ruru answered in a deep voice, "Yes, sir."

The second guard gave us an odd look. I turned my face away and hurried toward the tents with Ruru at my side.

I didn't want to do this part, least of all with Ruru. But not being a Dag or a woman, he had the best chance of getting close to soldiers without raising suspicion.

Loud laughter and male conversation emanated from between the tents. My skin prickled like I was walking back into the Den.

Just because these men didn't wear the masks didn't mean they weren't also wolves of a sort.

They may be wolves, but you are not prey. Aiden and Maz are counting on you.

I wanted to squeeze Ruru's hand for good luck, but couldn't risk it.

He grinned at me as though we were simply going to the market for some sticky bread.

We strode into the camp like we were meant to be there.

Soldiers in violet Rellmiran uniforms lounged around wooden tables, drinking and playing Death and Four. Others marched past in full armor. Their spears glinted in the firelight of many braziers that squatted near every tent. We skirted around a few soldiers on horseback who rushed through with taut brows and sharp commands to make way.

Keeping our heads down, we walked east toward the mine and the cliffs. Our distraction needed to be as close to the entrance as possible so Aiden and Maz could slip inside unnoticed.

Ruru swiped an abandoned mug from a table as we passed. He sniffed it. "Ale. Good enough."

Finally, we neared the end of the tents. A wide clearing encased by a high stone wall lay beyond. In the middle of it was a great hole, with steps descending into darkness. Guards with torches, bows, and swords stood at the entrance.

My throat suddenly felt parched. How many people were down there? What did the sunstone look like, still embedded in the rocky caves?

I glanced around, but didn't see Aiden and Maz. They must be hiding nearby. Waiting.

A small group of soldiers huddled around a barrel playing a heated game of Death and Four next to a few tents I hoped were theirs. A huge, red-haired soldier warmed his hands over a sizzling brazier, calling out colorful insults to the players.

"All yours," I muttered.

Ruru stumbled toward them, pretending to drink from his stolen cup. "Hey! Hey, I get next game."

The soldiers looked up. "Get lost, boy," one snarled.

"Yeah, border patrol can play with the infantry," the red-haired soldier sneered, jerking his thumb back the way we'd come. "Not the officers."

I edged toward the nearest tent and peeked inside. A shirtless man was sprawled across his bunk, snoring loudly. I nonchalantly walked to the next.

"Hey, I just got paid," Ruru said, slurring his words. He jangled a coin purse in front of their faces, which immediately turned greedy. "I want to play with *real* opponents. Not those baby infantry."

A soldier guffawed. "You're barely older than a baby yourself, boy."

"Wanna bet?" Ruru shook the coins under his nose.

He scowled. "Fine. Next game."

They would probably fleece Ruru, but that was part of the plan.

I checked two more tents while they focused on their game, pausing whenever soldiers walked or rode by. At last, I found an empty one within eyeshot of the entrance.

I darted inside. I needed to work quickly before Ruru ran out of coins, or the soldiers ran out of patience.

The tent held two wooden bunks, a chest, and a table with one chair. A lone lamp sat on the table, its flame turned down. The only light came from outside the tent walls.

Fingers shaking, I carefully took apart the metal lantern, preserving the smoldering, oil-soaked wick. Then I dumped the rest of the oil over every wooden surface in the tent. It wasn't nearly as much as I'd hoped, but it would have to do.

Raucous cheers and groans came from outside. Had Ruru lost already?

Shit, shit, shit.

I kneeled next to the oil-soaked chair and laid our last fireseed on it. Nikella said the fireseed would catch on any amount of burning material. And to run when it did.

Holding my breath, I carefully dangled the smoldering wick over the fireseed.

"Wait a moment!" a rough male voice came from just outside the tent. "I'm going to grab more wine."

I froze as a hand parted the tent flaps.

Nowhere to hide. I couldn't cover up what I'd done. He'd know it wasn't an accident.

"Liar!" Ruru shouted. "He's a cheat! He stole some of my coins and is probably going to hide them in his tent."

The hand disappeared. "What did you say, boy?"

Oh gods, Ruru, what are you doing?

I dropped the wick onto the fireseed. It ignited with a hiss and a loud *crack*. A flame speared upward, and I stumbled back, tripping over a heavy bag. The fire rippled down the chair and across the floor toward me.

I tossed the heavy bag aside. A bottle rolled out onto the oil-soaked rug. *The wine.*

Screaming silent curses, I flung myself at the back wall of the tent and cut a long slit through the fabric with Mother's knife.

I escaped the tent and raced around it. My eyes widened.

Two of the soldiers were holding Ruru by his arms to let a third soldier deliver punches to his face and ribs. Their makeshift table had overturned—ale, tiles, and coins spilled everywhere.

Rage burned through my veins. "Let him go!" I shouted.

The big, red-haired soldier who was hitting Ruru stopped and spun around. His eyes narrowed on Mother's knife, which was still in my hand.

"Where did you—"

Boom!

An explosion behind me knocked me to my knees. The soldiers' faces paled as they stumbled back.

"Fire!" the red-haired man screamed. "Fire! Ring the alarm!"

I twisted around to see a monstrous fire eating through one tent and flicking its many tongues at the ones next to it.

More men shouted, and somewhere a bell rang.

I crawled out of the road as men rushed out of their tents. The soldiers who held Ruru flung him to the side. He rose to his feet, wincing and eyes wide, looking for me.

I scrambled over to him. "Let's go!"

He nodded and kicked over the brazier, dumping burning wood and hot coals over the soldiers' spilled drinks. Another fire leaped up on the spot.

I grabbed his arm, and we raced back toward the horse pen.

Soldiers jostled us from every direction as they carried buckets of water toward the fires.

One slammed against me hard enough that I lost my helmet. My braid fell down my back.

Another soldier saw, and his jaw dropped. "You're a gods-damned woman!"

I brushed past him.

But he shouted. "Spy! She's a spy!"

"Run!" Ruru yanked on my arm, and we sprinted past the tents.

Something dull and heavy hit me in the back, but I kept running. Jek and the others were waiting, already atop their horses. Nikella held the reins of Ozlow and Ruru's horse.

Footsteps pounded behind us.

The two guards at the fence stared with open mouths.

"Stop her!" the soldier chasing us roared.

The guards whipped out their swords. Jek, Sigrid, and Yarina pulled out theirs and charged them.

Nikella aimed her bow and an arrow at us. "Split!"

Ruru and I veered away from each other, and she loosed her arrow. It streaked between us. A grunt, and something crashed to the ground.

Ruru and I swung onto our horses.

Metal clashed as the Dags fought the guards. Sigrid stabbed one while Jek and Yarina knocked down the other.

"Go!" Jek roared, jerking his horse to the north and taking off at a gallop.

The rest of us tore after him.

I twisted around to glance back at the encampment. No one

pursued us. Shouts and clanging bells still rose to the sky with the sparks I'd set.

We rode hard to the stream and splashed back through to the other side.

The plan was to wait here until Aiden and Maz were back.

We dismounted, panting and sweating. Ruru groaned, still on his horse.

"He was . . . injured," I said, breathing heavily.

"Get my supplies," Nikella said as she helped Ruru dismount.

I staggered to the bushes where we'd hidden our bags and other weapons near Wicked, Valiant, and our packhorse. I grabbed Nikella's bag.

But then a rough hand clamped around my mouth. Cold metal slid against my throat.

"Scream, and I'll gut you here and now, girl."

CHAPTER 29
AIDEN

The fire drew soldiers from every direction. Except two that stayed in front of the mine entrance.

I took a deep breath and stepped out of the shadows, Maz at my side. We strode forward like two Wolves who had every right and reason to enter that gods-forsaken mine.

One soldier's eyes darted to my mask, then away. He wouldn't risk stopping us.

We brushed past them and descended the stairs. Deeper. Deeper. The worn soles of our boots made little noise even in the stone tunnel.

No torches lit our descent. I always thought that was purposeful. To instill fear in the prisoners being dragged down here. I remembered scrambling up these steps like a desperate rat when we escaped.

The darkness pressed on my eyes like an invisible weight. The smell of dirt and decay hit me with a hundred memories.

I staggered on a step, everything in my body screaming at me to stop.

Get out. Now. While you still can. Trapped. Trapped forever. You'll never leave if you don't run. Run. Run.

Sweat rolled down my neck and chest. My heartbeat galloped like a panicked horse. Gods, I'd forgotten how far down it was.

Maz jerked to a halt. His muffled breaths drummed against his metal mask. He must be feeling the same way I was.

I grit my teeth together. I clenched his arm where his tree tattoo lay hidden. Reminding him.

I felt more than saw him nod. We continued.

The stairs gradually leveled out until they met dirt. Metal lanterns on hooks lined the passages ahead and to the right. The tunnel to the right was new. At least as of the last seven years. I was sure of it.

The slow drag and rattle of chains sent another bolt of fear through my heart. A bald man in threadbare clothes with manacles around his ankles carried a bucket from the passage ahead. He didn't even look up as he hobbled into the other tunnel. Chunks of sunstone winked at me from his bucket.

Either he didn't see us or didn't care. After all, when death was constantly looming, why care if it came from Shadow-Wolves, soldiers, or the very stone he had to mine every day?

I jerked my head, and we followed the prisoner. His shuffling gait made him slow, but I matched his pace.

The clang of hammers echoed toward us. Hope pricked my chest. The forge? Could it really be that easy?

The man stumbled into a large cave. The heat was intense, like Aquinon during Mynastra's season.

I glanced around. No guards. No Korvin. Just a few sweaty men immersed in their work.

The prisoner dumped his sunstone into a large bin filled with other ancient chunks of the night sky and left. Never looking up. Never changing expression. Like we were ghosts. Or he was.

Did he have a family? Were they still waiting for him, or did they assume he was dead?

Focus. Forge first, rescue later.

Scowling, I put my hands behind my back and prowled the perimeter of the cave. Two large furnaces took up the center. A stone chimney rose from them and disappeared into the cave ceiling.

Fire bloomed over pools of molten black sunstone, each in a stone mold the shape of a weapon or a piece of armor. A worker pulled one out with sunstone tongs and rapidly sculpted it. Much like I'd seen a glass blower shape an ornate bowl.

The sunstone gauntlets and chest plate I wore seemed to tighten. This was where they'd been forged.

A tall man wearing a leather mask and apron poured sunstone chunks into a large dipper, then threw a handful of something into the fire beneath it. *Fireseeds.* The fire roared, engulfing the dipper. Cracks, sizzles, and an odd screaming sound came from the stone as it melted.

Maz nudged me and tipped his head to where two soldiers were rolling a cart of finished sunstone armor and weapons up a smooth passage. Another way out?

None of the workers looked up to question us. They acted as if we weren't here. Perhaps they were used to Wolves coming to observe. Or they were too worried about hitting a quota to slow down, even for a moment. They probably assumed no one would be stupid enough or able to infiltrate this far.

Yet the first part of our mission had been shockingly easy. Kiera and the others had performed the harder task, hopefully making it out unscathed. Even if they had, they were still vulnerable, waiting for us.

Maz and I could leave right now. The soldiers were probably still distracted up on the ground. We had confirmation of why

Renwell had stolen the fireseeds. We'd seen his forge churning out large quantities of weapons and armor.

But that didn't solve the problem.

I needed to see the rest. I wanted to see the *cost*.

Like I'd told the others in Frieda's lodge, I didn't care what Renwell planned to use these abominations for. Terrible things, no doubt. Whether to keep the people of Rellmira in check or to bring the world to its knees, it didn't matter.

I wanted to stop him long before that could happen. I wanted to map this gods-damned mine like I had the Den. So I could tear this whole place down. Bury the evil that he forged here.

This mine was a stain on Rellmira's history, and I intended to remove it forever.

I marched out of the cave with Maz fast on my heels. I could almost feel him vibrating with things to say, but we couldn't speak here.

We passed another prisoner lugging a bucket of rock. I veered down the tunnel that would take us deeper into the mine. Purpose burned beneath my skin, leaching out any lingering fear.

The passage snaked downward, then opened up into the giant cavern from my memory. Soaring support beams pierced the cave ceiling. Wooden scaffolds wove over the rocky walls, prisoners lining them like ants. Sunstone shimmered in the rock like veins of black blood. Hammers pounded. Chains clanked. And the only human sound was that of helmeted supervisors barking orders from a raised platform in the middle.

It was like I'd stepped directly into one of my worst memories. Nothing had changed.

Except me standing here in an enemy uniform instead of the torn, dirty clothes of a prisoner.

But the burning in my heart was the same.

I needed to be here. I needed to end this.

"We should move quickly," Maz muttered.

"Ships, then prisoners."

He gave the barest nod.

We darted into one passage, then another, and then another. My breath came shorter, more stifled, with each turn. Gods, I didn't remember this many tunnels. Weylin, and then Renwell, must've dug deeper into the cliffs, and not just for access to the sea.

I started marking the ones we turned into with a slash of my sunstone knife. It cut through the rock like it was sand.

Occasionally, the walls shuddered around us. And every time, my whole body tensed. There had been several cave-ins when we were prisoners here. All of them deadly.

Perhaps Renwell would bring down the mine before I could. But he probably wouldn't get the prisoners out first.

I walked faster.

We ran into several dead ends, each filled with prisoners carving out tiny bits of sunstone.

Every time we backed out of a passage, I gave it another slash.

Finally, we chose a tunnel that smelled of the sea. My boots sank deeper into the damp earth, which gradually turned to sand.

The tunnel spit us out onto the beach.

A huge ship floated in the bay. The incomplete hull of another rested on a bed of logs.

We'd seen three when we rowed through the canyon. And the one at anchor didn't look like it'd been through a battle. Which meant the third—the one that had attacked the Urzost village—was elsewhere.

My scowl deepened.

Prisoners swarmed over the beached ship, hammering

boards into the hull. Renwell must have enough prisoners to work them in shifts, day and night.

Soldiers watched over them or sat around fires, drinking and eating.

No one had noticed our arrival yet.

I darted behind a large pile of rubble, Maz following, and we crouched, peering from behind the rocks.

"I count eighteen soldiers," I muttered. "In addition to those on the cliffs."

"At least thirty or forty prisoners," Maz breathed. "It's hard to tell them apart."

I nodded, staring at the floating ship, plans building in my head.

Maz pulled back and nudged me. "There's some fancy soldier down there by the unfinished ship. The general?"

I scuttled over to his side of the rocks. My gaze narrowed to where a short but broad man in polished golden armor and a long violet cape stood, gesturing at the partial hull.

Hatred seized my chest. High General Dracles.

The last time I'd seen him was amid the ashes of the people he'd massacred. He'd executed every other leader of the Pravaran rebellion in front of me. But when he came to me, he rested his bloody sword against my neck with a smile.

"Not you," he'd said. "I want your death to take as long as possible, serving the king the way he deserves."

He added me to a prison wagon with eight other strong young men. Two of them didn't survive the trip. Six of them died in the mine. I was the last of that rebellion.

I'd thought of hunting him down once or a dozen times. But my target had been Weylin. Then Brielle or her son would've forced him to retire, humiliated and unwanted. Which was worse than death for a man like him.

"Incoming," Maz rasped.

I jerked, hearing the stamp of booted feet almost too late. Maz and I scrambled around the rubble, partially exposing us to the beach, as two soldiers marched out of the tunnel.

I clung to the rocks like a beetle, praying we still blended in.

We needed to leave. Our luck was bound to run out.

As soon as the soldiers were clear, I tapped Maz's shoulder and pointed to the tunnel. We peeled ourselves away from the rocks and hurried back into the mine.

Seeing Dracles had rattled me. Shaken old memories loose. I felt like I had in those years trapped here. Mired in the dark, ugly feelings that had festered inside me every day.

I needed to tear this gods-damned place down. And I needed to bury Dracles in it.

But he had an army. I didn't. Because I was the dead son of a forgotten king. I was the sole survivor of a rebellion people only talked about in whispers.

No one. You're no one. The familiar whispers crept back into my mind. *Worse than that, you're a failure.*

I ground my teeth together and tried to force the old weakness away.

We came to the fork in the tunnels. I cut a horizontal line under my slash. A symbol that this was the way. Hopefully, we would be here again soon.

We followed my marks back through the tunnels, the distance somehow seeming farther than ever.

A row of prisoners that hadn't been there before lined the next tunnel. They sat on the ground, chained together, as a few others took pickaxes to a collapsed tunnel. A supervisor in a dented helmet stood nearby, head bent over a ledger while the prisoners sweat and bled.

My stomach churned. How many had died under the rocks just now?

I hated to leave them. We could easily cut down the supervisor, but we couldn't lead the prisoners out of the mine without being questioned. And a dead body could tighten security before our next attack.

I forced myself to keep walking. I made it a few steps before I realized Maz wasn't with me anymore.

I spun around to see him standing in front of a woman. Her hair was shorn to the scalp, but the tattoos on her bare arms and legs told me she was a Dag.

Dread curled my hands into fists. *Fucking Four, Mazkull, don't.*

She slowly looked up at his mask, a glimmer of hatred lighting her dull blue eyes.

I marched forward, about to drag him away, when he whispered, "Bruna."

Confusion wrinkled her brow.

Now that he said the name, I remembered her. Long brown hair and a merry laugh. She and Sigrid had been inseparable.

I jerked Maz's arm.

"Excuse me, did you just speak to one of my prisoners?" the supervisor demanded from behind us.

We both stiffened. Maz reached for his sunstone knife. I shook my head.

Stay calm. Stay quiet.

I turned on my boot heel and kept striding down the tunnel. This time, Maz kept even with me.

"Wolves aren't supposed to be here!" The supervisor's strident voice followed us. "Stop! Show me your papers this instant before I report you to the High General."

I halted immediately. Bold of him to threaten a Shadow-Wolf.

My muscles trembled with restraint as I sauntered back to the supervisor. The man's smug smile splashed scarlet over my vision.

"Good dog," he said. "You *must* show your papers when

asked. And according to my schedule,"—he waved his ledger in front of my mask—"no Wolf shipment is due for another three weeks. So let's have them." He snapped his fingers and held out his hand.

I'd strangled every carnivorous shadow that had stirred in my chest while creeping around this pit. But those demons reared their heads one by one as I stared at the man's outstretched hand. Then at the ledger of sordid deeds he carried, like he was measuring grain, not people's lives. Last, my gaze fell to the sunstone club at his side, so familiar I could almost feel my bones breaking beneath it.

As they had seven years ago, when another supervisor leered down at me, waiting for me to surrender.

Those shadows—every warped remnant of fury and hatred—swallowed the last bit of light from my mind.

I seized the supervisor's hand and wrenched until I felt several finger bones snap.

He shrieked, stumbling back.

I yanked the club from his belt and snarled, "Welcome to the Abyss." Then I cracked it against his skull.

CHAPTER 30
AIDEN

THE SUPERVISOR'S BODY COLLAPSED AT MY FEET, HIS HEAD A bloody clump. His helmet clattered against the rocky ground—a thunderstorm in the deadly quiet.

I stood, frozen, gasping for air. I felt like I was drowning in this gods-damned mask. Suffocating in my vengeance. That was who I was, deep down. A monster.

I dropped the club and faced Maz and the prisoners.

Maz had taken off his mask, his face white, his eyes grim. "The body," he grunted.

I hissed a curse between my teeth.

But then Bruna spoke up. "Mazkull? Is that really you?"

His face softened when he looked at her. "Sigrid sends her love. Don't tell her I spoke to you."

Bruna's eyes filled with tears. "She's out there? Are you here to rescue us?"

Maz darted a glance at me. "Soon, I think. Just hold on a little longer."

I grimaced. He shouldn't be making any promises. I'd disappointed enough people to give me a lifetime of regret.

"Help us move the body into the rubble," I said gruffly. "You can say a rock hit him when the tunnel collapsed."

Bruna slowly rose to her feet, wincing. "He already reported the cave-in. More supervisors and workers will be here any moment."

I growled, throwing my arms wide. "Then tell them there was a secondary collapse. You two, clear a hole," I barked at the two prisoners with pickaxes who'd stopped digging to gape at me.

"We'll have to spread the rubble more," Bruna said, her hoarse voice growing stronger as she helped the other prisoners to their feet. "And we'll have to create a few injuries of our own to be believable."

"Fine, just hurry," I snapped. *This is your fault,* that voice in my head taunted mercilessly. *They could be executed for this. You did this to them.*

Maz joined me in helping the prisoners clear out more dirt and rocks. Bits of sunstone glittered here and there. I grabbed a few and stuffed them into the supervisor's pockets before I dumped his body in the makeshift hole.

Let the others think he was stealing from the mine, barring further investigation. The man was likely a worse criminal than any prisoner here.

I considered taking his ledger, but then his death wouldn't look like an accident.

A few volunteers came forward and took turns smashing rocks against each other's faces. No one complained. If anything, they stared at me and Maz with the faintest ray of hope.

It felt like a fist around my gut.

"Go," Bruna said, now sporting a bleeding lip. "Before more come."

Maz put his mask on and clasped her shoulder. "Are the rest of the prisoners in the cells off the main cavern?"

Bruna nodded. "Fifty of us rest in there once a day, leaving a couple hundred working. But our numbers change daily. The innocent die quickly here, and they've been imprisoning anyone who looks sideways at a soldier."

"How many supervisors?" I asked, glancing up and down the tunnel.

"Thirty-seven, by my last count." Bruna's words came fast and frantic. "I don't know about Dracles's soldiers. Now go!"

Muffled voices echoed down the tunnel.

Maz and I darted forward, taking long strides toward the newcomers. Sweat trickled down my spine. What if this supervisor questioned us as well? We couldn't fight our way out. There were too many. Not to mention the army at the entrance.

I spotted a narrow tunnel and shoved Maz into it. We flattened against the craggy rock wall. I held my breath as boots thumped past, followed by the shuffle of bare feet and chains.

I didn't wait for the sound to disappear before I flew out of the tunnel. We all but ran down the passage, stopping only to check my tiny marks.

No shouts echoed behind us. Not yet. Gods, I hoped Bruna and the others wouldn't be punished for my mistake.

We slowed down once we hit the main cavern. Barely. I felt like I was running for my life again. My window to freedom closing with every harsh breath I took.

A shout rose in the main cavern. For us? For something else? I didn't stop to see.

Once we reached the uphill tunnel, my legs began to burn. We skirted around prisoners carrying their sunstone.

Almost there. Almost there.

My boots hit the stone steps. That thick darkness strangled my senses once more.

Holy Four, get me out. Let me breathe fresh air again. I need to live. I need to see her again. I need to find her.

The thought of wrapping my arms around Kiera, of looking

into her warm amber eyes, hearing her voice say my name—it flooded me with life.

I raced up the stairs with renewed vigor, Maz grunting and wheezing at my heels.

We burst out of the mine like the cornered wolves we resembled.

The two soldiers startled, eyeing us suspiciously. But we didn't wait for questions.

The camp still smoked up ahead. We cut to the right, aiming for the gap in their wooden blockades. After wriggling through, we fled into the cool night.

Once we were out of earshot of the camp, Maz ripped off his mask. "Fucking Four, Aiden! You didn't want me to kill him. You didn't want to leave a trail. And then you crushed the man's face! In front of all the prisoners! We were supposed—"

"I know!" I snapped, tearing off my mask and gulping in the grass-scented breeze. "I fucking know, Maz. But he wouldn't stop, and I had nothing else. No way out. I had to."

Maz kicked at a clump of grass. "I shouldn't have stopped in front of Bruna. It's my fault the supervisor even looked at us. I don't even know why I'm yelling at you. You only did what I wanted to do since I stepped foot in that gods-damned hell hole." He glanced at me, his eyes brimming with misery in the soft light. "Forgive me, brother."

My heart clenched, some of the darkness bleeding out of it. "There is nothing to forgive," I said with a sigh. "We can't always win when we fight our demons."

We lapsed into silence as we trudged back to our camp by the stream.

As we neared it, the hair on the back of my neck lifted. I stopped. Maz did, too.

The stream trickled peacefully by. Nothing but wind shifted the grasses along the bank. All was dark and quiet.

That was when it struck me. We hadn't seen any patrols on our way back. We'd snuck around one on our way in, but not on our way out.

I silently unsheathed my sunstone knife. Maz did the same. We crouched in the tall grass and slid into the stream. The water rushed around my boots as I took careful steps, never splashing.

A horse snorted on the other bank. I froze, waiting for a shout or an arrow to strike my chest armor. Nothing.

I eased up the other bank and crawled through the bushes. Two horses, one pale, one dark as night, turned toward me.

I breathed a sigh of relief. Wicked and Valiant. They were still here. But where were the others?

"Do you think the border patrol took them?" Maz murmured, turning in a circle.

My gaze landed on a discarded sword next to a crumpled body. My mind blanked. I seized the body and turned it over. A soldier.

"Not without a fight. And why leave our horses?" I swallowed hard. "Search for other bodies."

We combed through the brush but found no one else. Only the packhorse we'd taken. I left him untethered and happily grazing.

"Perhaps they were ambushed and headed for the gap back to Yargoth, like you told them to," Maz said hopefully.

I shook my head, studying the bent grass and tracks in the soft dirt. "Hoofprints go northwest. Farther into Winspere."

"Gods damn it," Maz growled. "Perhaps we would all actually survive if any of us could follow a fucking plan."

I didn't have the strength, or even the desire, to argue with him. My plans had never worked, anyway. Why would they now?

"What's that?" Maz asked, pointing his knife at a shadow streaking toward us through the grass.

I recognized that shadow. I watched for it every night.

I rushed forward and caught Kiera as she flung herself into my arms.

"You're alive," she whispered over and over in a choked voice. "You're alive."

I held her tightly, afraid to speak. Gods, she felt like a dream. Until something wet and warm trickled onto my cheek where it was pressed into her neck. The coppery scent of blood filled my nostrils.

I drew back and tugged her chin to the side, exposing her neck. The silver light glinted on a cut in her neck.

It seemed I would single-handedly be filling the Abyss tonight.

"Kiera," I said in a deep, deadly calm voice. "Who did this to you?"

Her throat pulsed beneath my fingertips. "He's dead."

I pulled her chin back until her gaze met mine. "He'd better be."

"Where are the others?" Maz demanded. "What happened?"

She slid out of my grip before I was ready to let her go. "Border patrol from the woods ambushed us when we came back. We got away, but they want revenge for the other patrol. They've been pursuing us. Nikella took us to a Winspere estate she knows. Sigrid, Yarina, and I circled back for you two." She paused from her rapid speech to take a breath. "But they're still looking for us. We need to go. Now."

Maz and I slid on our masks and grabbed our horses.

Kiera swung up behind me before I could offer. She pointed at the distant tree line to the north. "Yarina and Sigrid are waiting for us in there."

We rode across the plain, the horses' hoofbeats like thunder in the quiet night. Kiera held me tightly from behind. I handled Wicked's reins with one hand so I could lay my gloved palm over Kiera's cold hand.

We slowed down once we reached the end of the wall and slipped into the forest. Yarina and Sigrid met us with ready swords and twin sighs of relief.

"How did—"

"Later," Maz interrupted Yarina.

She frowned, but kept her mouth shut. Maz rarely snapped, but I was in no mood to talk about the mine yet either. Besides, we were running out of night, and I didn't feel like being hunted in the dawn.

Kiera slid off of Wicked and mounted Ozlow. "The border patrol is sweeping the woods, and they must've picked up reinforcements somewhere because there are fifteen of them now. We've been going slow and stopping to hide when they pass. We *cannot* let them trace us back to the Winspere house."

Oddly, my lips twitched in a smile. My little thief was directing us like a leader. Like I usually did. But I quite liked this change.

We rode in a single line through the trees. Twice, we heard a distant noise in the darkness and dismounted, but no one emerged.

Impatience gnawed at me. Part of me wanted to gallop to this house and battle the patrol if they saw us. Then we could cross a few enemies off our list.

I was tired of hiding.

The third time we heard a noise, the shadows shifted in the trees, and metal glinted.

Everyone else dismounted and led their horses to thicker brush. Running would be impossible through here.

My hand slid to my knife. They were already hunting us. Why not hunt a few of them?

I silently dismounted and crept toward the noise. They weren't using torches—probably to keep us from seeing them.

But they crashed through the woods like soldiers who hadn't grown up in a forest.

I had.

I glided over the pine needle-coated ground, darting from tree to tree until I found my mark. He was stomping over tree roots and breathing heavily through a severely crooked nose.

Ruru had told me about his escape from a border patrol.

I gripped my knife harder and waited until he passed by my tree. Then I stepped out behind him, wrapped my hand around his mouth, and slit his throat in one deft move.

He jerked and gagged, but no sound escaped through my fingers. I carefully laid him on the ground.

Kills like this were almost a relief. No horrible infectious guilt after. I didn't feel like a mindless monster, as I had with the supervisor.

This soldier hurt someone I loved and was intent on doing it again. The consequence was simple in my mind.

The swishing and cracking of the rest of the patrol carried on east. It might be a long time before they realized they were missing a soldier. And even longer to find him.

I hurried back to Wicked and found the others already mounted.

The air was thick with tension. Maz, Yarina, and Sigrid immediately rode on. Kiera waited for me to mount. I couldn't see her face, but I could feel her silence and the worry in it.

Perhaps she understood. Perhaps she didn't. But I would always do whatever it took to protect my people.

We rode without further interruption until we reached a large clearing in the woods, just as a gray, misty dawn rose.

A stone manor with wooden shutters and three smoking chimneys faced the plains of Winspere. Several other shorter stone buildings were scattered around the clearing. Workers in large, brimmed hats were already busy hauling buckets of feed to the animals within. Chickens darted about the yard.

I smelled bread baking and hoped to all the Four that Nikella's friend would feed us.

I was about to head for the stable when Kiera hissed, "Wait."

The others pulled up short and looked back at her.

Her gaze was fixed on the front of the manor where several saddled horses waited. None that I recognized.

"Those horses weren't there when we left," she whispered.

Nikella suddenly appeared between us. Kiera jerked to the side, nearly tumbling from Ozlow. But I wasn't surprised. Nikella had lived in the forest as many years as I had.

She looked up at me, a rare bleakness in her dark blue eyes. "Korvin is here."

CHAPTER 31
KIERA

Korvin is here.

Numbly, I followed her instructions and took my saddlebags from Ozlow's back. Two workers hurried toward us and led our horses into the stable.

Nikella assured us they would be taken care of. I kept a wary eye on the manor, waiting for Korvin to appear in one of the windows or to burst out of the front door.

I supposed we could keep running, but gods damn it, I was tired. We'd fought and ridden all night. My entire body ached and groaned with every step I took. The cut on my neck was my only injury from when that soldier first grabbed me. But I was coated in dirt and sweat, and the dead soldier's uniform smelled like his body was still in it.

But now Korvin had caught up with us.

None of the workers seemed terribly alarmed. As if soldiers stopped to check in regularly. Maybe they didn't know who Korvin was.

After we gathered our saddlebags, Nikella led us through the woods to the back of the manor. She fumbled through piles of dead leaves until she lifted a patch of them. A patch that was really a trapdoor in the ground, with grass and leaves threaded to it.

She gestured us inside, but her gaze never strayed from the back of the manor, which had no windows—only a simple door.

Sigrid and Yarina jumped into the tunnel, while Maz and Aiden balked for a moment. I couldn't see their faces behind their Wolf masks. Perhaps the mine tunnels had been harder to navigate than they'd thought.

I'd nearly cried with relief when I saw the two of them near their horses. Yarina, Sigrid, and I had just ridden back, and I thought we'd have to wait hours for them. But I'd seen Aiden's shadow and known it was him, even in his Wolf disguise.

Yet both of them had seemed different since coming back. Tense. Quick to lash out. Like wounded animals.

Aiden sneaking off to kill a soldier had unsettled me. As it seemed to unsettle the others. It was unlike him to be so reckless. To seek violence.

But I was coming to realize that everything Aiden did was to protect others.

Something had shaken him in that mine. Perhaps he would tell me once we were safe. If that ever actually happened.

Maz and Aiden disappeared into the tunnel, and I followed. The darkness and earthy smell reminded me of the tunnel between quarters in Aquinon. Collapsed now, according to Ruru. I prayed that Melaena was still alive and well since he'd left.

Nikella closed the trapdoor behind her, enveloping us in inky darkness. I gulped, feeling my way forward.

Gods, I hope there aren't any spiders in this tunnel.

"It's fairly straightforward," Nikella said quietly. "But watch your head."

There was a thud, and someone ahead of me grunted. "Earlier warning would've been nice," Aiden muttered.

A hysterical laugh bubbled up my throat, but I held it back. Not the time or the place.

Only a few moments went by before a shaft of light beamed down the tunnel. Yarina swung a small door open and crawled through. We emerged in a small, musty room lit by a single lantern. Wooden shelves laced with cobwebs lined the stone walls. A few kegs rested on the shelves, still plugged.

Several stone steps led up to a rusty metal door with a heavy chain and lock securing it. Perhaps it led to another cellar or the main house?

Nikella brushed past me to join Jek and Ruru in a corner where they'd piled up their cloaks and bedrolls. Ruru was snoring while Jek cleaned his weapons. Bruises were already darkening Ruru's jaw and cheek. His ribs probably looked worse.

I owed all three of them. Ruru for his distraction of the soldier. Nikella for killing the other soldier who had pursued me. And Jek for riding to my aid when I struggled with the soldier who'd held a knife to my neck by the stream.

I started toward them when a sudden movement caught my eye. A woman and a young girl gasped and scurried back into a corner, staring at Maz and Aiden in their Shadow-Wolf disguises.

I narrowed my eyes at the strangers. They seemed familiar somehow. But the dirty faces, the limp hair, the plain clothes . . . The girl clutched a box with holes in it and *Captain* scrawled across the side.

My heart dropped to my boots. Helene and Isabel. Lord Garyth's wife and daughter—the ones I'd helped flee Aquinon. What in the deep, dark, wandering hell were they doing here?

This couldn't be the friend Nikella had brought them to. It

would've taken her much longer to get here and back to Aquinon.

Aiden and Maz peeled off their masks and hoods.

"We're not Shadow-Wolves," Maz said gently. "We're with them." He nodded to the rest of our group.

Isabel relaxed, but Helene's tired eyes fixed on Aiden. "You," she whispered. "I wondered if you were still with her." She glanced at Nikella.

Aiden fidgeted with his gloves, taking them off more slowly than necessary. "It's good to see you, Lady Helene."

I couldn't say the same. I shuffled further behind Aiden and Maz. I wouldn't be able to hide from them forever in this tiny room, but I dreaded the inevitable confrontation.

The last time I'd spoken to them, they hadn't known who I truly was. Isabel had even begged me to save her father if I could. But I'd never seen him again.

Nikella had a brisk, murmured conversation with Jek while Yarina and Sigrid tossed down their saddlebags and slumped against them.

I turned my back to the room and slowly sifted through my bags, digging out my blanket and water pouch.

"When did you arrive?" Aiden asked.

"Last week," Helene replied. "Our situation in the south became compromised. Caddik was always a good friend to Garyth, so I felt safe coming here. Teacher Nikella told me . . ." Helene took a deep, shaky breath. I tensed, my blanket clutched in my hand. "She told me you were one of the last people to speak to my husband. Did he mention us?"

My heart cracked as Helene's voice did. Aiden was one of the last people to see Garyth alive? When? Where?

A heavy silence filled the room. Even Ruru's snores stopped.

I peeked over my shoulder at Aiden's stiff back. I wished I could see his face, but I could only see Helene's tearful one.

"He held on as long as he could for you," Aiden said softly. "He thought Renwell had captured you and your daughter."

Helene sobbed quietly, holding tight to a pale Isabel. "Was he . . . was he in much pain when he died?"

Aiden clenched a fist behind his back, his knuckles turning white. "He was relieved that you were safe. He died at peace."

I felt the lie between his words. But Helene seemed to take comfort from them.

I'd guessed that Lord Garyth was dead, but now I knew for certain. The knowledge carved itself into a wall of names in my mind—of the people I'd known and lost.

"Kiera? Where's Kiera?" Ruru's hoarse voice rose.

I squeezed my eyes shut. *Gods damn it, Ruru.* I rose and walked toward him, where he'd woken and sat up.

"I'm here, Ruru."

He relaxed when he saw me, but Isabel gasped and hurried over to me.

"Kiera! You're alive! Look, I still have Captain." She proudly shoved the box toward me. A thin pink tongue darted out of one of the holes.

I forced a smile at her. "I'm so glad, Lady Isabel."

Her smile drooped into a frown. "I *knew* your voice sounded familiar. Mama said it wasn't possible. That I was just imagining things. But I knew I'd seen you before." She pointed to my brace of knives. "You wore knives like that when you were in my father's study."

Everyone in the room turned to stare at us.

Holy Four, just when I thought every one of my betrayals had been revealed, another came to light.

But this presented a new kind of pain. I would be a monster in Helene and Isabel's eyes, much the same way Aiden had been one in mine. We'd both taken loved ones.

I glanced between mother and daughter. "Yes, it was me in Garyth's study. Renwell sent me there to spy on him."

Helene gasped and yanked her daughter away from me. "Who are you really?" she spat. "Are you still working for *him*?"

"No," I said quickly. "I did. For a while. I am—I *was*—Princess Emilia Torvaine. After my mother was killed, I gave up my crown to become a spy."

Helene shook her head as if she didn't believe a word I'd said. "Are you the reason Renwell attacked our house and arrested Garyth? What did you tell him about us?"

Truth, Kiera. Remember, no more lies.

Thorns seemed to grow in my throat, making it hard to breathe, to swallow. But I tried to keep my voice even. "I found some secret correspondence in Garyth's desk. I couldn't decode the letters, but I told Renwell about the People's Council symbol inked on them."

Aiden shifted next to me, but I couldn't bear to look at him. I hadn't told him any of this yet. This could extinguish what little trust we'd reignited.

Helene's eyes filled with anger. "It's your fault he died, then. You betrayed him. You betrayed his ideals. Why bother helping me and my daughter? Why not turn us in as well?"

Her words felt like knives to my stomach. I'd rather face down a border patrol—or even Korvin, if he were still lurking about—than a wife and daughter I'd caused so much grief.

"I didn't understand yet what a terrible man I was serving," I whispered. "I thought I was protecting my kingdom and my family. When I realized my mistake too late, I did the only thing I could and got you out of Aquinon."

"You could have warned us," Helene snapped. "You could've gotten *all* of us out of Aquinon."

I flinched, unable to argue with that.

"Renwell would've hunted you down and killed your entire family," Aiden said.

Helene flung her hand toward the locked door. "We're not exactly safe now, are we?"

No one answered her.

"And you. You defend her." Helene pointed a shaking finger at Aiden. "Who are you? Garyth spoke of this man in the shadows who was fighting for the same cause he was. He hoped your plans would help the People's Council rise again. But he didn't know who you were."

I tensed. Would he tell her the truth? I had shared my true name, but Aiden's carried a heavy weight as well.

He straightened, his jaw tight and his eyes fierce. "I am Aiden Falcryn, son of the late King Tristan and Queen Rhea. Nikella rescued me as a newborn and raised me in secret."

Relief passed through me as he rewrote history with his words. A new and strange reaction to a lie crumbling under the truth.

Nikella and Maz nodded their heads, approval in their eyes.

But a moment later, Helene turned accusatory once more. "You've been hiding. All this time. You are the true heir. You could've stopped all of this! You—"

"I've been trying to stop men like Weylin and Renwell for years," Aiden cut in, not without kindness. "I have failed many people many times, but I have never abandoned Rellmira."

"Rellmira has abandoned my family," Helene whispered, hugging her daughter close. Isabel burrowed her face into her mother's neck. "We have no home anywhere."

Aiden said nothing. He stared at them, but his mind seemed to be miles, or perhaps years, away.

After a long moment, I whispered, "I'm truly sorry for my part, Helene. Isabel." Then I retreated to my corner.

Aiden followed me with his bags. I sank to the ground, suddenly too exhausted to even want to change my clothes or wash the blood from my neck. Gods, all this arguing, and Korvin could still be somewhere in the manor. He could be moments away from finding us.

But not even fear could penetrate the hollow drum that stretched tight in my chest.

Aiden stripped off the sunstone armor he wore on his chest and wrists, like they were choking him. He stuffed them and his Wolf mask into his bag.

Then he yanked his shirt up over his head. My gaze couldn't help traveling over him. The sweaty muscles. The falcon tattoo. The many scars—including the new one above his hip where Father had stabbed him.

His hard green eyes caught mine staring, and I promptly looked away. He pulled on one of his usual short-sleeved black shirts, then settled next to me.

Strange. He'd heard what I said about Garyth. He should be angry as well, refusing to make any more eye contact, as Helene and Isabel were doing.

But his elbow brushed mine as he rested his arms on his knees like I did.

That small act of solidarity almost broke me. When I looked up at his tight expression, I wondered if I wasn't the only one withering inside.

Everyone else stayed quiet while we waited. And waited.

Then, someone knocked twice on the door, scratched once, and knocked three times.

"That's Caddik," Nikella said, rising with her spear in hand. "But Korvin could've forced him to reveal us." She handed a key to Jek, who also stood. "Unlock it and pull him inside."

He did as she commanded. He whipped open the door and yanked an older man into our room.

Nikella leaped out of the room, spear first. She came back a moment later. "All clear. He's alone."

"Of course I'm alone," Caddik grumbled, shoving Jek's hands off his collar. "That slimy weasel finally left after he ate my entire breakfast and drank my gods-damned tea."

His beady eyes glared around the room, taking us all in. "Now, does someone want to tell me why the king of the Shadow-Wolves was knocking on my door at dawn?"

CHAPTER 32

KIERA

BATHROOMS WERE EXCELLENT PLACES TO CRY.

I splashed water over my hands and face, washing away my tears with the sweat and dirt caked on my cheeks.

The others had followed Caddik into the kitchen for a meal while Nikella told him the story of my father and Renwell. It was a story I was tired of living.

But she would eventually come to the events of last night, which I wanted to hear.

First, I'd needed to release the tension that had been threading through my shoulders since the confrontation with Helene and Isabel.

Caddik had given me a stern look, but then told me where to find the bathroom. He gruffly added that he would find me some clothes if I didn't have any. I'd thanked him and hurried off before I fell apart.

The bathroom, unlike the exterior of the manor and the deep cellar we'd sheltered in, was cheerful and bright. Yellow wallpaper reflected light from the oil lamps. A porcelain tub sat at one end with a stone toilet and sink in the other. Thin towels were stacked by the sink. I used one to wipe my face and grimaced at the murky streaks I left on it.

If only guilt were so easy to wash away. Or pain. Or grief.

My eyes filled with tears again.

I needed some gods-damned sleep and food. That was all. I would be strong enough to fight my pain afterward. I had to be.

Someone tapped on the door I'd locked behind me.

I dashed away the fresh tears. "Just a moment!" My voice came out too bright and quavery, like a thin flame in a strong wind. I cleared my throat and tried again. "I'm almost done."

"I don't need the bathroom, Kiera."

I stilled, my heart thudding against my ribs. "Please go away, Aiden."

"If that's what you truly want."

It wasn't, and I didn't hear him leave. Slowly, I walked to the door and unlocked it. I hid the towel behind my back before I swung the door open.

Aiden leaned against the frame on the other side as if he were too weary to stand. Or perhaps he was hiding me from anyone in the hallway.

His gaze traveled over my stained face and salty eyes, reading me like a letter from a lover he missed dearly. His face softened.

"Let me look at your cut," he said.

We both knew it was shallow enough to heal in a few days, but I let him in, anyway. The bathroom felt much smaller with his tall, muscular body crowding me.

He grabbed a clean towel and wet it, then gestured for me to sit on the rim of the tub.

I obeyed and tilted my chin away to give him access to my neck.

He gently sponged away the dry blood, his black hair falling across his brow as he leaned over me.

I twisted the dirty towel in my hands. Why did he follow me? Why did I let him in?

When I couldn't bear the silence any longer, I asked, "How did Garyth really die?"

His hand wavered. Then he carefully pressed the damp towel into my cut. "I found him when we infiltrated the Den that night. Korvin had been torturing him for days."

Nausea rolled through my gut. I'd guessed as much, but hearing the details . . .

"He was in a bad way," Aiden continued, his voice soft and haunted. Like we were telling deep secrets in the dark. "He was dying, but he was relieved to see me. His words were jumbled at times, and I didn't catch everything. But he was grateful his family was safe. He admitted he told Renwell everything he knew to save his family. And he wanted to pass more quickly than Korvin was allowing him to."

I stiffened, turning my head to look at Aiden. His face was so close to mine I could count every black lash around his emerald eyes. My heart stuttered.

"He told them about you? Melaena? The People's Council?"

Aiden frowned. "He didn't specify, which is why I was so relieved when Ruru said Melaena was safe. Perhaps Renwell plans to use his information for other purposes."

Nothing good, I imagined.

"Did you . . . did you . . ." I faltered. *Did you kill Garyth the way you had to kill my mother?*

He turned away from me and went to rinse the towel in the sink. "I couldn't. Nikella did it for me."

My eyes burned again, and I stared at the smudged cloth I was strangling in my fingers.

I couldn't.

I knew why he couldn't even if he didn't say it. I remembered the way his expression had morphed into horror when I pleaded with him to let me go in the dressing room at *The Silk Dancer*. The way his knife had fallen to the floor.

He'd heard my mother in that plea, I was sure of it. Just as he'd probably heard her in Garyth's.

I remembered Davka slipping away from me, even though it wasn't my knife that stabbed her. Death always stole so much more than just life.

"Helene was right," I mumbled. "I should've warned Garyth sooner. Or Melaena. Or anyone."

In a heartbeat, Aiden was on his knees in front of me, tugging the towel out of my grip and replacing it with his hands. "Look at me, Kiera."

I lifted my gaze to his, our eyes nearly level with him kneeling.

"You did not kill him," he said softly. "Renwell and Korvin did. Garyth knew the risks. He was prying into Renwell's affairs long before Renwell sent you after him."

Tears trembled on my lashes, blurring his face. "I tried to fix it. I helped Helene and Isabel escape, but it wasn't enough. Renwell took Maz to punish me for my disobedience."

Aiden brushed his thumbs under my eyes, letting my tears slide down his skin. His expression was heartbreakingly tender. "You were defiant, Kiera, and I fucking love you for it."

The world hushed and stilled. I forgot everything else. Everything but those words. They changed me. From one beat to the next, my heart shifted, picked up a few of its broken pieces, and melded them together. It became something different. Something new and hopeful and . . . happy.

I slipped my hand around his jaw. He sighed and leaned into my palm.

Slowly, I eased closer to him. He let me come, heat flickering in his eyes. I halted a hair's breadth from his lips. His short, warm breaths pulsed against my mouth.

I fucking love you for it.

My eyes fluttered closed, and I pressed my lips against his. Softly. A shy greeting. A breathless agreement.

He kissed me back the same way, as if he didn't want to frighten me. As if there was more he could give, but wouldn't.

"Kiera," he whispered against my lips.

A knock sounded on the door. "Young lady? I have some clean clothes for you."

Aiden's brow furrowed, but he backed away from me. I wasn't sure if I was relieved or frustrated.

He opened the door.

Caddik poked his head in, checking to see if I was still in there. He cleared his throat and leveled a stern look at Aiden. "The others are looking for you in the kitchen."

Aiden shot a glance toward me, a myriad of unspoken words in it. Then he disappeared out the door.

Caddik handed me a stack of clothing. "These should fit you. Best hurry before all the breakfast is gone."

I thanked him, and he left. He'd given me a pair of hardy trousers, like the kind a worker might wear. There was also a thick, long-sleeved shirt. Someone had embroidered tiny yellow flowers growing out of the breast pockets.

I rubbed my thumb over the cheerful flowers. Did these clothes belong to his wife? Or a daughter, perhaps?

I'd have worn a sack if it got me out of this dead soldier's uniform, so I was profoundly grateful for Caddik's generosity. Even if he seemed curmudgeonly and had essentially tossed Aiden out of the bathroom.

My lips still tingled with awareness as I hastily changed clothes. So many things had happened in such a short time.

Aiden had said he loved me for my defiance. Was that all he loved me for? I wasn't completely ignorant of the feelings that still tethered us together. I knew he felt the same raw attraction I did.

But was there more?

CHAPTER 33
AIDEN

Gods damn it, why did I say that?

I ran my hands through my hair as I walked to the back of the house where the kitchen was. The hum of conversation mixed with the clanging of pots and pans.

I fucking love you for it.

I rolled the words around in my head. They were true. Too true. I hadn't meant to say that out loud.

Kiera was nervous around me. She still didn't trust me. Not completely. I wasn't even sure I completely trusted her.

But that didn't stop me from wanting her. Loving the pieces of herself she offered me. I had to fight for every piece, and I never wanted to stop fighting.

When she'd sat there looking so heartbroken and defeated, telling me of the impossible position Renwell had put her in, it'd stirred something deep inside me. Her desire to do right, her guilt in falling short, and her grief for others.

It was a deadly mix, and one I understood all too well.

But her story—our time in Aquinon—was making more and more sense. Her desperation to save Helene and Isabel. Renwell taking Maz. We'd been caught in a battle between master and apprentice.

And Renwell kept fucking winning.

I burst into the kitchen as if I'd been running.

Maz glanced up at me with a quirked eyebrow, his mouth full of shredded potatoes.

I shook my head and sat on an open spot of bench around the massive table. Jek handed me a plate. My mouth watered as I stared at the food before me.

Piles of crispy shredded potatoes. Thick cuts of bacon. A golden loaf of bread that was mostly gone. A collection of jars filled with a rainbow of jams and butters.

It wasn't grand, but it was a feast all the same. The sort of fare a worker might eat before toiling outside all day.

I filled my plate to the brim and began shoveling the food into my mouth.

None of us talked much other than to ask someone to pass some food.

The cook—a short man with an irritable scowl—barked orders at the two younger workers, a boy and a girl.

After a few minutes, the cook slammed down another loaf of bread in the middle of the table. "Gods-damned soldiers eating all my gods-damned food . . . not even a thank-you . . . such a waste . . ." He kept muttering to himself as he continued to terrorize the kitchen.

Caddik returned with a dark gray dog at his heels. Both of them sat next to Helene.

"How often do soldiers come here?" I asked him.

He snorted into the cup of tea he clutched with both hands. "Seems like every week now. Usually, it's just border patrols looking for a free meal or a roof for the night. They piss on my walls and rile up my staff."

I chewed my bacon thoughtfully. "So this was the first time Korvin knocked on your door?"

Caddik's scowl deepened. "That animal didn't knock. He just walked in like he owned *my* gods-damned house. I saw him ride up, though. Had just enough time to get everyone to the secret cellar." He nodded at Nikella. "Teacher already knew where the passage was."

"We're both quite familiar," Jek said under his breath with a twitch of his lips.

Nikella's cheeks pinked as she glared at him and kicked his boot into mine under the table.

I clenched my teeth to keep from laughing. Jek had been in love with my mentor since before I'd known him. Sometimes I was almost certain Nikella felt the same.

"He didn't even look around much," Caddik went on. He took a piece of bacon and fed it to the dog, who swallowed it whole. "His dirty soldiers raided my kitchen while he gave me some oily speech about who he was and who he was looking for. Then he drank out of my teacup and ate my food, never losing that creepy smile of his. Told me to have a good day."

Nikella dropped her fork and pushed her half-finished plate away. "He'll be back."

Caddik stared at her, idly stroking his dog's alert ears. "Oh, I'm sure he will until he finds you. And that one." He jerked his thumb at Kiera, who'd just entered the kitchen.

My heart thumped harder. She looked fresh and beautiful in her new clothes and her hair in a damp braid. The sun coming through the windows seemed to hug her, intent on making her glow.

But then Caddik's words registered.

"He's looking for her?" I demanded.

Kiera's gaze darted between us, startled.

"Fits the description he gave," Caddik said with a shrug.

I clenched my fork. Gods damn Renwell to the depths of the wandering hell. Sending his favorite hunter after two of the people he'd hurt the most.

Kiera met my eyes, uncertainty shining in hers. But I had no certainty to give.

Ruru made space between him and Nikella and waved Kiera into it.

"Should've just killed the weasel when he was here with only a few soldiers," Sigrid grumbled, tearing her bread into chunks and dipping them in the bacon grease on her plate.

Helene scooted farther away from the Dag warrior. "I don't want to be anywhere near a battle, thank you," she said icily.

Yarina eyed her with distaste. "Then you may not want to be anywhere near Calimber." She glanced between me and Maz with hard eyes. "Now tell us what you found in the mine."

Everyone around the table perked up. Even Helene seemed begrudgingly interested.

I met Maz's eyes, and he nodded for me to take the lead. Either to finish his second plate of food or because he didn't want to talk about it yet. Or both.

Swallowing my reluctance, I told them of the mine. The forge. The cavern. The prisoners. The beach. The missing ship.

Maz pitched in with details here and there. Others asked questions. When I started speaking of the prisoners, Helene sent Isabel to play with the dog and her lizard in another room.

Which was fortunate when I reached the supervisor.

"We followed my marks back out of the tunnels," I contin-ued. Maz tensed. "But a supervisor stopped us to ask for our papers. Said we weren't due for another three weeks with the next shipment of prisoners."

Maz shot me a look of relief, his shoulders dropping. There was no need to announce the reason we were stopped. The others didn't need to know about Bruna.

"What did you do?" Nikella asked, looking as though she already knew the answer.

I stared down at the empty stretch of skin on my finger. I hadn't worn my father's ring long enough to leave a mark, yet I still felt its lingering presence. It was good that I'd left it behind with Frieda.

You are not worthy to wear a king's ring, that voice from the Abyss said.

"We had no papers and couldn't speak without giving ourselves away, so I killed him," I said in a dull voice. "We made it look like a tunnel had collapsed on him."

Kiera drew in a sharp breath. "And no one saw you?"

I hesitated.

Maz sighed loudly, abandoning his last chunk of bread. "A few prisoners were there." He glanced at Sigrid. "I saw Bruna, and that's why the supervisor stopped us. She helped us hide the body."

Sigrid's eyes lit up. Then she scowled, pointing her knife at her brother. "You weren't supposed to talk to anyone, Mazkull! Fucking Four, it's not that hard! You could've—"

"She's alive, Sig," Maz said softly. "She's waiting for us to come get her."

Sigrid suddenly became very interested in the single piece of bacon left on her plate. Her heavy blond braids slid down to hide her face.

Yarina patted her on the back, then glared around the table at us. "We are getting Bruna out, right? And everyone else?"

"Aiden and Maz barely escaped last night," Nikella said. "A rescue would take a great deal of planning."

Yarina slammed her fist on the table, making Helene jump. "I say we just bury his fucking forge, along with the rest of his bloody sunstone, and take the prisoners with us when we're done!"

Sigrid nodded heavily. Jek grunted in agreement. I looked across the table to Kiera.

She was already staring at me. Her spine was straight, her eyes harder than I'd seen them. "Agreed. Can it be done?"

"Oh, sure, with a few thousand warriors and a couple of warships, we could take Calimber no problem," Maz said bitterly.

"We have a ship," I replied. "And that supervisor told us where we can get another."

Maz stared at me in disbelief. "The Shadow-Wolf prisoner ship?"

I nodded. The idea had been coming to me in bits and pieces since last night. "We use *Mynastra's Wings* to intercept the prisoner ship. Once we take it, we sail into the bay—Skelly's crew disguised as Wolves and us as prisoners—and anchor at the beach without raising suspicion. Then we infiltrate the mine, burn down the forge with the stolen fireseeds, and escape with the prisoners."

"And what of Dracles's army?" Jek asked, stroking his silver beard. "The supervisors would notice a fire and escaping prisoners and sound the alarm. Soldiers would overrun us before we made it back to the ship."

"That's why I said we *bury* them," Yarina growled. She gestured at Nikella. "You made excellent explosives for us in Aquinon. Why not for the mine?"

Nikella pursed her lips, deep in thought. "I could figure something out," she said. "But it would be dangerous. And the prisoners would have to be out of the mine before the explosions. The timing would need to be precise."

Timing was never precise in a battle. Especially one with this many moving pieces.

We would have to hide explosives around the mine and discreetly free the prisoners. Once we started escaping, the army would charge in after us. We'd need to set off the explosives without killing ourselves or the weak, confused prisoners. Skelly would have to fight the warship and any remaining soldiers to keep our escape route clear.

We could be crushed by the supervisors, the mine, Dracles and his army, or the warship.

It sounded impossible.

I rubbed my temples, exhaustion fragmenting my thoughts.

Caddik's chair screeched across the floor as he stood up. "Enough useless planning. That mine has stood for decades and won't be destroyed over breakfast. I have beds and cots for you all, unless Korvin changes his mind and burns down my house before lunch."

Kiera's eyes widened as if she didn't know whether that was a joke.

Unfortunately, I was sure it wasn't. We needed to rest while we could, but we had to keep moving before long.

In what direction, for what purpose, only the Four knew. But I wouldn't give up my plans. There was always a way.

Helene stood from the table first, reminding me of something.

"A moment in the cellar, Helene," I said, standing as well.

She eyed me with distrust and a little fear, but she nodded.

I opened the door in the kitchen that led down a set of stairs to the first cellar. Unlike the secret one, the room was full of fruits and vegetables, drying from the rafters or peeking out of barrels. Casks of wine layered the shelves next to sacks of flour and rice.

I pushed one of the shelves aside and pulled up the burlap cloth that hung over the metal door. It was well-hidden, yet Korvin hadn't even bothered searching the whole house. Instead, he'd sipped tea and eaten breakfast.

Shaking off my sense of foreboding, I opened the door and followed Helene into the secret cellar.

"Well, what did you need to say to me in this ghastly hole?" Helene demanded. She folded her arms tightly around her chest, the sickly lamplight aging her by a dozen years.

I grabbed Garyth's letters out of my bag. I'd found them after we left Yargoth. Ruru, or someone else, must've stashed them there. "I believe these were your husband's."

Helene gasped and gently took them out of my hands. "But . . . Melaena?"

"She's fine, the last I heard. She didn't want to get caught with them, so she sent them with Ruru."

Helene shuffled through the papers, an oddly fond smile lifting her lips. "This was one of his greatest achievements. He worked so hard to gather this group of people—men and women who would answer the call when the People's Council could rise again."

"His work was not in vain," I said softly. "Those names will be invaluable to the next king or queen of Rellmira. I will make sure of it."

She looked at me with sad eyes. "I was wrong to think you do nothing for your kingdom. But couldn't you accomplish more if you told our people the truth?" She waved the letters. "If you made allies of those who would support you, rather than scheming in the shadows?"

"There aren't many who would want to risk allying with me. The risk of death is too high."

"We are dying anyway," Helene whispered. "I want my daughter to grow up in the Rellmira that Garyth remembered, that he envisioned for the future. I would ally with anyone who provided that for my family."

Her words struck a chord deep inside my soul. It sang of

hope. Of a world where, one day, I wouldn't have to fight anymore. I wouldn't have to hide who I was.

But king?

"I am not worthy to sit on the throne," I said. "But I will fight for the Rellmira we both want until my last breath."

Helene sighed, clutching her husband's coded letters to her chest. "Then I pray the Four will keep your last breath for many years to come."

Hours later, after a quick bath and some much-needed sleep, I couldn't shake Helene's words from my mind.

The People's Council. The prisoners. Rellmira.

I had so much to fight for. So many hopes placed on my shoulders. This was why it was easier to stay hidden, so that if I failed, I wouldn't crush everyone else's hope as well.

Restless and irritable, I stole away to the one place I might find peace—Kiera's bedroom.

CHAPTER 34
AIDEN

Kiera had disappeared into a cozy yellow room before I'd found a bed in the same room as Maz.

I stalked through the manor, staying away from the windows, as Caddik instructed. He'd gone out with his workers to take care of the horses, cows, chickens, and whatever other animals roamed his land.

The sun was setting, and I seemed to be the only one awake in the house. I carefully opened the bedroom door and shut it behind me without a sound.

The fluffy curtains were drawn. Kiera was nothing but a lump under a pile of embroidered blankets in the four-poster bed.

Smiling, I eased onto the bed next to her. The wooden frame creaked under my weight.

She cried out and flipped over, aiming a knife straight for my chest.

I caught her wrist. "It's me, Kiera! You're safe. It's just me."

Her eyes focused on mine, and her arm went limp. I guided her knife hand to lie between us.

"Sorry," she mumbled. She rubbed her eyes. A pillow crease dented her cheek just below her new scar. Rage flickered in my veins at the thought of Renwell leaning over her to cut into her skin.

"Although," she continued in the same husky voice that made me forget all about my rage, "if you're here to drag me out of the first bed I've slept in since Yargoth, perhaps I should've stabbed you."

I grinned. "I wouldn't dream of it."

"Then why are you here?"

I leaned back on the pillow to stare at the ceiling. Swathes of yellow silk draped over the exposed beams.

"I couldn't sleep anymore," I admitted. "I didn't mean to wake you. I simply wanted the company."

"Maz isn't good company when he's snoring?" she teased.

"Not unless I'm tossing him into an icy river."

She chuckled.

For one bright, ludicrous moment, I imagined it was sunrise instead of sunset. That Kiera and I had just woken up together in our bedroom after a heated night in each other's arms. Teasing, laughing, content to stay in our warm seclusion.

That life blinked out in my mind. Replaced by Korvin and Renwell hunting us, an army devouring us, a mine collapsing on us, and ships destroying us.

I meant what I said to Helene, that I would keep fighting for a better Rellmira until my last breath.

But there were also moments like this where I wished for a quiet life. One of love and laughter.

It wasn't meant to be. I wasn't even sure that was the life Kiera wanted. Even if Kiera was the only one I'd ever envisioned that life with.

"We'll find a way," she whispered.

I turned my head to find her watching me. My heart leaped,

then sank when she added, "We'll destroy the mine and free the prisoners. It's what my mother would have wanted."

"Yes, we will," I promised.

Her eyes flicked to my mouth. I remembered our tentative kiss in the bathroom. Triumph had exploded in my chest when she'd closed the distance between us.

I wanted to give her so much more than one kiss. But if that was all she wanted from me, I would get back down on my knees and give her the best one I could.

Her stomach growled, easing the tense moment. She smiled and slid away from me. "Do you think Caddik will have some food around?"

I rose from the bed, trying not to show my disappointment. "Sun's almost down. I imagine dinner will be soon."

"Excellent, I'm already starving again," she said, sheathing her knife and pulling on her boots.

We headed back to the kitchen. The scent of roasting meat and vegetables reached us first.

Kiera groaned with excitement and hurried ahead of me, but then hesitated at the threshold.

I was surprised to see Helene and Caddik already seated at the table. Isabel sat with the dog on the stone floor near the hearth.

Caddik looked up at us, his dirty fingers clutching another cup of tea. "I thought the smell of food might wake you. My staff has already eaten, so it's your turn."

I nodded. "Thank you. No sign of Korvin or soldiers?"

He shook his head. "You've got a couple of real nice horses, though. Any chance you'd be willing to sell?"

"Not even a small one," I said with a smile.

Kiera and I took our seats at the table. Tense silence simmered as the cooks scurried about the kitchen. Helene's eyes looked red, and Caddik seemed lost in thought.

Kiera drummed her fingertips on the table for a few moments before she shot off the bench and joined Isabel at the sooty hearth.

"What's his name?" she asked the girl, holding out her hand for the dog to sniff. Which he did, thumping his tail in approval.

Isabel darted a look at her mother. "Pax. Caddik says he's part wolf because of his long legs and yellow eyes."

Kiera smiled. "He's the nicest wolf I've ever seen."

Isabel's eyes rounded. "Have you seen other wolves?"

They kept talking in low tones, both gradually relaxing. But the crease never left Helene's forehead.

Ruru stumbled into the kitchen, his hair sticking out in every direction. He collapsed onto the bench next to me.

"Sleep well?" I asked.

He nodded and stretched, his back bones popping. His bruises from the soldiers looked worse than ever, but he didn't complain.

Instead, he fixed me with his serious brown eyes. "I wanted to ask this morning . . . when you found Bruna, did you see a man a few years older than me? Looks like me, but with a birthmark just here?" He tapped his neck by his throat.

"No, Ruru," I said softly. "I didn't look too closely at the prisoners. But it's been years since Daire went missing. You don't even know if the Wolves took him to the mine."

Ruru set his jaw stubbornly. "The mine is where they take most of the strong, healthy prisoners, right? He could be there."

I swallowed back the words I didn't want to say. That I'd barely survived two years there. Most didn't survive one. Daire had been missing for three.

I clasped his shoulder. "If he's there, we'll find him."

Ruru nodded, my simple promise good enough for him.

The others wandered in one by one, Maz last of all. He thumped my back as he sat on my other side.

"Gods, it felt good to sleep in a bed. Eh, Nikella?" he said, yawning like a bear coming out of hibernation.

Nikella had taken a seat across from us and immediately pulled out scraps of paper that she was poring over. When he said her name, she looked up, gray shadows under her eyes.

"Couldn't sleep, so I worked," she said, her voice dazed.

I frowned. Was she worried about Korvin? Or was it something else?

Yarina peered over Nikella's shoulder. "How can you read any of that? What's that a drawing of?" She poked one of the sketches, smudging it.

Nikella whisked it away from her. "Ideas I had. For collapsing the mine." She looked at me, a grim certainty in her eyes. "But we need to go to Twaryn for the materials."

I grimaced. "It will take at least a week of hard riding to get to Twaryn, assuming we don't run into any patrols. Or Korvin. The Shadow-Wolf ship is due to arrive in three."

"Soldiers also created checkpoints along the river you'll need to avoid as well," Caddik added. "They make it bloody difficult to drive my livestock across for the markets. I wondered what they needed so much wood for. Warships," he grumbled, draining the rest of his tea.

Nikella scribbled something else in her notes, her charcoal pencil worn almost to a nub.

Jek reached into his pocket and pulled out a fresh one. He handed it to her. "Here you go, love. Sharpened it this afternoon."

She took it with a murmur of thanks and kept drawing.

Caddik seemed unsurprised by the interaction, like most of us, but Helene raised her eyebrows. She was probably used to the Teachers in Aquinon who kept to a strict code of behavior.

The cook—who seemed to be in a much more pleasant mood—placed a jug of water and a stack of cups on the table.

His young assistant added a few bottles of wine. Smiling, Kiera and Isabel joined us. Nikella kept working while the rest of us poured our drinks.

Suddenly, she whipped around to Caddik. "How big are the log floats? How many workers?"

He blinked and rubbed his dirty hand over his balding head. "Ah, the logs are three times a man's height, perhaps ten at a time lashed into a raft. One or two guards and four or five poor sods who look like prisoners. Shackles and whatnot, probably to keep them from jumping into the river."

I scowled. Of course, they would use more prisoners to raft their timber.

"Wait," I told Nikella. "You aren't suggesting . . ."

She nodded. "I'll need some way to smuggle in the explosives once I've created them. I can hollow out a log, like I did for my spear, and hide them inside. Then we just float them to the mine."

"But we'd have to overtake a raft—"

"And what of Skelly?" Sigrid interrupted. "Who's alerting him to the plan?"

"We'll have to split up," Kiera said quietly.

Silence fell over the table. No one liked that idea, judging by their various grimaces. But Twaryn was in the opposite direction from Yargoth and *Mynastra's Wings*.

"We should split up anyway," Nikella said, putting down her pencil. "Make it harder for Korvin to find us."

Yarina scowled. "And make either party easier prey. I don't like it."

Jek shook his head. "Me either. We're stronger together."

"I go where Kiera and Aiden go," Ruru announced, folding his arms over his chest.

We continued to argue as the cooks laid dishes of seared beef, fried peppers and onions, and potato bread in front of us.

Eating slowed the conversation. We still hadn't reached an agreement by the end.

Idea after idea was thrown out. Hunting down Korvin ourselves. Sending one messenger to Skelly. And on and on.

Gods, it was much easier to make plans when I was working mostly alone. Had my father dealt with situations like this as king? Forever arguing with his High Council or settling disputes in the People's Council. It was strange to imagine that I might have grown up learning how to handle those situations.

What would he think of me now?

I shook the thought loose. I'd never known my father. I'd never been a prince. I would not be king.

Making risky plans while on the run in a stranger's kitchen with a mixed group of rebels? That I could do.

Eventually, the cooks lit the lamps and candles and left the clean kitchen. Helene took Isabel to bed, and Caddik excused himself with Pax to check on the animals.

Nikella leaned back in her seat, rubbing her eyes. "We can't stay with Caddik much longer. We're putting him at risk."

"Agreed," I said.

"You should get some rest first, Nikella," Jek said gently.

"No." She bowed over her papers. "First, we need to—"

Caddik burst in through the back door, breathing heavily. "He's back. Korvin came back."

CHAPTER 35
KIERA

We stared at the old man in shock.

"Korvin is here!" Caddik bellowed. "With his Wolves this time! Go!"

Everyone leaped away from the table, drawing weapons as they went.

"How many?" barked Jek, wielding his huge sword.

"A dozen, maybe more," Caddik raced to the western window, Pax at his heels. "Gods damn it! They've set fire to the stables!"

Shouts and the thunder of hooves rose from outside.

"You three with me," Jek ordered Maz, Sigrid, and Yarina. "We need to save the horses."

Nikella stuffed her sketches into her pocket. I swore I saw her fingers trembling. I swept my own fingers over my knife brace, checking that they were still there. Ruru pulled out the short sword the Dags had given him.

"We'll bar the front door, slow them down," Aiden said.

Pax barked, reminding me of Isabel.

"I'll get Helene and Isabel," I said, already running out of the kitchen, "and put them in the cellar!"

I didn't stay to watch the others leave. There were no good-byes, no shouts of encouragement.

No time. No time.

I sprinted through the house. A window exploded to my left, and a torch fell inside. The curtains and carpet burst into flames. I shouted, "Fire!" and kept running. More windows exploded.

I bounded up the stairs. Crashes echoed, and I hoped to all the Four that Aiden was blockading the entrance.

Helene was already peeking out of her door when I skidded to a stop in front of it.

"Korvin," I panted. "Cellar. Now."

Her face blanched. She spun around and dragged Isabel out of bed. The girl woke instantly, brushing her red curls out of her wide eyes. "Where are we going? Are we hiding? Where's Captain?"

I snatched the lizard's box from a small table in their room just as their window shattered and another torch sailed through.

Helene and Isabel screamed.

Cursing Korvin and his Wolves to the depths of the wandering hell, I shoved Helene and Isabel out the door with Captain under my arm. We scurried down the stairs, smoke hanging like a gray cloud in the foyer.

Aiden, Nikella, Ruru, and Caddik piled chests and tables in front of the door while something slammed into it over and over.

The windows on the main floor were too narrow for a body, but that blockade wouldn't impede them for long. Especially with the whole house aflame.

For a moment, I thought of Mother. How she'd died, trapped. Someone tearing their way inside.

Fear clutched my chest, and I nearly missed the last stair.

Aiden grabbed my arm, his sword in his other hand. "Get

them out and hide in the woods. Grab what gear you can, but don't let anything slow you down. We'll hold them off until you're clear."

"But—"

He pressed his forehead to mine. "I'll meet you in the woods. I swear it."

Eyes burning, I crushed my lips against his, sealing that promise between us. Then I tore after Helene and Isabel without looking back.

Flames licked into the hallway, and we had to jump over burning bits of rug.

If Aiden and the others didn't follow soon, they wouldn't be able to.

We hurtled into the kitchen. The door burst open, and a Shadow-Wolf lunged inside with a sunstone sword. How had he made it past the Dags?

Helene shrieked and curled her body around Isabel's.

The Wolf's attention jerked from me to Helene. He darted toward her, sword raised.

"*No!*" I dropped Captain's box and charged into the Wolf with all my strength, gripping a knife. As we crashed into the hearth, I stabbed his sword hand.

He grunted and threw me off, still holding his gods-damned sword. I crashed onto the stone floor, gasping for air.

"Pax, attack!" someone shouted.

A streak of gray fur and gleaming teeth barreled into the Wolf. Isabel screamed as the two tousled, growls filling the air.

Pax locked his jaws around the Wolf's fist. The Wolf reached for a knife in his boot.

I flipped over and sank my blade into his neck. Just below his mask. He immediately went limp.

Pax backed away, still growling, and stood protectively in front of Helene and Isabel.

Aiden burst into the kitchen and heaved me to my feet, his expression furious. "There will be more. Go!"

Ruru helped me herd a sobbing Helene and Isabel, who snatched up her lizard's box. Nikella paced in front of the back door with her spear.

"Go with them, Caddik," Aiden ordered, guarding the burning hallway.

The old man shook his head stubbornly. "I'm dying where my wife died, whether that's tonight or in twenty years."

"Caddik! Please!" Helene called as I tried to shove her down the cellar stairs.

His face softened, but his eyes were resolute. He glanced at me lingering on the threshold. "Take Pax with you. Isabel knows his commands." He murmured something to the dog, who trotted past me to Isabel.

The girl clutched his fur, tears still streaming down her cheeks.

Another Wolf crashed into the kitchen. Nikella raised her spear just as Caddik slammed the door shut between us.

Fear bled out of every pore, but I pushed Helene and Isabel toward the secret cellar. Ruru had already heaved the shelf aside and opened it.

We hurried inside. I skipped the bedrolls and mostly empty saddlebags. Instead, I gathered up the extra weapons, strapping my sword to my waist and slinging bows and arrow pouches across my back. Ruru did the same. I also tucked the two long sunstone knives Aiden and Maz had worn into my belt.

One never knew when those would come in handy.

I handed Helene an ordinary steel knife in a sheath. "Belt it around your waist."

She did as I commanded, fumbling with the buckle. "Where are we supposed to go?" Her voice shook so badly I almost couldn't understand. "We have no friends left. No allies who could help us."

"The Dags will take you to Yargoth," I said firmly, entirely uncertain if that was true.

We had no plan. We weren't ready.

"To Dagriel? That will take days." Helene swayed.

Ruru smiled brightly. "It's an easy trip, and you'll love the mountains. Lots of animals there," he said with a wink at Isabel.

Helene stared at him as if he had two heads.

I slung Nikella's medicine bag over my shoulder. "It's death here or a short trip to Dagriel, Helene. Your choice."

The woman stiffened, a defiant gleam emerging in her eyes. She clutched at her chest, which crinkled strangely like paper under the bodice of her dress. "Very well. Lead the way."

I marched into the tunnel. Pax darted ahead of me, and the others followed close behind.

The sudden hush and darkness of the tunnel jarred me. But for the first time, I wished we could stay in it longer. Nothing good awaited us outside.

A wet nose nuzzled my palm. I clenched my teeth to keep from yelping. Pax must have decided the way ahead was clear.

Sweat tickled my skin as I trudged the last few steps, bumping into the ladder.

"Ruru," I whispered. I was carrying too much extra weight.

He slid past me and climbed up to push the trapdoor open. "All clear," he whispered back.

He heaved himself out. I handed him half of the weapons, then clambered into the dark forest.

No one jumped at me from the shadows, but that didn't mean they weren't watching.

Flames engulfed the manor and the surrounding buildings. Horses shrieked and galloped around fleeing and fighting figures.

Had Aiden and Nikella left through the back door?

I couldn't see their faces, but if there was still a fight, our people must still be alive.

Ruru reached into the hole and pulled out Isabel, who was still carrying the death-defying lizard, then Helene.

"How do we get Pax out?" he muttered.

Isabel leaned into the hole. "Pax, climb!"

A skitter of paws, and Pax vaulted out of the hole as if he'd run up the ladder.

I clutched my bow, peering into the melee in the yard. I hadn't practiced much with the bow, and I wanted to help, but I might hit the wrong person.

And *where* were Aiden and Nikella?

A shout rose, and my heart leaped in my chest. Maz. He lifted his bloody axe above his head and roared into the night.

They'd won. I counted three golden-haired Dags and the silver-haired Jek. They rounded up some of the panicked horses and urged them into the woods toward us.

"Help them with the horses," I told Ruru. "And give them these." I shucked off a few of the extra weapons I carried. They would have to sort them out later.

Ruru gripped my hand fiercely. "I'll be right back."

The yard was empty of everything but burning buildings and bodies. But the Wolves and their master were still on the hunt. Crashes and howls poured from the shattered windows of the glowing manor.

"We need to leave," Helene whispered. "They'll start searching the woods when they realize we're not inside."

"I know," I growled.

I paced around the hole in the ground. *Come on, Aiden, hurry.*

The Dags and Ruru rode up on their horses without saddles or bridles. Those were likely ash in the stables.

Maz swung down next to me. "Aiden? Nikella? Caddik?"

"Still inside. Take these." I handed him the last of the extra weapons for his sisters and approached Jek with his bow. "Will you take Helene and Isabel to Yargoth and pass our message along to Skelly? Tell him of the Wolf ship. To be at the mine in three weeks. We'll take care of the rest."

The warrior looked down at me with a solemn expression, studying me for a long moment we could barely afford. I knew he was weighing every cost and risk. But it was the only way.

"Very well," he said, taking his bow and a pouch of arrows. "You'd best be there, or we'll be slaughtered."

I grimaced. "Same goes for you. May the Four go with you."

He dipped his head. "Tell Nikella . . . Tell her I still feel how I felt on Arduen's Night seven years ago. She'll know what I mean."

I nodded, then helped Isabel onto Yarina's horse. Helene rode with Sigrid. No one seemed happy about the arrangement, but there weren't enough horses to go around.

"We should be sticking together," Yarina hissed.

"We don't have time for any more arguments," Maz growled. "I'll see you in three weeks, little sister. Rally our people. *Protect.*"

Yarina and Sigrid muttered the word back to Maz before they turned and rode after Jek into the dark. Pax ran nimbly alongside the horses. The last I saw of them was the glint of Yarina's scythes and the pink flap of Helene's skirts.

A moment later, the manor's back door flew open. I stepped forward hopefully. But then Shadow-Wolves poured out. My heart sank.

No . . . no . . .

Suddenly, Aiden rose from the ground, sweating and panting.

Maz yanked him upright. "Fucking Four, brother, I was about to come get you."

Nikella heaved herself out of the tunnel. "Where are the others?"

"NIKELLA!" a roar came from the manor. "Where are you and that little bitch princess hiding?"

My heart throbbed and my ears rang as Korvin dragged a bloody body out of the manor. His Wolves stood guard around him, facing the woods.

Korvin's face was twisted with fury. His black hair hung in wet strings, brushing the shoulders of his glittering sunstone armor.

Nikella drew in an uneven breath. "Caddik."

I reeled backward. "Why didn't you get him out?"

"He refused. Locked us inside the cellar." Aiden came to stand beside me. "The Wolves followed. We had to collapse the tunnel."

"Nikella!" Korvin shouted, holding Caddik up by his neck like a limp doll. "You know what happens when you fucking hide from me!"

Maz lifted his whistler, feeding a red-feathered dart into it. "I'm going to kill that sick bastard."

Nikella put a hand on his bow, lowering it. "No. Caddik made his choice. Honor his sacrifice by not giving us away."

Korvin threw Caddik's body to the ground. "Search the forest! The little rats got out through a tunnel! Find them!"

As one, we turned and raced for our horses. Ozlow was still alive, thank the gods. As were the others' horses.

I mounted awkwardly with no stirrups and slid sideways, but Ozlow shifted, catching me.

Thank you, Oz.

"The others?" Nikella demanded.

"Headed to Yargoth," I replied. "We're riding to Twaryn."

Aiden gave me a sharp look, but said nothing.

We tore off west, leaving destruction in our wake. And death on our trail.

CHAPTER 36
KIERA

WE RODE THROUGH THE NIGHT, CONSTANTLY LOOKING OVER OUR shoulders.

Dawn came, cold and distant. Hunger and exhaustion rattled through my body. But every time I closed my eyes, I saw Korvin's livid face and heard his dark threats.

He would never stop hunting us. A certainty that Renwell was no doubt depending on.

My lip curled. *Bastard.*

"We'll stop in Norford," Nikella announced as we continued west. "They will have food and supplies for the rest of our journey."

"I haven't got any coins," Maz grunted, stroking his beard, "and they won't like the looks of me."

Nikella cast him a weary look. "Unravel your braids and cover your tattoos. No one will notice you. The town is mostly working folk. We'll trade work for money or the supplies we need."

Maz grumbled curses, but did as she told him.

"We'll hide our more noticeable weapons outside of town,"

she added, glancing between Maz's axes and whistler and the sunstone daggers glittering in my belt.

I nodded, shifting on Ozlow's back to wake up my numb legs. Riding a horse without a saddle was torture. I had to knot my fingers in Ozlow's mane to keep from falling. Ruru had already slipped off his horse once.

Aiden rode like he didn't notice or care that he had no saddle. He hadn't said a word since we fled Caddik's manor.

But I knew Aiden. He was likely steeped in guilt. Another ally gone because of us. Another person he couldn't save.

We couldn't keep doing this. I had a plan. I just hoped he wouldn't fight me too hard on it.

We came to a fork in the road and stashed most of our weapons in the woods under a pile of dead leaves and twigs. Then we turned south toward Norford.

The small town lay nestled in a deep valley. Smoke curled from stone chimneys. Herds of people and animals plodded along the few dirt roads that intersected through the town. The cold morning breeze carried strong notes of dirty animals.

"Smells like shit," Ruru muttered, struggling to keep his eyes open.

Maz snorted. "Welcome to Winspere. I've only been in this province twice, and this is how it always smelled."

I didn't care how it smelled. I just wanted to get our supplies and get out. Gods only knew how far behind Korvin was.

"Where can we get work?" Ruru asked, looking a little more alert.

Nikella pulled up her long hood, signifying her Teacher status. Her spear was already hidden in its wooden staff. "Question the drivers or the stable owners. They always need more manual labor. I'll stop at the courier station and see if they need me to write any correspondence."

I could help with that, too, but that might look odd to be with a Teacher when I wasn't one myself. Teachers normally traveled alone.

"Do they have a tavern here?" I asked.

Aiden cut a glance at me.

Nikella nodded. "*Beards & Barley* on the north side of town." Her gaze flicked down to where I grasped the hilt of one of my small knives. "Be on your guard. Herd drivers make little coin, and they don't like to lose it. Especially the men."

"Do they ever?"

"I'll go with you," Aiden said.

I frowned. "For my protection?"

"For the Death and Four. There's bound to be a few games I can win."

Maz smirked. "And you two will get to cozy up in a tavern while poor Ruru and I do the back-breaking work."

I offered him one of my knives. "By all means, Mazkull. But have you ever beaten me at throwing?"

"No." He grinned. "I was thinking of using my other talents on a lonely barmaid or two. Get some food and a nice bed out of it."

I rolled my eyes. "Kind of defeats the idea of hiding that you're a Dag."

He shrugged. "I'll leave my shirt on, as disappointed as she would be. I haven't gotten that tattoo on my ass yet," he added with a wink.

I laughed. It sounded strange after such a horrific night, like a note of melody in a cacophony of screams.

Aiden quirked an eyebrow. "What's this now? An ass tattoo?"

"Just a wager between friends," Maz said.

"Enough." Nikella pointed to a signpost that announced the ways to the Medria River, Twaryn, and Calimber. "Meet here at midday. Then we'll go back for our weapons and sleep elsewhere."

We split in three different directions when we entered Norford. I peered after Nikella as she headed for a squat stone building with saddled horses out front and a quill-shaped sign above the door. Hopefully, I would have a letter to send soon.

Beards & Barley was easy to find. It was the largest building on the street with a painting of a large, bearded man drinking beer on the front.

Aiden and I tied up our horses and ducked inside. The thick smell of smoke and body odor made me cough.

Gods, how can anyone sit in here without convulsing?

But no one else seemed to mind. They *did* seem to mind two strangers walking into their tavern. Everyone stopped smoking, drinking, and talking just to stare at us like we'd come in brandishing our swords.

Most of them didn't seem heavily armed. Some didn't even look like they could stand up if it came to a fight. A few women were scattered here and there around the tables, so at least I wasn't the only one.

My muscles loosened a bit when I saw a target near the wide hearth. A few knives stuck out of it, but no one was playing.

"Norford must not get a lot of travelers from outside Winspere," I muttered out of the corner of my mouth as we claimed a small table in the back.

Aiden's gaze wandered around the crowd behind me. "They've probably had their fair share of soldiers. They drive their livelihoods through these lands. They don't want any troublesome newcomers risking that."

His suspicion was confirmed a moment later when the barkeep stalked over. He folded his arms over his burly chest and glared down at us over a thick beard. "You with a drive?"

"No," Aiden said with a smooth smile. He laid his hand over mine on the sticky table. "My wife and I came this way from The Hollow to visit her great-uncle Caddik."

His wife?

I gaped at Aiden, then quickly shut my mouth when his smile sharpened. It was a risky lie, but hopefully we'd be long gone before they heard about Caddik. As for being convincing . . .

I smiled up at the barkeep. "Yes, Uncle Caddik never leaves his manor, as you must know. But we wanted to visit as my mother worries for him."

The barkeep scowled at me. "Ole Caddik never mentioned a niece."

I shrugged, trying to ignore the way Aiden was stroking my hand with his thumb. "Does that surprise you? My mother always said you couldn't get two words out of the man unless it was about his animals."

The barkeep grunted, letting his arms fall to his sides. "Suppose you're right. Well, tell him to get his scruffy neck down here for a pint sometime. Gretchen wouldn't have wanted him to waste away out there."

My throat tightened, but I forced out a laugh. "I'll be sure to tell him."

"Food? Drink?" he asked.

Aiden laid two coppers on the table, never letting go of my hand. "Whatever this will get us. We've had a long journey."

The barkeep swept the coins into his apron pocket. "It'll get you enough."

He left, and I yanked my hand out from under Aiden's. My cheeks felt warm.

"Wife?" I demanded in a low tone.

Aiden leaned back in his chair, his expression guarded. "A married couple is much less suspicious than a man and woman who look like they've been hunted through the night." The corner of his mouth turned up. "Now he'll just assume we look tired for other reasons."

Heat crawled from my cheeks down my neck. I avoided meeting his intense gaze by peering around the hazy room. Most people had gone back to their business. But that didn't mean it would stay that way. We needed to hustle a few coins and get out of here.

"Gretchen was his wife's name," I whispered, rubbing my fingers over the yellow flowers stitched to my shirt.

When Aiden didn't say anything, I willed myself to look back at him. He was watching me with an indecipherable expression on his face. The dark stubble under his sharp cheekbones and curved jaw made him look wild and dangerous.

Which he was. But that was just one side of him.

"Nikella knew her," he said. "She died a few years back."

"I'm dying where my wife died, whether that's tonight or in twenty years."

"He must have really loved her," I said softly.

"A man in love is a dangerous thing."

Flutters erupted in my belly as if his deep voice had murmured the words straight into my soul.

I licked my suddenly dry lips. His gaze dropped to my mouth, his eyebrows pulling together. His jaw flexed like he was in pain.

"Two beers and some oatmeal," the barkeep announced, jolting me out of my daze. He thumped down two mugs and bowls.

I drained half my beer, grateful for the excuse to avert my eyes. It wasn't the best beer I'd ever had, but after a night of riding, it sank into my sore muscles like a hot bath. Holy Four, a hot bath would feel miraculous.

An image of me and Aiden soaking in the same steamy tub filled my mind, making me choke on my bland oatmeal. I gulped more beer.

Aiden smiled—a dark, secretive thing that seeped into me far deeper than the beer had.

"Everything all right?" he asked, sipping from his mug.

"You said a man in love is a dangerous thing."

His gaze sharpened. He leaned forward. "Yes?"

I took a deep breath and immediately regretted it when I inhaled more of the tavern's pungent smell. "I want to send a message to Henry."

CHAPTER 37

AIDEN

Henry. A message.

For a moment, my mind didn't grasp her words. Then I felt like a fool. Why had I thought she was going to say something about me? Us?

There was no us. Only in the lie I told.

I sat back in my chair. "I said no in Yargoth. I'm saying no now."

Her eyebrows pinched together as if I'd hurt her. I looked away.

"We barely made it out of . . ." She glanced around furtively and lowered her voice. "Of Calimber. We can't do this alone."

"We're not doing it alone. Isn't that why you sent off Jek, Yarina, and Sigrid? To join Skelly and complete their half of the plan?"

Her eyes grew wary. "Yes. But that plan only works if our timing, disguises, and explosives are perfect. Having more allies would be a wise precaution."

I shoveled some oatmeal into my mouth. Bland mush, more

like, but my body needed it. Especially if we couldn't pick up more supplies.

"Even if we could get him a message, and *if* he were willing to help us, too much time will have passed for him to march an army to Calimber." I glared at my soupy oatmeal. "Besides, I want to avoid an all-out war. I've seen Dracles cut down enough people to last a lifetime."

"Then how do you plan to get to Renwell?" she snapped, her eyes like fire and honey. "You think he'll just step down from the throne without a fight? Infiltrating the mine is hard enough. The palace would be impossible. Even I can admit that my earlier plan of sneaking in to rescue my brother and sister was foolish, with little chance of success." She gripped the edges of the table, as if she wanted to throw it. "Everett, Delysia, Melaena, and thousands of other people in Aquinon are essentially Renwell's hostages. Are we going to abandon them after all this?"

Sparks snapped beneath my skin. My blood had been simmering all night, but Kiera always ignited it further.

"We aren't abandoning anyone," I growled, practically nose-to-nose with her over the remains of our breakfast. "I just haven't planned that far ahead since I might be buried beneath a cliff before Arduen's Night."

Her cheeks paled, but she held her ground. "If that happens . . . If we both die in the mine, we need someone to carry on after us. Someone with allies who would risk death for their families and loved ones. Who would save Aquinon."

I swallowed hard, my gaze skimming over the scar on her cheek. "You truly think Henry would do that?"

The fire in Kiera's eyes turned silver. "I once thought that betrayal was the blade that cuts the deepest. But now I think it's love. Love will make a man face down his worst enemy simply to die in the same place as his wife. Love will defy birth, status, rules, sides, beliefs . . . even death," she whispered. "Love is the strongest weapon of all."

It will also drive a man to the brink of the Abyss and pull him back again. It will make him set aside those betrayals and lies for a truth that cuts too deep to survive.

It will make him want to sacrifice an entire kingdom for one woman.

You.

I slowly pulled away from her, my thoughts in ashes. "You're so gods-damned beautiful when you win."

She blinked, her lips parting. Fucking Four, how I wanted to swoop in and steal them.

"Did I?" she asked. "Win?"

I drained the last of my beer. "Tell him to meet us in Twaryn, wherever the logging camp is. He shouldn't look suspicious there if he gets caught."

Kiera nodded, her eyes distant, as if she were writing the letter in her mind. "I'll add a few words that allude to Delysia so he knows we're on her side. If he's as in love with her as I think, he'll come."

How easily she believed this soldier's feelings.

"We don't have long until midday," I said. "Let's win some coins and send your letter."

Two hours later, we had a pouch full of silver and copper coins. The patrons had surprisingly enjoyed competing with Kiera and her knives. Many congratulated me on such a fine wife. I smiled and enjoyed the role I played. Perhaps a bit too much.

I played a few matches of Death and Four and won easily. My most difficult opponent had been the one everyone in here was calling my wife.

I also asked a few discreet questions about the river checkpoints and the patrols who guarded them. Most of the drivers were only too willing to complain about the recent searches and rough treatment that made their jobs harder.

We left *Beards & Barley* with flushed smiles and led our horses to the courier's office. We found Nikella still there, a line of drivers waiting for her to pen or read a letter to them.

Nikella didn't acknowledge us as Kiera quickly wrote a letter with the quill and paper the officer gave her.

It reminded me of the days when it'd been just me and Nikella wandering the world. Occasionally, she'd have to pretend I wasn't her ward, to stave off the inevitable questions.

At first, it'd bothered me. She'd made it clear since I was a child that she wasn't my mother and never would be, but I cared for her like a son might.

Eventually, I realized her protection and guidance were her way of loving me, even if she never said the words aloud.

Sometimes I wondered if she was as scared to love as I was, given how cut off from it we'd been.

Kiera finished her letter and spoke quietly to the courier, likely telling him where to send it. She passed him a few more coppers than necessary. Probably for discretion. The young man nodded and took the letter and the coins.

We headed for the signpost, under which a very dirty and tired-looking Maz and Ruru waited for us. Their horses both wore faded bridles and saddles, with a few more clumped at their feet.

"No coins," Maz said wearily, all lightness scrubbed from his tone. "Fed nearly a hundred livestock in exchange for gear."

"Pretty sure I've swam in shit by now," Ruru said glumly.

I tossed him a silver. "You and Maz go get yourself some food and drink at the tavern while we wait for Nikella. Are those for us?" I pointed at the extra saddles.

Maz nodded. "Two saddles, one bridle. We'll have to buy the rest."

We split off again. I bartered a fair price for another saddle and two more bridles while Kiera bought some food, a few water canteens and bedrolls, and bags to put everything in.

The journey would be lean, but we'd have to make do. Lingering any longer would put us behind schedule. Or allow Korvin to catch up. Foreboding clouded my thoughts.

Would he track us? Or the Dagriel group? I was surprised we hadn't seen any sign of him all night. Surely he hadn't given up. I hated an unpredictable enemy. He'd already sneaked up on me once. It couldn't happen again.

The sun had slid west by the time we all met back under the signpost. Then we were off again. After we retrieved our weapons, I led us through the woods, riding toward the dying sun as I searched for a safe place to rest.

Eventually, I spotted a shallow cave, and we bedded down for a few hours, taking watches.

Then we continued to ride. And ride. Day and night. Stopping only to water and feed the horses, catch a few winks, and allow Kiera and Ruru to train with Nikella. Maz and I dueled off to the side like we were back at Yargoth.

To break the monotony of the ride, we discussed our plans for Calimber. What followed was essentially a four-day argument over each person's role in our mission.

Kiera was right when she said the plan had to go perfectly. And it put the people I loved most in danger. No matter how many times I tried to take the most perilous tasks, they shouted me down. They wanted to share the risk equally, and I had to accept that.

If I could destroy the mine single-handedly, I would.

If I could sneak into Aquinon and slit Renwell's throat while he slept, I would.

Instead, I was adding *Henry* to our plans. I'd told Nikella about the letter Kiera sent, and she immediately agreed it was a good idea.

Of course she did.

Kiera nudged her horse alongside Wicked as we rode together. "Brooding about the plan again, dear husband?"

Maz snorted behind us. Kiera had told everyone what'd happened at *Beards & Barley*, and Maz and Ruru seemed to think it was hilarious. I wasn't sure Nikella had even been listening. She kept glancing at the woods to the east. Behind us.

But Kiera's teasing title for me still made my stomach dip.

"No," I said sharply. "I just wish you'd let me be the one to—"

"Did you know my mother used to ask me to come with her to the Temple?" Kiera cut over my protest.

The unforeseen question made my mouth snap shut. *What did this have to do with the mine?*

I shook my head.

Kiera looked down at her scarred fingers, which were curled around Ozlow's reins. "She stopped—probably around the time she met you. But also because I always said no. I hated being anywhere near that square."

"I remember." Kiera had paled at the thought of going through it and had run away when she'd seen Asher's head.

"Father forced me to watch some executions there during the Pravaran rebellion," she whispered. "One of them was the first boy I fell in love with. Julian. His father was a People's Council member."

I ground my teeth together. Weylin's cruelty apparently knew no bounds in punishing his family and his people.

Julian. Julian. Why do I know that name?

"The boy you went to prison for," I said. "You said his name was Julian."

Kiera nodded. "That story was partially true. He was a boy

whose execution I tried to stop. His death was one of the reasons I hated my father."

Another truth from a lie. "Thank you for telling me. But why?"

"Because I feel like I could've saved their lives if I hadn't been so afraid," she said softly, gazing at me with her beautiful soul bared in her eyes. "If I had gone with Mother to the Temple, maybe she wouldn't have planned something so reckless. If I hadn't run away from my responsibilities, maybe she would've confided in me. If I had fought my father sooner, maybe I could've stopped those horrible executions."

My chest tightened. I recognized that guilt, that desire to do more and to do it perfectly.

I reached over and squeezed her arm. "It's easier to pass judgment when we're on the outside of fear. But that shouldn't make it any less real."

"Are you afraid?"

"Every day," I said without hesitation.

"I am, too. But for the first time, I feel stronger than my fear. And I want to do some good with it." She gave me a hard look, the fierce determination in it bolstering my meager hope. "Do you understand?"

You want to fight for our people. You want to honor your mother's and Julian's and all of Rellmira's sacrifices. And you don't want me impeding that.

I dipped my head, then set my gaze on the endless road. "I understand. No more brooding."

"Thank the Four," Maz grumbled behind us. "You really should listen to your wife more often, brother."

Ruru laughed. Kiera's cheeks turned pink, and she refused to look at me.

I dropped back next to Maz and gave him a shove. "For that, you get first watch tonight."

He shoved me back, the familiar gleam in his eyes. "Worth it."

"We should rest on the other side of that hill," Nikella said, pointing to a knoll off the road. "It'll provide excellent cover from anyone passing by."

We set up camp by dusk. I grabbed my bow and arrows to hunt for our supper when Nikella stopped me.

"You're fighting Kiera tonight."

CHAPTER 38
KIERA

I STUMBLED MIDWAY THROUGH AN EXERCISE, MY HAND LIMP around my sword hilt.

Fight Aiden?

Nikella had never pitted us against each other. He'd trained nearby when I trained with Ruru. I'd snuck glances at him when he and Maz fought, shirtless and sweaty. Aiden was all honed power and dangerous beauty when he whirled about with his sword.

I could only hope to be half as good one day. But now?

"Why?" I blurted out, watching Aiden with the same hesitation that lined his jaw.

Nikella's eyes were more serious than ever. The pale light cast tree shadows over her face and body. "I told you I would train your head, heart, and body. You have many emotional battles ahead of you. Therefore, you must master your emotions when you fight."

Aiden slowly set aside his bow and arrows and picked up his sword. I backed farther into the small clearing. He followed me, his eyes dark and his sword tip pointed to the ground.

He no longer looked like the warm, teasing man from the road. He looked like the wild warrior I'd seen in the mountain village. The one who'd emerged from the depths of the mine. The one from that night in the palace.

Was this his way of scaring me out of our plan, even though he'd said he understood my reasons?

I gripped my sword harder.

I am a warrior. I am stronger than my fear.

Aiden didn't wait for Nikella's word. He attacked. I blocked, shuffled my feet the way Nikella had taught me, and struck back. He easily deflected it and came at me with a series of strikes from all directions.

Sweat poured down my neck as I tried to keep up. I swung wide, and he kicked my foot out from under me. I crashed to one knee.

He whipped his sword at my neck, stopping a hair's breadth from my skin.

Fear gaped like a black hole in my chest. For a moment, it wasn't Aiden, but Renwell holding a blade to my throat.

Aiden must've seen the change in my eyes, because he immediately backed away.

"You're locking up," Nikella growled at me as I rose to my feet. "You're thinking too much. Try again."

We went again, and Aiden ended it by tapping the flat of his sword on my back, where an enemy would've sliced me open.

My legs shook with exhaustion. "He's much better than me. Faster. Stronger. I can't beat him yet. I need more training."

Nikella scowled at me. She'd never looked angry during our sessions before. "He might always be those things. Renwell and Korvin are also faster and stronger, as are most of the Wolves and soldiers and thousands more. Did that stop you when you charged that Wolf in Caddik's kitchen?"

"No," I said quietly.

"Did it stop you when you fought the Wolves in the alley in Aquinon?"

Shame curdled in my gut. "No."

"No," Nikella said firmly. "You used *your* particular skills without hesitation. You exploited the first weakness you found. Every fighter has one or several."

My pulse quickened. Her words closely echoed her brother's.

Gods damn your little weaknesses. You're looking for a weakness where there is none.

"I understand," I said, taking deep, slow breaths to calm my racing heart.

Maz and Ruru had finished setting up camp and now sat watching us. Aiden remained silent, his gaze flicking over me as if noting all of my weaknesses.

I sighed heavily and turned partially away from him, holding my sword casually.

The moment he shifted, I attacked without warning. He was still gods-damned fast, but I kept throwing him off. I leaned back when he did. Then I threw myself against him when he charged. I whipped out one of my throwing knives and jabbed the hilt into his ribs and neck. Then I dropped low and tripped him.

He twisted like a cat midair and rolled me beneath him as he fell, his sword edge at my neck once more. He panted through his grin, his eyes brighter than emeralds. "There's my sneaky little thief," he rasped.

I wriggled under him, trying to free my knife hand, which was pinned in the dirt beneath his knee. "I still lost," I tried to snarl, but it came out too breathy.

He was gods-damned heavy, and it felt too gods-damned good.

Nothing like being under Renwell's boot.

Aiden's grin softened. "If you hadn't used your knife hilt, I would at least be bleeding all over you right now."

My gaze dipped down to those bowed lips, the dark stubble that I remembered scraping deliciously over my skin. "It's not enough."

His body tightened over mine. "No, it's not."

A chorus of whistles and applause jerked my attention away. Maz and Ruru grinned from their seats as if we'd put on a spectacular show.

Nikella's expression was closely guarded. "Better. Again."

Maz and Ruru went hunting with Maz's whistler and simple metal darts, while Aiden and I fought over and over.

Aiden quickly picked up on my little tricks, so I had to keep getting creative. It was actually a bit . . . fun. And invigorating, despite my body feeling like one big bruise.

Nikella only let us stop when I sneaked in my first "killing" blow. By then, Maz and Ruru had already eaten their roasted quail and were now dozing next to the fire.

"No need to wake Maz," Nikella said, settling herself on a rock in the shadows with her naked spear. "I'll take first watch."

Aiden gave her a heavy look, his lips pressed tightly together. Perhaps I wasn't the only one who'd noticed Nikella's surliness.

But he said nothing and went to check on the horses, chewing on leftover quail meat.

I used my sleeve to wipe the sweat from my brow, then sat on the ground next to Nikella.

She said nothing, merely continued to stare into the dark woods.

"Are you worried about Jek and the others?" I asked quietly.

I'd told her what Jek had told me—about his feelings on Arduen's Night seven years ago. Her eyes had flared, and she'd ridden alone the rest of the day. She'd been more withdrawn than ever on this journey.

"They can take care of themselves," she said.

I clasped my arms around my drawn-up knees. "Is it Korvin then? Is that why you're pushing me harder than Ruru?"

"You asked for my help. Do you not want it anymore?"

I blew out a frustrated breath. Stubborn woman. "Of course I do. I'm just . . . I'm just worried about you, Nikella."

She finally looked down at me, surprise loosening the frown etched between her brows. She studied me for a moment in that way of hers. Then her shoulders relaxed under her long hood.

"The letter you sent to Henry," she said slowly. "It made me think of preparations I should make if Korvin accomplishes what he's wanted all these years and kills me."

"That won't happen," I declared.

She gave me a look that clearly told me she didn't need my reassurance. "It might. And it made me realize I need to prepare you as much as possible for what is coming."

"Why me?"

"Because my brothers are after you, too," she said, her eyes pained. "Not to kill you, but to make you a monster like them. I can't let that happen."

Did she think I would become Renwell's little soldier again, like Aiden had suggested on the mountain?

I clenched my jaw. "They won't. I feel nothing but vengeance for them."

"That's what I'm afraid of. Revenge only takes. It never gives." She glanced to where Aiden was bedding down for the night near Maz and Ruru. "What has revenge ever given Aiden? Or you?"

Loss. Betrayal. Pain.

"Should they get away with every crime they commit?" I demanded.

Nikella shook her head. "They should be held accountable for every atrocity. Justice is for the good of everyone. Revenge is only for yourself." She stroked her fingers along the gleaming silver of her spear. "Renwell killed our father."

I startled, my mouth falling open.

"He never admitted as much," she continued, as if patricide was common in her world. "But one night, our father wandered off, drunker than usual, and they found him the next day on the riverbank. Drowned."

"He might've just hit his head and fallen in," I said. Not to defend Renwell, but to offer Nikella some peace of mind.

She pressed her scarred lips together. "No other signs of injury. And he hated the river. Couldn't swim. Never went near water if he could help it. He'd also beaten Renwell rather badly that night. It was just like my brother to make someone's worst fear come true."

I remembered the way Renwell had occasionally protected me against Father's wrath, had told me I was better than him.

"Perhaps he was protecting all of you from your father," I said.

Nikella's gaze sharpened. "Your desire to see the good in people is admirable until it makes you willfully blind."

Wounded, I opened my mouth to argue, but she cut me off. "I told you before that Renwell doesn't care for you or me. That I was like you when I was younger. Any time he stepped between me and our father or me and Korvin, I thought he might love me. But he was simply playing with my emotions, the way Korvin played with my pain. He wanted to see how far he could twist them. I understood the truth when he left me with Korvin without a backward glance."

She broke off, breathing hard. Her eyes grew distant as she gazed east. "When you've experienced very little real love in your life, it's hard to see it even when it's standing right in front of you, asking you to choose it."

I frowned. Was she speaking of Jek? Of the feelings he told me to pass on to her?

My gaze fell to Aiden. I'd experienced love from Mother, Everett, and Delysia. With friends like Maz and Ruru, Melaena and even Nikella.

But with Aiden? Our shared past and broken trust. The new heated moments we shared. The teasing that felt too real. It confused me. Made me want to run toward it and away from it all at once.

"Or," Nikella continued, "when your heart is broken and even the smallest bit of comfort is addictive, it's easy to mistake a few calculated words and actions as the love we seek."

My heart rose to my throat. I knew where she was going with this.

Her eyes were kind as she said, "Renwell stepped in when you were vulnerable. He hardened and twisted your heart when it was at its weakest. He used you, manipulated you, and tried to forge you into a weapon he could leash to his side. That sort of treatment would cloud anyone's judgment."

I ducked my head to hide the tears that brimmed in my eyes. Every word rang so true, I felt deaf from their clamor.

She wasn't telling me she thought I was weak. She was telling me she understood. That her life with her family had shaped her in ways that still harmed her today.

Moments slipped by while I struggled to fit everything she'd said into my heart.

I lifted my head. "You want me to understand you. Understand him. So that I won't end up like any of you."

A small smile disrupted the scar that split her face. "Exactly. You have a future, Kiera. A good one, if you fight for it. One that could include love and happiness if you let it." Nikella purposefully glanced at Aiden. "You inspired him to want his own future for once. Your instincts are good. You'll learn to trust them again."

I blinked in surprise. Was she telling me to pursue Aiden? Did she think there was any world in which we could be together after all this?

Even as the thought crossed my mind, so did the image of the two of us exploring the world together. Sailing across sky-blue water. Scrambling over sandy rooftops. Watching Arduen's Mountain set itself aflame. All in each other's arms. Nothing between us and nothing in our way.

Free.

The campfire hissed and crackled, shattering the illusion in my mind. Such a life couldn't happen.

I refused to think of the darkest potential future. *Dead and defeated.* No. Aiden would be king. I knew it in my bones, even if he didn't. Rellmira needed him. Rellmira was his.

But me? I would take Everett and Delysia and we would start over somewhere new. Somewhere without terrible memories haunting us.

We would be free, yes. And I would be alone.

CHAPTER 39
AIDEN

I'd been expecting a handful of tents and a few guards, but this was almost a small village. A high wooden fence surrounded the camp, the tree trunks carved to sharp tips to deter anyone from climbing in—or out.

From my vantage point high in one of the tallest trees I could find, I spotted at least thirty prisoners scurrying about the camp in their faded clothes and clanging shackles. They hauled water from the rushing Medria River, sawed logs, and minded the camp. All under the watchful eyes of over a dozen soldiers. And that didn't count the ones who might be patrolling around the camp.

I'd been in this tree for nearly three hours, judging by the stiffness in my muscles. Sunset had come and gone. I was grateful for the cloak of shadows, but the darkness made it much more difficult to distinguish patterns.

Torches crowned the guard posts on the east and west sides of the camp. The guards were alert and well-rested.

Fucking rotten luck.

A low, trilling whistle told me Maz was descending from his tree. He was probably going out of his mind with impatience.

We'd pushed ourselves in the last week of riding, ever-conscious of the timeline we navigated. If Jek and the others had made it back to Yargoth and told Skelly of our plan, Skelly would be sailing to meet the Shadow-Wolf prison ship by now.

Nikella had two days to make her explosives. Then we needed to steal one of these log shipments and raft it right into the mine.

But walking into this camp would be suicide.

I silently swung down from my tree, the movements written into my muscles after years of climbing these trees growing up. Stepping back into the goddess's forest of Twaryn had felt like coming home. That first breath of rich, dewy air had eased an ache in my chest I hadn't even known was there.

Kiera had asked me why the trees didn't change color like the ones in Dagriel. Why the coming winter didn't seem to touch Twaryn.

I'd told her what Nikella had told me when I was a young boy. These were Viridana's trees, and she'd willed this forest to live forever.

I watched Maz's bulky shadow slide down his tree and land with a grunt.

"How are you so gods-damned quick?" he muttered.

I smiled in the dark. "Sheer talent. Let's go."

We slipped back through the thick forest to where we'd left the others with the horses. Nikella had chosen a grove far enough from the fortress that no one would see our fire. And if they did, hopefully they would assume we were simple Twarynites.

Ruru was standing guard when we approached. I whistled, and he relaxed. "All right?"

"It's locked up tight," Maz said, collapsing by the small fire Kiera tended. "Nothing goes in or out except the logs."

Ruru frowned. "Who floats the logs down the river, then?"

I sat next to Kiera. "A guard with four or five prisoners, as Caddik said. But they don't use the prisoners who do the logging, from the looks of it. A wagon arrived with a group of prisoners who hopped on the raft and started riding it down the river with the same guard who drove the wagon."

"So they use the same guards and prisoners on the river," Kiera summed up, dusting off her hands. "Probably to prevent many new faces they can't track."

I nodded.

"Which means we've got shitty luck," Maz said, glaring into the fire. "We can't take the shipment from inside the camp because they don't use the same prisoners. And we can't take it outside the camp because they *do* use the same prisoners."

"It's clever," I admitted.

"It's a problem," Maz countered. "We have eight days until we have to be at that fucking mine. Otherwise, my sisters and Skelly and the rest of them will be attacking a beach for no reason."

"We'll figure it out, Mazkull." I turned to Kiera. "Nikella?"

She shook her head. "Still not back."

The moment we'd set up camp, Nikella had disappeared into the forest with her notes.

She'd been more focused than ever on Kiera's training since the night she made us fight each other. I'd seen the two of them talking afterward, their expressions solemn. I hadn't asked what it was about, but both women trained like the world depended on it. Which it probably did.

Ruru trained hard as well, as if determined to prove he could do his part in the mine.

I was honored to be fighting this war with every single one of them.

"Is there some water nearby?" Kiera asked, glancing at me as she rose to her feet. "That isn't crawling with soldiers, of course."

Maz smirked at me. "I believe Aiden knows the perfect spot."

I resisted glaring at him. We'd passed a small stream earlier that I told Maz I needed to come back to.

I stood. "I'll show you."

Kiera nodded and grabbed everyone's water canteens.

"Bring us back a few, yeah?" Maz called to our backs as we walked into the forest.

"A few what?" Kiera asked, her light footsteps crackling behind me.

"You'll see." I reached back and slid a few of the canteens' straps from her shoulder onto mine.

My eyes grew accustomed to the dark, slivers of moonlight cutting through the tree canopy. In the distance, flecks of golden light danced through the thick bushes.

"Fireflies?" Kiera whispered. "Twaryn truly only knows one season."

My chest warmed, remembering the last time we'd been in the woods surrounded by fireflies.

The melodious sound of a stream reached my ears before we stepped into a wide clearing. Several large trees dipped their roots into the shallow water. Their stiff, shiny leaves hid the clusters of fruit I sought.

Kiera stood next to me. "It's so lovely. I can see why you'd want to live out your days here."

I glanced sharply at her. "Why do you think I'd want to do that?"

Kiera shrugged, not looking at me. "Something Melaena said once. And you always talked about this place with such reverence. Like you yearned for the peace you found here."

Something large and thorny took up residence in my chest. "I do yearn for peace, but I'm not sure where—or even if—I'll ever have it."

"There will be peace," Kiera said, finally gazing up at me. "Once there's nothing left to fight for."

I cupped the back of her head in my palm, then slowly slid her braid between my fingers. "There will always be something to fight for."

Kiera's throat tightened as if she'd swallowed hard. "Why did you tell Helene who you are?"

I frowned at the unexpected question. I pondered my answer as I walked to the stream. Kiera kneeled by the water and filled her canteens. She didn't ask again, as if she understood I needed a moment.

"I still don't want to be king," I said carefully. "But I'm tired of hiding who I am. Renwell tried to bury me—and my family— with more lies, and I just wanted someone else to know the truth. The truth Helene's husband waited and worked for."

Kiera sat back on her heels. "So many people want you to be king. My mother did, too." She drank from a canteen, then handed it to me. "Did you know my brother never had the desire to be king, either?"

I frowned and took a sip of fresh, cold water. Why had Brielle never mentioned that?

"I never understood it," Kiera continued. "As king, you would have all the power. Much more than I ever had as a princess. It was one of the reasons I was fine giving up my crown. I wanted to be High Enforcer instead. Someone with real power."

I sat in the thick grass next to her and took another long swallow of water. "And what if you were queen?"

Kiera stiffened.

It was like I'd struck a match. I let the question burn and burn between us, its implications billowing like smoke in a breeze. Then I doused it with one breath.

"If you had inherited the throne instead of your brother," I added.

Kiera's shoulders sagged. With relief? Her voice was still tight when she replied, "My father would never have allowed that, even if Everett put up a fight. I was never meant to rule. I never wanted to either."

Disappointment tunneled through my gut like worms. She was saying what I was, more or less. But I didn't like it.

"There was a time when I saw myself becoming king," I said. I'd never admitted this to anyone before, not even Nikella. "Back in Pravara, leading the rebellion. I thought we could defeat Weylin's soldiers and march on Aquinon, victorious. That I would parade through the gate and the streets with my allies. And that when I announced I was Aiden Falcryn, son of the last true king, they would cheer and welcome me with open arms. I would take my father's crown off Weylin's head and imprison him for his crimes. I would be the king that Rellmira loved, much as Nikella said they loved my father."

Kiera shifted, her shoulder pressing into mine. "But then the rebellion was massacred."

Memories clamored in their cages, but I didn't let them out. I didn't need to here in this forest, the crickets chirping softly, the trees swaying. Kiera's warmth anchoring me.

"And now?" she asked. "After we destroy the mine and kill Renwell, who will you put on the throne?"

I had no answer for that. At least not one I wanted to give her at this moment.

I rose, leaving my canteens by the stream. I extended my hand to her. "The throne can wait. But what I want to show you cannot."

She hesitated, staring at my bare hand. I vividly remembered a time not too long ago when she would've refused to take it.

But now . . . now she placed her hand in mine.

CHAPTER 40

KIERA

TINGLES SWEPT OVER MY SKIN AT THE WARM GRASP OF HIS HAND.

I forgot all talk of kings and queens, battles past and future. He gently led me to one of the great trees that fed its web of roots from the stream. Long, thick branches extended over us like benevolent arms.

I tilted my chin up and spotted clusters of white, like little moons, hiding under the dense leaves.

"Are those . . . moonblood fruits?" I breathed, hardly believing my eyes.

"Yes." Aiden's smile was clear in his voice. "I spotted these trees when we went to spy on the camp. Normally, they only grow in the heart of Twaryn, but Viridana wanted to spread their sweetness."

I grinned up at the fruit, excitement trickling down my spine. "I never thought I'd see one in my life."

"You're going to do more than see it."

I dropped my gaze. Aiden slowly backed me up to the tree trunk, our boots shuffling together. His eyes searched mine in a way that made my knees tremble.

Gods, I missed him.

We'd been together every day. Every night. We'd trained together again. We rode and slept side by side.

But I missed him like this. When we both blocked out the rest of the world. When I could forget his last name . . . and mine.

I missed him because I kept losing him. Yet we also seemed to keep finding each other.

"What are you thinking?" he whispered.

I drew in a shaky breath. "That you're going to make me do something dangerous."

"The only dangerous thing here is you."

His lips were so close. When had I risen to my tiptoes? Perhaps at the same moment I slid my hands up to his broad shoulders.

"That's not true," I murmured.

He grasped my hips and spun me around so my back was pressed into his hard chest. His bristled chin teased the sensitive skin of my cheek as he whispered into my ear, "I will never let you fall, Kiera."

Chills seared across my skin.

I will never let you fall.

His words from the Temple roof just before we walked out onto the parapet to touch the bells.

I will never let you fall.

And he never had.

Suddenly, he lifted me toward the nearest branch. I gasped and wrapped my arms around it like I was a hundred feet in the air, not ten.

His hands slid under my ass and pushed. My cheeks burned as I flailed my legs around the branch like I was mounting Ozlow.

The branch didn't even creak with my weight. It was thicker than Aiden and I combined, but I still sank my nails into it like a cat as I glared down at Aiden.

"A warning would've been nice," I said.

He grinned up at me, erasing my glare. "Perhaps I just wanted to hear that sweet gasp you make."

My skin now felt like a wildfire was coursing over it. "Am I to pick the fruit for us or—"

"Shift forward," he commanded.

Inner thighs trembling, I inched farther out onto the branch. "I still don't know how—"

Aiden backed up a few steps, then charged at the tree. I gaped as he *ran up* the trunk and grabbed my branch, swinging himself up on it.

He chuckled low and deep at the dumbfounded look on my face.

"Teach me that," I breathed.

He shook his head. "I like our way better."

I huffed and made a show of looking around my perch. I spotted a few moonbloods dangling overhead. I could reach them if I scooted further forward.

Jaw tight with determination, I stretched my arm as far as I could, my fingertips brushing the soft skin of the fruit.

Just a little bit . . . more . . .

I lunged, swiping at the fruit, and started tipping sideways off the tree. Before I could cry out, a powerful arm banded around my waist, anchoring me to the branch.

"So eager to test my promise?" Aiden murmured in my ear.

I scoffed like my hands weren't desperately curled around his arm. "How about you grab one, then?"

His arm slipped from my grasp as he stood up. He plucked one of the moonbloods. "Thank you," he murmured.

"Are you speaking to the tree?"

He sat down behind me again and drew back to lean against the trunk. He patted the bark in front of him.

Palms growing sweaty, I twisted around and crawled over to him. We sat facing each other, our knees and boots brushing together.

"Yes," he said. "When I was younger, I believed the trees were always dancing and whispering to each other. That they growled and creaked when danger was about. Moaned when they were sad." He looked down at the white fruit in his hand. "I always try to treat them well, and they treat me well in return."

I smiled, imagining a dark-headed boy with forest-green eyes whispering back to the trees. "Viridana must love you."

He shrugged. "These woods have given me a lot. There's no harm in being thankful, whether it was by her will or not. The legend says the goddess bled a few drops into the earth under a full moon and one of these trees sprouted on the spot."

I thought of the knife made of dead night sky in my boot. Of the fireflowers that burned on Arduen's Mountain. "I like having pieces of them with their stories. Makes them feel more real."

"Exactly." He pulled a knife from his belt and sliced through the moonblood. Dark juice ran down his fingers. He licked his knife clean, which did strange, burning things to my stomach.

My thighs tightened around the branch.

He must've noticed, because he smiled as he stowed his knife. "Close your eyes."

My heart trilled a warning, but I obeyed.

A breeze wafted through the tree branches, carrying the scent of wet grass and something deeply sweet. The leaves around us shivered as the crickets sang. It felt like peace.

Aiden pulled my hand toward him and placed something soft in it. A piece of fruit. "Don't look at it. Just taste it," he said softly.

I put the moonblood to my lips and nibbled at the sticky flesh. Gods, it was . . . it was . . . the sweetest thing I'd ever tasted. Like dark berries mixed with the lightest sparkling wine. The juices ran down my throat, quenching my thirst more than the water had. It made me hungry for more.

I opened my eyes, and my stomach swooped low and hard. If I was hungry, Aiden looked painfully ravenous. The rest of the fruit continued to drip through his fingers, but his gaze was fastened to my wet mouth.

Was it stained?

I wiped it with the back of my sleeve, my tongue darting out to sweep my lips clean. His nostrils flared as his eyebrows slammed together.

Oh. *Oh.*

I finished my piece of fruit and dropped the empty peel to the ground. Then I slid forward, hesitating when I couldn't get closer without—

He placed the rest of the moonblood beside him and lifted my legs over his, nestling me in his lap.

My heart pounded like I was in the heat of battle. But there was no fear. Only excitement. And something deeper, warmer, as I gazed into Aiden's eyes. Something I'd felt with him in Aquinon. In The Hollow. In stolen moments like this.

Something I thought had died a swift death the moment I realized he'd killed my mother.

But the feeling persisted.

"You should . . . you should have some moonblood," I whispered raggedly. "It's delicious."

Eyes burning with intention, he grasped my sticky fingers and slid the first one into his mouth.

I gasped, a bolt of heat shooting straight to my core.

His other hand tightened around my knee, pulling me closer.

He sucked hard on my finger. My body shuddered and rocked against him involuntarily, loving every hardened ridge.

A low growl rumbled in his chest as he released my finger. "You're right. Absolutely delicious." Then he stole another finger, working his lips around the tip.

Heat stacked in my belly, ember by ember.

His tongue swirled around my finger. My control snapped.

I yanked my finger out of his mouth and crushed my lips against his.

His responding groan poured into me as he kissed me back like his next breath depended on it.

He clenched his arm around my waist and seized the nape of my neck. As if I would go anywhere.

All I tasted was sweetness and heat. I was drunk on it. Craving more. His lips coaxed mine into a dance that felt perfect and familiar, new and dangerous all at once.

I plunged my fingers into his long, raven-wing hair, tugging him closer. His tongue curled into my mouth, deepening the kiss.

I wished it would go deeper. I wanted to feel him everywhere. His stubble rasped over my lips. I wanted it to burn over my aching breasts and between my thighs.

He dragged his mouth away and trailed searing kisses down my throat to my collarbone and behind my ear.

"Gods, I've missed you," he murmured between kisses. "Do you have any idea how long I've wanted to do this? How many nights I've dreamed of this? Fucking Four, I don't think I ever stopped wanting you, Kiera."

For some reason, tears burned behind my eyes. "That can't be true."

He captured my chin between his thumb and forefinger, pulling me to meet his gaze. "It is true. It will likely always be true. Maybe I'm a fool for it. Maybe I shouldn't want what I can't have. But you make it impossible to care about consequences."

I love you, Aiden.

I startled at the unbidden words in my mind. I pressed my lips together in case they tried to escape.

But it was true. I'd known the feeling, but now I'd named it. I loved him.

I didn't know for how long. I didn't know where it started and stopped. It simply . . . was.

My heart squirmed in my chest, uncomfortable with the heavy weight of this new truth.

Because he was right—we shouldn't want what we couldn't have. We had a job to do. A kingdom to save. People to free.

Nikella said I could have a future with love and happiness, but right now, it was marred by battles yet to fight.

This moment was likely all we'd get. And even then, it couldn't be everything I wanted.

What if you were queen?

I'd panicked, unsure what Aiden had meant with those words. But he wasn't asking me to be his.

My newfound feelings for the future king would likely remain just that—secret, unspoken feelings.

His thumb brushed my tight lips, his eyes growing sad and then guarded.

No, no. Don't leave me yet.

I grasped his tight jaw. "Kiss me again," I whispered.

His face softened. He cupped my face in his hands, his gaze roaming over it like he wanted to memorize every detail.

Agonizingly slow, he brought my lips to his. He kissed me, long and hard. Then soft and short. Fervent need and small caresses. I savored every single one. Warmth pulsed between us, drenching my mind with happiness.

Perhaps it was my imagination, but even the tree seemed to sway with us, whispering and singing through its leaves and long branches.

Like it was acknowledging the moment I realized I was in love with Aiden Falcryn. And that brought it nothing but joy.

Even as I mourned the future we would never have.

CHAPTER 41
KIERA

After we picked a few more moonbloods, we walked back to camp with full canteens, sticky fingers, and swollen lips.

My heart had not stopped skittering around in my chest after I'd realized my feelings for Aiden. It reminded me of when Melaena claimed that I loved him, and I'd immediately tried to deny it in my mind.

Had I loved him even then?

Maz grinned like we were bringing him a barrel of Sunshine and happily caught the moonblood Aiden tossed at him. "Had a nice walk, did you?"

I ignored him, and the heat crawling up my neck, and sat next to Ruru, who accepted the moonblood I handed him.

"Is that blood or juice?" he asked, pointing at his own neck.

I slapped a hand over the sticky stain on my skin. "Juice. They're, uh . . . a bit messy."

"Juice tends to get everywhere when you're . . . eating," Maz said with a solemn expression that belied the laughter in his blue eyes.

Aiden glared at him as he sat down by the fire. "Shove that fruit in your mouth before I do it for you."

Maz rolled his eyes and cut into his moonblood. "Gods, only you would still be cantankerous after tasting such delicious fruit."

Ruru slurped the crimson juice from his. "Holy Four, that is good. Like an orange, but so much better."

I smiled at him, grateful he was actually talking about the moonblood. "And a little sparkly, don't you think?"

He nodded, his smile drooping a bit. "I miss my sticky bread, though. Gods know when I'll ever have it again."

I squeezed his arm. "We'll get back to Aquinon soon."

"Do you really think this Henry fellow will march his army there?" Ruru asked.

We'd told the others about the letter I'd sent. But it could've gotten lost or seized. He could've decided not to come.

I swallowed hard. If I died in the mine, no one would save Everett and Delysia. Or Aquinon. Renwell would win.

"I hope so," I said thickly. I met Aiden's eyes across the fire. The same concern was etched between his brows.

"He'd better be here in the next two days," Maz said around a mouthful of bloody fruit. "We can't wait."

"I know that," I snapped.

His brows lifted.

"Sorry," I mumbled. "I just . . . need him to come."

Maz's face softened. "Of course, lovely. I'll keep watch with you."

"You're not doing a very good job of that," said Nikella as she appeared out of the darkness.

Maz waved his hand. "I knew you were coming."

Her lips quirked, the first sign of a smile in days. Her arms were full of leaves, branches, berries, and tools.

Ruru jumped up to help her set everything down.

"Did you find everything?" Aiden asked. He jutted his chin at the mortar, pestle, and hatchet she laid at her feet. "Where'd you get those?"

"Friends," she said. "You four will need to cut down a tree and create several hollow lengths to store everything in."

I gazed up at the massive trees surrounding us. "Won't that make Viridana angry?"

"We're not the ones taking more than our share," Nikella reminded me. "She'll grow back swiftly."

Suddenly, I very much wanted to see that.

We quietly ate dried pork mixed with boiled beans while Nikella stripped, ground, and sifted the flora she'd collected. She explained as she went, but I nodded off as she was showing us how to braid something called shiverroot into a fuse.

The next two days passed much the same, with the notable difference of not kissing Aiden again. We shared looks. We brushed past each other. We sat together by the fire. But our battle preparations consumed my thoughts.

Every hour I prowled outside that gods-damned fortress, every time I spied on the other side of the river, searching for a soldier who could be Henry, killed a little more of my hope.

We were also no closer to figuring out how to take a shipment without arousing too much suspicion.

We *did* manage to chop down a tree, cut it into three pieces, and hollow those out.

I'd winced when Maz had delivered the final swing that cracked the tree trunk from its stump. It landed with a mournful crash in the woods. Aiden had brushed his fingers over the jagged edges and whispered his thanks.

Ruru and I stared at the stump, waiting for the mythical tree to grow back. I almost didn't believe it would happen. But then, the edges smoothed and elongated, like pointed fingers reaching for the sky.

I gaped as Ruru whooped and danced around. Slowly, slowly, tender twigs curled out from the growing trunk. They hardened and lengthened. Leaves sprouted. The bark groaned and sighed, stretching back to its original height.

"Fucking Four," I breathed, my eyes wide. "I mean, thank you, blessed Viridana."

No wonder Father—and then Renwell—had gotten greedy with these woods. The goddess had made sure there was an endless supply.

But to feed a forge of deadly sunstone armor and weapons? To build warships? Things that would end countless lives?

No, the gentle goddess would've abhorred that. Just as Mynastra likely hated how Renwell was using her beloved pieces of night sky.

If only the Four were still here to fix things. But it was our mess. We had to clean it up.

We'll fix it, I promised Viridana's tree. *Aiden will stop this once he's king.*

Nikella had nodded with satisfaction when she saw our work. She worked from dawn into the deepest night on her explosives. She even ground a handful of black seeds from a blackrust tree into a powder she said wouldn't harm skin but would eat through metal.

I also wasn't the only one searching for someone.

Ruru usually accompanied me on my routes. He'd climb a tree almost as nimbly as Aiden and sit up there for hours. He noted routines and faces, but he was looking for one in partic-ular—his brother, Daire. Once, he thought he spotted a young boy he once knew, but couldn't be sure if he was the same.

I told him that if we were victorious, all of this would change. No more innocent prisoners. No more Shadow-Wolves stealing people in the night. We would make Rellmira safe again.

He'd smiled, but it hadn't quite reached his brown eyes. So I asked him to tell me more stories about growing up with Daire in Aquinon. He eagerly obliged, his usual spirit rekindling.

As the sun set on our last night in Twaryn, I paced by the fire while Aiden watched me, sympathy twisting the lips I desperately tried not to think about.

Nikella had finished her explosives. The logs were ready. The plan was simple and full of holes—steal a shipment along the river in the dead of night and hope we didn't raise any alarms.

But still no Henry.

"Perhaps he misread your letter," Ruru suggested, munching on a handful of nuts Nikella had picked.

"I was very clear," I said shortly, pacing a rut in the dirt.

"Perhaps he got lost," Maz offered.

I shook my head with a growl. A child could've understood my message, as innocuous as it was, just not its intent.

"Let's search one last time," Aiden said softly, getting to his feet and pulling his hood over his head.

Gratitude flooded me. I made sure I had my knives and shrouded myself in my cloak.

We slipped into the shadows. I walked between the trees that now felt like old friends and guardians instead of hiding places for our enemies.

But then I heard the clank of armor.

Aiden and I darted behind a wide tree. I unsheathed a knife and felt Aiden do the same.

We listened as the sound of booted footsteps and shifting armor grew closer.

Aiden tapped my shoulder three times. *Three people.*

I nodded.

They walked toward our tree. We slid around to the other side, flanking them as they passed.

They moved cautiously, but I didn't see the glint of weapons in their hands. No torches, either. Could it be . . .? They were headed straight for our camp.

"Henry?" I called without stepping out from the trees.

Aiden stiffened.

The movement stopped. "Who's there?" a man's voice barked.

"Friend or foe, depending on your answer," I replied. "What is your name?"

There was a pause, during which I held my breath.

Then: "Henry Avincourt, captain of the eighteenth. Now you answer me." Something rustled nearby, as if someone were creeping closer.

Aiden darted out and snatched a dark shadow, putting his knife to its throat. "The last person you'll ever see if you're lying," he growled.

The dim light revealed a man's face with a dark mustache and wide eyes. "I give you my word," he said quickly.

Metal scraped, and two other shadows leaped at us. I whipped out my sword.

"Stop!" the one in Aiden's hold cried. The other two hesitated. "Please tell me your name."

I stepped closer to him. "What is the name of the woman you love?"

"Delysia," the man immediately replied. "She has the most beautiful golden hair and blue eyes. Her favorite color is pink. She hates the dark and studying." He took a breath. "And she loves her older brother and sister more than anything."

A lump wedged itself in my throat. I blinked rapidly, trying to keep the tears at bay. I grasped Aiden's arm. "Let him go," I said hoarsely.

Aiden released him and backed away, but he didn't stow his knife.

Henry rose to his feet and peered at me in the dark. "Kiera?"

Kiera. Not Emilia. I hadn't signed the letter, yet he'd called me by the name Delysia did. She must've talked about me.

"Yes," I whispered. "I'm so glad you came."

"I almost didn't," he said. "I actually brought someone along who said he knows you. Just to be safe."

I jolted, lifting my sword. I didn't know any soldiers.

Aiden shifted in front of me as one of the other men stepped closer.

"Hello, Kiera."

CHAPTER 42

KIERA

MEMORIES JOLTED THROUGH ME. A GUARD WITH BRIGHT RED HAIR, standing at the bridge. Smiling at me. Sneaking me around the other guards. Stealing kisses and a few nights in his bunk.

"Shayn?" I stepped past Aiden, reaching for him, trying to see his face. "Holy Four, you're alive."

He gave a bitter laugh. "No thanks to your father and that prick of a High Enforcer calling himself king now."

I winced. "I'm sorry my father sent you away. I tried to find out what happened to you—"

"Forget about it. I should've known better than to get involved with you. I'm only here to verify who you are and see if you have a way to get me back to my family."

I deserved that. Of course, a short affair with me wasn't worth being torn away from the parents and sisters I knew he had in Aquinon. Still, I believed he was a decent man, especially if Henry deemed him honorable enough for this treasonous mission.

"How did you find us?" Aiden asked sharply.

"We passed through the fort," Henry said. "I figured you

hadn't crossed the river, so I told them I would take a night patrol and came north."

"Excellent," Aiden said brusquely. "Follow me. We don't have much time."

Henry straightened. "I came to talk to Kiera. I still don't know who you are."

"Aiden," he replied over his shoulder. "Aiden Falcryn."

Three heads swiveled to me. I sheathed my sword.

Getting used to sharing his full name, was he?

"He's been in hiding since his birth," I said quietly, leading the soldiers after Aiden. "He's fought for Rellmira longer than I have."

"I've never heard of him," Henry said in a clipped tone. "What fighting has he done?"

I shrugged, even though he probably couldn't see it. "I'll let him tell you that. But what we're doing now—and what we need to do after—is why I sent you that note."

We traipsed back to our little camp. Nikella, Maz, and Ruru looked up at our approach. Maz hefted the axe he was sharpening, rising to his feet.

I caught his eye and shook my head.

He winked at me. "Found your friends, did you, lovely?"

Henry pulled up short. "A Dag?" He glanced at Nikella and Ruru. "A Teacher and a boy? This is who you're fighting with?"

"We're who she'll be winning with," Maz said with a sinister smile.

Henry's brow furrowed, but he made no comment.

I sat next to Ruru, gesturing for the three soldiers to sit as well. Aiden leaned against a tree a bit out of our circle around the fire.

We made more introductions. The third soldier's name was Lionel, and he did little but grunt in anyone's direction. Their clothes and armor were dirty, and their expressions were haggard in the firelight. As if they'd traveled without stopping.

A kernel of hope wedged into my chest. Henry wouldn't have come all this way, risking his post and his men, if he weren't serious about helping Delysia.

"You told me you have something planned," Henry prompted, getting right to business. "What is it?"

I glanced at Aiden, his features shadowed. He nodded once.

"We're going to destroy the Calimber mine," I said.

Shayn's eyes widened in shock. "That's lunacy!"

Henry stroked his mustache, his brown eyes thoughtful. After a few moments, he said, "I can't help you with that. All my men are deep in Pravara. It would take weeks to get them here. Even if I could—even if they didn't desert at the suggestion— Dracles and his army would slaughter us before we reached the mine."

I nodded, not surprised after Aiden had argued the same thing at the tavern. "We have the mine covered. Mostly." I took a deep breath and looked at him with every bit of hope and solemnity I could muster. "We need you to march on Aquinon."

This time, Shayn was speechless. Lionel grunted and shook his head.

Henry's eyes softened. "To get Delysia? I would love nothing more than to rescue her from that . . . that *bastard*. But we can't just march on Aquinon. It would be war. Rellmirans fighting Rellmirans, which would be difficult for my men. Besides, Renwell would see us coming and summon Dracles's army before we reached the city."

"We're taking care of him, too," Maz said.

Henry's eyes narrowed. "How?"

"He and his men will be in or near the mine when it collapses," Nikella said, her eyes hard and sharp like the spear in her hands.

"You're going to bury an army?"

"Unless you think we can get them to desert Dracles," Aiden spoke up.

I frowned. We'd never discussed that possibility.

Henry shook his head. "Not those men, no. Dracles hand-picked every one of them. The strongest, the cruellest, the most bloodthirsty. Animals more than men, the lot of them. I was glad to quit Calimber when they arrived."

Like Delysia had said. Suddenly, I wanted to know everything about how they'd met and fallen in love. Holy Four, if anything happened to Henry, I would hate to tell my sister of my part in it.

"Tell me, why Calimber? Why not go to Aquinon yourselves?" Henry asked.

I grimaced. "Things are more complicated than we realized." I told him of Renwell's attack at Arduen's Mountain. Of the sunstone armor and weapons. Of the forge and the prisoners in the mine.

He listened with an expression that grew more and more grim. Shayn shook his head and muttered curses. Lionel simply stared into the fire.

"I see," Henry said when I finished. He stroked his mustache again. "I see. So you want to destroy the mine and as much of Dracles's army as you can manage. Then you want me to march my men to Aquinon to liberate the city."

"Yes," I whispered. "If I don't make it out of the mine alive, I need someone I can trust to defeat Renwell and save Delysia and Everett."

"And if you survive?"

"If we survive, we'll meet you in Aquinon," Aiden said.

My heart leaped. I glanced toward him to find him already watching me. The flames flickered in his green eyes.

"With what army?" Henry said, gesturing at our group. He didn't say it cruelly. Just stated the obvious.

But Maz still bristled. "With every warrior we have left, which will be more than enough."

"We'll come by sea," Aiden added. "We should have several ships by then."

My eyebrows lifted. He must've been thinking about what I'd said in the tavern these past few weeks. Thinking and planning. Even Nikella looked surprised . . . but also pleased.

Henry leaned back, a gleam of excitement in his eyes. "And what of the cliff gate? I was born in Aquinon. Lived there most of my life. Once that gate is down, it's impossible to get through it."

"We had a few guards we bribed before," Maz said, cutting a look at Aiden, who shook his head.

"Those men are probably dead or on the run after what happened," he said.

Henry nodded. "I know a few of the men posted there, and one of them sent me a letter after Renwell took the throne. He told me it was likely the last letter I'd get from the inside, as Renwell was barring all communication to the outside. We'll have to send someone in."

I opened my mouth, but Nikella beat me to it. "I'll go inside and disable the gate." She shook her small bag of blackrust powder. "I can partially meld the chains inside the drum so that the winch can't turn and the gate will be stuck open."

Holy Four, she'd been strategizing the battle for Aquinon, too.

But not together, from the look of Aiden's hardened jaw. "No. You won't be able to enter the city without someone raising the alarm of who you are," he said. "Don't forget who's hunting you."

Everyone went deadly quiet.

"I have been hunted all my life. That has never stopped me

before," Nikella said in a soft, cold voice that reminded me of Renwell. I shivered.

Aiden's jaw flexed, but he said nothing.

Henry cleared his throat. "May I ask who—"

"Korvin," Nikella said.

Henry's throat bobbed. "Fucking Four," he muttered.

Shayn's face paled, and he grasped the hilt of his sword, glancing around the dark woods as though Korvin was hiding behind a tree.

Which I supposed he could be. But we hadn't seen or heard anything of him since Caddik's manor.

The scars on my back itched.

"Yes," Nikella said, waving away their fear. "We're also on a tight schedule. Can we count on you in Aquinon or not?"

I pressed my lips together to keep from begging. I could think of no one else who would risk going toe to toe with Renwell and his Wolves. And soon, it would be too late. He would be too powerful with too many resources. The world would slowly fall to him. As Father had. As I had.

"If you fail to defeat Dracles's army," Henry said slowly, "I will not march on Aquinon. I would be leading my men to destruction. Many of them are from Pravara and had family who were massacred after the rebellion. They will not be keen to do so again." He gave me a pained look. "As much as I love Delysia, I cannot ask my men to sacrifice themselves for her. We need at least a chance of success."

My heart ached, heavy with disappointment. "I understand. She wouldn't want you to do that either."

"Move your men in groups," Aiden said. "Get them close to Aquinon without looking like you're advancing on the city. When you see our ships, send a messenger to the main gate, asking for their surrender. I do not want our people slaying each other. We're there to eradicate the Shadow-Wolves and the man who has seized control of our kingdom and who will make war on the world if we don't stop him. We must lay siege to the throne, not the city."

My lips parted. I'd never seen Aiden so animated. Everything about him glowed with the fervor he felt for his mission, for his kingdom. He truly was a king.

If he is to be king, where does that leave you? a small voice whispered. *To be in love with a king is to love a man who will always put you second.*

"Falcryn," Henry murmured, assessing Aiden, who met his scrutiny without a trace of tension. "Would victory include putting you on that throne?"

"It should," Maz muttered.

Nikella and Ruru nodded. My heart whispered *yes* and *no* at once.

After a long moment of everyone staring at him, Aiden said, "I don't do any of this to wear a crown."

"Why then?" Henry asked, his expression curious.

Aiden glanced at me, then back at Henry. "At first, out of a desire to wipe out tyranny when I fought in the Pravaran rebellion. Then out of revenge when I was imprisoned in Calimber for two years. I nearly had it, too. I almost killed Weylin, the man who murdered my parents and caused so much pain in Rellmira. But Renwell had other plans."

And me. I had plans that ruined yours.

"You stole everything from me, little thief."

I could still remember the fury and betrayal in his voice when he growled that at me.

Aiden sent me a heated look, as if he could hear my thoughts. The tenderness in his eyes, his taut brow. It wasn't the face of a man who blamed me anymore.

"Now I do it for a better Rellmira, for those who fought for the kingdom and the people they cherished," Aiden said softly. "I do it for the hope of peace. And love."

My heart burned. He was probably talking about people like Mother and Garyth. But something in his eyes told me his last words were meant for me.

Henry blinked rapidly, looking between me and Aiden. "That's . . . er, a lot take to take in. Pravara? And a prisoner for two gods-damned years. And Weylin . . . fucking Four."

Aiden straightened away from the tree. "If you don't believe me, mention my name to some families in Pravara, particularly around Tiersen and Chalmont. They'll remember me."

"I will," Henry said, rising to his feet. "But I believe you. And I wouldn't mind a king like you." He stretched out his hand.

After a moment's hesitation, Aiden grasped it, and they shook firmly.

It was so simple. A mutual agreement. But I felt as though it was one of Aiden's first acts as a king.

Judging by the range of proud faces from Maz, Nikella, and Ruru, I wasn't the only one.

Then Henry turned and kneeled before me. "If you sail on Aquinon, I will be there. I swear to the Four." He lowered his voice. "And if you're not, I will never stop trying to find a way to Delysia. And Everett. I swear that as well, Kiera."

Tears sprang to my eyes, and I clasped his hand. "Thank you. I'm so glad she has someone like you."

He smiled. "I was going to say the same about you."

Aiden cleared his throat, breaking us apart. "We have one last problem you might be able to solve. We need to steal a log shipment to take down the river to the mine, but the fort is too well-guarded."

Henry nodded. "Leave that to me."

CHAPTER 43
AIDEN

I hated to leave Wicked behind.

Kiera seemed to feel the same way about Ozlow. She whispered into his alert ears as she handed him over to Nikella.

But we couldn't bring horses where we were going.

I rubbed Wicked's nose as he butted my chest. "One day we won't have to say goodbye, old friend," I murmured.

He huffed.

I smiled and handed his reins to Ruru, watching until they disappeared into the forest.

Nikella and Ruru were bringing the horses to her Twaryn friends who lived nearby. We'd also left them with our saddlebags and weapons that wouldn't suit the mine—like the bows and arrows and Maz's whistler. Nikella assured us the forest dwellers would take good care of everything until we returned.

If we returned.

Henry and his men had already left to make arrangements for us. We were to meet them at dawn, which was fast approaching.

Kiera scattered the ashes of our fire and tucked the last of her knives into the third log. She sealed it with one of the wooden caps Maz had whittled for each hollow log. Now they looked like all the others floating toward the mine.

Maz and I carried them to a low, grassy bank along the river, away from the eyes of the fort.

We spoke little, focused on our tasks. But the air was crackling with tension.

I could see the way it darkened Maz's eyes and danced in Kiera's fingers. It lived in my jaw and my chest.

So much hinged on this going right. Plans built on spindly twigs that could collapse everything we hoped for.

And now I had Henry and his men to worry about.

I'd liked the captain well enough. He'd seemed as Kiera said —honorable and in love with her sister.

But it didn't sit well with me to place so much trust in a stranger so quickly. Until I'd looked at Kiera's hopeful eyes and grateful smile ... and taken the leap.

"Done," Maz announced, dusting his hands on his pants. He stared at the wide, deep river. "Think it'll work?"

I also gazed at the rushing water. We'd chosen a place along the bank that seemed the easiest to swim to, but one never knew with currents. All I could think about was Kiera trying to swim through it.

"It'd better," I said. "It's the only way we're getting on a shipment."

Dawn rose in molten orange over the eastern horizon, glowing like the forge we meant to destroy.

Maz grasped my shoulder. "Before we go, I just wanted to say I'm proud of you."

I frowned at him. "For what?"

"For finally owning up to who you are. You've been burying that shit since we met."

"With good reason."

Maz fixed me with a hard stare. "Why? Because you've faced defeat from time to time? You've been a rebel, a prisoner, a spy, an assassin, but you've always been a king, Aiden. A good king fights for the wellbeing of his people, which you've always done. A better king owns up to his mistakes and still tries to make the better choice." He poked me in the chest. "That's you, brother."

Something deep in my soul twinged. It'd been waking for days, a long-buried hope. A raw desire caged by fear.

I clapped Maz on the back. "I wouldn't have made it this far without you."

"I know," he said with a brief grin. "But only because you saved me from that mine. I'm with you to the end. Your Highness."

I chuckled, some of the earlier tension waning, and shoved him away. "If you ever call me that again, I'll use you for target practice."

He guffawed, then turned serious again, his eyes on the horizon.

"We'll get there in time, Maz," I said. "Your family will be safe, and you will get to go home soon. For good, this time."

He gave me a sad smile. "I've already lost half my family. I don't relish losing more. Will you . . . will you watch over them if I die?"

I frowned. "Of course. But this isn't goodbye, Maz."

"And it never will be."

We trudged back to the dismantled campsite to find Henry and his two men standing with Kiera.

Shayn—her ex-lover, judging from the earlier discomfort between them—stood closer than necessary to her, talking enthusiastically about something.

I ground my teeth together, a hot, sickly feeling stirring in my stomach.

"Easy, brother," Maz muttered under his breath. "Don't kill him before he helps us."

"Wasn't planning on it," I growled, stalking up to the group.

I didn't care about the red-haired soldier. I'd probably never see him again after this. He certainly hadn't seemed to care about Kiera last night. Saying he should've known better than to get involved with her.

Kiera was worth far more than his sullen regret.

"Got everything?" I demanded.

Henry faced me, the sun of his captain's badge glimmering in the dawn. "Yes. We have a shipment ready. Just meet it downriver within the hour. Here, I brought these." He pointed to a pile of dirty, threadbare clothes. "Shayn will put the shackles on once you board."

I forced myself not to flinch. It was my least favorite part of this plan. But we had to make it look real for any patrols and checkpoints.

"This is where I leave you," Henry continued. "With any goodwill of the Four, I'll see you in Aquinon, Falcryn."

I shook his outstretched hand. "Thank you for this. And your alliance."

He nodded and moved on to say a quiet goodbye to Kiera.

Within moments, they disappeared again.

We stared at the wispy pile of clothing.

"At least impersonating a Shadow-Wolf had better clothes *and* weapons," Maz said mournfully.

It would take about five or six days to get to Calimber, and we were going to spend every one of them wet and cold and shackled.

For Rellmira.

I snatched what could laughably be called a shirt and trousers.

"Boots?" Kiera asked, running her finger over the yellow stitching on her shirt as if reluctant to part with it.

"We can't." I stripped mine off. "None of the prisoners wore shoes."

"Makes it harder for them to run off, I suppose," she said bitterly. "I'll have to strap Mother's knife to my leg when we get to the mine."

Maz grabbed another set of men's clothes and patted Kiera's shoulder. "Better than between your ass cheeks, lovely. Someday, I'll tell you the story of how Aiden and I escaped Calimber."

Kiera wrinkled her nose and selected her own clothes.

The three of us stood staring at each other.

"Bit of a memory, isn't it?" Maz said with a forced grin. "When I freed you two from the Den?"

Kiera's lips twitched. "We helped."

"A bit." He waved his finger in a circle. "Shall we all turn around again, or just me, since the two of you have already seen each other naked?"

Kiera's cheeks reddened. A memory of her smooth, naked body against mine sent a rush of desire through me.

"Not the time, Mazkull," I growled and pivoted my back to them.

I yanked off my shirt and pants and put on the prisoner's garb. The pants fell just above my ankle. The shirt collar was torn at the front, revealing my chest. The thin material let in every breath of breeze and smelled of a dozen campfires.

"Done," Kiera called out softly.

"Same," Maz said.

I turned just as they did. My jaw clenched.

Kiera's curved torso was clearly visible beneath the threadbare shirt. Her breast band offered little protection from leering eyes. I was staring, too, but the cruel supervisors in the mine would likely have far worse intentions.

"Where will you hide the keys?" I rasped. "You have no pockets."

Kiera crossed her arms in front of her chest, dislodging my gaze. "Between my cheeks, if I must," she quipped.

Maz snorted.

I nearly bit my tongue in half to keep from telling her to stay back.

"This is the only instance I'm glad they have Dag prisoners," Maz grumbled, picking at his shirt.

I'd left him the larger one, but it still clung to him like a second skin. His tattoos were visible, as my falcon one likely was. But for once, no one would care. We were just two more prisoners.

A moment later, Nikella and Ruru rejoined us. Nikella dropped a bulging sack on the ground.

"Where's your cloak?" I asked.

"Left it with the horses," Nikella said, her eyes not meeting mine.

She looked strange without her long hood. But we would get it back. This wasn't goodbye.

She and Ruru grabbed their prisoner disguises and changed behind trees. Then we stuffed our old clothing into the sack. Nikella cinched it shut and hid it behind a nearby bush.

"We should go," I said, my voice hoarse and uneven. *Whatever happens, I'm proud to have known and fought with each of you.*

All four of them looked at me, silent understanding in their eyes.

We walked away from the campsite. My callused feet didn't mind the thick, rough grass. But the cold dew that wet my skin sent a shiver down my spine. The Medria was going to be even colder.

We hid in the tall grass by our logs. We didn't have to wait long for a log raft to nose its way around the river bend. Four prisoners struggled to paddle while a soldier in a glistening helmet stood in the middle.

I held my breath until I recognized the red hair curling out from under the helmet.

"Shayn," Kiera whispered.

I waited until the raft was closer, then I stood and whistled. The prisoners stared at me with wide eyes. Three men and one woman. Gaunt and starved of hope.

"Bring the raft to him," Shayn ordered.

They hastily obeyed.

Maz and I leaned out and tugged the raft to our bank. Shayn was already kneeling by the woman's feet and unshackling her.

Kiera gestured to her. "Come. You're free to go."

The woman's eyes filled with tears, and she clasped hands with Kiera, who pulled her onto the bank. "Th-Thank you. Thank you," she kept murmuring over and over.

"You'll find some clothes a short walk that way." Kiera pointed toward our old campsite.

"And some food," Nikella added.

Maz and I helped the other three prisoners off the raft and gave them the same directions. I watched them disappear, that stubborn seed of hope growing in my chest.

"Four down, only a few hundred to go," Kiera said.

I smiled down at her. "Easy."

Shayn helped us lash our three logs onto the raft with thick leather straps and buckles. Then he snapped the hated metal cuffs around our ankles, using an extra set he pulled out of his pack for me.

Unease slithered back into my veins as I stared at the chain connecting them. A prisoner once more. Perhaps I was always doomed to die as one.

I shook myself. *No. You won't die. You won't let them die. You are free. You are free.*

But the words were like a weak dam fighting against a mighty river.

We took up our paddles and awkwardly maneuvered our larger raft back into the current.

What followed was a sort of fever dream. Always cold. Always wet. Always wearing the gods-damned shackles. Steering the raft east, yet Calimber never seemed to get closer.

We talked little, miserable as we were. We stopped even less. Shayn handed out the hard bread and dried meat the fortress had allotted him. Sleep . . . sleep passed me by like the never-ending river.

We encountered a checkpoint two days into our journey. The soldiers on the wooden bridge lowered a barrier until Shayn hopped off the raft and handed over his paperwork. The soldiers scrutinized him and the paper and peered at each of us.

"This says three male and one female prisoner," one soldier said.

Kiera tensed next to me, and I clenched my oar, ready to use it as a poor weapon if necessary.

Shayn shrugged. "The girl was causing trouble, so I took her off the fort's hands."

The soldier stared at Kiera for a moment longer, something unpleasant in his gaze. But then he returned Shayn's paperwork. "The mine will beat that trouble right out of her. Off you get."

The soldiers raised the barrier and waved us forward. I forced my quivering muscles to relax.

Gods, I hoped that was the worst of it.

As each day brought us closer to Calimber, the number of patrols along the river increased. They shouted to Shayn, who answered their questions with ease. Whatever the man's faults, I was glad Henry had chosen him for this.

Nikella ducked her head every time one of the patrols passed. But they never examined us too closely.

We came to another checkpoint two nights later. Once again, they lowered the gate, and Shayn disembarked, papers in hand.

The rest of us waited, huddled together for warmth, grateful for the break.

Angry voices rose beyond the torchlight on the bridge.

"Problem?" Maz asked hoarsely.

I slowly stood, the cold metal around my ankles rasping against my skin.

Shayn stood with a few other soldiers, waving his arms and talking loudly. They argued back, pointing emphatically toward the raft.

Gods damn it. I sank down. "Something's wrong," I muttered.

"Fucking Four." Maz grasped his oar with blue-tinged fingers.

Kiera's shivering body pressed into me. I wrapped one arm around her, giving her what little warmth I had left. Ruru huddled against her other side, his wide eyes on the bridge above us.

Footsteps tromped overhead, and two soldiers came down the bank with long, hooked poles. My chest seized as they stabbed the logs and dragged us up the sloping shore.

I heard a small splash behind me, but I was too busy searching for Shayn. Surely he hadn't betrayed us? Abandoned us?

I didn't see him. But I did see a figure who made my blood run ice cold.

Long, greasy, dark hair. Dead black eyes. A triumphant smile.

Korvin had found us.

CHAPTER 44
KIERA

Such intense terror was nauseating.

I never thought I'd meet death weak, shivering, shackled, and defenseless. But that was certainly how Korvin liked to deal it.

His toothy smile and bared muscles made him look like a monster ready to devour us.

The soldiers dragged our raft up the shore. I held onto Aiden and Ruru, my nails digging into their arms. Maz was as pale as the moon above us, still as stone. Where was Nikella?

Four more soldiers with spears herded us up onto the bridge with Korvin. They shoved us to our knees before him.

Korvin glanced behind him to where two Shadow-Wolves held a red-faced Shayn. "Your papers said four prisoners—three men and one woman."

"That is what you see before you," Shayn said through clenched teeth.

Don't anger him, Shayn. You don't know him like I do.

Korvin smiled as if very pleased with this answer. "How strange when the western patrols tell me that there were three male prisoners and *two* female prisoners. The likes of which matched the descriptions I gave them."

My heart sank. They'd been watching for us and reporting back. They let us slip through their fingers so that we would land in Korvin's clutches.

Where in the deep, dark, wandering hell had Nikella gone? She was still shackled. She could be drowning right now, in the same river her father had.

Shayn visibly swallowed. "They were mistaken. My papers say three men and one woman, as you see before you."

I grimaced. *Brave, stupid man.* Perhaps he knew Nikella might be our only hope.

Korvin's smile dropped faster than an executioner's axe. He sauntered over to Shayn, pulling a long, thin sunstone blade from his belt.

Shivers ricocheted through my body, and I struggled to stay upright.

"Where is she?" Korvin demanded softly. "Where is the other woman?"

My heart beat frantically, willing Shayn to just tell the truth. Korvin would look for Nikella, anyway. He would always look for her. She wouldn't want anyone dying on her behalf.

Shayn shook his head, his jaw set. "There was no other woman."

Korvin growled and shoved the knife through Shayn's chest to the hilt.

I stifled my cry, hunching my shoulders and hanging my head. Ruru inhaled sharply, and Aiden's fists clenched on his thighs.

Shayn had a family in Aquinon. He would never see them again.

Because of me.

No. Because of *them.* Because of the choices Shayn made.

Because we were all fighting to be rid of these murderous men who had stolen so much from us.

I lifted my head, eyes burning with hatred.

Korvin was already staring at me. He tilted his head to the side, a smirk back on his dry lips. "Princess. My brother will be so happy I caught you. I was a bit too hasty with my first attack. Patience, Renwell's always telling me."

He wiped off his blade on Shayn's limp body. "I suppose he was right this time. I tracked you to Norford, and a few idiot drivers there told me you were interested in the river checkpoints. So I set myself up at this one and waited." He licked his lips and nodded at the Wolves.

They tossed Shayn's body in the river on the other side of the barrier.

Korvin watched it with glee. "He'll be the only one to reach Calimber, I'm afraid. If that was truly your intended destination. He'll tumble right off the cliff into the sea."

He chuckled, sauntering toward us. It took every ounce of willpower not to lean away from his sweaty bulk.

"Who else have I caught in my trap?" he murmured. "A boy. A princess." He halted in front of Aiden. "Ah, the prisoner Renwell wanted all to himself. Are you the monster who shot my brother with an arrow?" He pivoted to Maz, and his eyes gleamed. "Or was it you, Dag? This is going to be such fucking fun."

Korvin stepped back and jerked his head at the two Wolves. "Take her."

"No!" Aiden, Maz, and Ruru shouted at once.

The Wolves shoved Aiden and Ruru aside and yanked me away. My numb body didn't protest.

"Don't fight them," I begged Aiden as I twisted around to look into his furious green eyes.

The Wolves handed me to Korvin, who snared my wrist in a grip that could easily crush it.

He stroked my cheek, right over the scar his brother had given me. "Chain up the others by the fire. I want my sister to find us quickly. I'll take this one."

Needles of panic prickled over my cold skin.

This was a nightmare. It had to be. I was dreaming of him again. I would wake up and be safe in Aiden's arms by the fire.

But I was trapped in Korvin's hold. He smelled of oil and blood and death.

"Renwell s-swore," I stammered, hating the weakness in my voice. "He swore he'd n-never let you hurt me again."

Korvin's eyes were soulless pits. "Renwell said you'd say that. He told me to pass along a message. 'You broke your promise to me, so I'm breaking mine to you.'"

Memories of Korvin's sunstone whip assaulted me. The agonizing pain across my shoulders.

Not again. I can't. I won't survive.

A feral shriek exploded from my throat. I snatched his knife from his belt and plunged it toward his chest. He caught my wrist, wrenching it backward. Pain sliced through my arm. I dropped the knife.

Madness seized me, and I flailed against him, trying to jab at him with my knees and elbows. I sank my teeth into the taut tendons of his forearm.

He roared.

Then . . . darkness. And silence.

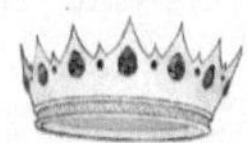

Light flickered through the darkness, followed closely by pain and the taste of blood.

So cold. Colder than the river around Arduen's Mountain. My feet were too heavy. Was I drowning?

Muffled sounds rumbled against my ears. Yes, I was underwater. Why was I tasting blood instead of water?

Korvin.

My eyes flew open. I coughed and spat onto the dry ground. A fire danced before me.

"Kiera," a beloved voice whispered.

Aiden, on the ground nearby with his wrists now shackled to his ankles. Maz and Ruru with him. The relief on their faces didn't soothe me.

We were all going to die.

My gaze fell on Korvin, who was pacing the dirt around the small clearing between tents. Blood dripped down his forearm.

I convulsed again and tried to spit out the lingering taste of his flesh in my mouth.

"Where is she?" he hissed as I wiped my mouth.

I stared at him. "Who?"

He stalked over to me and slapped me hard across the face. "My bitch sister, of course."

"Enough, Korvin!" Aiden shouted as I held my stinging cheek. "She's not fucking here! She drowned in the river this morning when we hit a rock."

No, no, Aiden. Lies won't work.

Korvin sneered at him. "My men told me they saw two women yesterday. You can't lie to me."

"The last patrol we saw rode past before she died," Aiden said, his voice full of conviction.

"That's right," Ruru piped up. "Our guard lied about having two women because he wasn't supposed to have an extra."

Korvin's face sagged with disbelief. "My little Nik would never drown. You're trying to keep her from me."

"We're telling the truth," Maz growled, his chest expanding.

"We told you the truth about the log. Why would we lie about this? Besides, your men haven't found her either. No one can swim with shackles on."

The log? I craned my neck from where I was curled up on the ground. A log from the raft lay shredded behind Korvin.

Disappointment crashed over me. The tins of explosives. The fuse ropes. The pouch of blackrust powder. They were all strewn on a table next to the gutted log.

Our plan for Calimber was now exposed to our worst enemy.

"I don't believe you," Korvin snapped. "And I can't kill you until I lure her in."

He stomped over to me and yanked me upright. Pain seared through my head. He must've slammed his fist into my temple.

He set the edge of his sunstone knife against my jaw. I stopped breathing.

"Perhaps I can teach this one a lesson while you shout for my sister," he said to Aiden.

Rage twisted Aiden's face. "If you spill one more drop of her blood, I will flay every inch of skin from your body with your own gods-damned whip."

A horrible laugh rumbled from Korvin's chest. His sticky fingers tightened on my face. "Call for her."

Fear hammered through my body. *It's just a face. My face. Just skin. It doesn't matter. The pain doesn't matter.*

Aiden's eyes burned into mine. His lips parted.

I was gasping for air, but still managed to cry out, "Don't, Aiden! He won't kill me, but he *will* kill all of you."

"Shut up," Korvin growled. "Now, call—"

"I'm here, Korvin."

Everyone twisted to see Nikella standing on the south side of the tents.

She was dripping wet in her prisoner rags, her ankles still chained together. And she carried her silver spear.

Korvin tossed me into the dirt, his eyes on Nikella. "Sister. At last."

Her nostrils flared. "You shed whatever blood I shared with you a long time ago."

"And what of the Wolves I sent searching for you?"

"Dead."

Korvin smiled. "There's my naughty little Nik. I'm so glad our brother finally let me hunt you down. I've wanted to for years. All the blood I spilled. All the pain I caused. All the death I delivered. I always thought of you."

While he spoke, I slowly crawled to the table with our explosives. Maz and Ruru sent me panicked looks, and Aiden jerked his head to the side, *stop*.

I ignored them. I was the only one with unbound hands.

Just a few more feet.

My chain rattled. I froze and peered back at Korvin. But he was fully focused on his favorite prey.

"Of all the scars I've etched," he said, gesturing at Nikella's face, "I cherish that one the most. I hope it reminded you every day of who you are. Who you'll always be. Mine. Forever."

Bile burned the back of my throat. I slid up to the table and grabbed the powder Nikella had shown me.

Praying to the Four with all my might, I dusted some over my heavy chain. The metal hissed and peeled, shedding bits of rotted metal into the dirt.

Korvin started to turn, but Nikella stepped toward him, her spear lifted.

"It's my favorite scar, too," she said. "Because it was the one that set me free. From my fear and from you. It gave me the courage to leave you and become a Teacher. To save the future king of Rellmira. To destroy everything greedy, spineless men desire. Now the rest of the world will be free of you as well. You didn't make me who I am today. I did. My choices. My will. My scars. Me."

Tears sprang to my eyes. She was everything I wanted to be.

My chain fell apart just as Korvin rolled his shoulders back and pointed his sunstone knife at Nikella.

"It doesn't matter, Nik," he said softly as I crept toward them. "I told you, little girls don't survive."

She edged toward me. "No. That's why we become women."

Korvin lunged. Nikella ducked and threw herself toward me. I scrambled forward and smattered some of the black powder on her chain. It sizzled and started to disintegrate as she danced away from Korvin's furious blows.

I sprinted toward Aiden, Maz, and Ruru, my chains beating against my bare feet.

"Guards!" Korvin screamed as he fought Nikella.

An answering shout came from the light beyond the tents. The bridge.

One of my chains tripped me, and I crashed to the ground in front of Aiden. Some of the precious powder spilled onto the ground. I swore loudly.

Aiden snatched it from my hands. "Get a weapon!"

I staggered to my feet—my knees and hands scraped and bleeding. But I hurried back to the table, dodging the vicious fight between brother and sister.

Nikella shoved Korvin into the fire, and he howled. He tossed a handful of embers at her.

There were no weapons. No weapons on the table. Only our bombs. Our weapons were in a different log, and Korvin was using the only other blade I could see.

"Fucking Four!" I shouted, frantically searching.

The guards raced toward us, their spears gleaming. Aiden was still shaking the last flecks of powder onto Maz's chains while Ruru wrenched apart his crusted shackles.

I seized one of the bombs, trying to remember what Nikella had said about them. But I had no time.

"Run!" I screamed, cocking my arm back.

Aiden's eyes widened when he understood my intention. He grabbed Ruru by the collar and flung him away from the fire. He and Maz threw themselves behind a tent just as I tossed the can into the fire in front of the soldiers.

I raced in the opposite direction. *BOOM!*

An invisible force lifted me off my feet and hurled me into a tent. Heat seared me from behind. I crashed into a heap of canvas and broken wood. Screams rose in the night.

I lay still for a moment, panting. Something warm dripped down my leg. I ignored it, trying to swim out of the tent that had swallowed me.

More screams rose, and the clash of weapons.

I thrashed harder. *We will not die here.*

I slowly crawled to freedom and found a gruesome scene. Several soldiers lay in twisted, molten heaps by the blown fire. Aiden, Maz, and Ruru battled the remaining three with stolen swords and spears.

Aiden ran his opponent through and spotted me, his face twisting with relief. "Find Nikella!" he shouted, then turned to help Maz and Ruru.

I unsheathed a dead soldier's knife and stumbled in the direction I'd last seen Nikella and Korvin hurtling.

I found them down a grassy hill, still at war. Their movements were slower, as if they were wearing out.

"You can't defeat me," Korvin shouted, slashing at Nikella. "We are the same. Monsters, the pair of us. Born of the same monster. You can't defeat what you are."

I flipped the knife and caught its tip, ready to aim it at Korvin's throat.

"No, Kiera," Nikella said sharply.

I hesitated.

Korvin used her distraction to stomp on her lagging chain and trip her.

My heart shot up to my throat. My grip grew sweaty on the blade. I didn't care what she said. I'd kill him before he killed her.

But Korvin didn't go in for the final blow. He stopped, wheezing for air. The sweat pouring down his back glistened in the moonlight.

"Admit it," he said. "Admit we are the same monster, and I won't draw out your pain for too long."

Nikella slowly rose to her feet with the aid of her spear. "You are the monster, Korvin. And you're a liar. Because I am something you never chose to be."

"What? Good? Kind?" he sneered.

"Merciful."

She stabbed at him. He evaded. She spun and plunged her spear through his chest, impaling his entire body.

CHAPTER 45
KIERA

Relief buckled my knees.

Korvin choked and gurgled, then collapsed over Nikella's spear.

He was dead. At last. And I was free. Alive. He couldn't hurt me anymore.

Nikella let his body slide off her spear like a dead fish. She was breathing heavily, and her spear shook.

I clambered to my feet and stepped around Korvin's bloody body. I pried the spear from Nikella's grasp and laid it in the cold grass. Her eyes were wild, fixed on her dead brother. Sweat clung to her scars, carving silver paths on her face.

I clasped her trembling hands in mine. "It's over, Nikella. You saved the world from a monster. He's gone."

Finally, she looked at me. "I had to do it. I had to be the one."

I nodded. "Are you hurt?"

"No. But you are." She pulled her hands out of mine and pointed at my leg.

I glanced down to see blood dripping down my thigh, a long sliver of wood stabbing through my skin.

My stomach rolled as the pain registered once more. "Oh. Right. From the explosion . . ."

"You set off one of my bombs," Nikella said sternly.

I winced. "Couldn't find any weapons."

She sighed. "We should get back to the others and make sure the other explosives and logs are safe."

She picked up her spear and led the way back up the hills to the burning camp. I glanced back once. Just to make sure Korvin was still lying in a dead heap.

Aiden, Maz, and Ruru met us on the edge of the campsite, weapons still drawn, chains flapping about their wrists and ankles.

Aiden's gaze darted between me and Nikella. "He's dead?"

Nikella nodded.

Ruru let out a tired whoop.

Maz clapped Nikella on the shoulder. "I would've liked to slice off a few pieces of him, but you deserved that victory."

Aiden wore a look of savage triumph that turned to concern when he noticed the splinter in my leg. "Gods damn it, Kiera. Why didn't you tell me?"

"We were a little busy—"

He grasped my arm and pulled me into tent after tent—the ones that weren't destroyed—until he found one with some healing supplies.

He sat me down on a chair and tore the hole in my pants wider. As he worked the splinter out, pasted my skin, and bandaged it, I tried to breathe the fear and pain from my body.

"Thank you," he said, "for freeing us the way you did. We would've died without your quick thinking."

I frowned. "You never have to thank me for that." An echo of the truth he'd spoken to me out of anger.

He gave me a soft smile, his black hair sticking to his forehead and cheeks. "At least we know the bombs work."

"But now we have less of them."

"We'll figure it out," he whispered. "Don't give up, little thief."

A corner of my mouth quirked. "Never."

He finished my leg, which was already throbbing less. Then he pulled me to my feet, a conflict raging in his eyes. His jaw flexed as if he were the one in pain.

I cupped his bristly cheek in my hand. "What's wrong?"

His brow furrowed, and he gently folded me into his arms. "When he hit you . . ." he murmured into my neck. "When he held his knife to your face . . . I would've done anything to save you, Kiera."

He pulled back enough to stare deeply into my eyes. "I could say I would burn this world for you, but the truth is, *I* would burn for you. To keep that beautiful heart beating, I would burn until I was nothing but ash and a name on your lips."

My heart beat wildly as if trying to escape my chest. Was he saying what I thought he was saying?

He loves me. Surely he must love me as I love him.

But I didn't just love him.

I trusted him. The words he spoke. The fervor behind them. That anguish didn't stem from a promise to my mother, but from something deeper.

He had bared his heart to me over and over. And each time had sealed tiny shards of my broken trust back together.

But had I healed his shattered trust in me?

I tried to speak, but no words came out. I licked my lips and tried again. "Aiden, I—"

"We found the shackle key," Ruru announced as he burst into the tent, holding a rusty key aloft. His eyes widened when he found us embracing. "Oops. I'll, uh . . . be out here."

"No, Ruru," I said quickly. "I'll take it." Aiden probably hated still being shackled.

Ruru handed it to me and disappeared.

Aiden smirked and lifted one of his cuffed wrists. "Would you like to free me a second time, little thief?"

I smiled back at him. "And I didn't even have to steal the key this time."

"No. Just everything else."

I inhaled sharply, gazing up at him. The way he said it, soft and deep, was far different from the way he'd said it right before he'd kissed me, drunk and bitter. Now those words held a treasure mine of emotions and meanings.

I unchained his wrists and handed him the key for his ankles. But instead of releasing his shackles, he kneeled down and inserted the key into mine.

His fingers grazed the inside of my ankle as he unlocked one, then the other. Chills raced along my skin.

I made a small noise in the back of my throat. He looked up at me, those green eyes practically glowing in the soft light.

I wanted a thousand things in this moment. And all of them included him.

But we were running out of time.

"We won't have shackles for the last leg of the journey," I rasped, gesturing at the broken, discarded chains. "We won't look like true prisoners."

Clenching his jaw, he bent to unlock his ankle cuffs. They sprang open. "We'll just have to hope they don't notice. Or don't care."

Several other problems crowded my mind. We didn't have Shayn or our papers. We'd used some of our supplies. And this delay with Korvin could make us late.

I stretched out my hand. Aiden grasped it, and I helped him rise.

"We need to talk to the others," I said.

We found them gathered around the fire. They had contained its spread with large stones. Their discarded shackles lay in a heap by the table that was now empty of our bombs.

"I moved everything into one of the other logs," Nikella said, wrapping a strip of fabric around a bleeding cut on her arm. "What was left, anyway."

I cringed. "I'm sorry, Nikella. I—"

She held up her hand. "It was smart. We still have enough bombs for the mine, especially if we supplement with some fire-seeds from the forge." Her brow creased. "As far as the blackrust powder, I'll just have to think of something else for the cliff gate. Losing Shayn is far more troublesome—may the gods find his soul."

We all murmured the same farewell.

Aiden walked over to one of the dead soldiers. He picked up his helmet and put it on his head. "I'll be our new guard."

"What about our bloody papers?" Maz asked between gulps of water from a canteen. "None of these men had any on them."

"We'll have to go without," Nikella said grimly.

"Perhaps they'll be too busy to check," Ruru added with a shrug.

Unlikely. But we'd spin that lie when needed.

Another problem was that, if Aiden was our new guard, he wouldn't be able to help me and Ruru free the prisoners.

I glanced at Ruru.

He nodded solemnly at me. "We can do this."

"We'll need more time," I told Aiden.

"I'll think of something." He glanced at Maz and Nikella. "That means you'll have to hold off on lighting the fuses a bit longer."

"We'll wait for the signal, brother. As long as it takes."

I fidgeted with the end of my braid, then dared to ask, "What if Skelly and Jek and the others aren't there?"

Maz scowled at me. "They'll be there."

"But if they're not?"

"Then we'll try to steal one of their ships anyway," Aiden said quietly. "Escape with those we can and destroy everything else."

The silence crackled between us like the fire.

We were probably headed to our deaths. The memory of the prisoner woman's face from a few days ago surfaced in my mind. Her desperate gratitude, her shock at being free.

There were a hundred more like her in the mine. Plus thousands of frightened Rellmirans in Aquinon.

They needed us.

"We should go," I said. "But first, we need to burn the bodies to cover our tracks."

Nikella shook her head. "Leave them. We'll lose too much time. Even if a patrol comes by and spreads a warning that reaches Calimber, our mission will already be over."

I nodded, relieved at her reasoning.

Aiden stripped the soldier of his uniform and donned it over his rags. I swept up the shackles and dumped them into the river while the others heaved the raft back into the water. My thigh throbbed as we scrambled on board.

On the bridge, Aiden cranked up the barrier, then leaped onto the raft as we passed through.

He looked strange in a soldier's uniform, almost like the night of our heist when he'd dressed as one of Asher's guards.

We'd worn so many disguises, yet I always knew who he was underneath. Just as he knew me. More and more, until nothing could hide us from each other.

We paddled away from the smoldering tents and empty bridge. Away from the lone body in the cold grass. The husk of a defeated enemy.

"How did you survive the swim?" Ruru asked, glancing at Nikella as he pushed the raft away from the riverbank.

Her shoulders tightened. "When I was a young girl, I learned to hold my breath for a very long time."

My little Nik would never drown.

My lip curled. I hoped the Four would throw his soul into the Abyss, where it belonged.

We paddled as long as we could and slept in shifts, trying our hardest to reach Calimber in time. The journey was much more bearable without the shackles. But the added fear of being discovered almost outweighed it.

A patrol passed us, heading west, and we crouched down to hide our unshackled legs. They shouted to Aiden, who shouted back, using similar replies to what Shayn had.

They were eager to report to Korvin, bloodthirsty grins lighting up their faces. Little did they know of the carnage they were going to find.

We saw the smoke spirals of a dozen fires at dawn. Then the mass of tents and blockades came into view. The river picked up speed, rushing us toward the cliff and the waterfall that spilled over it into the Niviath Sea.

I barely had a moment to breathe before our raft raced up to the dock. Soldiers hooked it with their long poles, pulling us in, while Aiden tied us to the mooring posts.

Calimber. Gods, we'd made it. Soldiers and prisoners bustled everywhere. Horses tramped through the mud, pulling carts and carrying riders. Men ran through shouted drills with their swords and spears in the field next to the river.

How in the deep, dark, wandering hell were we supposed to defeat all this?

My legs shook as Aiden stepped onto the dock. A thin man with wild gray hair hurried up to him with a ledger.

"Twaryn, load 713?" he snapped, already scribbling something down.

"Yes," Aiden answered immediately and with much more calm than I felt.

"You'll have to use your own prisoners to unload and chop the wood. We're short," the man spat, as if this were Aiden's fault.

Aiden frowned. "Didn't the Shadow-Wolves arrive with more prisoners?"

"Clearly not, otherwise I wouldn't be asking you," he sneered and hurried off, barking at someone else.

My heart sank to my toes. They weren't here. Skelly, Jek, Yarina, Sigrid . . .

I glanced at Maz. His face was whiter than bone as he stared at the distant, empty horizon.

We were alone.

CHAPTER 46

KIERA

WE CARRIED OUR LOGS TO THE CHOPPING STATION.

Dozens of prisoners and soldiers crowded around, sawing and carving wood into distinct shapes. Like the bones of a ship.

A hulking soldier bellowed. "You there! Stop!"

We halted as one and turned. Aiden stepped forward, his expression annoyed. "What is it now? We have a schedule to keep."

"Watch your tongue, boy. I outrank you," the soldier growled. He nodded at my bare feet. "Prisoners must be shackled in Calimber."

I stiffened.

Aiden's eyebrows rose. "Truly? That's not what my commanding officer in Twaryn said. But if that's the way here..."

"It is," the soldier griped. "Get them shackled before you chop your wood. When you're done, take it to the bastards in the forge. They've been begging for more fuel."

Aiden led us to where the soldier gestured. A box of shackles sat near a pile of bark shavings. After hesitating for a split second, Aiden grabbed a pair and locked them around my ankles.

"I'm sorry, Kiera," he whispered.

I bit my lip and tried to keep my rising fear in check. I'd hoped they wouldn't notice. Gods, those keys had better be easy to steal.

Once all of us, except Aiden, were shackled again, we lifted our logs onto our shoulders and carried them to an empty stand.

While Maz and Ruru sawed the normal logs, Nikella and I hurried back for the hollow ones. We discreetly emptied our weapons and supplies into a cart. Then Ruru tossed the chunks of wood on top.

Aiden, in his partially burned soldier's uniform, barked orders and snapped at us to hurry. My limbs shook as we wheeled our two carts down into the mine.

I felt blind at first, blinking in the darkness. My bare feet appreciated the packed earth over the piles of wood shavings and sawdust. But I hated the now-familiar bite of metal on my skin and the drag of the chain between my ankles.

We stepped into the blaze and brightness of the forge. Two sweaty men poked at the roaring fire and hissing weapons. Neither of them looked up at our entrance.

Aiden sauntered toward them, pretending to observe their work, as we unloaded the wood from our carts. We added to the small stack of wood they already had, which was covered by a leather blanket—most likely to prevent sparks from catching.

Maz dipped his hand to the bottom of a cart and pulled out his small axe. He hid it behind his back.

My stomach in knots, I hurried to the other end of the cave to peer into the tunnel beyond. No one was there.

I nodded to Aiden.

He slipped up behind one man while Maz slid up to the other. I looked away when Aiden unsheathed his soldier's sword.

A thump and wet gurgles joined the forge's grumbling.

I flinched, staring determinedly into the empty tunnel. Death was necessary, but it wasn't pleasant.

By the time I glanced back, Aiden and Maz had stripped the two limp men of their forge aprons and sturdy boots and dragged their bodies to the woodpile. The leather blanket hid them perfectly. We just had to hurry in case more deliveries came.

Nikella and Maz donned aprons over their prisoner garb.

"We'll have to cut away our ankle cuffs to wear these," Nikella said grimly, hefting the boots. "We can't wait for you to bring back a key."

Aiden grabbed a pair of wickedly curved sunstone shears from a worktable. "These should work."

Ruru scowled. "You'll gouge their legs with that."

"We'll be fine, little brother," Maz said with a reassuring smile. "I've lost a lot of skin already. What's a bit more?"

Nikella nodded.

Aiden kneeled at Nikella's feet and carefully angled the shears around one of the thick metal bands.

A soft groan drew my attention away. A prisoner stumbled through the tunnel toward me, carrying a bucket.

"Shit," I hissed under my breath.

I hurried forward. "I'll carry that the rest of the way."

The old man looked up at me, startled. He shook his head.

"Please," I begged. "If I don't make myself useful, the supervisors will whip me again."

The man's face softened, and he handed me his bucket. I took it gratefully and waited until he'd shuffled back the way he'd come.

The bucket was full of sparkly sunstone bits. I blinked at it. Father would've locked this in his vault or sold it for hundreds of gold coins.

It'd been worth more to him than the lives spent to attain it. And now Renwell continued that tradition on a grander scale.

I scowled at the sunstone and carried it into the forge cavern.

Nikella was limping slightly in her heavy boots as she sprinkled fireseeds around the glowing furnaces. Then she strategically tucked her bomb tins throughout the cavern. Ruru helped her coil the fuses out of sight.

Maz growled between clenched teeth, while Aiden slowly sliced through his remaining shackle. "Gods damn it, go faster."

"Hold still, or you'll lose more than just skin," Aiden said, his gaze focused.

The metal clanked to the ground with Maz's sigh of relief. I emptied the sunstone bucket into the glittering pile of night sky.

"I'll use this as my cover," I said, waving the bucket.

Aiden nodded. "Since the Wolf ship hasn't arrived—"

"They'll be here," Maz snapped. "They're just late. We can stall until then."

Aiden's face hardened. "When you hear my whistle, Mazkull, you will run up to the soldiers and tell them there's a breakout— whether that ship is here or not. I'll fight our way onto one of their warships alone, if I have to."

"Don't be stupid," Maz snarled. "I'm not letting you fight alone, and I'm not saying to wait that long. Just give them a minute to get here, Aiden."

I glanced between the two of them staring stone-faced at each other while I strapped Mother's knife to my leg. I slipped the rest of my small knives into my waistband. Uncomfortable, but hopefully they wouldn't be there long.

Ruru and Nikella also hid weapons on their person, trying to ignore the tension.

"I'll give them as much time as I can," Aiden finally said.

Maz nodded stiffly, turning back to the forge.

Nikella tucked several canisters with their fuses into my bucket, covering them with a cloth.

Aiden slid a few more into his pockets, then marched into the tunnel. "Let's go."

Ruru hurried after him. I followed more slowly, glancing back at Nikella and Maz, suddenly worried I would never see them again.

Maz's scowl softened. "Go on, lovely. This isn't goodbye."

I smiled tremulously and whipped around before I lost my nerve. I had to hop awkwardly to catch up with Ruru. Stupid fucking shackles.

We descended deeper into the mine. I could almost feel the press of the earth around us. Earth that would come crashing down soon.

Aiden led us into a huge cavern. My jaw dropped at the enormity of it. The sunstone. The pillars. The *people*. It seemed too much, too many.

This mission suddenly felt almost impossible. Especially without our ship of allies.

That familiar edge of panic began slicing into my calm.

Focus, focus. One thing at a time.

I recognized the supervisors from Aiden's descriptions. All with helmets and sunstone clubs. A few with ledgers and signal horns. But I only cared for the keys dangling from their belts.

Just a twitch of your fingers, Kiera. Nothing you haven't done before. Get close. Steal them. Get out.

But first, we had to hide the bombs.

We split up like we planned. Aiden sauntered off in one direction. Ruru and I in another.

Ruru grabbed a bucket like mine. We quickly found the line of prisoners waiting to fill their buckets with sunstone. It snaked around the rim of the cavern under the scaffolding, which was perfect because it protected us from the rocks that frequently tumbled down.

The other prisoners didn't pay us any mind. Just hobbled forward with their empty buckets and emptier eyes.

I wanted to whisper that they would be free soon. That they needed to be ready. I wanted to see hope reignite in their souls.

But I didn't want to cause a ruckus. I needed to wait, wait, wait. Gods-damned waiting.

I discreetly slipped Ruru a few of the explosives. Once he was close enough to a pillar, he casually shuffled toward it. He blended in with the other prisoners who picked over the rocky floor, looking for any bits of sunstone that might've fallen and adding it to their buckets.

When the next cry of "Rocks!" came and everyone ducked, he darted forward and nestled the canister in the rocky hole from which the pillar sprouted.

We did that three more times, alternating who slipped out of line. Always making sure the supervisor's back was turned.

By the fourth time, we'd gotten several curious stares from other prisoners, but they said nothing.

I breathed a sigh of relief once all the canisters were hidden. I waited for the bucket of sunstone to be lowered from the top of the scaffolding, then transferred the sunstone into my bucket and stepped away.

I hesitated, wanting to wait for Ruru, but the supervisor prowling the wooden platform in the middle of the cavern noticed.

He leered down at me while grasping the handle of his sunstone club. "Haven't seen you before, girl. Must be new if you haven't turned ugly yet."

Imprisonment in this abyss tends to do that, you sick bastard.

Stomach churning, I lowered my eyes and trudged past him.

He jumped down behind me with a heavy thud and grabbed my arm. "How about I come find you later?"

His keys jangled against my hip. Fucking Four, if only I had a hand free. But if I dropped my bucket...

"Did you hear me, girl?" he demanded, his rotten breath nearly making me gag. "Which cell—"

"Supervisor!" a rough voice shouted.

I looked up to see Aiden striding toward us, murder in his gaze. He gripped the hilt of his sword.

I sent him a panicked look. *Gods, no, Aiden! You'll give us away!*

He ignored me, halting almost too close to the leech of a man holding me. "Need I remind you we are behind schedule, and you harassing the prisoners will only make it worse. Get fucked on your own time, or I'll report you to High General Dracles."

The supervisor stiffened. His wide eyes traveled over the badges decorating Aiden's chest. He took a step back and threw my arm away from him.

"Get back to work," Aiden snarled at me. Then he turned and left as if I were nothing to him.

I stumbled back toward the main tunnel on shaky legs. Gods damn it, that was close. If only I'd gotten the fucking keys. Now I'd have to get close to one of them again. Me, not Ruru. I wasn't letting him anywhere near a bastard like that.

I glanced over my shoulder. The supervisor was watching me go, dark, violent thoughts twisting in his gaze.

I'd earned an enemy. One who would be hard to hide from.

So be it. If he came after me, I'd take more than his gods-damned keys.

Ruru caught up to me as we plodded back to the forge. "Are you all right? What happened?"

"Stay away from that one," I said shortly.

"I already picked my mark. He's half-asleep or drunk. I'll

stumble into him on our way back." Ruru shoved his sweaty hair out of his eyes. "You sure you're all right?"

"I'm fine. Now stop talking before they punish us," I muttered under my breath as two soldiers approached.

They peered into our buckets as we passed, but said nothing.

The tightly coiled fear in my chest eased a bit when I saw Maz and Nikella were still in the forge, pretending to work. Maz flashed me a smile.

"Is everything ready?" Nikella asked in a low voice as I took my time pouring my sunstone into the pile.

"Bombs, yes. Keys, no," I said. I quickly told her where the bombs were located.

She gave me a short nod, her brow furrowed. For a moment, I thought I saw a flicker in her eyes of the same fear that was crushing my chest.

If someone discovered the bombs . . . If we couldn't steal the keys . . . If we couldn't free the prisoners . . . If our ship didn't come in . . .

One terrible scenario after another haunted my thoughts as Ruru and I walked back into the cavern.

I joined the line again, but Ruru diverted, aiming for a supervisor who was leaning heavily against the stone wall. A tiny woman holding a bucket of water stood next to him as he slurped from a cup.

Make it quick and smooth, Ruru.

I couldn't help searching for Aiden as I shuffled forward in line, but I didn't see him. The loss of his familiar face notched my fear higher.

"Rocks!"

I pressed myself against the wall, cowering under the scaffolding like the others. Rocks showered down. Then a large body smacked into the ground.

I jerked backward, gasping. Several other prisoners whimpered.

The body was a shattered, gory mess. Chains around the ankles.

I swallowed back the urge to vomit. The prisoner must've fallen from the scaffolding when the rocks broke free.

The perverse supervisor hurried over, swearing, and kicked the body in disgust. He shifted the helmet on his head to peer up at the scaffolding. "Do you have another to take over?" he bellowed.

"We'll manage," someone from above shouted back.

The supervisor glanced around. I made myself small, but it didn't matter. His dark eyes lit up when they found me.

He jabbed a finger at me and the man in front of me. "You two. Clean this up."

The other prisoner immediately shuffled forward, his shoulders hunched. I followed, putting him between me and the supervisor.

My stomach pitched and rolled like I was back on *Mynastra's Wings*.

How am I supposed to clean up a body in pieces?

I shuddered and gingerly picked up a bony arm that separated from the rest of the body with a horrible squelch.

Bile seared past my throat with a vengeance. I coughed it up, tears springing to my eyes.

The supervisor laughed and climbed back onto his platform.

The other prisoner and I carried pieces of the body to a cart that already held several other bodies. I tried not to sob, gently laying the arm in the cart.

I'm sorry we didn't get here sooner. I hope the gods find your souls and give you peace.

After a few more trips, we finished our grisly job. I was covered in blood and other things I didn't want to think about.

Truly, I didn't want to think about this gods-damned place ever again.

The supervisor blocked my path when I tried to re-enter the line. His eyes narrowed cruelly, sliding over me. "Let's get you cleaned up," he breathed.

I opened my mouth to protest, but he seized my arm and yanked me toward a dimly lit tunnel that burrowed deeper into the earth. Gated cells pockmarked the dark walls. He flung me against an empty one at the end.

I stumbled over my chain, barely catching myself as I used the movement to grab Mother's knife.

A lone lantern shone over his repulsive face. He licked his lips greedily, his eyes dipping lower. "I'm going to enjoy this."

My body felt cold and hard, a sword without feelings, only purpose. "So am I."

His face went blank.

I darted forward and shoved my jagged knife into his chest. Right into his worthless heart.

He jolted, his eyes wide in disbelief, his mouth gaping in a death rattle.

"From one Abyss to the next," I whispered and twisted the knife.

He crashed to the ground, as dead as the poor soul I just scraped off the cavern floor.

My hands shook, covered in even more blood. But I felt no shame, no regret.

His keys glimmered at his waist. I yanked them off his belt. Just as footsteps pounded around the corner. I whipped the keys and knife behind my back.

A soldier burst into view, sword at the ready.

Aiden.

I sagged in relief. A raw mixture of terror and rage twisted his beautiful face.

He stopped short when he saw me standing over the supervisor's body. "Did he hurt you?"

I shook my head, strapping my blade and the keys to my leg. Hopefully, my rattling chain would cover any noise the keys made.

Aiden didn't lower his guard. "They're still not here. The ship. I checked."

My heart fell. What if they'd been hurt or captured or killed? What if they never came?

"We should—"

"You there! Soldier!"

I stiffened, all the blood draining to my toes. Two supervisors with their sunstone clubs aloft stood in the tunnel.

Aiden's face softened at the panic on my face. "Save the others. Leave me behind if you must."

What?

He dragged his sword through the dead supervisor's neck, coating the metal in blood. Then he whipped around with a snarl.

"My name is Aiden Falcryn, and I've come to kill High General Dracles."

CHAPTER 47

AIDEN

I LOST THE ENSUING FIGHT AS QUICKLY AS I COULD.

The supervisors knocked my bloody sword out of my hands and hauled me to the place I hated most in the world. One I swore I'd never dwell in again—a frigid cell in the deepest part of the mine.

The darkness was so complete I'd often felt that I was going mad when they locked me up here years ago. There was no beginning or end to it. No sound. No way to anchor myself other than the clutch of cold metal.

I rattled my chains to a steady rhythm, humming deep in my throat. Anything to keep the terror at bay.

And I thought of Kiera. Of the horror on her face when I'd told her to leave me behind. But she didn't know. She didn't know the agony I felt when I arrived back in the cavern to find her gone.

I'd gone to check the beach, to hold up my promise to Maz. I'd been bitterly disappointed to see no other ships than the warships—one at anchor, one being built on the shore. After waiting a few minutes, I started drawing suspicious stares.

I'd hurried back to find Ruru frantically gesturing at me, then to a tunnel off to the side. I didn't see Kiera ... or the supervisor scum who'd harassed her. I'd pelted into the tunnel, someone shouting at me as I drew my sword. But I didn't stop until I reached her.

My beautiful Kiera was alive and still fighting, covered in death and gore.

She was going to set those prisoners free. I'd promised her a distraction, and this was it. The supervisors had already suspected me, but claiming to be here to assassinate Dracles was more than enough for them to throw me down here.

Perhaps I'd bought her and Ruru enough time. Perhaps Ruru would whistle, and Maz and Nikella would alert the soldiers. They'd set off their bombs, unaware that I was chained up in this pit.

Perhaps ... perhaps ...

I kept rattling and humming until a faint blob of light swayed toward me, closer and closer. Was my mind playing tricks on me? It had before.

But then I heard the creak of the lantern and the steady stomp of boots. I saw the arm holding the lantern and the face that accompanied it.

"Ah, just the man I wanted to see," I drawled, as if we were meeting in a tavern over a cold, foamy pint.

Dracles squinted at me, holding his lantern closer to the bars of my cell. He looked older than what I expected after spying on him as a Wolf. The lines in his jowly face looked almost as deep as Nikella's scars.

But his fierce gaze was the same. "I laughed when they told me some lunatic was here to kill me. But then they told me the name you gave them. Aiden Falcryn."

"And you just had to come verify for yourself," I said, stepping as far into the light as my chains allowed. "Was I lying?"

He studied my face, his jaw hardening. "You look like him. The eyes. I suppose I should've guessed that his stupidity was hereditary."

My fists tightened. He'd known my father. But I also knew my father was anything but stupid—from stories Nikella and other older folk told.

"We've met before," I said, fighting to keep my voice as even as his. "Do you remember?"

It took him a moment, then recognition lit in his eyes. "Ah, yes, the young rebel from Pravara. I didn't recognize you as Tristan's spawn then, half-dead as you were. How the hell did you survive here for seven years?"

I smirked. "Oh, I wasn't here all that time. I escaped five years ago."

"That's impossible," he snapped, his back straightening into his soldier's posture. "No one has ever escaped Calimber."

"Not that they told you, anyway. I suppose the men here aren't as loyal as you think."

He growled and paced in front of my cell. I smiled, thoroughly enjoying getting under his skin. If I died down here, at least I had gotten this small revenge.

"Renwell and his bloody secrets. He must've known," Dracles grumbled under his breath.

"Trouble with your new master?" I taunted.

He stopped pacing and glared at me. "I am High General, boy. I've held that title since before you could walk." He clasped his hands behind his back. "So you came back here to kill me, is that it? Just you?"

I leaned forward, so he could see every bit of hatred in my eyes. "I wanted to be the one to watch the light leave your eyes. I would never let anyone else share that victory with me."

"Victory." Dracles released a short, hard chuckle. "I'll show you what victory looks like, young Falcryn. Guard!"

They released me from the cell and dragged me back through the tunnels, my hands and feet still shackled.

My heart pounded heavily, as if realizing these might be its last beats.

All I asked for was one more glimpse of Kiera. If I could look into those fiery amber eyes one last time, I could die with peace and hope in my heart.

As they hauled me back into the main cavern and up onto the supervisors' platform that had served as the location for many beatings, my mind flickered through everything that could've been. Storming Aquinon. Defeating Renwell. Wearing my father's crown. Getting to know the palace he and my mother had fled.

But those hopes were overshadowed by my brightest dream —having Kiera by my side through a coronation, a wedding, a life. Falling asleep beside her. Waking up next to her. Playing Death and Four in our rooms. Eating biscuits on a roof somewhere. Touching, kissing, never letting go.

Fucking Four, was this how Brielle had felt before she died? Plagued by the dreams of a life she desperately wanted but would never get to live?

An ache blossomed in my chest as they forced me to my knees on the wooden platform.

I frantically searched the crowd of prisoners and supervisors for Kiera's familiar figure. One more glimpse wasn't enough. I needed her to know. Even if I couldn't speak the words aloud.

I didn't hear what Dracles shouted. I didn't care about the soldiers encircling me. I didn't fear the sword poised at the back of my neck.

I feared not telling her. I feared losing her before she knew.

At last, I spotted her—one more dirty, scarred face among the many that surrounded my hasty execution. But her eyes burned into me like the sun I would never see again.

I locked gazes with her.

I love you, Kiera. I would give anything to have a life beyond this moment with you. My soul will never stop trying to find yours.

I love you, my little thief.

Her face crumpled for a moment, as if she'd understood some part of what my eyes were trying to tell her.

But then it hardened when Dracles shouted again. "Behold the last rebel of the Pravaran rebellion! He thought he could escape his fate, escape his punishment—the same one that you all bear now. He dies today to remind you that you cannot escape."

He bent down to whisper in my ear. "This is what victory looks like—the better, stronger man standing over the weaker one as he dies at his feet. Just as your father did. Just as your other rebels perished. *Weak.*"

I ignored him, my gaze fixed on Kiera's murderous one. She'd pushed her way to the front row of prisoners. Something glinted in her hand.

She wouldn't—

"Kill him," Dracles ordered.

The sword lifted. Kiera cocked her arm back.

"We're under attack!" someone shouted. "Enemies on the beach! We're under attack!"

Everyone froze, except the soldier panting and waving his arms.

Then chaos unleashed.

"Sound the alarm!" Dracles bellowed.

Supervisors blew their horns. Prisoners scattered.

I started to rise, but Dracles knocked me back down.

"Finish him," he snarled at the soldier behind me.

The soldier lifted his sword again, then jerked backward, a knife sticking out of his throat. He collapsed.

Dracles drew his sword and slashed at me. I rolled to the

side, tumbling off the platform. A pair of gentle hands caught me.

Kiera.

She sawed through my chains with her sunstone blade like they were mere rope. She thrust a sunstone club into my hands. "Fight, Aiden," she growled.

A shadow shifted over us. Kiera looked up and blanched, shoving me to the side. Dracles's sword screeched against the rock between us.

"Go!" I shouted, rolling to my feet. "Get them out!"

The general's eyes widened when he realized this was about much more than an assassination.

He roared, spittle flying from his mouth as he attacked me. We fought furiously. I had no blades, but the club protected me from his steel blows.

People shouted and fled around us. More soldiers poured down the main tunnel.

It was time.

I ducked and whirled away from Dracles's blows. His face was nearly purple with rage. He swung wide, and I bashed my club into his sword hand. He released it with a howl. I snatched it up and drove it through his armor into his chest.

"For Pravara," I whispered.

I withdrew the sword before his last breath. I didn't care to watch him die. I cared only for my people.

"Aiden!"

I glanced over to see Nikella and Maz racing toward me in a throng of soldiers.

Then an explosion rocked the whole cavern.

CHAPTER 48
KIERA

THE GROUND TREMBLED BENEATH MY FEET, BUT I KEPT RUNNING.
I'd sliced through my chain the moment I saw them haul Aiden
to that platform.

After the supervisors had taken him, another one came and
tossed me into the empty cell. He didn't even bother to search
me—possibly because I was sobbing hysterically. It took little
effort to be convincing.

He locked me in, glared at the dead supervisor, then walked
away, muttering that he'd find someone else to clean up the
mess.

Ruru had found me just as I'd unlocked my cell. I told him
what happened, and together, we opened the rest of the cells.

We freed the prisoners from their shackles, but told them to
wait for the first explosion before fleeing. Ruru handed our two
stolen Wolf knives to a few Dag women, instructing them to cut
anyone's chains they could. I also passed out a few of my small
knives.

We hurried back to the main cavern, where I fully
intended to search for Aiden. But then they'd dragged him

out and ordered everyone to gather around for an execution.

I'd given the keys to Ruru, telling him to unlock as many shackles as possible and to arm the prisoners with whatever tools and weapons they could find.

But I couldn't leave Aiden to die, no matter what he told me.

Now I prayed to all the Four that he was close behind me. Along with Maz and Nikella, after they lit the bomb fuses in the main cavern.

Ruru was somewhere ahead of me, leading the prisoners to freedom amid the anarchy.

Soldiers shouted, eyes wide and wheeling. Some ran back toward the explosion. Others kept stampeding toward the beach. They shoved the prisoners out of the way to reach the greater threats.

They probably figured there was no escape regardless.

But enemies on the beach? That *had* to be Jek and Skelly and the others.

A woman running next to me stumbled and lost her grip on the sunstone pick she carried. I grabbed it and shoved it back in her hands. "Keep going! Split any prisoner's chains you can before we reach the water."

She nodded, her face determined despite the blood smeared on her cheek.

I slowed down, shoving the stragglers along. I cut what chains I could with Mother's knife. This was the best use this gods-damned knife had ever seen.

A soldier crashed into me. I fell to the ground, and people trampled over my body. Pain pounded through me. I cried out, dragging myself into a side tunnel.

I clutched my knife, trying to catch my breath. The next explosions could happen any moment. But I hadn't seen Aiden, Maz, or Nikella.

I squeezed my eyes shut. Panic threatened to drown me.

Breathe. Breathe. Keep moving. Get out. Save the others. Breathe. Breathe. GO!

I hauled myself to my feet, staggering as pain wailed through my body. Gritting my teeth, I tailed the stream of soldiers and prisoners. No need to use Aiden's markings.

I found the body of one prisoner, then another. Trampled. I prayed for them as I snatched up a discarded sunstone axe.

The salty smell of the sea and the stench of burning oil hit me the moment I stumbled out of the tunnel into blinding sunshine.

Screams and shouts battered my ears. A battle raged on the beach between me and a dark ship.

Shadow-Wolves and Dag warriors clashed with soldiers. Arrows whistled through the air. Steel and sunstone drew blood. Bodies dotted the sand like flies.

"Kiera!" Ruru waved to me from the water. His arm hung at an odd angle.

I raced forward, dancing around soldiers and warriors.

"I can't swim," he panted, sweat trembling on his upper lip. "Keep leading them."

The prisoners were wading toward the stolen Shadow-Wolf ship, but a few of them balked at the Wolves standing at the railing. One of them yanked off their mask, revealing red hair.

"Climb up!" Skelly shouted, waving at the rope ladder he'd let down.

I sheathed Mother's knife and threaded my arm around Ruru's waist. "We'll lead them together."

I plunged into the cold water. It dragged at my heavy ankles and the remnants of my chains. But I kept charging through.

Ruru groaned, doing his best to stay upright. A few of the prisoners slipped under the water before flailing above it again, still clutching their makeshift weapons.

"Drop them!" I screamed. "Just get on the ship!"

One man—the same one who'd helped me clean up the body—dropped his sunstone chisel to the bottom of the bay and paddled for the ship. Only for an arrow to sink into his back.

My last thread of calm shredded. I beat at the water, kicking my exhausted legs, keeping a stranglehold on Ruru's waist.

They will not kill me. They will not kill us. We will not die here.

I thrashed my way to the ladder. Prisoners clambered up it and onto the ship. I shoved Ruru onto it.

"Climb," I gasped and turned around.

"Kiera, don't!" he called.

But I'd already started swimming back to the beach. There were more prisoners to save. I wasn't done yet.

A series of explosions ripped through the white stone cliffs. Rocks ground together like giant teeth. The cliff buckled.

My heart stopped.

The tunnel coughed out dirt, shuddering.

And then—

A handful of figures burst out of the tunnel. Soldiers and Aiden, Maz, and Nikella.

I nearly sobbed with relief. They were alive. They'd made it.

But the mine was still collapsing, spewing stones at everyone on the wide beach.

The battle halted as the fighters raced for their ships. The soldiers retreated to their warship, and the Dags and fake Wolves splashed their way to our ship.

Maz threw an older woman over his shoulder and kept running toward the water. Spear in hand, Nikella snatched up a skinny girl and followed. Sprinting hard across the beach, Aiden seized the arm of a boy younger than Ruru.

A woman called out, thrashing in the water, trying to get to me. I swam toward her. An arrow grazed my cheek.

I jerked back. Rellmiran archers were still shooting from a

corner of the beach. Until a massive chunk of the cliff crushed them.

I struggled toward the woman, then clasped her hand and towed her to the ship.

Maz had beaten me there. He carried the old woman all the way up the ladder. I let the other woman go first, then followed her on the slippery rungs. I glanced down once to see Nikella and Aiden and the people they'd saved below me.

We're going to make it. We're alive. The mine is dying. We saved as many prisoners as we could. We've won.

Rising hope pushed me up the last few rungs onto the ship. The deck was crowded with Dag warriors and half-dressed Shadow-Wolves and prisoners. People bled and cried in huddles. Skelly yelled from the captain's wheel to get everyone below. Prisoners scuttled down the hatch.

The cliff devoured the beach and slammed rocks into the bay, violently shaking the ship.

"We need to get the fuck out of here!" Skelly roared.

A barrel with a lit fuse crashed onto the deck in front of me. My mind blanked.

Maz seized it and threw it over the railing. It exploded, raining bits of wood and boiling oil over us. I threw my arms over my head, whimpering as my skin burned.

"Fucking bastards!" Maz roared across the gap of water between us and the warship.

Yarina and Sigrid, in their Wolf garb but without masks, stepped up next to their brother and fired arrows at the soldiers.

Aiden and Nikella clambered onto the ship with the boy and the girl, whom they shoved down the hatch.

I snatched an abandoned bow off the deck and yanked an arrow from Yarina's pouch.

"Good to see you, princess!" she shouted and loosed another arrow. It hit a soldier, sending him into the churning sea.

But they were loading the catapult with another lit barrel.

"Shoot the barrel soldiers!" I yelled, firing at one of the men. I missed. But Sigrid didn't.

The barrel exploded in the soldiers' faces.

Maz cheered, lifting his battle axe above his head. He beamed down at us.

Just as an arrow slammed into his chest.

CHAPTER 49
AIDEN

All I heard was Kiera screaming. Endless and agonized, like her heart was being ripped from her chest.

I let go of the man I'd been helping into the hatch and whipped around.

Kiera held Maz in her lap, screaming and sobbing. He was so pale. So still. Blood covered his chest and side. An arrow.

Yarina and Sigrid stood frozen in shock, their weapons limp at their sides.

I stumbled toward my friend. My brother.

"No," I rasped, cupping my hands around his wound. "No. We made it. We fucking made it, Mazkull. Everyone did. Just like you said. Don't do this to me. *Please.*"

Kiera shook as she clutched him. As if she could keep his soul in his body if she just held on hard enough.

I continued to mumble to him. Trying to staunch the blood. Too much blood.

Another crash rocked the ship, and Skelly shouted something. But I couldn't look away from Maz's closed eyes and still face. I pressed my trembling fingers to his neck.

A faint pulse fluttered against my touch. He moaned something.

"Wake up, Mazkull," I commanded him. "Open your eyes."

His eyes slowly opened. "Brother . . . I'm sorry."

"Don't you fucking dare," I snarled. "This isn't goodbye, remember?"

"And it . . . never will be." His eyes slid shut.

"No. No!" I threw my head back and roared in agony, shredding my throat.

Fucking Four, the pain. I'd never felt such pain. So deep no one could heal it, even if they tore me open.

His sisters dropped to their knees, sobbing. Kiera stared at him, glassy-eyed, like her horror had carried her away from her body entirely.

Another gods-damned barrel hit the railing near us, showering fire over the deck. I threw my body over Kiera's and Maz's. I barely felt the sizzle of my skin.

I rose to my feet, staring at our ship, frantically rowing toward the canyon. And then theirs. We would never make it out of here with that warship on our heels.

Limbs shaking with grief and rage, I stalked toward Nikella, whose spear dangled in her limp grasp. Tears laced her scar as she stared at Maz.

"Give me the last bomb," I growled.

One of the bombs in the cavern had lost its fuse, so Nikella had grabbed it in case we needed it.

She looked at my bloody hand, then at the warship chasing us. "You can't blow it up, Aiden."

"I can and I will. Give it to me."

"You'll die."

"I don't care, gods damn it!" I shouted. "I will not stand by while we *all* die!"

Emotions warred in her eyes until nothing but resignation

remained. She cupped my cheek in her hand. "A leader must always make sacrifices. A good leader knows which sacrifice to make."

I frowned, her words not making sense. Grief and fear clouded my thoughts. "I *am* making the right sacrifice."

For Kiera. For Maz. For his family that I'd sworn to protect. For the prisoners we'd saved and the warriors who'd fought for them.

I would do this for them all.

Another barrel crashed into the ship, which groaned and pitched. Cries sounded from below.

"Give it to me," I said through clenched teeth.

Nikella straightened, her eyes sadder than I'd ever seen them. "Aiden Falcryn, may you be a man like your father and as strong as your mother. May you be a king, the greatest among your ancestors. May you have love, as they did. Love that no knife, no arrow, not even a gods-damned war can break." She glanced at Kiera, who stared at us with eyes swimming in pain.

I shook my head in confusion. "What are you . . . Why are you saying this?"

Nikella squeezed my hand once, the closest she ever came to a hug. "It's what your mother told you as she lay dying," she said, her voice strong. "I've fulfilled my promise to your mother. You were never alone. You were always loved. And you always will be."

The reason finally dawned on my mind. "Nikella, don't—"

Tears fell over her scars once more, flooding her eyes with light. "Tell Jek I love him, too."

I grabbed at her arm, but she wrenched away and jumped over the railing. Her spear clanged to the deck.

"Nikella!" I shouted, rushing over to peer into the water.

She bobbed to the surface and immediately struck out for the warship.

I clung to the railing, tempted to jump after her.

Fucking Four, Nikella, why? Why?

A wave slammed her up against the warship, and she latched on. She pressed the last canister to the ship's hull.

"I have to shoot it," Sigrid said in a dull voice, coming to stand next to me. She'd lost her eye patch, her eye socket scratched and bloody.

She didn't wait for my agreement. She simply loaded a burning arrow into her bow.

Don't, please. There must be something else . . . She can't die. I need to save her, too. I can't lose someone else.

But the words wouldn't rise to my mouth. This was Nikella's choice. To protect me one last time. To save Rellmira.

Sigrid's arms shook as she aimed at Nikella's hand holding the canister in place. I could barely see Nikella's eyes across the water, but I stared hard at her face. The only face I'd known my whole life.

Sigrid fired. The arrow landed next to Nikella's hand.

Nikella yanked it out and shoved it into the canister.

My heart stilled. The explosion followed a moment later. A ball of heat and white flames ripped through the warship's hull and bellowed against the walls of the trembling canyon.

The warship burned and sank, soldiers leaping off.

I swayed on my feet, unable to look away from the spot Nikella had been a moment ago.

My heart twisted and slowed. Too wounded. Too much loss.

"May the gods find your soul," I whispered. "Please, Mynastra, carry her home."

As soon as the words left my lips, a strange wind rose. A whispered song. It rushed through our ship and eased my pain for just a moment.

Skelly shouted in alarm as the ship hurtled through the

water, twisting through the canyon as if guided by the cool, sweet, strong wind.

A wave swelled beneath us and tossed us out of the canyon, into the sea. Then it pulled away, rushing toward the cliffs. The stormy gray water rose higher and higher. The wind billowed and howled, and the cliffs trembled.

More people shouted in dismay, but I simply watched. I felt no danger.

Vicious waves crested like a thousand spears and stabbed at the cliffs. Their harsh faces shattered, spilling out black stone like blood. It tumbled into the roiling sea with a great sigh.

Violet clouds darkened to obsidian between one breath and the next. Bolts of lightning darted out like Nikella's spear, impaling the cliffs. They shrieked and crumbled.

The army encampment—a smudge on the cliffs—fell into the furious sea.

The battle between sea and sky raged until the waves swallowed every trace of Calimber.

Mynastra had reclaimed her night sky.

The sun parted the black clouds, lighting upon a glittering sea—and a rough cliff face bisected by a jagged scar. Just like Nikella's.

Perhaps it wasn't. Perhaps I'd imagined it all. Perhaps it was simply a strange storm.

But I chose to believe it was a goddess honoring the sacrifice of a Teacher who spent her life defeating monsters.

I staggered away from the railing, ignoring the open-mouthed expressions of everyone on deck.

I collapsed next to Kiera, who still held Maz.

Tears poured down her cheeks. "He's still breathing."

And Maz continued to breathe. All the way to Yargoth.

CHAPTER 50
KIERA

Grief clung to me like the shackles at my ankles. Cold, hard, unyielding.

In the blur of my fear for Maz, I hadn't heard Nikella's last words. I caught her last glance, though. The warm, kind one I felt I didn't deserve.

I'd never thanked her for what she'd done for me—the stories she told me or the training she'd given me. I'd never told her how much her courage inspired me.

I hoped she knew. I hoped she was watching us sail back to Yargoth. I hoped she was proud of the mark she left behind on our lives.

During the three-day journey back to Yargoth territory, I rarely moved away from Maz. I watched his chest rise and fall, praying for the next one. I felt for his pulse so many times, I eventually just left my fingers on his neck.

Aiden searched the Wolf ship for any medical supplies and gently removed the arrow from Maz's chest. He staunched the blood flow until it stopped, then packed it with a poultice and bandages.

He also shoved Ruru's arm back in its socket and fashioned him a sling until it healed.

His movements were swift and practiced. But his eyes were haunted. His mind far away under the crushed cliffs of Calimber.

I said nothing, mired in my own memories, which turned into nightmares.

Yarina and Sigrid sat with me and told Maz stories or sang songs. A tall Dag woman named Bruna never left Sigrid's side.

Ruru often wandered through the ship, looking for Daire, but always came back with a defeated look on his face.

The other prisoners seemed to be in various stages of shock, grief, and joy. Some had lost companions or loved ones in the escape or during their imprisonment. Others embraced each other, happy to be free at last. Most looked forward to landing and finding their families once again.

And Jek. The proud warrior had crumbled when he climbed up to the deck only to discover that Nikella was gone.

He'd fallen to his knees, clutching her spear, and shouted his grief to the waves and to the sky. When Aiden told him what Nikella had said—that she loved Jek, he'd hung his head and wept.

I'd cried again just witnessing his soul-wrenching loss.

Yarina told me a great many Dag warriors had shown up to help destroy Calimber. Jek had led them into battle and kept their losses low.

That victory felt hollow now.

We arrived on the shores of Dagriel, broken-hearted once more. *Mynastra's Wings* followed close behind, a little worse for wear after the capture of the Wolf ship. Skelly practically threw himself into the first rowboat to head back to his beloved ship.

The Yargoths greeted us with horses and longboats. But no Wicked. No Ozlow.

Strangely enough, I spotted Helene and Isabel in the crowd, next to Frieda. They both looked calmer than the last time I saw them, fleeing through the woods. Helene wore a fur jacket, and Isabel's red curls were flying loose in the wind. Pax—the ever-faithful wolf-dog—sat next to her, tongue lolling.

I helped ease Maz onto a makeshift stretcher we lowered over the side of the ship. The Yargoths below caught him and gently carried him to a waiting longboat.

The rest of the injured followed.

Aiden caught my arm before I could clamber down the ladder. "I need to speak with you when we get back to camp."

His eyes were hard and determined. My stomach sank. Was something wrong? Holy Four, I didn't think I could handle any more bad news.

I nodded, my throat tight. He released me, and I hurried down to the beach. My broken chains rattled over the pebbles. Yarina assured me we'd destroy them when we reached camp.

Isabel barreled into me, flinging her arms around my waist. "You're alive! Oh, I hoped you were! Mother said you saved our lives at Caddik's manor and that we should pray for you."

My seemingly endless tears rose again. I hugged her tightly, smelling snow and smoke in her hair. "Thank you, little one. I'm so glad you and your mother are safe as well."

She pulled away, beaming. "We quite like it here. Ruru was right—there are so many animals, and my job is to take care of all the horses and dogs and chickens. Pax helps. I even have a pet rabbit! He likes carrots. Do you want to see him when we get back?"

I gave a watery chuckle. There was something blissfully sweet about listening to a happy child. "Yes, but I need to help my friends first."

"Of course," Isabel said, nodding solemnly. "Mother says we are to help first, then play later."

I looked over Isabel's head to where Helene was watching us, a tentative smile on her face. The dark circles under her eyes were gone.

"Caddik?" she asked.

I shook my head.

Sorrow creased her eyes. "May the gods find his soul. Anything you need us to do, just ask."

I bit my lip. "The Rellmiran prisoners need food and water and possibly someone to ask about their families."

"I would love to." Her chin quivered, but then she lifted it. "Is Calimber truly destroyed?"

I thought of the monstrous waves and explosions and lightning storm. "Every bit. No mine will ever exist there again."

A few tears dripped over Helene's smile. "That's good. Very good. Garyth would be . . . He'd be so pleased."

"I wish he'd gotten to see it," I said softly.

Helene stroked her daughter's curls. "He didn't want it only for himself."

I offered a small smile, then moved out of the way as more warriors and prisoners disembarked.

Soon the beach was full. The injured went in the first longboats while the rest of us waited our turn. Aiden went with the injured to lend his healing skills.

Exhausted to my bones, I watched the light fade from the sky, huddled under a thick blanket Frieda had given me. The old woman's eyes were sad. She'd likely received a list of the dead. One that included Nikella's name.

Wrapped in his own blanket, Ruru sank down beside me. "I've looked everywhere. I've asked everyone," he said glumly. "He's not injured. No one recognizes his name or me."

I squeezed his uninjured shoulder. "I'm sorry, Ruru. But perhaps Daire was never at the mine. Perhaps they sent him elsewhere."

"Like the prison tower in Aquinon? He would've been executed by now, and I always checked. I never saw him at the logging camp. I don't know where else he'd be." Ruru dropped his chin to his bent knees.

Dead. But, gods, the last thing I wanted to do right now was steal the last bit of hope Ruru had of finding his brother.

"You said Shadow-Wolves took him, right?"

Ruru nodded.

I pointed at *Mynastra's Wings*, where the crew had started unloading the prisoners they'd taken from the Wolf ship. "We should ask the sailors from the Wolf ship if they remember Daire from any of their voyages. Then we'd know if he left the city by boat."

Ruru perked up. "Brilliant idea, Kiera." He immediately threw off his blanket and splashed into the freezing water to help pull the rowboats to shore with his one good arm.

I smiled and helped people out of the boats.

Ruru asked each of them if they'd ever seen a young man who looked like him named Daire. They all shook their heads.

But then the next boat came, and he assisted an old man to the beach, asking the same questions.

"Eh?" the man shouted, cupping his ear. "Oh yes, handsome lad, but he's dead, isn't he? Got killed in the battle."

Ruru paled. I felt the blow to my chest like a drum. Hollow and loud.

"Gods damn it, I'm sorry, Ruru," I whispered, embracing him.

He trembled in my arms and gave me a fierce, one-armed hug. "I . . . I can't believe I found him. And he's gone. I thought . . . I thought I would know if my brother was dead. But I guess not."

My heart ached. I used to think the same. That if something happened to Everett or Delysia, I would know. But I'd been sulkily eating a grand dinner when Mother died. I had no idea she was gone until Renwell came back and announced it.

Ruru pulled away, wiping his eyes. "Thanks for helping, Kiera." He turned back to the old man, who wore the thin garb of a prisoner and was sitting on a large stone nearby, catching his breath.

"I'm sorry to bother you again," Ruru said. "But you seem like you knew Daire, and I really want to know more about my brother."

"Daire?" The old man looked confused. "I thought you were asking about Tarel. But yeah, sure, I know Daire. He's right there, isn't he?"

He pointed a gnarled finger at *Mynastra's Wings* to where a young man with brown hair and brown skin climbed the rigging. I couldn't see his face in the murky light, but Ruru let out a strangled cry.

He ran into the water. "Daire! DAIRE!"

The young man glanced over. "*Ruru?*" He dove off the rigging and sliced through the water.

I grinned, tears falling like rain to my bare feet.

Daire swam to his brother while Ruru kept waving and shouting. They met in a splashy hug, jumping and yelling with joy.

And just like that, my heart healed a bit.

Ruru dragged his brother toward me, wearing the biggest grin I'd ever seen. Daire wore a matching one. He looked to be a few years older than Ruru, scars and weather aging his face. His long hair swept his broad shoulders. A brown patch of skin marred his throat.

"Kiera, this is Daire," Ruru said proudly, shoving his brother toward me. "Daire, this is one of my greatest friends, Kiera. She's saved my life a few times now."

Daire's eyebrows lifted, but he threw his arms around me. "Then it's the highest honor to meet you, Kiera."

"The honor is all mine," I said, "to be his friend."

Ruru smiled at me over Daire's shoulder. "Now, come on, come on, tell me everything!"

Daire laughed. "Still as impatient as ever, little brother." He plucked at Ruru's sling. "Seems like you have a few tales of your own to share."

"More than a few," Ruru said, his eyes gleaming.

We sat on the beach and traded stories under the rising moon.

Daire had been in the mine for a few years until last year, when the Wolves had lost some of their sailors in a storm. The mine let them have replacements, and Daire volunteered, saying he was an excellent sailor.

Ruru laughed. "You've never sailed in your life!"

Daire grinned. "They didn't know that, and I learned quick." He sobered. "You had to on that ship. The Wolves weren't very forgiving."

He told us about the fight between Skelly and the Wolves, and how he'd helped defeat the Wolves and switch the warriors with the prisoners. He'd offered to go back to free the mine, but Skelly had told him to help sail *Mynastra's Wings* instead.

Daire shrugged. "Turns out I'm pretty good at sailing. And I love it. When those gods-damned Wolves aren't whipping us every day." He nudged Ruru. "Now tell me how you got caught up in this."

Ruru hadn't even reached the part where he met me by the time the longboats returned. Daire happily joined us for the trip inland.

My heart warmed at the familiar sight of the Yargoth camp. I immediately checked on Maz, who seemed to breathe more easily in his bed, but was still shockingly pale.

The fear of losing him wasn't likely to leave me until he opened his eyes.

I kissed his cold, sweaty brow and whispered that I'd be back.

I nodded to Yarina, Sigrid, and Bruna, who had already set up their beds around Maz in his lodge. Aiden and Ruru would have to find somewhere else to sleep.

I trudged through the camp, nodding to people I recognized. I found Aiden by the fire, pressing a molten iron to Ruru's remaining cuff. A pile of twisted, melted shackles lay in a heap next to them.

Steam rose from the metal. Ruru's face tensed as he breathed hard through his teeth. Brow creased, Aiden removed the iron, and Daire wrenched open the remaining shackle.

The brothers grinned with relief. Daire shook Aiden's hand and helped Ruru toward a table full of food.

Aiden's gaze met mine, and his face softened. He gestured for me to take a seat.

I did, extending my feet toward him as he reheated the iron. "This already feels too familiar," I said, my throat suddenly feeling parched.

"It will never happen again if I can help it," he said quietly.

His tone, his manner . . . He was acting strangely. Did he regret the mine? Or was he second-guessing our future plan? Henry would hear of Calimber's destruction and start gathering his forces. We'd promised to meet him in Aquinon.

Aiden carefully pressed the iron to one of my shackles. The heat soaked through the metal and into my skin.

More to distract myself than anything, I asked, "What did you want to talk about? Now that we're back at camp."

He stayed focused on his task. "It can wait until you're free and fed. Perhaps after some sleep as well. It's not a conversation I want to rush."

I swallowed hard. Gods, it must be bad.

Suddenly, I remembered I used to share a lodge with Nikella. The weight of her death slammed into my stomach yet again.

"I don't want to sleep in my old bed," I whispered.

"Helene and Isabel took that lodge anyway," he said. Then he snapped the shackle off my ankle. He looked up at me, his eyes tide pools of sadness and yearning. "You can sleep in my lodge, if you wish."

My heart tapped faster. "I'm pretty sure Maz's sisters and Bruna have taken over that one."

"I found another," he said, thrusting the iron back into the fire without breaking our gaze. "It only has one bed, though."

I swallowed and almost choked on my dry throat. Gods damn it, I needed some water. My whole body felt like the metal rod he held—submerged in embers.

"Only to sleep," he added gently, then turned his focus to my other shackle. "I sleep better with you next to me."

My soul brightened. "I do, too."

His smile felt like a victory, since I hadn't seen it in days. He broke off my other shackle.

I didn't stand immediately. Instead, I kneeled down and gently took the iron out of his hands. Then I hugged him as tightly as I could, pouring every unspoken thought, word, and emotion into the embrace.

He let out a deep sigh and crushed me to him.

My sore body needed many things—a bath, food, sleep. But my heart was in far worse pain. And it yearned for Aiden most of all.

He pulled back and rested his forehead against mine. "I was going to wait, but I can't. I have to tell you now."

CHAPTER 51
KIERA

My heart hammered in my chest.

His eyes burned with a ferocity I'd never seen before. "If Nikella's death taught me anything, it's that I shouldn't wait. I was so worried in that gods-damned mine when I thought I was going to be executed. I worried you would never know."

"What is it?" I murmured, clasping his jaw, feeling frightened. "Tell me, please."

"I'm in love with you, Kiera. Since we met, I've loved you in small ways. As I came to know you, I loved you in bigger ways. Life-altering ways." He brushed his thumb over my cheek.

I couldn't stop gaping at him, his words exploding in my ears and through my body. *He loves me? He's IN love with me?*

The corners of his mouth quirked. "I'm in love with the light you bring to my world. I'm in love with your courage and your defiance and your kindness. The way your heart shares the pain and joy of those you love." He took a deep breath. "I once told you that you stole everything from me. And you did. I wasn't ready to give up my heart. I didn't think I ever would. But you took it anyway. And now . . . now I'm surrendering my heart to you willingly and fully, with no expectations. I love you, Kiera."

He spoke the final words with such tenderness and awe, as if he couldn't believe he was saying them aloud, but so happy that he was.

I'd never expected such words in my life. Not even from him. I'd hoped. I'd dreamed. But this was more.

His brow creased again as tears lined my eyes. "What's wrong?"

"Do you remember how you told me that a few of my words could pierce the darkness?"

He nodded.

"Now I know what that feels like," I said with a smile.

His expression smoothed, and a tentative hope grew in his eyes. "Does that mean—"

"I love you, too," I whispered. "I couldn't name the feelings I had for you in Aquinon, as twisted and complicated as they were with all the lies. But I came to you that night to admit who I really was, because I was choosing you, Aiden."

He pulled me into his lap, still holding tightly to me. "I know that now. I was too hurt to see it then."

I looped my arms around his neck and played with the ends of his hair. "I knew for sure in the moonblood tree."

His eyebrows rose. "That was over a week ago. I thought we were done keeping secrets from each other, little thief."

"I was going to tell you. I just didn't want it to change our plan." *Or have you leave me behind, for my sake or yours.*

He seemed to hear my unspoken words. "Loving each other doesn't make me want to put you in a cage, Kiera. It means I'll guard your life above my own, and where you go, I will always find you. In life and death."

My throat tightened as I gazed down at our clasped hands. Death was a possibility that never seemed more than a day away.

Even with the beautiful things we were admitting, our future was uncertain. We still had more to do. Aquinon. Renwell. Everett and Delysia.

Loving each other couldn't change that either.

The fate of Rellmira rested on our shoulders.

"Don't worry, I don't plan to give up either of our souls for a long time," Aiden whispered, drawing my chin up. He pressed a soft kiss to my lips. "Now eat quickly, so I can hold you in my arms all night."

A warm glow suffused me from the inside out.

As we walked to the food table, I noticed the approving smiles aimed our way. Perhaps they hadn't heard every word, but we weren't exactly hiding when we confessed our love to each other.

Love. It didn't feel real. Like I couldn't possibly forge such a precious bond with a man like Aiden.

But I believed every word he said and trusted every emotion that spilled from my heart to his.

This was real.

We ate as fast as we could. Something tasty I didn't remember. Aiden was barely out of arm's reach the entire time.

After we finished, Helene handed me a new outfit. She'd been passing them out all evening, a flushed smile on her face. The Rellmirans and Dags both seemed to like her and Isabel. I was glad they'd found a home here. And a purpose.

I changed inside one of the outhouses. The thick white shirt and black trousers were nothing special. Though they made me think of Gretchen's yellow-flowered shirt. I hoped the woman we freed from the log raft was wearing it now on her way home. The boots and stockings chafed my raw ankles a bit, but I'd never been happier to have them.

I also used some soap and water to clean my skin. It wasn't a full bath, but it was enough for now with exhaustion dragging at my limbs.

After the destruction of Calimber, Nikella's death, and worrying over Maz, I'd barely slept. The thought of sleeping in a real bed with Aiden almost made me giddy.

He was waiting for me outside, also refreshed in new clothes. "You can burn those," he said, nodding to my prisoner rags.

"Gladly." I walked to the nearest fire and tossed them in.

I wished the memories were just as easy to burn.

I put my hand in Aiden's, and he led me to a small lodge that looked newly built.

The camp had expanded since we were last here, overtaking nearly half the snowy meadow. Most likely to make room for the visiting warriors and refugees.

One day, I wanted to visit under more pleasant circumstances, not after another heartbreaking battle.

I'd been so angry and hurt the first time we came here. So eager to leave as soon as I could. Then, after the battle at Arduen's Mountain, I'd wanted to crush Calimber to honor my mother's sacrifice.

I was still laden with grief—old and new. And with fear for Maz and the battles we had yet to face.

But I also had love. Because of the man at my side. Love was worth every battle I fought.

Snowflakes kissed my cheeks before I ducked into Aiden's lodge.

A bed barely wide enough for two people took up most of the space. A small table and a stool consumed the rest.

Any possessions we had left were with our horses in Twaryn.

"Do you think we'll be able to retrieve Wicked and Ozlow soon? And the other horses?" I asked.

Aiden rolled back the heavy fur blankets and quilts on his bed—*our* bed. "One day, I hope. After."

After Aquinon. Would he be king then? Would I be . . .

I shook my head. *Enjoy this now while you have it.*

Aiden kicked off his boots and turned down the overhead lamp. I gingerly removed my boots in the darkness.

"Aiden?" I whispered.

A warm hand grasped my elbow and guided me to the bed. "I told you I'd always be able to find you, even if you were one with the dark."

I smiled and crawled into the bed. His large body quickly followed. I curled into his arms as if we'd be doing the same motions for years. He dragged the blankets over us.

"Does the darkness bother you? After everything," I whispered.

"It helps to have destroyed that place." The words rumbled in my ear. "But I fear nothing with you in my arms."

I snuggled deeper into his arms. I had many new fears, but he was right. I was at peace in his arms.

"I love you, Aiden."

His arms tightened. He kissed the top of my head. "I love you, too, Kiera."

I fell into a deep sleep. I dreamed of training with Nikella in a snowy meadow. She smiled and laughed, her eyes glowing with happiness. She touched my shoulder when we were done.

"Defeat the monsters, Kiera," she whispered.

I woke up, my heart pounding, sweat tickling my spine. Aiden still slept soundly next to me, even as light threaded through the cracks of our door.

Defeat the monsters, Kiera.

Gods, that dream had felt so real. It stirred an unease deep in my gut. The only monster left was Renwell. And we had plans for him. Henry would be at Aquinon in about three weeks. Giving us plenty of time to recuperate, fix the ships, and sail to the royal city.

But we'd lost Nikella.

She'd wanted to sneak in first and disable the cliff gate so Aiden and I and our forces wouldn't be stuck on the steep cliff road.

We couldn't blow it up without decimating ourselves. We could wait for Henry to let us in, but what if he didn't make it through in time? We'd be like snared rabbits at the mercy of the Wolves.

Defeat the monsters.

I stilled, hardly daring to breathe for fear of disturbing Aiden.

I needed to be the one to go into Aquinon. I needed to cripple the gate. But before that, I needed to confront Renwell and make sure Everett and Delysia were out of harm's way before the attack.

Then I could defeat Renwell myself.

The plan notched into place in my mind as if my dream had given me the perfect pieces.

I gazed at Aiden's sleeping face. My heart burned with longing, with fierce protectiveness, with a deep desire to see us victorious on the other side of this battle.

He wouldn't like it. But I needed to do this.

Quietly, I wrapped a blanket around my shoulders and slipped out of our lodge to visit Maz. His sisters and Bruna were snoring near him, but his eyes were open.

"Maz!" I threw myself at him, careful to avoid his heavy bandage.

He coughed. "Hello, lovely," he rasped. "Water."

"Of course." I dipped a cup in the bucket of cold water near his head and tilted it to his mouth.

He sipped slowly, grimacing. "Gods, everything hurts."

My throat constricted, those moments flashing through my mind again. "Thank you. For saving me from the barrel."

His eyes filled with soul-deep kindness. "No, thank you, Kiera. For saving me from Korvin and Renwell. I should've said that a long time ago."

My eyes burned as his words soothed a hurt I didn't know I still carried.

Sniffling, I nudged his good shoulder. "You need to stop doing this to us, Mazkull. I almost lost my mind. Again."

He let out a laugh that was more of a sigh and leaned back, closing his eyes. "Can't help it. Such a desirable target."

"Or just lousy defensive skills," I retorted.

"Eh. Get Nikella to teach me."

My heart cracked, and I bit my lip.

Maz peered at me through heavy eyelids. When he saw my expression, he groaned. "No."

"She saved us," I whispered. "We wouldn't have made it without her."

Tears leaked from Maz's eyes into his golden hair. His face contorted. "Aiden?"

"He's alive," I said quickly. "And Ruru. He found his brother, Daire. We rescued one hundred and fifty-three prisoners from the mine and the Wolf ship. Helene and Isabel are here and happy. Your sisters are safe. And Jek."

"Ah, Jek. He must be heartbroken." Maz frowned. "Gods, Nikella. I thought nothing could defeat that woman."

"She chose to save us," I corrected him gently. "Perhaps if you're very good and heal properly and don't get yourself gravely injured *again*, I'll tell you the story of how Mynastra swallowed Calimber whole."

His eyes widened. "You've got a story, lovely? You know what I say about a story well-told."

I smiled. "Yes, but first, drink more water. And eat something. And let Aiden examine you."

"Bossy," Maz griped. "One would think you're already queen."

I froze.

Guilt flashed through Maz's eyes. "Sorry, sorry. I didn't mean—Aiden!" Relief strengthened his voice. He coughed again, trying to lift his hand, but couldn't quite manage it.

"Good to see you, brother," Aiden's deep voice said from behind me.

"Told you it wasn't goodbye."

My cheeks heated as Aiden stepped up behind me. He wrapped an arm around my waist and growled in my ear. "When I said I wanted to hold you in my arms all night, should I have specified I meant the morning as well?"

Maz's eyebrows shot up, and a satisfied smirk curled under his beard.

"How long have you been standing there?" I asked breathlessly. Did he hear what Maz had called me?

"Only a moment or so," Aiden murmured and released me.

"Don't you two have your own lodge?" Yarina grumbled sleepily, throwing her arm over her eyes.

"Hey, little sister," Maz rasped.

Yarina bolted upright. "Fucking Four, Mazkull! Why didn't you wake me?" She beamed at Maz, then kicked Sigrid's foot. "He's awake!" she shouted.

While his sisters and Bruna converged on him, and Aiden tried to hold them off so he could examine Maz's wound, I slipped out of the lodge.

I walked toward the open meadow, my mind pacing faster than my feet.

Queen.

The word rattled me. I'd barely allowed my thoughts to touch on such a dangerous idea. The title. The palace. The *marriage.*

When I thought of a queen, I thought of Mother—confined, desperate, dead. Aiden would be a better king than Father, but I'd left that life for a reason.

Loving a future king meant I'd have to make a choice one day. But not now.

I reached the meadow where Nikella had trained me. Dozens of hoofprints and footprints riddled the thick layer of snow, especially where the Yargoths had piled branches and kindling into a large tower.

Jek was standing in front of it, his shoulders slumped. Nikella's spear shone in his fist. I wondered if he ever relinquished it.

Pale sunlight glittered across the snow, making it look as though I were wading through diamonds as I trudged toward him.

He didn't glance at me, but I noticed his red-rimmed eyes. "We can't burn her body," he said, staring at the mountain of wood. "But I suppose Mynastra claimed Nikella for herself in the end."

"I'm sorry, Jek," I whispered. "She really did love you."

He shook his head. "Not more than her duty. I knew that. I knew I would have to let her go again and again until she was gone for good. But I hoped . . . I hoped we would have more time between."

My throat tightened. I remembered how she'd always looked east when we were traveling. How she said her heart could barely recognize love when it was standing in front of her.

She'd wanted a life of love, but never let herself have it.

"I'm sorry," I said again, the words feeling paltry.

He drew in a deep breath and straightened his shoulders, the air of a warrior returning to him. "Perhaps when my soul joins hers, I won't have to chase her anymore."

I brushed my fingers over his arm. "Not too soon, Jek. We need you here. We need you for the battle ahead."

He looked down at me. "I'll be there. I have one score left to settle on her behalf."

Renwell.

"She believed in you," he said gently. "She read people's hearts, and I think she saw the warrior in you."

My nose stung as I tried to hold back a fresh wave of tears. "Then I hope she was right."

"I see it, too. And I pray you do not have to give everything as she did."

I bit my lip. I prayed for that, too.

Jek nodded to the woodpile. "For Arduen's Night in five nights' time."

My brow furrowed. "I've heard you perform a special dance around a fire, but I've never celebrated that way." The closest I came was dancing in Asher's ballroom.

A faint smile quirked Jek's mouth. "You'll enjoy it."

Five nights. And then I would ride for Aquinon.

CHAPTER 52
KIERA

The next five days passed too quickly.

Aiden was busy with healing. Ruru and Daire went back to the ships to make repairs and restock supplies. Yarina and Sigrid spent every waking moment with Maz and their long-lost Yargoth friends and relatives and the Dags from other clans.

I told Maz the story of Calimber's collapse after he begged a few more times. He wept again for Nikella, but was awestruck when I told him of the storm.

I also spent a great deal of time with Helene and Isabel, caring for the freed prisoners. It brought me joy and pain to listen to their stories and stoke their hope of reunion with their friends and families.

I met Isabel's rabbit and helped her tend the horses, missing Ozlow. I hoped Frieda wouldn't mind lending me another for my journey.

But I had yet to say anything of my plan to anyone.

The shadows in Aiden's eyes always melted away when he saw me. He'd give me a warm smile and a lingering kiss as we went about our days. At night, we collapsed into bed together. I felt a growing need for him in other ways, but we were taking our time with each other, savoring every moment we had.

I didn't have the heart to tell him I was determined to go back to Aquinon this time. He'd hated the idea before. He hadn't even wanted Nikella to do it. But someone had to, and I was the best choice.

The selfish, cowardly part of my heart wanted to enjoy these few days of peace before we had to go back to war.

The morning of Arduen's Night, Aiden woke early and dressed.

"Where are you going?" I asked, barely able to keep my eyes open.

"To check on the ships' progress," he said, bending down to give me a gentle kiss. "I'll be back before the festivities start. But before I go . . . I have something for you."

I perked up and scooted to the edge of the bed while he dug something out of a sack he'd set on the floor before we'd gone to sleep.

He turned up the lamp, filling our lodge with cozy light. His face was utterly serious as he lowered himself to one knee in front of me.

He held out a beautiful crimson scarf. Stitched in colorful thread, symbols danced over the fine cloth from end to end.

I gasped, running my finger over them all. A key, a mask, a bell, a wave, a lily, a group of trees, a firefly, a moonblood, an axe, a small knife, a lizard, a mountain, a fireflower, a spear, and a falcon.

"What is this?" I whispered.

"It's us," Aiden said softly. "It's our story. It's our love for each other and from others."

I couldn't breathe. Tears blurred my vision as I kept stroking the silky cloth.

"It's tradition to give someone you love a scarf like this on

Arduen's Night," Aiden continued. "I threaded most of the symbols myself the past few days. Maz, Ruru, Jek, Yarina, Sigrid, Frieda, Helene, and Isabel all added their own. I would love to get Everett and Delysia to add a few as well."

I crumbled, tears racing down my cheeks. "It's the most beautiful thing I've ever seen."

Relief thawed the tension in his face and shoulders. "If you accept my token, wear it to the dance tonight."

I reverently took it in my hands, gazing up at him. "Thank you. I will."

He kissed me one more time and left for the coast.

I sat and stared at the scarf for a long time. I'd noticed other men and women with them around camp. I'd thought perhaps it was just a traditional decoration. But I'd also seen Dags clutching them at funerals of loved ones.

Still in awe, I tucked the scarf in my pocket and went to visit Maz.

"You seem distracted, lovely," he said as we sat together in his lodge. "Are you not excited for tonight?"

He looked much better than he had when we first arrived. His skin had lost its pallor, and his appetite was voracious. He crammed freshly cooked venison in his mouth even now.

Being home was good for him.

"Yes," I said, picking at a loose thread in the quilt wrapped around my shoulders. *Except I'll have to tell Aiden my plans tomorrow.*

"Aiden said I could attend," Maz said around a mouthful of meat. "Can't dance, of course, but watching is fun, too. Has he . . . spoken to you today?"

I narrowed my eyes. "Yes. This morning before he left. Why?"

Maz hummed and avoided my gaze.

I sighed. "He gave me the scarf, Maz. He told me you helped him with it."

Maz beamed. "I did. Did you like my axe? My needlework is normally smoother, but my hands are still shaky."

"It was perfect."

He frowned, licking his fingers clean. "Then what's with the sad eyes? Do you not want it?"

"Of course I do. I'm just worried, is all."

"He loves you, Kiera," Maz said gently, patting my knee.

"I know that, and he knows I love him. I'm worried about what happens next."

Maz waved his hand dismissively. "Oh, the dance is easy to learn. Just follow Yarina's lead. Or Bruna's—Sigrid gave her a scarf two days ago."

I froze, my thoughts torn from Aquinon. "I have to dance?"

"Yes, it's tradition. When one gives another a scarf, they do the fire dance on Arduen's Night." He cocked his head to the side. "Aiden didn't tell you that?"

Nerves bundled in my stomach. "No. He just said to wear it."

"Don't worry. I'll walk you through it."

Maz explained what would happen, and my apprehension grew.

"Is this more serious than just a declaration of love, Maz?" I asked cautiously.

He hesitated. "It can be. But anyone can give anyone a scarf. I gave one to Yarina. A mother might give one to her daughter. Deeply bonded friends can. Lovers who might want to be more."

"More?" I squeaked.

"Not always," he said quickly. "But some lovers use it to promise themselves to each other before a wedding."

"Like a *betrothal*?"

Maz looked slightly panicked now. "Again, not always. Fucking Four, I'm making a mess of this. It's not a betrothal, Kiera. Unless you both want it to be."

I tried to breathe steadily through my nose. Aiden had said

nothing of a betrothal. The scarf was merely a symbol of the love we'd already professed.

"If it was, would that be so bad?" Maz asked, his blue eyes tender.

"I don't know," I murmured. "He's not just a man. He's a king."

Maz nodded. "That life frightens you still."

My heart warmed to have a friend who understood. "Yes."

Maz took my hand in his. "Just remember, lovely. You haven't experienced that life with him yet. The one you knew is gone."

I gave him a bleak look. "I still have one left to destroy."

"Then think about it afterward."

Too late. I likely wouldn't stop thinking about it.

At that moment, Yarina and Bruna burst into the lodge, out of breath. "Time to get ready!" Yarina sang, dragging me away from Maz. "Don't move until we come back," she ordered her brother.

A few hours later, I huddled in the snowy woods with a group of men and women. Night had fallen, and a large crowd had gathered around the unlit bonfire.

My scalp ached from the brutal brushing and braiding Yarina had subjected me to, but I had to admit the results were beautiful. My hair glowed and fell in a soft, wavy blanket down my back. Red and orange ribbons cascaded from the woven crown on my head.

She'd also given me a dark blue blouse with long, flowing sleeves and a black skirt. I hadn't worn a skirt since the last time I'd danced. The thick material kept my legs warm as we waited.

Yarina hurried to each of us and pressed a single fireseed into our palms. "Your scarf, Kiera," she hissed at me.

I dug my lovely scarf out of my pocket and knotted it around my waist with trembling fingers. Gods, I couldn't believe I was doing this. Yarina and Bruna had practiced the dance with me.

We'd laughed and twirled, and I realized how much I missed Melaena and Delysia.

I would see them again soon.

"All right, it's time," Yarina barked. "Follow me."

We trailed after her, each of us wearing an outfit of the same colors and displaying our scarves.

We snuck through the woods until we stood closer to the crowd. They had backed away from the wood piled in the center of their circle, leaving a narrow walkway.

Half-naked men and women formed a ring around the pyre.

Yarina had told me that, traditionally, the givers started the dance barefoot and bare-skinned as the god Arduen once had.

A slow drumbeat rolled through the clearing, and the crowd hushed. Frieda walked forward and thrust a lit torch into the stack of wood. Once it caught fire, she backed away.

The drums beat steadily. Louder, then softer, like deep breaths. The scantily clad dancers linked hands around the growing fire.

My heart leaped when I glimpsed Aiden. His tan, muscular back with its scars and single falcon tattoo drew me in like a beacon. His black pants rode low on his hips, and his bare feet glided through the snow.

He looked as he had the night we met.

The dancers swept inward, blew on the fire, then drifted back. Kindling the flames like a bellow in a forge.

But only one kind of weapon was forged here. Something stronger than steel or sunstone.

Love is the strongest weapon of all.

The dancers circled and repeated the motion. As the fire grew, they danced faster. Eventually, they broke hands and leaped and spun, as if urging the fire with their movements.

Warmth trickled through my body as I watched Aiden. The way he bowed to the fire and kept time with the drum. His face was a flickering mirage. He looked as wild as these mountains. He looked as regal as a king. He looked like the man I loved.

My fingers wandered along the scarf he'd made for me. No matter what happened, Aiden would always be the right choice.

My heart lifted with the rising beat of the drum.

"Almost time," Yarina whispered next to me, her eyes glowing. "Are you ready, princess?"

I grinned. "Let's go."

More drums joined the song, and Yarina swept out of the woods. I followed her, dancing through the crowd. Everyone smiled and clapped.

The first dancers backed away as we approached. Aiden beamed more brightly than the bonfire, his chest heaving, his skin flushed.

I smiled back before concentrating on the dance. We formed our own circle around the fire, twirling back and forth. Then, one by one, we threw our fireseeds into the flames.

The crowd cheered every time the fire roared higher. The heat caressed my skin, making my body feel languid and powerful.

Once all the fireseeds had gone into the fire, it rose as tall as the trees.

Then it was time to find our partners.

Yarina hurried over to where Maz sat on a throne of furs and waved her scarf at him. Everyone else clasped hands with their people.

Suddenly, Aiden filled my vision. He looked more beautiful than the god of love himself.

He offered his hands, his emerald eyes sparkling.

I clasped his fingers, and together, we danced the same push-and-pull fire dance we'd done apart.

"You look beautiful, Kiera," Aiden said as we pressed

together. "Somehow more beautiful than the last time I watched you dance."

I quirked my eyebrow. "You mean when you spied on me?"

He chuckled. Gods, how I'd missed that sound.

"Yes," he admitted. He twirled me, and then I him.

"Did you know I wondered what it would be like to dance with you?" I asked breathlessly. "When you blindfolded me?"

The heat in his eyes burned more fiercely than the fire at my back. "Did you?"

I swallowed hard. "Yes. But then I told myself we would only end in betrayal or death. But as fate would have it, we now dance beyond both."

He held me closer, brushing the tip of his nose against mine. "I foresee only dancing in our future. Especially the kind we did in The Hollow."

I gaped at him and accidentally stepped on his foot.

He laughed again, spinning me about with his warm hand clamped on my waist.

Sparks of desire whirled through my body. I wanted them to incinerate me.

Aiden's eyes darkened, and he held me even closer. Closer than the dance was supposed to be.

"Give me tonight, Kiera," he whispered. "Make love with me until the sun rises. Let me show you just how much I've missed you."

My core clenched, and a soft groan escaped my lips. "Yes. Please."

He flashed a wicked grin down at me. "Then run away with me, little thief."

CHAPTER 53
KIERA

We left without a word.

Everyone else had joined in the dancing while we talked. And no one called out to us as Aiden grabbed my hand and tugged me away from the fire.

We ran through the snow back to our little lodge. My heart pounded as hard as if I'd raced a mile.

Aiden swept open the door flap and pulled me inside. His lips were on mine before I could catch my breath.

But I didn't care. I wanted him to steal my breath, my heart, my body.

I wanted him to have every part of me.

We kissed with a desperation that knocked over the stool and made the lamp swing wildly. I nearly fell back on the bed, but Aiden caught me.

He hauled me upright and cupped my face in his hands. His tongue swept over my lips, then dove into my mouth.

I curled my tongue around his, and he groaned, long and deep, as we devoured each other. My belly fluttered, and I scraped my nails over his bare chest and back.

He tried to slow the kiss, to gentle it. I pulled away.

"No," I said huskily. "I can't go slow right now. I need . . . I need everything. Fast. Hard."

"Gods, yes," he growled.

He picked me up and tossed me on our bed. He yanked off my boots, then settled himself over me. His lips found mine once again, warm and needy. He dragged up my skirt, caressing my bare skin as he did so.

I whimpered into his mouth. *Too slow, too slow. Please, Aiden.*

He cupped me through my undershorts. I ground against his hand shamelessly, embers already smoldering in the pit of my stomach.

"What do you want, love?" he murmured as he kissed down my throat. "One finger, or two?"

"T-Two," I stammered.

Aiden hummed in approval. "Greedy little thief." He pulled my shorts aside and slid in one finger, then two.

I gasped and jerked.

He chuckled and curled his fingers, then started sliding them in and out. Over and over.

Gods, I was wound so tight. Every nerve ending on fire. I broke in moments with a loud cry.

He curled his fingers harder, pulsing with my inner walls.

Pleasure ricocheted through my bones, hummed through my veins, drenched his hand.

Then his fingers—along with my undershorts—disappeared as I lay gasping.

I heard a rustle, then felt something hard and warm press against me.

"Are you protected?" he whispered.

"Yes," I breathed.

"Do you still want hard and fast, beautiful?" he murmured against my lips.

I hooked my leg around his hip, my skirt falling back over my waist. I pulled him in for one kiss, then another, and another. Gods, he was so addictive.

"Love me like a summer storm," I whispered. "Lightning and thunder so fierce you take my breath away."

He thrust into me, hissing between his teeth as I gasped. "Keep your breath, Kiera. Keep it, so you can scream my name."

I nearly came again on the spot. But then he thrust into me again and again. Hard and fast. Like lightning strikes. Each one sent a bolt into my core. He growled and kissed me. He nipped at one of my breasts through my shirt. I moaned at the pinch of delicious pain.

He pumped harder until I couldn't keep up. Until the lightning struck closer and closer together, setting me ablaze.

"*Aiden!*" I cried out.

He answered me with a roar of his own, like thunder. He threw his head back, and his body stiffened, upright between my legs. The perfect vision of a man unraveling in ecstasy.

The sight made me fall in love with him all over again.

"I love you, Aiden," I whispered, brushing my fingers over his taut stomach.

He looked down at me with something like adoration. It squeezed my heart. He kissed me, soft and slow. "And I love you, Kiera. Always."

Always.

How long would "always" be with another battle on the horizon?

Aiden pulled out of me and lay on his side, playing with the ends of the scarf he'd given me. "Were you nervous about dancing tonight?"

I didn't bother to adjust my skirts, merely rolling toward him. "Yes. But seeing you wiped it away. I couldn't wait to get to you."

He smiled and brushed my sweaty hair away from my cheeks. "And now I never want to let you go."

Guilt nipped at my heart. "Aiden, I . . . I need to—"

He kissed away the words on my lips. "I know what you need to say, Kiera. But please . . . say it in the morning. I want my one night."

My throat tightened, and I nodded.

"Good. I need to make up for months of wanting you. Wishing I could comfort you. Wishing I could forget everything else and just live in the feelings I had for you."

He stood up and stripped off his unlaced pants. Then he turned the lamp to its brightest.

I blinked at the sudden light. And at the sight of him standing before me, naked, and with a wet, already-hardening cock.

"I didn't get to really see you before," he murmured. "I promised myself the next time we were together would be in a proper bed. But now that we've had that, I want to see you in the light, Kiera."

Butterflies erupted in my stomach. I slowly rose, discarding my shirt as I did so.

His eyes darkened with hunger as he stared at my taut breasts. Instead of reaching for them, he loosened the scarf's knot and used the ends to pull me closer to him.

He hummed, a deep, melodic sound. "Perfect." He kissed his way from my mouth to each breast, dropping to his knees. His lips grazed my stomach as he pinched my skirt button open.

The heavy material fell to the floor. His fist kept my scarf— and me—in place. He swept his mouth over my center and licked away some of the moisture on my thighs.

I trembled, clutching his silky hair. Gods, the pure joy I felt with him. I'd thought perhaps nothing could surmount our time in The Hollow. But knowing he loved me, after everything we'd been through, filled me with a fierce hope I hadn't allowed before.

Aiden rose, his lips dragging along my skin as if he couldn't bear to part with it. His glowing eyes captured me in their depths. He pulled the scarf harder, yanking our bodies flush against each other, our arousal evident between us.

"You are the most beautiful thing I've ever seen," he murmured, echoing my words about the scarf. "And I'm going to savor every inch of you. I'm going to map every cry you make, so I know just how to elicit it again. I'm going to make you mine, Kiera."

I wrapped my arms around his neck, my heart full to bursting, my body on fire for him. "I'm already yours, Aiden."

His eyes flared. Our mouths crashed together. This time, his hands wandered where they willed. Twisting in my hair. Brushing my hips and ribs. Circling my nipples. Clutching my ass.

I didn't hold back either, marveling at every taut muscle, every inch of smooth and scarred skin, every place that made him gasp and groan—particularly when I wrapped my hands around his cock. He thrust against my fingers as if he couldn't help himself.

I grinned and slid him into me like he belonged there.

He growled and grasped my knee, whirling me, until I was bent backward over the small table. The wood scraped my ass, but I didn't care.

"So good. So fucking good," I mumbled deliriously as he stroked into me.

I propped myself up, pushing my breasts forward. He immediately devoured one and then the other, never stopping his deep, pounding rhythm.

Gods, I'd never seen anything so erotic as Aiden bent over

me, lost in his frantic desire for me. Wave after wave of pleasure rocked through me until they reached a cliff-shattering height.

I let out a ragged cry, the waves still pummeling me as mercilessly as he did.

"More, sweetheart, more. Take as much as you can," he commanded gently.

His hazy green eyes soaked in every moment of my writhing until I started to calm and quiet. Then he picked up his pace, his brow taut. I lifted my legs over his shoulders, easing him farther in.

He swore and gripped my hips, slamming into me. His thumb circled my most sensitive flesh. I jerked under another shock of lightning just as he released with a long, agonized growl.

He leaned against the table, buried in me. Sweat dripped down his face that I brushed away with my thumbs.

"How's your map looking?" I whispered.

He smiled and kissed my thumb. "Incomplete. I'll need more than tonight. It must be perfect."

I smiled back. "I hope it takes many, many nights then."

He glowed with happiness.

I'd all but forgotten what I needed to tell him tomorrow. The contentment was too thick, too rich—it blocked out everything else.

Tonight, I was just a woman in love with a man who didn't need to think about tomorrow.

CHAPTER 54

AIDEN

I HAD THOUGHT IT WAS IMPOSSIBLE FOR SOMEONE TO LOVE ME LIKE this. Like Kiera did. With her whole heart, mind, and body.

We made love for hours. The way she looked at me felt like she was touching my soul, which added new pleasure to something that already felt like ecstasy.

In between bouts, we talked. And ate, when she made me get dressed and sneak out for some food and mead. We'd made a mess of the lodge, but I tucked away her scarf to keep it safe.

I told her stories of my childhood with Nikella in Twaryn. She told me stories of Brielle, Everett, and Delysia. It helped to hear happy memories of her mother. To layer them over the painful ones so that wasn't the only emotion I associated her with.

Thinking about how things had been between us two months ago, I was amazed we could be here now, lying naked, telling stories. And yet, it somehow felt inevitable. As if our souls were meant to collide. We just had to clear away the rubble of our old defenses first.

But as dawn came, and Kiera drifted off to sleep mid-story,

the tension crept back into my shoulders. I gently stroked her hair, trying to keep myself anchored to her.

If Henry was marching toward Aquinon as he'd promised, he would arrive at the gate in two weeks. That left little time to re-gather our forces, finish the ship repairs, and sail for the harbor.

Renwell likely had his remaining warship patrolling there, and our ships didn't have catapults like his did. We had our warriors with their weapons. But that wouldn't matter if we couldn't make it into the city.

It'd matter even less if we couldn't make it through the cliff gate.

I kissed the tip of Kiera's nose. I knew that was what she wanted to talk to me about. I'd drawn the same conclusion she must have over the past few days. That someone had to be in Aquinon, and there was no better person than her.

I just hated it with every fiber of my being.

I'd already lost Nikella. I'd nearly lost Maz. If I lost Kiera . . .

The thought of her being in Renwell's clutches again, listening to his oily words, fighting the pain he seemed to inflict on her so easily.

It killed me.

But I'd told her that loving her didn't mean I'd keep her in a cage. And I meant it. I refused to be like her father or Renwell, who tried to imprison and control her. Her choices, her life, were her own. I just hoped to all the Four that she chose me at the end of this.

I must've fallen into a fitful sleep because the next thing I knew, Kiera was kissing me awake.

She looked thoroughly loved . . . and nervous.

"You can say it now," I murmured, gazing at her across the pillow.

"I'm going to Aquinon," she blurted out, as if she had to get the words out quickly or not at all. "I want to leave tonight."

My heart flinched, but I tried not to let my emotion show. "That journey will take a week by horse, if you ride fast."

"I can do it."

"And don't forget the border patrols. The soldiers. They will stop you at the city gate."

"Then I'll tell them the truth—Renwell is looking for me."

I couldn't hide my grimace this time. "Kiera . . . he might kill you."

Her eyes tightened. "He won't."

I stroked the scar on her cheek. "We destroyed his forge, his weapons, his ships, his mine, his brother, his general. That's enough loss to change anyone's intentions."

"He still has Everett and Delysia. I can't abandon them, and he knows that. He'll keep me alive as long as he has a way to make me be useful to him."

My dread grew. "He could do terrible things to you. Make you do things you'll regret forever. You're one of the strongest people I know, but everyone has a breaking point."

Kiera bit her lip. "I know. I will do what I can to avoid that, but not at the cost of my siblings or our plan. You and Henry will lay siege to the city, and I will be the key that lets you in."

"And what is your plan this time, little thief?" I asked, trying to infuse lightness into my voice. Just to see the smile come back to her face. And it did.

"When Henry was saying goodbye, he told me the names of his two soldier friends who stand guard on the city wall. They'll have access to the cliff gate. Dredger and Mankmen."

I frowned. "You're going to ask two strangers to sabotage the gate?"

She shook her head. "Just to let me in while I damage the gate chains, as Nikella intended. They rarely lower that gate. No one should be the wiser until you arrive."

"How are you going to get to the gate if you're stuck in the palace with Renwell?"

Kiera pursed her lips, uncertainty growing in her eyes. "I haven't quite figured that out yet. I'm hoping Melaena can help me with that part. Maybe Renwell will let me visit her."

My jaw clenched. Not likely. Unless he got something from her in return. Or he shadowed her every step of the way.

Kiera smoothed my wrinkled brow. "I'll find a way, Aiden. I always do."

I captured her hand and kissed her palm. "But you'll be alone. One warrior in a palace of wolves."

"I'll have Everett and Delysia. And you won't be far behind me. Right?" she asked in a worried voice.

"No warship, no Wolf, no army, no gate will keep me from you, Kiera." I kissed her lips. I needed to while I still could. "Even if I have to storm the palace alone, I will come for you."

She smiled, something shining in her eyes that I never thought I'd see—trust. "Perhaps I'll fight my way to *you*. If Everett and Delysia are out of harm's way, I might just kill the usurper king myself."

"I fully support that goal, especially if he threatens you in any way. Then I hope you tear him to shreds," I growled.

Kiera kissed me again, immediately softening me. "I must admit," she murmured between warm kisses, "I thought you would put up more of a fight."

"It's hard to fight you when you're so good at distracting me, little thief." I grabbed her shoulders, pinned her to the bed, and kissed her long and hard. "But I certainly won't say no if this is how you'd like to conduct all our fights in the future."

She grinned. "If only I'd known that this was how we could both win the fight, I might've tried sooner."

She hooked her bare leg around my waist and twisted us so

she sat on top of me. Her glorious, ribboned hair fell over her bare breasts, and I lost all threads of what we were talking about.

A very pleasant hour later, she reminded me by slipping out of my grasp. "I need to prepare," she said gently.

But she let me pull her in for one more lingering kiss. "I'll help you."

We both dressed, stealing glances at each other. It felt playful and sweet, but a hole was already growing in my heart. Right next to the wounds from Nikella and all my other losses.

Love always left a scar.

I reluctantly followed her out of our lodge to where half the camp was having breakfast by the main fire. Maz and his sisters were already there, looking as tired as we felt.

But Maz brightened the moment he saw us. "Good morning, you two! I see you've already misplaced your scarf, lovely. Or was that Aiden's doing?"

Kiera's cheeks turned pink as Yarina guffawed with her brother.

I fought a smile. "This is why you keep getting gravely injured, Mazkull."

Maz puffed out his chest like a ridiculous rooster. "Because of my dazzling wit and distracting good looks?"

"Your big mouth."

He shrugged. "Still alive, aren't I?"

"Thank the gods," I said quietly.

He heard me anyway and grinned. "No, thank your little lovely. Yarina said that if Kiera hadn't yanked me backward, I would've fallen into the water."

"We would've fished you out," Sigrid grumbled under her breath.

I glanced down at Kiera, whose cheeks were still pink. "You didn't tell me that."

"I forgot," she said, the truth clear in her amber eyes.

"All your screaming probably erased the memory," Yarina said. "You've got quite the pipes, princess."

Kiera frowned, as if she couldn't believe Yarina was teasing her about such a horrific moment. But it was the Dag way. Most especially the Maz and Yarina way.

Kiera shook her head. "Thanks, but I prefer dancing."

"I'll bet you do." Yarina winked at her, then grinned at me.

Sigrid, meanwhile, hadn't stopped staring at Kiera with her one eye. Finally, she rose and stretched out her hand. "I never thanked you for what you did at the mine for Bruna and the prisoners and for Maz." Sigrid swallowed hard. "And Davka. But . . . thank you. And I'd be honored to fight at your side in Aquinon."

Kiera solemnly shook her hand as if this moment meant a great deal to her. "I don't need your gratitude, but I will take peace and respect between us."

Sigrid dipped her head in acknowledgement, then sat back with Bruna.

Kiera took a deep breath and straightened her shoulders. "I won't be going with you to Aquinon. I'm going to ride ahead. Today."

Every gaze swung in my direction.

I crossed my arms over my chest and scowled at all of them. "This is her choice, and I fully support it."

Maz's brow furrowed as he looked between me and Kiera. "But . . . Renwell."

"You bring up a valid argument, Mazkull," I said, my lips twitching. "But she knows how to handle him. She also has a plan to make sure the cliff gate isn't a problem for us."

Kiera sent me a grateful look. Probably glad I hadn't mentioned the gray areas in said plan.

"I don't like it," Maz groused. "And Ruru will hate it."

Kiera gave him a loose hug, minding his bandage. "You'll see me soon enough on the battlefield. I expect you to be in full armor this time."

"He will be," both his sisters said.

Maz rolled his eyes. "Fucking Four, you almost die a few times, and suddenly you're as fragile as glass."

We finished our breakfast and secured a horse and supplies for Kiera. She said a brief goodbye to everyone at camp and instructed me to tell Ruru and Daire that she would see them soon.

We walked to the edge of the woods in silence.

My grip was sweaty and tight on the horse's reins. "You have my map?"

Kiera patted the saddlebag next to her head. "Right here."

"All your weapons? Do you want more food? I can—"

Kiera wrapped her arms around me, her warmth chasing away the snowy chill. "I have everything I need, Aiden. Except you. Hurry to me as soon as you can."

I crushed her against me, kissing the top of her head and inhaling her sweet scent. "There's nowhere you could go that I wouldn't find you."

"There's nowhere I wouldn't want to be found by you."

"Stay alive," I choked out.

She drew back and studied my face with soft eyes and a teasing smile. "Is that a command from my king?"

My heart swooped low and hard. *My king.* I was only her king if she agreed to be my queen. "It's a request from the man who loves you and would cross any battlefield to reach you."

"We will be together again, Aiden," she whispered and kissed me once. Hard and resolute. Then she mounted her horse, her eyes silvery and her chin trembling. "I love you."

She urged her horse into the woods, leaving me behind. I

stared after her until I couldn't see her. Until she was far beyond my reach.

Then I marched back to camp. The final battle for Aquinon now had a prize more important than a crown.

Kiera.

CHAPTER 55
KIERA

The journey to Aquinon was fairly uneventful.

I thought I would come across border patrols like we had last time. But perhaps the fall of Calimber had scared them off. Or Renwell had called them back to Aquinon to defend it.

Regardless, I was happy to keep my sword in its sheath for the whole journey.

When I passed the gaping hole that used to be Calimber, I said a prayer for Nikella and any other lost souls. Then I added another to Mynastra for luck with our next battle.

I caught my first glimpse of Aquinon a week after leaving Yargoth. A long, cold, lonely week.

But staring at the royal city with its warm stone walls and sparkling palace and formidable city gate, I wished the journey was longer.

"This is it," I whispered to my horse, a friendly roan mare. "Hopefully, you have a better time than me."

She huffed and kept carrying me to the gate. To whatever fate lay beyond.

The gate was—unsurprisingly—shut, with archers on top aiming at me as I rode up to them.

"Nobody gets into Aquinon by order of the king," a voice boomed down to me.

"My name is Kiera Torvaine. Renwell is expecting me."

The guard didn't bother to correct my purposeful lack of a royal title for Renwell. Instead, the archers lowered their bows.

The gate doors cracked apart, startling me. A guard in the violet Rellmiran uniform slipped out. The sun beamed off his helmet, nearly blinding me. He had a thick mustache for a mouth that moved when he said, "He's been expecting you for weeks."

My mouth went dry. Of course Renwell had. He still held Everett and Delysia captive. He knew I couldn't stay away forever.

"Dismount and leave your sword," the soldier barked when I said nothing.

I slid off the mare and handed over the reins. They could take my sword, but I would put up a fight if he demanded Mother's knife.

But he said nothing. Didn't search me. Just gestured me to go ahead of him through the narrow gap between the gate doors.

I fought the sudden urge to get back on the mare and ride hard for The Hollow to meet up with Henry. Come back with an invading army, rather than alone.

But Aiden needed me. Everett and Delysia needed me. As did Aquinon.

I have monsters to defeat.

I squared my shoulders and stepped back inside Aquinon. And into the sharp embrace of a dozen guards with spears.

They marched me through the city like a prized prisoner. Even if my shackles were invisible, they were still there.

We passed dozens of Shadow-Wolves prowling through the

streets. Hardly any other people roamed about. Perhaps Renwell sensed a coming attack and had ordered them to stay inside. But a city could not operate without its lifeblood—the people.

My heart ached unexpectedly as I strode past new and old memories. Things I now saw in a different light. Like the white dome and four bell towers of the Temple. Aiden and I had climbed to those towers. The Temple was where he'd first met Mother.

The taverns were dark and quiet, not full of life and laughter as they'd been when Aiden, Maz, Ruru, and I had met up at *The Weary Traveler.*

Maz would be so disappointed he couldn't get a pint of Sunshine. But he wouldn't be here for the mead when he came.

I remembered how it felt to fly across the Old Quarter's rooftops. And to fight the Wolves who now patrolled in the daylight.

We passed the Market Quarter, which no longer smelled like the sticky bread I used to get with Ruru. The colorful awnings flapped in the breeze like a flock of restless birds.

The Noble Quarter gate was more heavily guarded, but they let us through without a word.

Hope sprang in my chest when I saw *The Silk Dancer,* still bright and untarnished. Was Melaena in there now? Would she hear of my return before I could meet with her? Would she be glad I was still alive or angry about what I'd done?

One of the guards shoved me hard in the back, forcing me to pick up my pace.

No nobles strolled through the streets of this quarter, either. Even though the fountains were still running and the gardens remained manicured, there was no one to enjoy them. Except the guards posted at every corner.

Then Garyth's mansion came into view. I winced at seeing the shattered windows and smashed door. A rotten tooth in a gleaming smile. Renwell had probably left Garyth's mansion like this as a message to his neighbors.

Everyone was hiding. Except me.

My escort tightened around me as we neared the bridge. We squeezed past another dozen guards at the bridge gate.

I could barely see the bridge as we walked over it. Just the guards at my side and the palace ahead of me.

The thundering waterfall washed out the sound of my heart drumming in my ears. I had no time to fear traversing its fury with something worse waiting for me inside those walls.

The soldiers marched me up the stone steps, through the double doors of the palace, and into the familiar throne room. It hadn't changed since the last time I was here. But now there was a different monster on the gold throne.

Renwell sat alone, an impassive look on his darkly bearded face. But I knew from the calculating gleam in his eyes that a messenger must've told him I was coming. He'd wanted me to see him like this—casually lounging on the throne, the Rellmiran crown on his gray-streaked dark hair.

He wore a finely tailored tunic belted over trimmed pants. A heavy velvet cloak rested on his shoulders. All black with a few threads of gold and purple, as if the darkness had almost swallowed Rellmira's colors.

I was so used to him hovering in the wings in his austere, hooded cloak, forever a fleeting shadow. But somehow, he looked just as comfortable playing at the role of king. Yet his boots were scuffed as always, as if he couldn't give up all his ways despite his stolen status.

A smirk slowly grew under his gaunt cheeks as I drew closer on the black-and-white marble floor.

He waved off the guards as if fully confident he didn't need them. Mother's knife rubbed on my ankle inside my boot. I could still kill him if he tried to kill me. The way he'd done to Asher the last time we'd been in this throne room together.

Once we were alone, Renwell rose to his feet, towering over me on the black marble dais.

My body screamed at me to take a step back, to snatch my knife. But I didn't. I stiffened my spine and lifted my chin to meet his dark gaze.

"Welcome home," he said.

My eyes narrowed. What game was he playing now?

His eyes drifted to the scar on my cheek. An emotion I didn't understand flickered over his face.

"Where are Everett and Delysia?" I demanded, my voice filling the huge, domed space like a bell.

He smiled smugly, as if he knew this would be my first question. "I'll take you to them."

Fear bled my courage. Was he keeping them in the palace dungeon?

He descended the dais and walked through the northern doors. I hurried after him.

"My soldiers found Korvin's body at a checkpoint on the Medria River," Renwell said calmly, striding through the golden hallways.

I almost stumbled, but then anger snapped to the surface. "You mean your *brother's* body?"

Renwell raised an eyebrow at me. "Nikella told you, did she? I'm guessing she was the one who killed him. Spear wound, they said. How is my little sister faring now that she's destroyed her childhood tormentor?"

I came to a sharp stop, my boots squeaking on the glossy floor. "She's dead."

I hadn't meant to state it so baldly, but I had no desire to shape the words into something more palatable.

Renwell slowly faced me. His cheeks hollowed as he worked

his jaw. "How?"

"Saving us," I said, willing myself not to get emotional. "And destroying your precious mine."

I had no trouble interpreting the rage that steeled Renwell's features. He stepped toward me, his hand going to the hilt of his sunstone sword. "I knew that was your doing at Calimber," he spat. "But how? How did you get an explosive strong enough to gouge such a mass out of the coast?"

I balled my hands into fists to keep them from reaching for my knife. "Our explosives only took down part of the mine. Mynastra did the rest."

He stared at me for a moment, then threw his head back with a laugh I'd never heard before.

It unnerved me more than his anger.

"Mynastra? Gods damn it, your rebel lover must've taught you to be a better liar, you seem so convinced. But choose a more believable lie next time. The few soldiers who escaped Calimber's fall told me nothing of a goddess. Only explosions."

My heart tripped over itself at the mention of Aiden. I tried to keep my face and voice neutral. "It's the truth. After Nikella sank your warship, a vicious storm crumbled everything else into the sea."

Renwell cocked his head to the side and studied me. "Why do you continue to choose him?"

I didn't need to ask who he meant. I kept silent.

Renwell stepped even closer, his voice dark and soft. "I protected you. I trained you. I gave you a purpose—"

"I was simply a blade you forged and sharpened to keep in a sheath at your side," I snarled in his face. "You only released me when you wanted to use me for your own gain."

"Is that not what my sister has done to you as well?" Renwell breathed, his eyes like chips of sunstone. "She turned you against me, filling your mind with lies, thinking that even in death she'll best me."

My nose wrinkled in disgust. "This isn't about 'besting' anyone. I chose to come here. For Everett and Delysia." *Although I'll gladly kill you when it's time.* "And she didn't need to turn me against you. I already hated you, Renwell."

His face shuttered, turning perfectly cold and blank. "You hated me once before. And you still came to care for me."

My stomach twisted as if he'd wrenched it. I tried to breathe evenly, but I couldn't. He'd known all along of my naïve trust in him, and he'd used it against me as he was doing now. I'd never felt so ashamed.

"I shouldn't have," I whispered. "I should've stayed away from you after what you did to Julian and the rest of the People's Council."

"But you didn't. You needed me. You will come to care for me again."

He was so sure of himself. He spoke as if he knew my mind better than I did. Had I really been so ignorant all those years?

"Care for you?" I croaked out, my anger and hurt stripping my voice. "The man who betrayed my mother and lied to me about it?"

"I'm not the one who killed her."

"You killed my father in front of me."

The corner of Renwell's mouth quirked. "Yes, I killed a man you despised who would've executed you."

"You threatened Everett and Delysia," I snapped.

He shrugged. "Empty threats to halt your attacks on me."

"I don't believe you." My fists were shaking with the effort of holding back from grabbing my knife, from striking him with my bare hands.

"I don't believe you either," Renwell said softly. "You don't hate me. You can't. I saved you when no one else would. You will never hate me for that."

My rage boiled over, flooding my body with heat and my mind with blood. I snatched my knife from my boot, but Renwell had me against the wall in a flash, his hands like shackles around my throat and wrist.

I gasped, tears rising to my eyes. "You destroyed that mountain village. You've killed innocent men, women, and children. You sent Korvin after us, told him to punish me. You have no excuses for any of your crimes, and *I will never forgive you.*"

"You forgave *him*," Renwell growled in my ear. "He killed your mother. He used you to further his rebellion. He's using you to get to me just like he did with your father, and you *still* don't see it."

Darkness crowded the corners of my vision as I struggled against his grip. "Aiden loves me. *You* never cared for me at all."

The deadly look in Renwell's eyes made me wonder if he would kill me here and now. Banish whatever plans he might've had in store for me.

Instead, he loosened his grip so I could breathe. "Didn't I?" he whispered.

CHAPTER 56

KIERA

I gaped at him.

For a moment—just one horrible moment—my old self lifted her head with hope. *He cared.*

Then I squashed that thought like the poisonous spider it was, trying to draw me back into his web of lies.

This was what he did. This was how low he would stoop to trick my mind. To win this game he played with my life.

"You lie," I whispered as if we were playing a game of Death and Four and I was calling his bluff.

"Do I?" He wrenched Mother's knife from my hand. "I'm leading you to see your brother and sister. Alive and well in their rooms, just as you left them."

"Because you needed to dangle them in front of me like bait." I lunged for my knife, but he was faster, stepping out of my reach.

He stared at the glittering weapon. "I wondered what it would take for you to reveal this, to show your true intentions."

I grit my teeth. Was that what this had been about? If so, I'd failed spectacularly.

"Strange to think I won't be able to make more of these, thanks to you and"—he smirked—"*Mynastra*. But no matter, I have more than enough weapons for whatever vengeful plans are swirling in your head, my little apprentice."

With that, he turned on his boot heel and strode off down the hall. I followed more slowly, shaken to my core.

I'd come here with such confidence, such surety of my thoughts and emotions. That he wouldn't be able to break me.

But he'd already cracked me open.

He walked up to Delysia's bedroom door, where two guards stood outside. He knocked instead of barging in like I expected him to.

"Come in," Delysia said from the other side.

I shoved past Renwell and burst into the room. And there she was. With Everett. Alive and well, just as Renwell said.

Delysia was facing the door in a plain pink dress, her face drawn and tired. But she lit up when I barreled into her, throwing my arms around her. I cried, unable to help myself. Delysia's body, which seemed thinner and less curvy than before, was shaking.

Everett wrapped his arms around both of us, his scent of books and ink immediately soothing me.

"We thought you were dead," Delysia whispered. "When Renwell told us of the mine, we thought you were dead, Kiera."

I drew away, looking over my shoulder. But Renwell was gone, along with my knife, and the door was closed. "He told you about Calimber?"

Delysia nodded, wiping away her tears with a wrinkled handkerchief.

Everett kept his hand on my shoulder. "He said it's completely destroyed. That you were likely with the rebels who did it, except no one made it out."

My upper lip curled. He hadn't been surprised when he saw

me. Someone had to have reported our ships fleeing. He'd only said such things to hurt my siblings.

I will always hate you, Renwell.

"I thought perhaps he'd already captured you, before the loss of Calimber," Everett said, rubbing his ink-stained fingers on his unshaven chin. "He spends a lot of time in the palace dungeon."

I frowned. "How do you know that?"

"We . . . follow him sometimes."

My eyes widened, and I glanced at Delysia.

She nodded. "We use the secret passages. Mostly the ones we're sure he doesn't know about. We were trying to see if he knew anything about you he wasn't telling us."

"That was incredibly brave *and* incredibly stupid," I said, even as my heart warmed at their concern. "Do you have any idea what he might've done if he'd caught you spying on him?"

Delysia's eyes, so like our mother's, hardened. "We were right next to him when he paraded our father's head and body around the city. We knew what kind of man he was during the Pravaran rebellion. We *both* tried to warn you about him."

I staggered back a step. Her words peeled the thin skin off a barely healed wound.

She was right. They'd shared their misgivings several times. I'd thought they were jealous at first, that I was to train under such a powerful High Enforcer. That I wouldn't have to fill the role Father wanted me to, as they did.

And then I tossed their worries away because I feared if I accepted them, I would have to admit my own mistakes in trusting Renwell.

But the damage was already done, and far from over.

"I'm sorry," I said quietly. "I should've listened. I just . . . couldn't in those moments."

Delysia's face softened. "I know. When Renwell said you had

joined the rebels who had tried to assassinate Father, it gave me pride, not disappointment, as he probably intended."

I smiled. "I hope Mother would have felt the same."

Delysia frowned. "What do you mean?"

I sat down on one of Delysia's—Mother's—settees. Everett and Delysia joined me as I told them what our mother had done, how Aiden had helped her, and how our father had covered it up.

Delysia wept into her handkerchief. Everett dashed at his eyes with the embroidered sleeve of his jacket.

"Is that why you went with them?" Delysia asked, her eyes pink and swollen. "Because you found out what really happened with Mother?"

I shook my head. "Not at first. But I knew I needed to after Arduen's Mountain. I helped free the prisoners and destroy the mine for her. And for Rellmira. Now I'm going to do the same for you."

Delysia and Everett shared a look. It pinched my heart that I was on the outside of it. They'd had to survive in a different way than I had. It'd clearly brought them closer.

"We don't have anywhere to go," Everett said, leaning back in a velvet armchair. "Renwell's announcement of Father's usurpation, coupled with our lack of relationships outside this palace, has truly sealed our fates here."

I stared at him in disbelief. "You want to stay? With him? After all the warnings you gave me—"

"He doesn't hurt us," Delysia interrupted. "He lies to us, keeps secrets, sure. But what good would we do on the street? Who could we trust to help us? We can trust Renwell to be untrustworthy. And we were hoping—before he surmised you'd died in Calimber—that you would come back and we could help you overthrow him." Delysia smiled, a distant look in her eyes.

"Then I would run away with Henry, and Everett could be a Teacher in one of the Temples."

I glanced at Everett with raised eyebrows.

He smiled sheepishly. "It's what I've always wanted. I just never thought it would be possible with becoming king and all."

It made sense. And judging by the ink stains on Everett's fingers, Renwell was still allowing him to use the library. Giving Everett what he wanted until Renwell needed something in return, no doubt.

"But . . . I need to get you out of here," I said, still surprised I had to argue with them on this. I'd thought they'd be desperate to leave. "It's going to be too dangerous for you to stay."

"Why?" Delysia demanded, crushing her soiled handkerchief in her fist. "Is that why you're here now? What are you going to do?"

I hesitated. "I shouldn't say it here."

"Closet," both my siblings said.

I chuckled. Mother's large, stuffed closet had been where we used to go for private conversations because all her clothes muffled our voices.

Perched in the narrow room, amid Delysia's dresses and shoes, I told them our plan.

We talked long into the night.

At some point, a knock interrupted us, and a guard brought in enough food for six people. Roasted chicken with seared vegetables, potatoes fried in garlic and rosemary, and fresh biscuits with a bowl of soft butter.

Delysia looked at me with wide eyes. "Renwell must know your favorite meal."

I scowled. "I would've preferred my knife back."

But I ate as much as I could, anyway. I'd barely eaten in the last week.

Delysia was excited about our plan and kept reassuring me

that Henry was up to the task, even though I was the one who'd summoned him.

"And Aiden truly is a Falcryn?" Everett asked, still amazed at what Aiden had done to try to make him king.

"The last one," I said. "He may not know it yet, but he will be one of the greatest kings."

Delysia smiled with those sappy eyes I used to tease her for. "You love him."

This time, I didn't hesitate to admit it. "Yes, I do."

"He'd better treat you well," Everett said, his profile suddenly stern in the firelight.

"He does, Everett. I pray you'll meet him soon."

However this battle ended, I wanted everyone I loved in the world to be with me under one roof, even if it didn't last.

Once we were done and had talked ourselves out, Everett and I left.

A guard stepped forward. "My lady, the king requested I escort you to your room."

My eyes narrowed. "I know where it is."

Renwell was undoubtedly looking forward to watching my every move from his study next door. Unless he'd moved to Father's.

The guard, an older man who'd been working in the palace since I could remember—Pierce, shook his head. "Not your apprentice room, he said. He thought you'd be more comfortable in the room you had since you were a child."

I pursed my lips. Or perhaps he feared my spying on him more than he wanted to spy on me.

But it certainly wasn't for my comfort.

"Lead on then," I said. I wished Everett a good sleep and followed Pierce to my old bedroom just down the hall.

He opened the familiar arched door for me. The scent of

lilies and fresh air washed over me. I wandered inside, and Pierce quietly closed the door behind me.

It was surprisingly clean after years of being vacant. Fresh blankets covered my bed. The silk awning looked clean and smooth. My small fireplace was swept and loaded with chopped wood. Fresh purple lilies in vases on every table were an expert finishing touch.

Renwell had been expecting me, after all.

I tiptoed through my room as though I might disturb someone.

Mother was everywhere in here. My lavender walls displayed her dreamy paintings of flowers and vines. A brush still lay on my dressing table, left there since the last time she'd brushed my hair.

I opened the narrow doors to my balcony, breathing in the cool, salty air. It smelled like home. Or at least the home from my memory. Where I was happiest for a time.

My windows faced west over the cliffs the palace sat atop, overlooking the plains and the river.

I'd spent so long staring at this view, wishing I could go beyond these walls and explore the world. Ride a horse across that plain, like a driver from Winspere. Sail down the river. Stand in the mystical forest of Twaryn. Meet new people. Experience new things.

I'd done all that. Not in the way I'd always imagined. But daydreams rarely included the mess of suffering and loss.

The iron chairs and stone table on my balcony were also clean. As if Mother had just eaten her breakfast with us this morning before disappearing into her garden.

I sat on a chair and closed my eyes. Listened to the gentle breeze. And dreamed new dreams.

The next morning, I awoke to a knock. I'd changed into my

thickest sleeping gown before going to bed last night, but I still threw on a dressing robe.

I knew who it was before I opened the door.

Renwell stood in my doorway, looking well-rested in similar clothing to yesterday's. But without the crown or the cloak. A familiar wooden box was tucked under his arm.

He smiled, soft and pleasant. A lie. "Play with me?"

Memories nipped at the back of my mind. He'd asked me the same question in the same stance many times during our years of training.

But everything else had changed.

"No."

His smile grew. "Not even to get your precious siblings out of Aquinon?"

My breath snagged. This was his plan? To get me to wager their freedom? For what?

It didn't matter when neither of them wanted to leave just yet. But Renwell didn't need to know that.

"And if I lose?" I asked.

"Then you will grant the favor I ask."

Dread churned in my stomach. This was precisely what Aiden had worried would happen. "What favor?"

Renwell's eyes narrowed with predatory confidence. "Play with me and find out."

CHAPTER 57
KIERA

Renwell had thought of everything.

When I went to change clothes, I found my old training outfits, instead of my princess dresses, in the closet.

My lip curled.

Clearly, he was trying to make me comfortable—leaving me alone with Everett and Delysia, giving me my old room and my preferred clothes, asking me to play our usual game.

I might as well let him think it was working until I got what I wanted. I had six days left before Aiden and Henry were supposed to arrive. I needed to make them count.

I slipped into a comfortable pair of brown pants and a black, long-sleeved shirt that hugged my skin. He'd also left me a new pair of boots, but I laced on my worn ones, just as he still did.

Moments later, I entered Renwell's study without knocking.

He sat behind his desk, the Death and Four tiles already scattered facedown in front of him. A steaming teapot, two cups, and a simple breakfast of eggs, sausage, and toast sat on a tray at the edge of his desk.

The food smelled amazing, but Renwell's scent was steeped

in the simple furniture and black rug—rose petals and candle smoke. The dangerous reality living under the calm surface.

The heavy curtains were drawn, and a fire warmed the room from the hearth. No matter what time of day it was outside, night always reigned here.

Everything was as it used to be, down to Renwell's intense gaze as he watched me sit down on the other side of the desk.

"Eat or play first?" he asked, but the gleam in his eyes told me he already knew the answer.

I grabbed a piece of toast and spread apple jam on it with a knife that wouldn't pierce even the most tender of flesh. "Why didn't you take Father's study? It's bigger. More regal."

Renwell poured us both tea and put sugar and milk in mine the way I liked. "I have no need for a bigger office. Despite what your father thought, ruling is not all about appearances. It's about action."

"Like stealing a stolen throne?"

Renwell leaned back in his imposing chair. "I am more equipped to rule this kingdom than your greedy father or your traitorous lover."

The toast was too dry in my mouth, even with the sweet jam. I downed my tea. "The Falcryns were chosen by the Four before they left this world."

"And everything the gods have done is for the best?" Renwell shook his head. "Do you not weary of obeying orders from dead gods? Did you not shed the role of princess to take on High Enforcer—the very first royal in Rellmiran history to do so? You tire of the same irrelevant rules that I do. So, yes, I believe we're both better suited to power than those that came before."

My appetite suddenly deserted me. There was a time I wanted power—more than what I had as a princess destined to be auctioned off to another man. I wanted to be High Enforcer and bring justice to a world that had killed my mother.

Now? I still wanted power. But I didn't want it from Renwell. Power wasn't true if it was simply a token meant to mollify and control. I had no desire to walk from one cage to another.

I brushed the toast crumbs from my lap. "If I win this game, I want to visit Melaena at her club tonight. Alone."

Renwell studied me as he drank the rest of his tea and set it aside. Probably calculating all the reasons I'd want that instead of freeing my siblings.

"Done," he said.

"How can I trust that you'll honor our wager?" I'd never forget that he'd told Korvin to punish me after swearing he wouldn't allow it again.

Renwell reached down, then laid my knife atop the smooth black Death and Four tiles. "Kill me if I lie."

I snatched the knife before he could take it back. Instead of tucking it into my boot, I rested it across my lap. Just in case.

"Then let's play," I said.

We picked our tiles. After swapping a few, I held Terraum's bearded head, two sevens, and a six.

Renwell placed a tile facedown. "Mynastra." He smirked as if he were still laughing at me for what I said about the fall of Calimber.

I selected my six. "You lie."

He flipped over his tile. Mynastra's fierce face stared back at me, outlined in gold. Gods damn it. Three Duels left.

"Nine," I said evenly, shoving my Terraum tile forward.

"Liar." Renwell tossed Viridana's sad face onto the desk.

Fucking Four. I had to win or draw the next two Duels.

Renwell laid down another tile and tapped it with one pale finger. "Seven."

I studied his face. It'd always been hard to read him. If it hadn't, I probably wouldn't be in this mess.

But there could only be one other seven since I had two. Which also meant it didn't matter what I played.

"Truth."

He nodded and showed me his matching seven.

I could still win if his last tile was less than seven. My fingers trembled as I revealed it.

He stared down at it without a flicker of triumph or defeat in his gaze.

I fisted my knife in my lap. I had no intention of using it against him—yet. But holding it was a comfort all the same.

He gently laid his last tile next to mine. An eight. He won.

Fear quickly chased my disappointment away. "What favor do you want?" I whispered.

His smile sent a shiver ricocheting between my shoulder blades. "I'll show you. But you have to wear this."

He pulled something out of a drawer and tossed it on top of the tiles, making them bounce and skitter away.

A black metal Wolf mask snarled up at me.

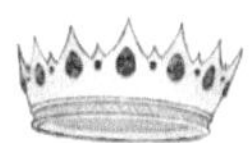

THE MASK MADE IT HARD TO BREATHE.

But perhaps that was for the best as I walked through an alley in the middle of the Docks Quarter. Rotting fish, congealed urine, and a thousand other smells assaulted my nose through the holes in the metal snout.

I hated the mask. I wished I could say I hated the Wolf uniform, too, but it was gods-damned comfortable. Soft and loose, and the boots barely made a sound on the uneven cobblestones.

A long sunstone sword, inconspicuous in its sheath, tapped against my leg as I walked.

Renwell touched my shoulder. I stopped and glanced at his matching mask.

I'd nearly backed out of our wager when he met me at my door that evening, also dressed as a Shadow-Wolf. But if I could kill him for reneging, then he would likely do the same.

"No talking" had been his first rule. "Follow my lead" had been his second. When I asked what we were supposed to do, he simply said, "Keep Aquinon safe."

I highly doubted our idea of safety was the same.

Renwell pointed to where a group of sailors swaggered down another alley adjacent to ours. Their loud jokes rattled against the stone walls like the cluster of bones tied to their waists.

I fell in step behind Renwell as he tailed them.

So far, we had done nothing but prowl the streets. Other groups of Wolves did as well. I wondered if they still lived in the Den after the battle two months ago. Renwell pointed out we couldn't use the faster passage from the royal bedchamber to the Den because Aiden had destroyed it when we escaped.

I hadn't replied.

Instead, I'd darted my gaze everywhere I could, hidden by the mask. I'd observed the cliff gate—raised as always. I'd peered into the harbor to see what defenses Renwell had set up but saw none, other than the two watchtowers.

I didn't see his third warship.

Even if I did, I had no way of contacting Aiden. Holy Four, I was glad he couldn't see me now.

We tailed the group of sailors until they piled into one of the busy taverns. Renwell swapped targets for a thin, mousy man who scurried between pools of light.

Why were we following this man? He looked harmless.

But then I spotted the bulging sack at his waist that rang with the sweet sound of coins, no matter how carefully he walked. He must've won a great deal tonight.

Surprise fluttered in my belly. Strange that Renwell seemed to be protecting this man, rather than stalking potential criminals.

After another turn down an alley, we lost him. Renwell held up a fist to stop me. We listened.

Muffled thumps and yells came from ahead.

We drew our swords and darted toward the sound. The mousy man was on the ground bleeding while a large, bald sailor snatched at the coin bag.

Renwell slid his sword under the bald man's chin. The man immediately froze. He followed the sword's glittering edge to its owner. The blood drained from his face.

He dropped the bag. Coins spilled every which way, rolling in the muck around the unconscious man.

"I-I wasn't . . . I didn't mean to—" The sailor tried to back away, but Renwell twitched his hand and cut a red stripe across the man's chest. He gaped at the blood dripping down his front, then bolted down the alley.

Renwell strode back the way we came without looking at the beaten man.

I kneeled and pressed my gloved fingers to his neck. A strong pulse thrummed. He would live.

I hurried after Renwell.

Why punish the would-be thief instead of putting him in the city prison? He had beaten a man unconscious, after all. This sort of brutal justice was wildly unbalanced and could lead to anarchy.

But I kept my mouth shut. For now.

A short while later, we came upon a brawl outside a tavern. They tried to scatter, bleating with fear, but Renwell wouldn't let them. He used his fists and feet freely, punishing each man with crushing blows. His mask hid his expression, but I swore I could feel his pleasure, as if he relished fighting in the street.

One of the cornered men took a swing at me, and I smashed his face with my metal Wolf mask. He dropped like a stone next to the other brawlers. Renwell grunted his approval.

Perhaps this was his new method of inducing fear, now that he couldn't ship them off to the sunstone mine.

We left the men there as patrons gaped from the tavern windows.

When we neared the harbor, we spotted two men slashing at each other with curved knives while a woman wept against the sea wall. I raced toward them, drawing my sword. But one sank his knife into the chest of the other. The woman screamed.

Renwell slammed the hilt of his sword against the murderer's temple. He fell face first in his victim's blood.

I hurried over to the woman, offering a gloved hand to help her up. She gasped with fear and cowered against the stone wall.

Right. I'm just another Shadow-Wolf out here.

Feeling dirty with guilt, I stepped away from her.

Renwell threw back his head and uttered a shrieking howl. The fine hairs on my arms and neck lifted.

Two more Wolves came and dragged away the unconscious man. Renwell moved on while I whispered a prayer over the other man's body. As we left, I glanced over my shoulder to see the woman crawl over to him.

Who was he? Why had they been fighting?

I felt like I'd invaded several ongoing stories tonight and hacked them all to threads without knowing why.

It was disconcerting, leaving a sour taste in my mouth.

Was the whole city this bad, or had Renwell taken me to the worst part? But even with this amount of violence, his swift execution of momentary justice felt like trying to contain a waterfall in a teacup.

I hurried to catch up with Renwell when someone jumped out of a darkened doorway between us.

The man wore a sack over his face with holes cut out for his eyes and mouth. He brandished a long, wavy knife at me.

Gods, the man must be insane to attack a Shadow-Wolf.

I whipped out my sunstone sword and sliced it through the air a few times, warning him what I was capable of. The long black blade felt as it had in the mountain village—too comfortable, too deadly. And my recent training only made it more so.

But the man didn't heed me. He lunged. I blocked his knife with my sword, and the steel burst. Without missing a beat, the man pulled out another knife and came at me with furious strikes.

Whoever he was, he knew how to fight well.

He backed me down the alley as I tried to shatter his other blade, but I kept missing it. Panic crept into my mind. I tried to fight it as Nikella had taught me. But I already felt unraveled in this awful uniform, doing Renwell's dirty work.

The man seized my sword hand and slammed it against the stone wall behind me. Pain crackled through my body.

I shouted and kicked his thigh as hard as I could. He didn't budge.

A sword tip pierced my chest . . . *through* my assailant's chest. He glanced down at it, gasping, the sack on his head drooping.

Renwell's masked face appeared over his shoulder. He yanked the man off me and threw him against the wall, where he crumpled. Dead.

Renwell spun back to me. I flinched, lifting my sword.

He could kill me just as easily, and no one would know.

Renwell stiffened, then he slowly lifted his Wolf mask. His features were drawn tight, his eyes dark with rage.

"Did he hurt you?" he demanded in a hoarse whisper.

Confused, I shook my head. He told me not to talk.

Renwell lifted his gloved fingers and gently stroked the cheek of my mask.

My heart hammered. Why was he showing concern? This had to be a ruse. A trick to make me forgive him. He didn't care for me.

"Didn't I?"

I turned my face away. His fingers dropped.

"We're done for the evening," he said in a deeper voice, backing away and sliding his mask back into place. "I'll take you to *The Silk Dancer* now, if you wish."

My brow furrowed. He was going to let me see Melaena even though I hadn't won our game?

"I want to see his face first," I said, gesturing to the dead man.

I waited for Renwell's wrath, for his hand around my throat. But nothing.

He nodded.

I bent over the blood-soaked man and removed his hood. A stranger. Thin, dirty brown hair and a crooked nose. He had strange pink scars above and below his closed eyes.

Why had he targeted me?

"Come, Kiera."

I left the man in the alley and followed Renwell to *The Silk Dancer.*

He led me up the steps and held open the door for me. I balked for a moment. I hadn't realized he meant for us to visit *right now*.

I would have to meet Melaena dressed as a Shadow-Wolf at Renwell's side. Gods damn it, she'd probably think I'd surrendered my loyalty to him.

I slipped into the busy atrium of the club. An immediate hush fell over the crowd. Nobles wrapped in fine silks, velvet, and furs stared at us. Jewelry glittered at their necks and wrists like my sword glittered in its sheath.

A small girl nearby stared up at me with stark terror on her face.

That fear hurt worse than anything else had tonight. *I must look like a monster to her.*

Perhaps that was Renwell's goal all along.

Renwell sauntered past the quivering nobles to the side corridor. The familiar crimson carpet and ornate doors soothed me the tiniest bit.

The door at the end of the hall burst open, and Melaena emerged, calling over her shoulder, "Ten minutes, ladies! Finish up!"

She caught sight of us and stopped, her plum-colored silk dress whirling about her. "What are you doing here? Renwell assured me—"

"*King* Renwell," he said, pulling off his mask. "I brought you a surprise."

Feeling strangely guilty, I tugged off my mask. "Hello, Melaena."

CHAPTER 58
KIERA

Melaena's face slackened, then crumpled. With a muffled sob, she rushed toward me, her arms outstretched.

Relief pounded through my aching body as I happily embraced her. Her gold earrings tickled my cheek, and her long, curly black hair enveloped us both.

"I was so worried," she whispered. "Everything . . . the explosions. Everyone was gone."

"It's all right, Melaena," I murmured. "Please." *Please stop talking. Please don't ask questions. Not here.*

She seemed to remember who was standing at my shoulder and hastily backed away from me. She glanced between me and Renwell. "Can Kiera come back and say hello to the other dancers?"

Renwell pressed his lips together. "No. They can greet her out here if they wish."

Melaena's eyebrows drew together as if she were putting the pieces together. Renwell didn't trust me, nor I him.

But I might not get another chance.

Thinking quickly, I smiled at her. "You're doing a show tonight, yes?"

She nodded. "The Ballad of the Lotus Wars."

"Holy Four, that's my favorite poem!" I turned my smile on Renwell and brushed my fingers over his forearm. "Would you mind if I danced with them? I . . . I've missed it these last few months. It would mean the world to me if I could do it again. One last time."

His eyes flicked to where my fingers still touched his arm. His jaw tightened, but he didn't remove my hand. Instead, he addressed Melaena. "Are all the dancers back there?"

"Of course," Melaena said.

Tension rippled through Renwell, and just when I thought he'd refuse, he jerked his head in a nod at me. "You may go. I'll watch from the front row."

I grinned, tightening my grip on him for a moment. Then, deciding it could only help my cause, I leaned forward and whispered, "Thank you. And thank you for saving my life."

Some of the tension melted from his face. He didn't smile, but his eyes softened in the way I remembered whenever I conquered a new skill or beat him at Death and Four.

"You're welcome."

I released him and grasped Melaena's hand as we darted into the dressing room.

She closed the door and leaned against it, her chest heaving. "By the Four, I thought he was here to haul me off to the executioner's stand, after all."

I winced, trying to ignore the stares of the other dancers. I opened my mouth to speak, but she shook her head the slightest bit, glancing at the bouquet of beautiful women.

Right. Ruru had said she didn't trust them all anymore.

Melaena clapped her hands, fluttering to the middle of the

room. The women stopped applying makeup and jewelry and focused on her.

"Olivia, you'll be joining the divine group. Kiera will take your place as a background dancer. Since it will take her a moment to get changed, please perform the opening dance from Arduen's Night for our guests."

A memory echoed in the back of my mind, of Melaena inducting me into her dancers for another performance. But this really would be the last time.

Melaena herded her dancers out the door. A few tried to argue, but she insisted that they not let the "king" get bored waiting.

I noted Jayde glaring at me as she left. Tullia gave me a cautious wave that I returned. The two women hadn't been my friends exactly. They had no idea who I was. And to turn up dressed as a Wolf wasn't likely to win me any allies.

"Get in the bath," Melaena said briskly, turning on the tap. "We can talk while we work."

While I bathed, I caught her up on everything since I'd last seen her. She mentioned Aiden had told her I'd betrayed them, but she didn't know how, only that he looked like a man whose heart had been destroyed.

She grew much happier when I told her of how things were between us now. How Ruru and Maz were doing. And what we'd accomplished at Calimber.

After my bath, she brushed out my knotted hair and braided it into an elaborate crown, much like Yarina had done for the fire dance. Tears pricked my eyes, but I blinked them away.

"Hold still," she commanded as she dusted powder over my cheeks. "You have terrible red marks on your face. What did Renwell make you do?"

"I slammed my mask against a man's face," I admitted. "Only because he tried to hit me."

"You don't have to justify yourself to me, Kiera," she said gently, applying makeup around my eyes. "Just tell me what you need before that murderer comes back here."

I relayed our battle plans. "Henry also gave me two guards' names: Dredger and Mankmen. I need one of them to get me a disguise and a cover story that will allow me to disable the cliff gate."

"Dredger and Mankmen," she murmured. "I'll find them. When do you need to do this?"

"The fifth night from now. I don't want to risk anyone checking the gate before Aiden arrives."

She frowned, scrubbing at a spot on my face. "And how will you get away from Renwell?"

"Any way I have to. But I'll be here." Perhaps he'd be willing to make another wager. If I lost again, I wouldn't have to suffer the consequences too long.

"Be careful, Kiera," she whispered, cleaning her hands on a towel. "The way he looks at you . . . He means to keep you. One way or another."

Unease trickled down my spine. "I can handle him. Now, what am I wearing this time?"

A few minutes later, I was waiting backstage with the other dancers. They whispered and giggled while I stood alone, peering around the gold curtain.

I wore a dress of black silk edged in gold. It clung to my arms, neck, and torso and flared around my legs. This dress was more opaque than the one I wore for Asher. I wasn't sure if that was because Melaena wanted to cover more of my scars and wounds. Or if she knew I wasn't here to seduce Renwell, no matter how much I played to his ego.

Gold necklaces laced with artificial black feathers cascaded over my chest. My feet were bare and adorned with gold ankle bracelets. They helped cover the marks left behind by the shackles.

I was the crow of death, the scavenger of war. A fitting role.

Renwell was easy to spot in the crowd. He sat at his own table in the front, lounging with one dirty boot propped up on the pristine velvet bench. His mask and sword rested on the table, glaring symbols of his power. The other guests were crammed around tables the farthest they could sit from him. The conversation was minimal and carried on with forced smiles and shaky hands.

Renwell smirked at the pale boy who placed a glass of wine in front of him. The boy fumbled a bow and ran back down the aisle.

Renwell stared directly at me and lifted his glass, as if toasting me. Then drained it.

I let the curtain fall back, hiding from him again. Gods, I felt as though I were back in the mine, the walls thundering around me, ready to crumble.

How far would he go to win back my trust? How far would I have to go to convince him he was succeeding?

The musicians played the opening notes as we hurried into our positions. I was perfectly happy in the back.

Melaena had told me to perform a few of the leaps and twirls I'd learned for Asher's dance. Nothing too grand. Just be a beautiful crow.

And I was. I danced on stage, waving my arms, flying, leaping, twirling in the winds of war that carried me. I pretended I was free, flying to my love with his crow-wing hair and brilliant green eyes.

Home, at last.

Melaena insisted I wear the costume back to the palace.

Renwell's eyes swept me from head to toe, his nostrils flaring, but he didn't argue. I carried my Wolf uniform, apart from the boots that I wore under my dress. Once again, a group of soldiers escorted us across the bridge.

Was Renwell worried I would jump? Or did he remember I feared the bridge and wanted me to feel safe? Neither felt right.

He walked me to my door without a word.

My stomach tightened. Did he want something else from me?

"Thank you for tonight," I said, handing him my Wolf uniform. I twisted my doorknob.

"Kiera."

I allowed a grimace to pass over my face before I glanced back at him.

He held my mask in his gloved hand, rubbing one finger over the cheek of it. "I wanted you to come with me tonight to see the good we could do together in Aquinon. You once desired to be High Enforcer of Rellmira more than anything else. I'm offering you that job now."

Shock made my lips part. "Why?"

"To have what we always talked about when I was training you. I want you at my side as we rule Rellmira. You could have all the power you crave." He held up the Wolf mask. "If you wish to disband my Wolves, you can. If you prefer to patrol the streets yourself, to protect those you deem worthy, then you must. If you demand change in our justice system, I will grant you the power and resources to do that."

He was handing me everything—everything I'd wanted for years. All that savage hope I'd kept bottled inside as I trained and waited for my moment, and he was finally rewarding it.

Impossible.

"And in return?" I croaked.

His face tightened. "You swear your loyalty to me. To never instigate nor aid a plot against me or my rule."

I shook my head wearily. "That is not power, Renwell. That is another cage."

Anger flickered in his eyes. "Power always comes at a price. I am asking a very small one for a very great honor."

I pretended to hesitate, thinking long and hard. But really, I knew better. I had seen too many of Renwell's crimes, dealt with too much of the pain he'd inflicted, to believe that I would be powerful. That I could actually make the changes he suggested.

It was as though he handed me a sword while cutting off my legs.

And I hadn't missed his other insinuation. If I swore loyalty to him, he would demand I tell him any plans regarding Aiden. But if I told him no, he might extract that information through other means.

"I'll think on it," I told him. "Good night, Renwell."

"Sleep well, Kiera."

I entered my room and closed the door in his face. I sank onto my bed, staring into the fire a servant must have lit. The weather never got as cold as it did in Dagriel. But the fire chased away the chill that emanated from my heart.

A soft knock came at the door.

I grabbed Mother's knife from my dressing table and hid it behind my back as I opened the door.

Everett's tired face greeted me.

I ushered him in and locked the door. "What's wrong?"

"Nothing," he said with a jaw-cracking yawn. "I was waiting in one of the passages until Renwell left. I've been in the library all day."

I shot him a stiff smile. "Of course you have."

He sat on my bed and seemed to notice my outfit for the first time. "What are you wearing? And why? Did Renwell make you do this?" His voice rose.

"Hush, no. I was at *The Silk Dancer*, telling Melaena what I needed for the gate."

Everett's gray eyes cleared. "Ah, yes, that's why I'm here. I found an old account of when Aquinon was built. The architects and engineers sketched the buildings, like this palace and the Temple and the layout of the quarters. Very interesting, actually. Terraum himself must've helped with their work, as some passageways are clearly marked. Perhaps he didn't mark them all on purpose—"

"Ev, I'm dying to get out of this dress and these feathers. What did you find to help me?"

"How to immobilize the gate." He revealed a small leather book from his jacket and pulled out a piece of paper. "The architects never drew the gate mechanism, but simply described it. I sketched the gatehouse as close to their words as I could. Tampering with the winch mechanism or the chains would either take a long time or send the gate crashing down. But in a tiny footnote here, an engineer mentioned locking pins that anchor the gate to prevent too much tension on the winch. If you sever those with Mother's knife and put the pieces back in, they'll jam the gate in place when the guards try to pull the pins out."

I stared at the carefully inked sketch. The gate system was a mess of pulleys and chains. "Like breaking off a key in a lock."

"Exactly. But make sure you cut the pin just right so it doesn't fall out the other side."

I bit my lip. "What if someone sees what I've done? Then they'd have plenty of time to fix it before Aiden arrives."

"Try to disguise it, if you can. And pray to the Four they don't inspect it too closely." Everett sat back in my chair, rubbing his bloodshot eyes. "If they discover it, they'll be able to reach through the gate and cut through the rest of the pin with a Wolf's blade, as I'm sure they've also realized sharpened sunstone has more uses than death. There are too many problems to solve, but this is the best plan I have over a dozen others."

I wrapped my arm around his shoulders and pulled my brother close. "It'll work, or it won't. Either way, I will do everything I can to shape this battle in our favor."

He gave me a wan smile, then kissed my forehead. "I'm with you, little sister. Either way."

I wanted to burst into tears at the rare show of affection and curl up in his arms like I had when we were younger. But I couldn't lose my nerve now. I had to be strong until the end. Like Mother.

After Everett left, I shimmied out of my dress and carefully laid it over a chair. Maybe Renwell would let me use the excuse of returning it to go back to the club.

I sat in front of my mirror and washed off the thick makeup Melaena had painted onto my face. She'd tried very hard to hide the red marks in my eyebrows and on my cheeks from the Wolf mask.

I froze, staring at my half-washed face. I'd just seen marks like this. But as deeper scars. Like the ones someone would get if he wore a Wolf mask for many hours.

The man who'd tried to kill me was a Shadow-Wolf.

CHAPTER 59

KIERA

I SHARED MY DISCOVERY WITH EVERETT AND DELYSIA THE NEXT morning over breakfast on my little balcony.

I thought about keeping it to myself. But I didn't care for secrets anymore.

It was actually a relief to discuss it with them, rather than spin questions around in my head.

"Perhaps he used to be a Shadow-Wolf, then grew disgruntled with Renwell and deserted," Everett suggested, buttering his toast.

"I don't think any Wolf has ever deserted. If they did, it wasn't for long," I said grimly. "Remember, they sign up for the money or for darker desires. Few men change their minds about that."

"Renwell set you up," Delysia declared, peeling a cooked egg. "You said he's trying to get you to forgive him for some twisted reason. He wanted to save you, like Aiden saved you." Every time she mentioned Aiden, her voice turned dreamy, even though she'd never met him. I couldn't help but smile each time.

"I agree. Renwell likely paid that man to attack me," I said, picking the fatty bits off my bacon. I only liked the crispy parts.

"But what mercenary would willingly sacrifice his life? You don't get paid in the Abyss."

Everett shrugged, the sun glinting off the gold thread in his jacket. "Perhaps Renwell lied to him, too. He could've told the Wolf that he would only fight him off, not kill him."

"That sounds more like him," I muttered. "But I plan to keep my suspicions to myself and pretend to warm up to his ideals until I get his gods-damned permission to go back to Melaena's. There are too many guards on the bridge for me to sneak past."

Delysia nodded. "They've been all over that bridge for weeks. For a while, they didn't let *anyone* cross it. Renwell must have thought you or Aiden would try to sneak across the bridge, since it's the only way in or out now."

"When Aiden crosses that bridge, he won't be sneaking," I said firmly.

Delysia smirked at me. "No, he'll be sprinting toward you."

I flicked a piece of fatty bacon at her.

She shrieked and launched backward in her chair. "Do you have any idea how hard it is to remove a grease stain from silk?" she cried.

Instead of laughing like I might've when we were younger, I held my hands up. "You're right, I'm sorry. I wouldn't want to create more work for the maids. I suppose I'm not used to caring for fine clothes anymore."

Delysia settled back in her chair, fluffing her skirts with pink cheeks. "I didn't mean to get hysterical. I guess it's still a reflex from when Father used to criticize all my dresses for any little wrinkle or stain."

Even though he was gone, Father still cast a shadow over us as he had our whole lives.

I reached across the table and clasped her hand, then Everett's. "When this is over, I promise I'll do whatever I can to make sure you both get to lead the lives you've always wanted.

No more worrying about late nights in the library or ink-stained fingers. No more stress over a secret lover and perfect appearances. You'll be free. I promise."

"You should also have the life you want, Kiera," Delysia whispered, a breeze toying with her golden hair.

Everett nodded, squeezing my hand.

I gave them a weak smile. All I wanted was for Rellmira to be free. To get my friends and family through this last battle alive. Beyond that, my dreams were wisps of light—vague hopes of love and happiness and freedom . . . and Aiden. But those dreams kept dancing out of reach in my mind, frightened of the darkness that still held it captive.

Later that night, I knocked on Renwell's study door. The two guards flanking it didn't look at me. Nor did they seem to care that I had a knife in my boot.

"Come in, Kiera," Renwell called.

My eye twitched. *Always reminding how well you know me, aren't you?*

I opened the door, forcing my expression back to its calm facade. "I'm here for a rematch," I announced.

I sat in the chair in front of his desk, tossing my braid over my shoulder as if I hadn't a care in the world.

Renwell's narrowed eyes took in my perfectly still hands and loose posture. Gods, it was almost painful not to fidget.

The fire in his hearth crackled in the silence, but I didn't fill it. Just lifted an eyebrow at my former mentor.

He wore the crown this time, making me wonder if he'd come from a meeting. Who remained on his High Council if Korvin and Dracles were dead? Perhaps he meant to have no High Council as well as no People's Council. To rule alone and independently.

Except he had offered me the position of High Enforcer. He wanted *me* at his side.

It's not because he cares for me. He doesn't. He hasn't. He never will.

Renwell withdrew the box from a drawer in his desk. "Stakes?"

"I want what I wanted before. An evening with Melaena. *Alone.*"

The corner of Renwell's mouth lifted. "Did you not have enough time to discuss your rebel business before your captivating dance?"

Heat crawled up my neck, but I didn't break eye contact with him. "I told her who was still alive. And who wasn't. As well as what happened at Calimber. Seems your subjects aren't very well-informed."

The other side of Renwell's mouth ticked upward. "A lapse in judgment you'd like to rectify, High Enforcer?"

"One of many," I said.

Renwell dumped the Death and Four tiles onto his desk. "If you think you can turn the people against me, you'll find that they know exactly who I am and what I've done. Fear is an axe to the tree of discontent."

"Do they know you murdered your father?" I asked, nonchalantly flipping tiles over.

Renwell froze. His pale cheeks were like marble. "My sister truly unburdened her mind before she surrendered the fight."

The cold way he spoke of Nikella's heroic sacrifice hardened something inside me. "She told me the truth. She wanted me to know who I was dealing with."

"And do you understand me now?" Renwell breathed, leaning over the desk. His eyes were nearly black with leashed rage. "Have you found a weakness yet? Something to use against me?"

"I'm sorry your father beat you," I whispered, clutching the seat of my chair to keep myself from bolting. "No father should do that to a child."

"Is that your play?" Renwell sneered. "Your father had you beaten once, and you think we suffered the same."

"No, I—"

"You know what my father used to say to me? Or did Nikella not tell you that?"

I shook my head.

"He used to say, 'one man's weakness is another man's power.' He told me that every time I cried when he kicked me and whipped me with his belt. Because I feared him, he had power over me." Renwell suddenly broke off and sat back in his seat, his expression as placid as glass. "So I took his advice. I stopped being afraid. I dragged him to the river he so feared and drowned him while repeating those very words."

Disgust crawled through my veins. Disgust for such a horrible man, but also for the son he turned into the monster before me.

"Are we the same?" Renwell asked softly. "Would you have wanted to kill your father if I hadn't gotten there first?"

I shook my head. I'd hated Father, but to actually kill him? I didn't know if I could've forced his heart to stop beating.

"Come now, admit it." Renwell's smile was venomous. "You tried to kill me, after all. The night Aiden killed your mother, I found that wild, raw hatred and helplessness inside of you and knew exactly how to sculpt it."

I shook my head again, even though he hadn't asked a question.

"Shall I tell you more about myself? Perhaps you'll find another weakness. Or another way we are alike." He took the crown off his head and studied it in the firelight. The bits of sunstone embedded in the gold flickered with their dead stars.

"As a miner's son, I would never be more than a miner. The

same as every boy and girl in the village of Calimber who toiled for someone else's gain and accepted their scraps. But I was cleverer than all of them, including my siblings, and twice as ambitious. I refused to waste that on the life I was born into."

His eyes refocused on me when I said nothing. "That's why I partnered with your father when I left Calimber behind. Weylin already had the connections I needed and the bone-deep desire to get us there. I simply had to play on his considerable weaknesses to ensure our victory."

"Just like you used Mother's death to cut me away from the rest of my life," I rasped.

"You chose that. If anything, you used me."

I barked a humorless laugh. "As a mentor. Not a weapon."

"We both had to play our parts." Renwell placed the crown back on his head. "I grew tired of pretending I wasn't stronger and smarter. I grew weary of constantly herding lesser minds, of not just *taking* what I wanted." His gaze gleamed with an almost feverish look as it slid over me. "Aren't you tired of pretending, Kiera? Pretending you don't want *more*?"

I licked my dry lips. His eyes snapped to the motion like a snake's.

"I do want more," I said. *But not from you.* "I want peace. I want freedom. I don't want to be held captive in a role that carves away pieces of who I am to make me fit. Freedom means *I* will carve my place in the world to fit exactly who *I* am."

My voice cracked, and I looked away, staring into the fire. I hadn't meant to speak such truth, to let a sliver of my soul escape through my words. Fucking Four, I hadn't even realized that was what I wanted so badly.

Renwell leaned forward, drawing my attention back to his hard eyes. "Then I will hand you the knife, Kiera. All I ask is one simple promise."

I hesitated, letting my gaze wander over his furrowed face as if I were thinking it over. Renwell didn't seem to breathe. The Death and Four tiles lay abandoned between us.

He wants me to trust him. For some unfathomable reason, he wants me at his side. Willingly. Whether that's because he truly cares or not, I can use it against him the way he did to me.

"Give me one night alone," I said. "*Show me* you can honor your word, and I will swear an oath to you the next day."

Triumph flared in Renwell's eyes. "Done."

CHAPTER 60
KIERA

I waited in agony for four days.

I desperately wanted to claim my night of freedom immediately, but Everett and Delysia agreed with my first instinct—to wait. The timing had to be just right.

Melaena needed time to find the two soldiers and set up a disguise. Aiden and Henry needed time to get here. And I needed to give the guards as little time as possible to find the flaw in their gate.

But it also meant giving Renwell time to change his mind.

I avoided him as much as possible for this reason, pacing my room and then Delysia's, until she threatened to tie me to a chair.

I visited Everett in the library, where he showed me sketches of the city walls and battlements, ensuring I'd know my way around. He'd make an excellent Teacher, someday.

When the day finally came, I marched into Renwell's office at dawn and demanded my night. He nodded, a small smile on his face.

I ignored the ominous feeling in my belly and left to send Melaena a message, telling her when to expect me.

As soon as the sun set through my window, I shoved Mother's knife in my boot, threw a cloak around my simple outfit, and left, carrying Melaena's costume and jewelry.

I balked at the main palace doors. A dozen guards stood in the foyer like they normally did. Everett and Delysia said the guards had stopped them from leaving, but not forcefully.

Now they stepped aside and opened the doors for me.

Giddy with success, I hurried through. A group of soldiers waited to escort me across the bridge, but they didn't follow me once I was in the Noble Quarter.

I checked for lurking shadows on my way to Melaena's, but saw no one. I swept past the bronze dancer, touching her foot for good luck.

Melaena met me in the atrium, her smile full of relief. "Thank you so much for returning my costume," she said loudly, probably for the benefit of the few patrons relaxing in armchairs. "If you carry the dress, I'll take the jewelry."

I handed over the small pouch of jewelry. We walked back to the dressing room.

Melaena quickly locked both doors. "I gave the dancers a night off to spend with their friends and families. Even the two I suspect of being spies were eager to go."

"Thank you. And thank you for taking such a risk, helping me. I don't deserve—"

"Stop that right now," Melaena ordered, grasping my scarred hands in her smooth dark brown ones. "I can't begin to understand what your life was like. I only know my side of things, which was always more clear than the murkiness you faced. I won't begrudge you a few mistakes when you have done so much to rectify them."

Tears welled in my eyes. "You are truly the best of friends, Melaena."

She smiled. "Now let's turn you into Dredger's wife."

Less than an hour later, we walked out the front door.

The plan was simple—I would pretend to be Eleanor, Dredger's wife, who usually delivered his supper around this time.

Melaena had made my face paler with powder and drew lines in my face to age me. She tucked my hair in a floppy cap that belonged to Eleanor. The simple brown cotton dress with deep pockets was also hers. I kept my boots with Mother's knife. I also carried a basket with Dredger's meal.

Melaena walked me to the Noble Quarter gate and gestured for the guards to open it. "So good to see you, Eleanor. Tell your husband hello for me."

I nodded and shuffled through.

I kept a slow, even pace down the main street. Wolves stalked by or slipped into alleys, but they didn't follow me. I briefly wondered if Renwell was among them or if he'd truly kept to his word to allow me my freedom.

I took a circuitous route to be safe. But nothing seemed out of place. No warnings snaked down my spine.

I hurried past the silent taverns until I reached the city gate.

Keeping my gaze down, I approached the guard at the foot of the wall steps. "Good evening, Locklean. Just delivering Dredger's supper."

Melaena had told me precisely what to say, per the real Eleanor's instructions. If this worked, I would personally deliver whatever reward the couple asked for.

The guard, Locklean I hoped, nodded. "Right, Eleanor. Any extra sausage?"

I pulled out the extra link Eleanor said she always set aside for the friendly guard.

"Thanks very much!" Locklean happily stepped aside, already chewing on his prize. "Just be quick, yeah? The captain has been more strict lately."

I nodded and hurried up the stairs that criss-crossed up the wall to the top.

Archers lined the battlements, shifting close to the large braziers to stay warm. I eased past them and walked toward the cliff gate, feeling like I was inside one of Everett's sketches.

My heart pounded the closer I got. Melaena had given me a detailed description of Dredger, but I would look immediately suspicious if I passed by my own "husband."

He found me first, thank the Four. Dredger, a heavily bearded man built like a bull, waved from his post near the stone gatehouse.

"Ellie, so good to see you, my sweet," Dredger said a little too loudly as I approached.

I smiled through clenched teeth. "You don't need to announce it to the whole city, darling."

He coughed, his cheeks like two red apples. "Right, er, I'll take my supper now."

"What, not even a kiss first?" I said teasingly.

Sweat poured down the man's face beneath his helmet. "Uh, of course." A few of the other guards snickered. "Somewhere a little more private."

The other guards whistled and cheered as Dredger towed me into the narrow gatehouse.

"Is there really going to be a battle tomorrow?" he asked in a desperate whisper, clutching my basket. "My wife, my children . . . This city can't burn. I just want the gods-damned Wolves gone. And—"

"Enough," I hissed, frantically looking over my shoulder as I scurried around the winching mechanism. The metal gate was enormous, anchored by thick chains. "We're helping free the city right now, you and me. Now watch my back."

I crouched on the musty floor where the gate disappeared

into a crevice. The meager lamplight showed two huge square metal rods skewering the gate against the wall.

Gods damn it, the pins were thicker than I thought. More like metal branches than the slender twigs they'd seemed in Everett's sketch.

They were also bent upward at the end, like twin snakes ready to strike. I tested one, and it didn't budge—the iron stubbornly clinging to its home in the gate.

I would just have to sever the metal where it sat against the stone floor. But perhaps that was for the best.

"Hurry," Dredger muttered from where he peered at both entrances of the gatehouse. "Mankmen is watching the other side, but the captain could come by any moment."

"Keep talking as though you're murmuring to Eleanor," I whispered. "Drown out any noise."

And keep you from talking to me.

Dredger muttered nonsense to himself while I grabbed my knife. I set the glittering blade as close to the gate as possible and started sawing through one locking pin. It was like slicing a tough steak with a butter knife. Much more difficult than the prisoner chains.

Sweat gathered under my warm dress. My face felt sticky. Gods damn it, if my makeup melted, the other guards would know I wasn't Eleanor.

I gritted my teeth and strained. Finally, my knife sank through to the stone with a light squeal. I caught the metal handle before it could fall.

Holding my breath, I waited for any cries of alarm as Dredger's amorous mumbling increased in volume.

No one came.

I carefully laid the severed handle next to the rest of its body, aligning them to look whole.

There. That's the best I can do, Everett.

Scratching at my sweaty cap, I hurried to the other pin.

"Hey, Dredger, did Eleanor bring you those berry muffins again?" someone called from the other side of the gatehouse.

I jerked upright, my wide eyes finding Dredger's.

"Leave him alone, Wottel," said a gruff voice. "Give the man a minute with his wife."

"Ah, come on, Mankmen, you know you want one as well," Wottel said cajolingly. "Eleanor's cooking is the only good food left in Aquinon."

I flew over to Dredger and flung my arms around him as if we were in a passionate embrace. The poor man's arms shook as he held me tentatively.

"Later," Mankmen growled.

There was a scuffling noise just behind us. I gripped Dredger tighter, hiding my knife behind his back.

"Oh, uh, I see what you mean," came Wottel's embarrassed voice. "I'll give you a minute. Fucking Four, don't make a fourth baby right here in the gatehouse. Captain would be right pissed."

I flinched. They had three children? They must truly be desperate to risk their lives helping us.

Holy Four, I hope it's all worth it.

"He's gone," Dredger breathed in my ear, immediately shaking me off.

An honorable man. And a dead one if I didn't hurry.

I raced back over to the second pin and sawed as hard and fast as I could. It seemed like hours, but was probably only seconds until I'd severed the handle and replaced it.

Dredger nearly melted into a puddle of relief when I reemerged, tucking my knife into my boot.

"Go, go!" Dredger pleaded, shooing me like a lost chicken.

I hurried out, blowing him a kiss. "See you at home, darling!"

The guards hooted and teased, then converged on a flushed Dredger and his basket of food.

No one questioned me as I left the wall. Locklean waved and wished me a good night. I replied in kind. Gods, I hoped these guards would join Aiden and Henry when they arrived. We needed all the good soldiers we could get.

I strode back the way I'd come, not daring to leave the main road. The Wolves didn't stop me, but the guards at the Noble Quarter gate did.

"Oh, silly me," I said in a quavery voice. "Somehow, Lady Melaena's earring ended up in my basket. I need to return it to her." I held up the ornate gold earring Melaena had given me.

The guards shifted their spears toward me. "Did you steal it?" demanded one.

"Oh, Eleanor, there you are!" Melaena called, hurrying toward us. "I was about to come looking for you. I believe I dropped my earring—"

"I have it right here," I said, waving it under the guards' noses.

"What a good friend you are. Please let her in." Melaena smiled at the guards, but even I heard the thinly veiled command.

They grumblingly did as she said.

We hurried back to *The Silk Dancer* and collapsed into undignified heaps on the dressing room chairs.

"Is it done?" Melaena asked, fanning herself.

I handed her the earring. "We are ready for an invasion."

"I pray we survive it."

"I pray we are victorious," I said grimly. I would die fighting before I succumbed to another cage.

Find me, Aiden, before it's too late.

CHAPTER 61
AIDEN

I stood at the bow of the Shadow-Wolf prison ship as if I could get to Aquinon faster by leaning as far out over the water as I could.

Two weeks. Two gods-damned weeks without Kiera.

I'd barely slept. I wouldn't have eaten much if Maz hadn't threatened to force it down my throat. His arrow wound had healed enough that I considered his threat genuine.

My worry for Kiera existed in every beat of my heart. In everything I did. I couldn't get her out of my mind as I gathered weapons and warriors and repaired our two ships.

I saw the same worry on Jek's and Maz's faces as they prepared for war. Even Yarina and Sigrid seemed more subdued after Kiera left. Ruru hadn't spoken to me for a full day after I relayed Kiera's goodbye. He'd been distraught that she'd left without him and sat by the river all day with his brother.

Eventually, he came back around, throwing himself into preparations. He'd helped stitch the flag that now flapped from a line at the bow. I'd designed it myself. A violet background with

Rellmira's sun at the top, my family's falcon and the joined hands of the People's Council beneath.

The new symbol of the union I hoped to achieve today upon the sacrifice of so many.

I twisted my father's falcon ring around my finger. I hadn't taken it off since retrieving it from Frieda's safekeeping. I wore it to honor the family I'd never known—and to remind myself of the family I fought for.

"Be with us, Nikella," I whispered to the salty breeze that whisked us over the stormy gray sea.

Black clouds swirled overhead. Thunder rumbled like gathering war drums.

Maz stepped up beside me, his eyes on the sky as well. "She never could resist toying with you on her seas."

"Let's hope her storms favor us again," I said, dropping my gaze to the southern horizon. We should come upon Aquinon in the next hour. "Are they ready?"

"More than that, brother. They're eager to get their weapons wet with the blood of Wolves."

I nodded. We had over two hundred Dag warriors from several clans. They had heeded the cry for vengeance for the Urzost village. A dozen prisoners who were strong enough and eager to fight for their home city were also aboard. Another few dozen of Skelly's bone-rattlers rounded out our small invading army.

"Henry had better be there," I muttered.

"He will be," Maz assured me, as he always did. "As will Kiera."

I glanced at him and tapped his new steel breastplate. "Looks good."

"It's bloody uncomfortable," Maz grumbled, adjusting it on his shoulders. "Dag armor isn't usually so thick."

I grinned, having heard this complaint many times now. "You

know the deal. Get through the battle without damaging it, and you can toss it."

He grinned back at me, looking fierce in his warrior paint. "Easy."

Ruru tapped me on the shoulder and pointed at the horizon. "Ship ahead."

I squinted, barely making out a distant speck. A speck that morphed into tall sails with a purple flag on top. "Looks like we found Renwell's third warship. Warn the others."

Mynastra's Wings and the Wolf ship raced toward the warship, the wind filling our sails. Warriors lined the deck, bristling with weapons. Maz with his axes, at least three broad knives, and a shield strapped to his arm. Ruru carried a bow and a pouch filled with arrows, knives strapped to his waist like a row of teeth. Daire stood next to him, similarly armed. Jek hefted a huge shield, Nikella's spear in his other hand.

I had two swords strapped across my back, two curved knives sheathed at my waist, and one each in my boots. I readied a bow as well, with an oil-dipped arrow.

"Remember," I shouted to the warriors. "Don't shoot until my order!"

I lit my arrow in the brazier that sat in the middle of the deck. I flexed my fingers around the thin wood, angling the arrow higher. "Carry it, Mynastra."

The warship was near enough I could see soldiers scurrying about, bringing their catapults to bear on us.

I fired. The arrow sliced through the air—and pierced the warship's hull. Triumph burst through my veins. They were within range.

I raised my arm. "Fire on the catapults!"

Dozens of fiery arrows nocked into place, then whistled through the air. Some hissed into the choppy water. Others peppered the ship's hull with scorch marks. A few found soldiers and the catapults they had already loaded.

Gods-damned catapults.

"Spears!" I shouted.

A group of Dags stepped forward with long, stout spears that took two of them to wield.

The catapults fired. Lit barrels passed through our second cloud of arrows toward us.

But before they could reach the ships, the Dags leaped forward and speared them out of the air. They exploded safely away from the ships.

Everyone cheered.

"Brilliant idea, brother!" Maz shouted.

I'd thought of it while watching the Dags spear fish off the coast. But the barrels were only the first problem.

I turned back to the warship just as they released their own swarm of arrows. "Shields!"

Everyone ducked under their assigned shield-bearers. I took cover under Maz's. Jek covered Ruru and Daire. Arrows thumped down around us like hail.

Lightning flashed, and the sky growled again.

Fucking Four, if it rained, our fire would be useless. But so would theirs.

I yanked on Ruru's arm. "Signal Skelly to circle now."

He nodded and grabbed another flag we'd made, a red one threaded with a black triangle in the middle. He waved it back and forth, the cloth snapping in the vicious wind.

Skelly shouted orders, and *Mynastra's Wings* veered off to cut around the warship. Roark, the bone-rattler from Skelly's crew, spun the wheel of our ship. The wood creaked and groaned beneath my feet as the ship turned broadside in the waves.

The warship slowed as the soldiers readied all four of their catapults to aim at the tempting target we presented.

"Come on, Mynastra, come on," I muttered, gazing up at the black clouds.

"Aiden," Maz growled, gripping his axe.

The other warriors readied their spears again. The roaring waves crashed into our ship, pitching the deck at a steep angle.

"Aiden!" Maz shouted.

The catapults flung their burning barrels. Just as sweet, glorious rain flooded the sky. The barrels lost speed, their flames sputtering out before they crashed into the sea.

Everyone cheered again, thrusting their weapons into the downpour.

"Right us, Roark!" I bellowed.

The sailor was already battling with the wheel, his neck straining. Our ship slowly turned with the waves. But the warship was too close.

I grabbed the deck railing. "Brace!"

Everyone latched on to something.

The two ships crashed together in an explosion of wood. The force of it nearly threw me overboard. Cries sounded from both sides.

The ship shuddered and groaned as it swayed against the warship.

"Our hull's cracked like an egg, Aiden!" Yarina shouted from the other side of the deck. "We're taking on water!"

"Board the warship!" I roared. If we were to survive, we needed at least two working ships. Theirs would do just fine.

I yanked our flag from its line and tied it around my waist.

Jek handed out grappling hooks. The soldiers seemed to have recovered from our collision as they began shooting arrows down at us.

Cries of pain tempted me to turn around, to save whoever it was, but I stayed focused. I flung my grappling hook over the warship's railing and started climbing up. A dozen other warriors did the same—Maz and Ruru on either side of me.

We hauled ourselves onto the warship as sailors swung from our mast to theirs like monkeys. I unsheathed my swords just in time to cut down a soldier who lunged at me with his own sword.

Rain pummeled us as we shouted and fought our way through Renwell's soldiers. No Wolves. No sunstone weapons.

Skelly's crew took advantage of their distraction as I intended and boarded the warship, brandishing their weapons. Outnumbered, the remaining Rellmiran soldiers surrendered.

"Cease!" I roared until our forces backed down.

"We don't have time for prisoners," Maz muttered to me, his axe coated in blood and his armor undented.

"There's always time for mercy," I replied quietly, staring at the drenched, miserable men huddled on deck. "I will not make enemies of my people if they don't wish to be so."

Maz nodded and shouted for the warriors to collect the soldiers' weapons and march them belowdecks. We locked them in the brig and brought the rest of our warriors over from the rapidly sinking Wolf ship. Skelly's crew returned to *Mynastra's Wings*.

We set sail once more. The storm cleared enough for me to see the Rellmiran palace glittering in the distance. Was Kiera there, watching me?

My gut clenched. If so, Renwell could see us, too. He'd know we were coming.

CHAPTER 62
KIERA

The knock came with the first clap of thunder.

I'd been pacing my room since dawn, waiting for news of Aiden and Henry. Or for guards to escort me to the palace dungeon, if Renwell discovered my treachery with the gate.

What happened to me didn't matter as long as the plan worked. It *must* work.

I'd already barricaded Everett and Delysia inside one of the secret passageways they were sure Renwell didn't know about.

I'd fought with them all night on this plan, and they'd eventually given in, knowing I was the one Renwell wanted. That I couldn't do what needed to be done if they were around to use as hostages.

Pierce opened my door before I could answer his knock. "Apologies, my lady, I'm to bring you to the throne room."

It was time. All the Death and Four tiles were laid out. All the truths and lies would be revealed. No more hiding.

I drew my shoulders back, even as my knees trembled. Mother's knife was safely tucked into my boot. My hair was tightly braided, and I wore the pants and shirt I'd arrived in.

Taking one last glance around my room, I followed Pierce to the throne room. I brushed my fingers along the glass doors that led to Mother's garden.

Be with me, Mother. Give me your strength. Help me defeat the monsters, Nikella.

I tried to breathe steadily through my nose. Tried to align my head, heart, and body as Nikella instructed me. But the fear was an icy river, determined to suck me down. The names and faces of everyone I loved and my fear of losing them drowned out every other thought.

Pierce gestured for me to enter the throne room without him and shut the doors behind me.

The cavernous room was empty. The gold throne bare.

A brutal storm lashed at the many windows that faced the sea.

Unable to help myself, I hurried over to them and peered out. The rain made it difficult to see anything in their shifting gray curtains. But . . . was that a ship?

It was there, and then it was gone. Shadows chased each other under the lightning. Or it was my imagination.

"He's coming for you," came a deep voice behind me.

Gasping, I whirled to see Renwell standing a few feet away. Crowned and armed with a sheathed sword. His face was unreadable. The wind howled against the windows I pressed against.

"But he can't have you," Renwell said, an eerie echo of what Aiden had said to me when we escaped Aquinon. "Your loyalty belongs to me now."

"What are you talking about?" I whispered.

He tilted his head to the side, looking like a merciless crow determined to scavenge his due on the battlefield. "I gave you one night of freedom. You used it. Now you owe me your oath."

My hands shook behind my back. I'd thought Renwell would

be too concerned about the battle to care about the oath I'd promised.

"But . . . Aiden . . ." I fumbled with my words.

"He's being dealt with." Renwell waved me forward. "Come." He strode up the dais and sat on the throne.

Holy Four, did he really think I'd bow to him now? Was he truly so confident in his victory?

His eyes glittered as he leaned forward. "One simple vow, and you'll have all the power I promised. But I will retract my offer if you make me wait much longer."

I opened my mouth to tell him I couldn't when the southern doors banged open.

"Not now," Renwell snarled at the red-faced soldier. "I already know of the invading ships."

"Not . . . the ships," the soldier panted. "Army. Heading to the main gate."

My heart leaped with hope. Renwell cut a glance at me, his face so full of wrath I stepped back.

"Stay here," he growled. Then he swept out of the room.

I had nowhere to run. I could hide with Everett and Delysia and pray for victory. But I needed to stay. I needed to end Renwell before Aiden and Henry suffered too many losses.

I slid out the knife that had started it all twenty-seven years ago. The knife that had defeated a kingdom and destroyed families. But it had also saved my life and set Calimber free.

And now, it would defeat Rellmira's greatest enemy.

CHAPTER 63
AIDEN

We sailed into Aquinon's harbor, so fast the watchmen didn't have time to fire on us.

Instead, they blew the warning horns. I didn't care. I hoped Kiera heard them and knew I'd come. I hoped they bolstered Henry's resolve as well. If he was here.

As we neared the dock, my eyes widened in disbelief.

"What in the deep, dark, wandering hell . . ." Maz muttered.

"Do *not* fire!" I bellowed to my warriors. "Do not attack!"

Everyone scowled, lowering their weapons upon seeing what awaited us on the dock. Rows and rows of men, women, and children. Unarmed. Stark terror in their gazes as they watched our ships coast up to the dock.

"Renwell, you sick bastard," I growled under my breath. What kind of monster used his people as a human shield against an invading force?

"Coward," Ruru snarled. He carried our flag on a pole he'd tied it to. "I don't see him or his Wolves."

I shaded my eyes against the renewed sun. The cliff gate was still open. Either Kiera's plan had worked, or something else was afoot.

"Get off the ships!" I commanded, making sure my voice carried to both ships. "Do not fight unless you are attacked!"

Somewhere on the dock, a child cried.

My gut churned like the storm we'd just passed through. Gods, this would be worse than the Pravaran massacre if fighting broke out.

We docked and ran out the gangplanks. I was the first off the warship. The city folks pulled backward, creating a pocket of space around me.

I kept my sword steady in one hand, lifting the other in a placating gesture. "We're just passing through. We will not harm you. We want only to destroy the Wolves and the man who calls himself your king."

No one responded. The strained, battered silence unnerved me further. I stared at every face in the crowd, looking for soldiers and Shadow-Wolves.

I saw none.

Had Renwell done this just to slow us down?

The crowd shifted along the docks as more of my warriors followed me.

"Are you daft?" Maz growled at one man, shaking his shoulder. "Go home!"

The man shook his head rapidly, like a frightened bird.

They were being threatened. By whom? Something was wrong.

I spun in a slow circle, just as a man lunged at me from the crowd, strange scars on his face and a familiar black blade in his hand.

I evaded the blow and slammed my sword into his back. Screams rose, and people stampeded in every direction.

"Wolves!" I shouted. "No masks! Sunstone blades!"

Maz cursed and pushed his back against mine as we spun in the horde of panicked people.

Another Wolf attacked, and Maz slaughtered him with his axe. Ruru cried out as two Wolves attacked him and Daire.

I swore and fought my way to them as Daire's knife shattered under the Wolf's. I tore my sword across the Wolf's throat, spraying Daire with blood.

"Th-Thanks," he stammered. Ruru and Maz took down the other Wolf.

The docks slowly emptied as the city folk found refuge in homes and taverns. We fought our way through unmasked Wolves until there were none left.

They'd killed several of our warriors, and a handful of men and women who'd gotten in the way. No children, thank the Four.

"Fucking bastard." Maz kicked one of the Wolves' knives into the harbor. "Renwell loves his gods-damned surprises."

I nodded wearily. "We should assume nothing going forward." I lifted my head and spoke to the other gathered warriors. "Stay alert and watch each other's backs. To the cliff gate!"

Please, Kiera, tell me you got to it in time.

We marched up the steep road, our extra weapons and shields making the climb worse. Near the top, I heard shouts.

I whipped my head up to see the gate still open. Soldiers peered over the wall, but didn't fire upon us. A few of them gestured to the flag that Ruru waved proudly.

Perhaps they were trying to fix the gate. Or fighting among themselves. They had just watched us slay a group of men—whether the soldiers knew they were unmasked Wolves was unclear.

I held my breath as we crept closer. The heavy gate shuddered as if someone was hitting it from above. But it didn't budge.

Maz squeezed my shoulder. "Kiera did it. She fucking did it. Your future queen is quite the rebel."

A wild grin burst across my face. "That she is." *My queen.*

Our warriors cheered and formed ranks behind me. I raced forward, only to stop short. Everyone halted behind me as well.

A small contingent of soldiers waited for us on the other side, their faces pale but resolute. They pointed their swords downward in a gesture of surrender.

Their leader stepped forward, his eyes darting to our flag before meeting my gaze. "Are you Aiden Falcryn?"

"I am."

He let out a long breath. "I'm Dredger. I helped your spy with the gate, sir."

Some of the tension eased from my shoulders. "Then you have my deepest gratitude, Dredger."

The stocky man drew himself upright, his flushed face sincere. "We're here to join your fight to free Aquinon, sir."

The other soldiers nodded and murmured their assent.

I strode forward and stuck out my bloody hand. "I would be honored."

Dredger shook it with a quick grin that showed the genial man he likely was outside of battle. Then he was all business. "There's an army contingent outside the main gate, requesting entrance under your orders. No one has fired a shot yet, but—"

"Lead the way," I commanded.

He nodded and marched ahead, his men falling into place behind him.

I glanced back at the cliff gate. A few soldiers ran along the wall to the main gate. Likely to warn the rest that we were coming.

Maz walked at my side, his eyes darting around the market

stalls that huddled on either side of the road. "That couldn't have been all the Wolves at the docks."

Certainly not.

"Ruru," I called quietly, gesturing him forward. "Give the flag to your brother and scout ahead to the Noble Quarter for more Wolves. *Stay hidden.* Report back."

He nodded, then did as I said, disappearing into the labyrinth he knew well.

We reached the main gate without further hindrance. But the top of the gate wall bristled with archers and armed soldiers. More of them formed a thick ring in front of the gate doors, spears at the ready. But pointed at us.

My stomach crawled with unease. One wrong move, and this could turn into a bloodbath no one wanted.

A tall man in full armor, apart from a helmet, stood on the stone steps between the ramparts and the ground. His furious gaze was fixed on Dredger.

"What is the meaning of this, soldier?" he bellowed. "You betray your kingdom and your brothers in arms by leading these rebels here."

"I'm trying to bloody save them, Captain!" Dredger roared back.

I stepped up next to him, flipping my sword hilt so that I held it pointed to the ground. "Dredger is right," I said, lifting my voice to be heard as far as possible. "My name is Aiden Falcryn. I come to our royal city to destroy the man who has captured Aquinon and kept it in terror for many years beyond that. I do not want to shed any Rellmiran blood other than that of Renwell and his murderous Wolves. Join us, and we will reclaim the city!"

The soldiers stared at each other and me, uncertainty rippling through their ranks. The captain's jaw worked furiously, as if trying to decide whether to give the order to attack.

"Listen to him!" Dredger cried. "Captain, how many times

have you lost men to Renwell and his Wolves? And you, Locklean. They murdered your sister in front of her children! Wottel, Mankmen, Grindall, Cabbot, all of us have suffered at the hands of Weylin, Renwell, and the dogs that do their bidding! We have a chance to end it here and now. I say we take it!"

Some of the soldiers nodded and lowered their weapons. A few of my warriors shouted and cheered their approval.

But the captain remained stone-faced. "And you would trust this man?" he demanded, gesturing to me. "He may shackle us with the same fear we suffer now, or worse, we will fail and be branded as traitors. Our families will suffer and die for this!"

"They already are!" Dredger shouted back. "I would rather fight for them now, instead of waiting for those gods-damned Wolves to take them from me!"

Silence fell over the crowd.

I stepped closer, putting myself in range of their spears. I felt Maz shift into place behind me. "You don't know me, but you know of me. I fought in the Pravaran rebellion. Many of the soldiers waiting outside lost friends and family in that fight. I was also a prisoner in the Calimber mine. The same mine that my allies and I have now destroyed, along with the High General who massacred and imprisoned our people."

"It's true!" yelled one of our warriors, stepping forward. I recognized the man as a prisoner who'd volunteered to fight. Varyn, I believed his name was. "They freed us from Calimber and obliterated the whole gods-damned mine! This man is the true king we've been waiting for!"

Murmurs broke out among the soldiers. Awe and understanding cleared away the suspicion in their gazes.

The captain kept his arms crossed, his fingers tapping on his arm in a way that reminded me of Kiera. My heart lurched. Fucking Four, we didn't have another moment to waste. But I needed these soldiers.

Someone touched my shoulder, and I turned.

Ruru's eyes were wide, his breath coming in pants. "Wolves in the Noble Quarter. More than I could see. Armed to the teeth. Waiting."

Gods damn it.

"We have no more time," I roared. The soldiers in front of me took a step back. "The true enemy waits for us in the Noble Quarter. Let our allies in, and we will finish this!"

The warriors behind me stamped and yelled.

The captain debated for another agonizing moment. If he waited much longer, I would push through these soldiers and tear open the gate myself.

He muttered something under his breath, then raised his voice with the sharp bite of a commanding officer. "Any man who does not wish to join the fight will not be thought a coward. Open the gate, and may the gods find our souls!"

Cheers rose as the gate creaked open. The soldiers parted to allow Henry and his small army to march inside.

Henry strode forward and shook my hand. "Gods, am I glad to see you. For a moment, I thought this wouldn't work."

"For a moment, so did I." I lifted my sword in the air as Daire raised our flag and waved it. "To the Noble Quarter!"

"Slay the Wolves!" Maz thundered, beating the broadside of his axe against his shield.

The other Dags took up the war cry. Then the soldiers. Until we were a single mass of fury bearing down on the Noble Quarter gate. Which stood wide open.

Row upon row of Wolves awaited us. Sunstone weapons glittered in their hands. Their black metal masks snarled at us in a uniform expression of hatred.

Our battle cry sputtered against their wall of silence.

I gripped my sword harder, glancing at Maz.

"Onward, Your Highness," he murmured, a steely glint in his eyes. "For Davka," he said to his sisters.

They nodded grimly. "For Davka."

"For Nikella!" Jek rumbled, lifting Nikella's spear.

"For Daire!"

"For Meryl!"

"For Lana!"

More and more soldiers cried out the names of their loved ones, likely ones they'd lost at the hands of the enemy facing us.

"For Mother, for Father," I whispered. "For Pravara. For Brielle." My voice grew louder. "For Nikella. For Kiera! *For Rellmira!*"

I charged forward, bloodlust roaring through my veins.

A thunderstorm of answering bellows and stampeding feet followed me as we crashed into the Wolves.

CHAPTER 64
KIERA

I WAS SITTING ON THE THRONE WHEN RENWELL STORMED BACK into the room.

He glared up at me. "Get. Down."

I tapped Mother's knife on a shimmering arm of the royal seat. "No."

"Do not make me remove you," he snarled, slowly climbing the dais.

"I won't run from you, Renwell," I said, my muscles tensing. "I won't hide either. I mean to kill you."

Renwell halted, surprise darting across his face. Quickly replaced by rage. "Why? Because your lover is on his way? He will die before he reaches this palace."

"He has an army," I snapped, fear biting into my words.

"So do I. An army of Wolves awaits him before the bridge." Renwell eased up the last few steps. "You may have destroyed my mine and half my army, but you will not win this battle. Surrender to me now, before it's too late."

I laughed. "I was never going to swear an oath to you, Renwell."

"Pity," he said softly, his lips bloodless. "We could've done such great things together."

He lunged just as I lashed out with my boot. I kicked him in the throat. His neck folded around my boot heel, then he flew backward down the dais. The crown fell from his head with a sharp *clang* and rolled away.

Savage satisfaction filled me. This was why revenge was so easy to seek. Attaining it felt too good.

"Now you know what it's like to be under someone's boot," I seethed, stalking down the steps toward him as he staggered to his feet, clutching his neck. "Did you really think I would forgive you again after you humiliated me? *Scarred* me?" I gestured at my cheek.

He ripped his sunstone sword out of its sheath. "You did the same to me. A scar for a scar. A lie for a lie."

I circled him with my small knife. He was just as fast as me and stronger.

Surprise him. Keep him off-balance, Nikella's voice urged me in my head.

"I think in your own dark, twisted way, you do care for me," I taunted him. "You were so eager to get me back here, not because you needed me, but because you missed me. You crave my attention, the control you had over me. I looked up to you. Respected you. And you loved me for it."

Renwell's sword shook in his fist. "I do not love you, stupid girl. I have *never* loved you. This is the same, desperate search for a weakness. *I do not have one.*"

"Oh, but you do," I said, circling closer. "You've let me live countless times when it would've been easier to get rid of me. You've lured me back to your side, knowing full well I intend to destroy you. You tried to get me to care for you in return— pretending to save my life, offering me the power I always wanted, treating me with basic kindnesses. It was all a ploy to make me care for you because you see feelings as a weakness. And you needed me to be weaker than you."

"You *are* weaker than me," Renwell snarled. But he still didn't attack.

I pushed a little closer. "Nikella was wrong—you care for me. You always have."

"Nikella wanted to believe I loved her as well," Renwell spat, looking slightly deranged. "And where is she now, Kiera?"

"You sent Korvin after her because you were afraid of her, of what she could do to you."

"I'm certainly not afraid of you."

"You should be," I whispered. "You took control over me at my weakest. I will defeat you at your strongest."

"You will die as she did. As your mother did. As Aiden will. Weakened by love." He leaped at me.

I slid to my knees and sliced at his leg. He roared and kicked me in the ribs. I skittered away, springing to my feet. He was on me in a moment, swinging his sword with deadly efficiency. I blocked and evaded and retreated under his fury.

Until he stumbled on his bleeding leg. I darted in and slashed at his ribs. He grabbed my knife hand, kicked out my legs, and slammed me to the floor.

I cried out and tried to throw off his heavy weight, but I was pinned. Panic rose from the depths of my mind, fogging over my senses as I thrashed. Gods, I couldn't die like this. I refused.

"Shut up," Renwell growled. He snatched Mother's knife from my hand and slid it into his boot. "Even if you did manage to kill me, your lover would never make it across the bridge. I made sure of it. Or rather, Librius did."

Librius? He was still alive? How could Librius—

Suddenly, it all made sense. The bridge. The guards. The secrecy. The time Renwell spent in the dungeon. Why he was so sure Aiden wouldn't reach him here.

Renwell's snarl melted into a smile at my growing horror.

"You rigged the bridge to explode?" I choked out.

"Fitting, isn't it, that I learned of Librius's special skills because of Aiden and my sister. The same people who destroyed my most valuable resource with their irritating explosives. Now, they will both have died from them."

Tears slid down my temples. "Please. Please tell the guards not to set them off."

Something dark and malicious glowed in Renwell's eyes. "Are you begging me, Kiera?"

I swallowed my pride. "Yes."

"See, this is what love does," Renwell murmured. "It has you begging beneath a man you claim to hate."

My hatred for him was deeper than ever. But my love for Aiden knew no depths, no bounds, no rules.

"If I kneel before you and swear my loyalty, will you call off the guards?"

Renwell hesitated, then slowly nodded. "Yes."

You lie. But so do I.

Renwell rose to his feet, blood coating his pant leg and his side. But he held himself upright and proud. He'd never needed a crown to rule over those he saw as lesser than him.

I slowly gathered my body, kneeling at the tips of his boots. I gazed up at his victorious smile.

"Before I swear myself to you, you should know," I said, inching my hands upward, "that the only reason I would get on my knees before you would be to"—I snatched Mother's knife from his boot and rammed it into his gut—"steal a knife from your boot."

I ripped the blade out, and Renwell staggered backward, clutching his stomach. I raced out of the throne room, my heart screaming in my chest.

Am I too late?

I sprinted down the steps, suddenly seeing what Renwell had prevented me from noticing before—fuses trailing over the sides of the bridge. Guards with torches stood in the middle of the bridge, waiting.

Shouts and clashing weapons reached me from the far side of the bridge, where a battle raged in a crimson tangle of steel and sunstone. A familiar black-haired man fought his way through the Wolves like a demon.

Trying to reach the bridge. To find me.

I screamed as I ran across the bridge, waving my arms to get his attention. "Aiden! Don't cross the bridge! Aiden! It's a trap!" But the roaring waterfall swallowed my voice.

The guards shifted uneasily as I charged toward them.

"STOP HER!" Renwell bellowed from behind me.

One guard stepped in my way. I cleaved through his arm, snagging the torch before it landed on a fuse. I kept running. I waved the torch, trying to catch Aiden's attention.

He finally looked up, his face breaking into a relieved smile at the sight of me. Which morphed into a look of fury a moment before someone slammed into me from behind.

I fell hard on the stone, trying to keep the torch and my knife from hitting as well.

Renwell's heavy breathing had a rattle to it as he seized my legs and started dragging me off the bridge. "Blow it as soon as that man steps on it," he ordered the nearest guard.

"No!" I screamed, kicking my legs until I crushed Renwell's hand against the stone.

He swore and let me go. I scrambled to my feet. Aiden was so close to the bridge, fighting as hard as he could to reach me.

My heart pounded, heavy and sad and lost. "I love you, Aiden."

I lunged past the guard and pressed my torch to the fuse in the middle of the bridge. It spat and sizzled out of sight.

I met Aiden's eyes one last time before an explosion ripped through the air. The ground buckled beneath my feet.

Something snagged my collar and hauled me backward. The bridge between me and Aiden crumbled away into the ravenous waterfall, carrying the screaming guards with it.

I twisted around to see Renwell on his knees behind me. The part of the bridge leading back to the palace was gone, too. We were stranded in the middle of the waterfall on a wide, precarious pillar that shuddered harder with every passing moment.

"Even now," he rasped. "Even now, at the end, I can't let you go."

His face was stark white. Crimson blood dribbled from his lips to his beard. But something had fallen away in his dark eyes, like the bridge that had collapsed into the sea.

A vulnerability he'd never allowed to show until his life and his soul were already forfeit.

My heart beat hard and slow, suspended in my chest like a bell ringing its final hour. Yet I couldn't look away from the dying man who'd saved me yet again.

"I hate you," he whispered, the words crystal clear over the deadly waterfall. "I hate that I failed because of you. That my plan was perfect until you burrowed under my skin and drove me mad." His eyes crawled over my face, latching onto the scar across my cheek. "Gods damn my weakness for you. I have failed because . . ." His lips contorted into a bitter, bloody smile. "Because I care for you. You have won our game, at last. Only too late, as we shall both die for our weaknesses."

I stared down at the man who had twisted my mind until I wasn't sure if I could trust it. The man who said I was better than my father, but who'd been worse himself. I felt the smallest drop of pity in a waterfall of resolution.

"You didn't fail because you care for me," I said. "You failed because you didn't care enough."

The pillar wobbled as stone crunched and split.

"KIERA!"

I looked back at Aiden, who held onto one of the bridge posts and stretched out his hand to me over the abyss.

"It's going to fall this way!" he shouted. "When it does, jump!"

Jump? I waited for the needles of fear to set in, but they didn't. I felt strangely calm.

A wet cough brought my attention back to Renwell. His eyes dulled with the certainty of death. "You will fall."

I will never let you fall.

"No," I said. "My wings are too strong for your weak cages. Your knives will never be sharp enough to carve away my freedom. I will rise. I will fly. Over this abyss and any other. It is you who will fall."

I glanced at Mother's knife, then tossed it into the waterfall. Let Mynastra have her stars back. I didn't need them anymore.

I had a better weapon now.

The bridge cracked and crumbled, pitching forward.

Aiden shouted and stretched his hand out further, his face taut with desperation, his fingers curling toward me, grasping.

I charged over the falling stone.

Faster. *Faster.*

My heart pumped harder.

Free. *Free.*

Fly!

My feet didn't hesitate. I threw myself off the edge. Toward Aiden.

CHAPTER 65
AIDEN

Time slowed. The bridge fell. My love flew over an abyss.

Yet her fiery eyes were full of hope and trust. Her beautifully scarred fingers reached for me.

Too far.

My muscles strained and popped. My boots slid toward the edge. My voice shattered over her name.

And then . . .

Her hand landed in mine.

CHAPTER 66

KIERA

AIDEN CRUSHED MY HAND AS THOUGH HE MEANT TO NEVER let go.

I cried out as my shoulder wrenched in its socket and my body slammed into the stony debris left from the bridge.

Aiden roared, his muscles contorting as he lifted me up.

We collapsed together at the edge of the watery abyss.

"You're alive," Aiden murmured, brushing my hair out of my face. "You're alive."

Then he sealed his lips against mine. I'd never felt such relief in a kiss. Such life. Such joy.

I smiled against his lips. Tears trailed down my cheeks as he gazed at me like I was the most precious thing in the world.

I held his face in my hands. He was alive. He was whole.

My body shuddered with exhaustion, but I couldn't let him go.

"I almost lost you," he murmured in a broken voice. "Why, *why*, did you blow up the bridge, Kiera?"

I pressed my forehead against his. "It was the only way to save you."

"When you jumped . . ." He swallowed hard. "I'd never been so afraid in my life."

I brushed my thumb over his taut brow. "I wasn't afraid because I knew you would catch me."

"Always." He caressed the tears from my cheeks. "I plan to capture you in my arms at least once a day for the rest of our lives, my love."

My heart stuttered. I stopped breathing. What was he saying? Forever?

"Kiera!"

I turned my head just as Ruru wrapped his thin arms around my shoulders.

"Fucking Four, you made it!" he cried hoarsely, as if he'd been shouting for hours. He smelled of blood and sweat, reminding me of the battle.

I pulled against Aiden's arms, which tightened for a moment before releasing me.

We all stood up. Ruru and Aiden supported me when pain seized my body, particularly my wrenched shoulder. My body would be one large bruise tomorrow. But I was alive.

I surveyed the destruction of the Noble Quarter, my heart falling.

The battle had ended, presumably around the time I'd jumped from the bridge. Dozens of Shadow-Wolf bodies lay like bits of charcoal among other bodies. Rellmiran, Dag, and Eloren ones.

A familiar hulking figure stepped forward amid the crowd of soldiers still standing.

I cried out and rushed to embrace Maz. He clutched me against his shiny armor. "Ah, lovely, don't cry. It's over. We won. *You* won. And I can hardly wait to get that heart tattoo on my ass."

I gave a watery chuckle and stepped back. Immediately,

Yarina, Sigrid, and Bruna engulfed me in a big, sweaty hug. They were bloodied, their clothes torn, and they held a few fractured weapons, but they were beaming.

Daire waved to me from a mansion stoop where Jek leaned heavily on him, a bloody wound on his leg and Nikella's spear still in his hand.

They were all alive. Gods, I could hardly believe it.

We did it, Mother. We finally won.

"Are we secure?" Aiden asked, coming up behind me.

Maz nodded. "We were already winning when the bridge exploded. The rest of the Wolves ran for the Noble Quarter gate."

Henry jogged up to us, his uniform torn and a bloody scratch on his neck. "We routed the Wolves from the city, killing who we could."

"Good," Aiden said. "We'll send out a warning for any who escaped. Their reign, as well as Renwell's, has ended."

Henry gave a slight bow, startling me.

That was when I noticed how all the other soldiers were staring at Aiden. With hope and respect in their eyes. Shedding enemy blood and protecting each other in battle would do that.

The snap of fabric drew my attention upward. An older soldier carried a strange flag that danced above the gruesome Noble Quarter. Strange, yet so familiar.

A falcon, a pair of clasped hands, and the half sun of Rellmira gathered on the field of deep violet. It was a flag that proclaimed Aiden's royal heritage and what he stood for. From the looks of the surrounding soldiers, he had won over a fair amount of the garrison from the city walls and gates.

His claim to the throne was no longer an idea. It was reality. It was his.

I shifted the slightest bit away from him, wary of what people might think to see me so close to the future king.

Aiden glanced down at me, his brow furrowed, but he said nothing.

Henry's eyes widened as he realized who was standing before him. "Delysia?" he asked desperately.

"Alive," I said with a tight smile. "But in the palace with no way for us to cross over."

He released a heavy breath, his shoulders dropping. "Thank the Four. We will find a way to cross, I promise you."

"I'll construct a rope bridge immediately," Aiden said, his gaze never leaving the side of my face.

I nodded, my throat tight.

I hadn't seen any Wolves in the palace, only guards. Hopefully, Everett and Delysia would be safe there.

A soldier approached, older and weather-beaten with a stiff spine. He wore a captain's badge. "Shall I declare the city safe, King Aiden?"

Another tremor shook my heart. He wasn't crowned yet, but these men clearly assumed that was just a formality.

Aiden nodded. "Have any able-bodied soldiers spread the word. Tell them the city is ours. That we will celebrate soon, but right now we need food, medicine, and shelter for the wounded. And a pyre for those we lost."

I slipped away as they continued speaking. There was one person I needed to share the good news with.

I picked my way across the bloody battlefield that seemed so at odds with its noble surroundings. Faces peered down at me from polished windows, but I ignored them.

Passing the bronze dancer, I brushed my fingers over her foot just as the doors of *The Silk Dancer* burst open.

Melaena stood framed in the doorway, her usually flowing curls pinned into a tight bun. Gone were her silks, replaced by supple leather and a knife at her hip.

Tears pearled in her blue eyes as she stared down at me. "Is it . . . Did we . . ."

I nodded.

She cried out and ran down the steps, wrapping me in a tight hug. I hugged her back.

"Your mother would be so proud," she whispered.

My jaw dropped as I stared at her. "You knew her?"

Melaena smiled through her tears. "Why do you think I hired Aiden and Maz? Your mother sent them to me."

I smiled back, a sense of peace stealing through me. I felt, in a way, that I'd finished what Mother had set out to do. And I truly hoped she was as proud of me as I was of her.

"Kiera!"

I turned to see Ruru rushing toward me, his face split in a huge grin.

"Your brother and sister!" he shouted, waving me toward him. "They're calling for you!"

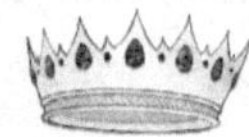

T HE NEXT FEW DAYS WERE GLORIOUSLY BUSY.

As word spread that the city was free from Renwell and his Wolves and now under the protection of the Falcryn king, life breathed back into Aquinon.

Everyone helped to clear the streets and burn the dead. Nobles and city folk alike shared food and medicine with the injured and opened their homes to those who needed it. Melaena took in widows and newly orphaned children, caring for them in the opulence of her club.

Aiden cleared out Asher's mansion, which Renwell had been using as a garrison for his Shadow-Wolves. Now, Rellmiran soldiers mingled with Dag warriors and Eloren sailors on the once-pristine grounds.

Pride swelled through me every moment I witnessed the city come together in a way I'd never experienced. It was amazing how life flourished once the heavy shadow of fear dissipated.

I helped as much as I could, but I constantly drifted by the waterfall. After I'd ensured that Everett and Delysia were alive and well—through much shouting and dancing and more tears, I grew impatient for the temporary rope bridge to be finished.

Aiden had started its construction immediately, as he said he would. Our archers had shot many ropes across the perilous gap, and Pierce and a few other friendly guards had anchored it on their side of the bridge.

Daire and several brave sailors, who were used to climbing the ropes of their ships, ventured out to twist the ropes into a bridge. We secured the workers to our side with ropes around their waists, but I still watched them with my heart in my throat.

Sometimes—my favorite times—Aiden would keep watch with me. He'd sneak away from his many tasks, wrap me in his arms, and stare at the palace with me. The beautiful prison, with its sunrise-colored stone turrets and gleaming windows, was something we'd both avoided our whole lives.

And yet . . .

We didn't speak of it. But the future loomed as large as the palace.

A question needed to be asked. And answered.

Occasionally, I'd glance down to where the waterfall pounded into the sea, knowing that Renwell was dead at the bottom. Like that woman from Mynastra's Tide so many years ago. My old mentor was another sacrifice Mynastra had gladly taken. But she probably preferred the other one we gave her.

Before burning the Shadow-Wolf bodies, Aiden ordered some soldiers to toss all the sunstone armor and weapons into the sea. Just as at Calimber, the weapons of the night sky met the sea with a sigh. As if Mynastra were exhaling in relief. The water glittered in the dying sun, the remnants of a dark legacy melting away.

On the third day, Aiden shook me awake from where I slept in one of Asher's rooms. I typically collapsed into whatever bed was empty—Aiden joining me in the brittle hours before dawn.

He swept a kiss over my brow. "Come to the palace with me, Kiera."

CHAPTER 67
KIERA

The rope around my waist felt too thin and fragile. Aiden expertly knotted it, his fingers brushing over my hips with soft yearning.

"See you on the other side," I said breathlessly.

He tucked a stray hair behind my ear. His eyes were full of thoughts that I'd seen gathering the last two days, like water in a dam. "I'll be right behind you."

"Don't worry, we've got you," Ruru assured me from where he and Daire stood by the sturdy post that held our ropes.

I nodded shakily. *Breathe in. Breathe out. And look to the other side.*

Delysia and Everett waved to me from the palace steps.

"Why are you smiling?" Aiden asked close to my ear.

"That's all I ever needed," I said. "Someone who loves me waiting for me on the other side of the abyss."

"And someone who loves you to cross it with you."

My smile widened, and I gave him a quick peck on his stubbly cheek. Then I dropped to my hands and knees and crawled out over the waterfall, with Aiden close behind.

Bits of cold spray struck my face like the driving snow of Dagriel while Rellmira's sun warmed my back.

The braided rope ladder swayed under our weight, pitching my stomach with it. But I gritted my teeth and kept crawling.

You've watched Daire and the others do this for days. It will hold you.

For once, I appreciated the unceasing roar of the waterfall. It grounded me. I had no desire to soar through the air again.

Hands grasped my arms and hauled me upright before I registered that I'd reached the other side.

Everett crushed me in a hug so unlike him that I squawked in surprise. Delysia laughed and clutched us both, talking so fast I couldn't hear her over the pounding of my heart.

But I *did* hear her gasp, "Oh!"

We all turned around to see Aiden step onto solid ground, a grin on his ruggedly handsome face. He untied his rope and looped it around a post.

Delysia tugged on my sleeve. "Introduce us," she hissed out of the corner of her mouth.

I tried to hide my smile. "Aiden, this is my younger sister, Delysia, and my older brother, Everett." I squeezed both of them. "Everett and Delysia, this is Aiden Falcryn."

"I think you mean *King* Falcryn," Delysia murmured, dipping into a perfect curtsy.

Aiden bowed, his black hair sweeping over his brow. "I haven't been crowned yet. But I'm so pleased to meet you both."

Everett bowed as well. "After everything you've done for Kiera, our mother, and our kingdom, the honor is ours."

"I wouldn't be here without your sister," Aiden replied, his gaze flicking to me. "I hope—"

"Oh!" Delysia gasped again, much louder this time.

She broke away from us to throw herself at the third person who'd crossed the bridge. Henry clutched her in his arms, his face buried in her long golden hair. They murmured things to each other we couldn't hear. Delysia fussed with his torn uniform while Henry smiled down at her.

Something tugged in my chest.

I glanced at Aiden, who was already looking at me.

That dam was close to breaking. I could feel the words pushing and straining against the fears that held them back.

Ducking my head, I busied myself with untying my rope.

Everett cleared his throat. "There's someone waiting for you inside," he said to Aiden. "A Teacher named Librius."

Aiden's eyebrows drew together, and he nodded. With swift steps, he led us up the stairs. I wondered how he felt entering the palace. Not an assassin in the night, but as a king returning home.

Some of the palace guards were gathered outside, their armor gleaming in the sun. They bowed as Aiden passed. Had their loyalties changed that quickly, or had they always wanted to serve someone better? The latter seemed more prevalent in the soldiers and city folk. But I wondered how much opposition Aiden would face in the coming days, months, years.

You could face it with him.

I shoved the stray thought back behind the dam.

Everett directed us to the throne room. Someone had picked up the crown I'd knocked from Renwell's head and nestled it in the golden lap of the throne. And a lump of brown fabric lay at the foot of the dais.

No, it was Librius hunched over, his long hood enveloping his head.

At our approach, he unveiled himself. I bit my lip at his gaunt appearance. The hollow eyes and wasted skin reminded me of the prisoners in the mine.

"Librius," Aiden said, getting on his knees to grasp the man's shaking hands. "What happened?"

"Forgive me, Aiden," the Teacher whispered. "I built the bombs that destroyed the bridge."

"Renwell forced you to," Aiden said firmly.

Tears filled Librius's eyes. "He came to the Temple shortly after you left Aquinon. The High Teacher pointed him in my direction as someone who had the knowledge to create the bombs that had destroyed the Den. Renwell took me. Put me in the palace dungeon. Ordered me to create what he wanted. Tortured me when I refused." Librius wiped his eyes. "I kept refusing until he brought a young woman before me and . . . and killed her. He said I would force him to kill more unless I obeyed."

Everett flinched next to me.

My lips twisted with revulsion. *Another crime you have finally paid for, Renwell.*

Aiden bowed his head. "You saved lives, Librius."

"But I also ended them. And for that, I beg forgiveness."

"I must also beg yours," Aiden said quietly. "It's my fault they discovered you."

Librius shook his head vehemently. "I always knew that was a possibility, dear boy. I simply ask that you allow me to return to the Temple, where I may live out my days serving Aquinon to atone for the pain I've caused."

Aiden drew him to his feet. "Of course. Also, I believe the position of High Teacher just became vacant. I'd like you to fill it when you're ready."

My heart warmed with happiness, and I beamed at Everett, who was watching the exchange with something akin to awe mixed with deep yearning.

"Oh . . ." Librius blinked rapidly. "That is very generous. May I think about it?"

"Of course," Aiden said. "For now, please find somewhere to

rest." He glanced over his shoulder at Everett. "Is there enough food and water here, or shall I have some carried over?"

"We've enough to feed everyone here for a month, maybe more," Everett said. "I can show Librius back to his room and get him something to eat."

And ask how one becomes a Teacher, I surmised, seeing the light in my brother's eyes.

Aiden nodded, and the two of them left.

Leaving Aiden and me to stare at each other in an empty throne room. Sun burst through the tall windows in warm shafts, setting the golden throne aglow like a fireflower behind Aiden.

But he didn't look at it. He stood there in his rough black clothes, the rebel I'd met, the assassin I'd betrayed, and the warrior I'd fought beside.

All of whom were the man I'd fallen in love with.

"This is it, then," I said softly.

CHAPTER 68
AIDEN

I frowned at Kiera's words. Was she saying goodbye?

I stepped closer to her.

She bit her lip, her fingers dancing on her thighs before she gestured around the cavernous room. "Is it everything you thought it would be?"

Something had shifted in my mind when I'd walked up the palace steps and entered its royal halls.

This was where my father and mother had reigned. And generations of my family before them. They had tread these marble floors and held court in this domed room that reminded me a bit of the mine. Yet this place was full of light and without shackles.

But I didn't care about the room. Or the palace. Not like how I cared about why Kiera was suddenly nervous.

"There is only one throne," I said in a husky tone, easing close enough to touch her. "One crown."

Her throat slid up and down in a swallow as she stared over my shoulder at the lonely chair and ornament. "Yes, well, Father removed Mother's throne from the dais and dismantled her crown after she died. He claimed it was out of grief. That he would never take another queen. But now I know it was out of spite."

I gently caught her chin and shifted her attention back to me. "I do not want to rule alone."

Her amber eyes were lined with silver. "Aiden," she whispered.

My heart trembled before the sword of her rejection. But she needed to know, in no uncertain terms.

"Marry me, Kiera," I whispered. She gasped and swayed. I snaked an arm around her waist, anchoring her to me. "Stay with me. I will always love you from afar, if that is what you wish, but I want to love you as close as possible. So close I never have to go another day without your smile. Your touch. Your heart and soul. Please . . ." I didn't care that I was begging. My whole being yearned for her too deeply. "Please, marry me."

Tears rolled down her cheeks. "You can't marry me, Aiden. I'm the daughter of the usurper king everyone hated."

I grasped her face in my hands, my eyes burning. "I don't care who your father was. I love *you*. The kind of love that no knife, no arrow, not even a gods-damned war can break. Tell me you don't feel the same."

"I do," she whispered, clutching my wrists. "I do."

My heart soared, and our mouths met in a scorching kiss.

I panted against her searching lips, kissing her again and again as I spoke the words that had been forming for days. "I want to give you everything, Kiera. I want to show the world the amazing woman you are. I want to live in the light with you, scars and all. For Nikella, who never could. For my parents, who wanted better for me. For us, because we had to hide parts of ourselves our whole lives. I want to be all of who we are, together. I want to change the world with you."

Kiera smiled up at me through her tears. "I told Renwell I

wanted to carve my place in the world, to make it accept me as I already was. And he said he would hand me the knife. But I don't want a knife. I don't want to force my place in the world. I want to create a world where everyone can live without fear." Her brow furrowed. "Yet something still holds me back."

"What, my love?"

"Being in this place, so full of bad memories. Being trapped in a role, caged by others' expectations." She gently swiped her thumb over my cheek. "Not being the queen you need."

"You are the queen I want," I growled, hating that she didn't see herself the way I did. "You will rule however you see fit. We will fill this palace with friends and family and allies, with love and laughter and better memories across every single inch of it. Our home is what we make it. And when we need an escape, we'll explore the world as far as you want to go." I pressed my forehead to hers. "Everything I offer is freely given. It will always be your choice to accept or not."

"I never thought I'd want this," she whispered. "I thought I was destined for a life where no one really knew who I was or accepted me for it."

"I see you, Kiera," I murmured. "If you were the sun, I would be the moon—to always remind you how brightly you shine."

"And if I wanted to be the moon?" she teased, her eyes sparkling up at me.

"Then I would be the stars to ensure you're never alone."

She made a tiny noise in the back of her throat as the tension melted from her body. "I can't imagine a life without you, either. Whether it's the two of us in a cabin deep in Twaryn or roaming the palace halls together, I just want you, Aiden. I want to take the advice Nikella gave me and choose the future I want most—a life filled with love."

"What are you saying, my little thief?" I needed her answer like I needed my heart to keep beating.

"I'm saying yes, Aiden Falcryn," she said with a smile, so soft and sweet I couldn't breathe. "Yes, I will marry you."

The world crystallized with light. I felt as though I were made of wind and fire and pure, healing joy.

I kissed her and spun her around, listening to her laughter echo in the marble hall.

Today was just the beginning.

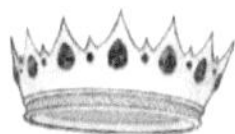

WE SPENT HOURS WANDERING THE PALACE HALLS.

Kiera showed me her old bedroom, and I glimpsed who she'd been before I met her. The young princess who loved her mother and her siblings. Who used to look out of her windows with hope and longing.

It only made me love her more.

She took me through the secret passageways, delighting in making me find their entrances.

Parts of the palace were still destroyed—such as the royal bedchamber I'd set on fire and the tunnel leading away from it. But I didn't mind that. I wasn't planning on sleeping in Weylin's old room anyway without remaking it.

I made a mental note of every place that caused Kiera sadness or anger so that I could include it in our plans of renovation. If this was to be our home, then we would change it until it felt like ours.

Everett and Delysia rejoined us, adding their own stories for the benefit of me and Henry. When Kiera told them of our engagement, they embraced us with cries of happiness. It made me ever fonder of my soon-to-be family.

Eventually, as the sun set, we crossed back into the city where Maz waited for us outside Asher's mansion. The rest of the Dags stood with him, dressed for departure.

Last night, he'd told me the other Dags were eager to return home, and I could see in his eyes that he wished to go with his people. Yet, sadness still leaked into my heart.

I forced a smile and tapped my friend's chest. "Not taking your armor with you?"

Maz snorted. "I tossed that hunk of metal in the heap as soon as I could."

"Must you leave so soon?" Kiera asked, her eyes watering again.

Maz's face softened. "How else would I find a stitcher for that tattoo I need to get?" When Kiera didn't smile, he pulled her into a bone-cracking hug. "I'll come back, lovely. I expect you to visit as well."

"Of course," she mumbled into his chest.

"We both will," I said firmly. "But perhaps not until after our wedding."

Maz's eyes widened. "Fucking Four!" He thrust Kiera away to gape at her. "Is it true? Did you say yes?"

She laughed, wiping her cheeks. "Did you know he was going to ask?"

Maz grinned. "It was inevitable. I knew from the moment you two emerged from that cell with unlocked shackles you would be sharing a story for a long time. After you came back from The Hollow, I knew it would be a lifetime. I felt it." He rubbed his stomach as he had that first night.

Kiera and I laughed.

"What's all the ruckus?" Yarina demanded, poking her head into our little huddle.

"They're engaged!" Maz boomed out.

Kiera's cheeks reddened as the news spread like wildfire.

Ruru nearly tackled both of us, beaming with joy. Dags, Elorens, and Rellmirans alike congratulated us. I could see the hope and excitement in the city folks' faces of not only a new king but a new queen as well.

We paraded in a celebratory fashion to the docks, where we said our goodbyes to Maz and the Dag warriors. Some were carried aboard Skelly's ship on stretchers, including Jek, who was still healing from his leg wound.

The older Dag warrior gave me a firm handshake and a solemn promise to always uphold the alliance between Dagriel and Rellmira as long as my family ruled.

I thanked him, feeling a strange rush of eagerness for the future. No more raids between our countries. No more trade bans. We would be free to engage with each other as we wanted.

Our new world was already taking shape.

Kiera and Ruru said their tearful goodbyes with Maz while I said goodbye to his sisters.

"Keep him out of trouble," I said, returning Yarina's brisk hug.

"Unless it's entertaining, of course." She winked.

I chuckled and held out my hand for Sigrid, who shook it and went so far as to squeeze my shoulder. Her one blue eye looked brighter than I'd seen it.

My throat tightened. "I never thanked you for helping Nikella. With the final bomb. And me. I would've found what you did very difficult."

"I did what had to be done. You were willing to sacrifice your self for everyone. I was willing to shoulder a portion of your pain." She pinned me with a hard stare. "We protect our family."

I dipped my head in acknowledgement of the sentiment.

Then it was my turn to say goodbye to Maz. We stood an arm-length apart on the dock, the sea lapping against the wood.

"Gods-damned strange," he said with a rueful smile. "Leaving you here."

I tried to tease him. "It's been seven years. Surely you could use a break from me."

"I never needed one, brother. But, Fucking Four, does it make my soul sing to see you so happy. To leave you in the home you always wanted."

My eyes burned, and I took a deep breath. "I wish the same for you, Mazkull. That you're able to lead a life that's not so dangerous or lonely."

"Ah, what's life without a little danger?" He shrugged his massive shoulders. "I'm sure I'll find some. But I sure as hell won't be lonely because I never was. All these years . . . I was always with my family."

I embraced him hard, slapping his back. "So was I."

He thumped my back as well, and we pulled apart, swiping at our eyes.

Maz cleared his throat. "I expect the finest room in the palace when I return."

I grinned. "And flagons of fresh Sunshine delivered every morning."

He roared with laughter. "See you soon, brother."

He walked up the gangplank, followed by his sisters. They waved from the deck as Skelly shoved off into the starry night.

Kiera slipped her hand in mine and continued to wave until the ship was out of sight. "It's not goodbye," she whispered, almost as if reassuring herself. "We'll see them again. Many times."

I kissed the top of her head. "Whenever you wish. We never really say goodbye to the ones we love. If our eyes don't meet, our souls will."

She looked up at me, hope warming her amber eyes. "I'm so glad I'll never have to say goodbye to you."

I smiled. "And I you."

We kissed under the stars to the tune of the waves, and I felt it for the first time in my life, just as Maz said.

I was finally home.

CHAPTER 69
KIERA

Wearing a royal gown, no matter how beautiful, was still a pain.

"You'll get sweat stains on the silk if you keep pacing," Melaena reminded me for the second time as she lounged on my bed, eating grapes.

I huffed and made to throw myself in a chair before remembering to sit carefully. Wrinkles were almost as bad as sweat stains.

"The wedding is in one hour," I said. "Delysia will never forgive me if she misses it."

Melaena shrugged one bare shoulder. Her strapless turquoise dress hugged her body like water. "Then we'll dawdle as best we can. The kingdom will wait for its queen."

"I'm not sure its king will," I grumbled, but I couldn't stop my smile.

King. Queen. Holy Four, this is really happening.

Melaena giggled. "Probably not. Aiden will storm the palace and carry you to the Temple if we don't show on time."

I kicked off my golden slippers. "Could be entertaining, though."

"When was the last you heard from your sister?"

"I received her letter two days ago. She wrote that she and Henry were on their way back from the southern coast. They were going to stay the night in The Hollow before getting here." I glanced at Delysia's curly handwriting in the letter on my table. "She seems very happy."

"I imagine she is. A sweet little wedding to our new High General followed by a honeymoon along Rellmira's finest coasts is very romantic."

I smiled, gazing out of my open balcony doors. A playful breeze toyed with my silk skirts, smelling of fresh grass and endless possibility.

It'd been two months since Aiden had proposed to me.

We would've married sooner, if not for his insistence that we construct another throne and crown for me first. My throne, the twin of his, now also sat on the dais, waiting for me. My crown was likely at the Temple, also next to his.

Meanwhile, construction continued on a more permanent bridge between the palace and the city.

I'd grown quite adept at crossing the rope ladder, but I was excited for the day I could walk on solid stone once more.

After Henry and Delysia had returned from cleaning out the Twaryn fort, with Wicked and Ozlow in hand, they asked to get married quickly and with little fanfare.

Aiden and I agreed.

Everett, even though he was one of their newest Teachers in training, helped perform the ceremony in the Temple. Librius, our High Teacher, presided. I brought as many fresh flowers as I could from Mother's garden.

I spent much of my spare time reviving the garden she loved so much. The only battles I fought anymore were against the weeds that never gave me rest. Aiden helped when he could, crawling on his hands and knees through the dirt, sweat on his brow, despite his new status.

More often than not, we ended up stealing kisses amid the lilies and jasmine and would run to the bathing pool covered in dirt.

It was sheer bliss.

With each passing day, we carved away more of Father's and Renwell's influence and memory and created something beautiful in their place.

I didn't feel the need to skulk through the crested halls as the forgotten princess or the shameful apprentice. I held my head high and greeted those I walked past with mirrored smiles. I strolled arm-in-arm with Aiden, laughing and telling him a story from my day and discussing everything under the sun.

I looked forward to every part of the day, meals with Aiden or with friends like Melaena and overseeing repairs to the city and the reintegration of former refugees and prisoners.

At night, I would attend a show at *The Silk Dancer* or throw knives at *The Weary Traveler* or lounge on the Temple roof. Always with Aiden.

Then we'd spend the last few hours of the day wrapped in each other's arms, whispering our hearts. Every morning began with a smile and kiss before the day's work.

I had never felt freer—or happier—in my life.

And today . . . Today I would get to promise forever.

Yet, this last hour was taking forever to pass.

I rose to my bare feet and padded around my room once more. I smiled at Aiden's dirty, everyday boots that he'd left by his side of the bed. He'd be wearing a new, shiny pair today. Waiting for me in the Temple.

Anticipation bubbled under my skin, and I cast about for a

distraction. "Have the votes come in yet?" I asked Melaena as she idly twirled her long black curls.

She pursed her lips, clearly pondering on what answer to give, which could only mean one thing.

I sank onto the bed next to her. "They did! Tell me."

"I didn't want to until after your wedding."

"I need a distraction, or else I'll keep pacing and ruin this dress." I started to rise in mock threat.

She laughed, pushing me back down. "Very well, very well. The votes came in and . . . I have been nominated as a People's Councilor for Aquinon."

I gasped, my hands flying to my cheeks. "Melaena! That is wonderful! Of course, I figured you would get it, but I'm so happy for you. And for Aquinon. You will do amazing things on the Council."

Pride shone in her eyes. "Thank you. It's such an honor to be chosen. To carry on the People's Council as my parents hoped for, that I've fought for. It's a dream come true, Kiera."

I threw my arms around her, dresses be damned. "It truly is. For all of us. Do you know the other councilors?"

We pulled apart, and she dabbed her eyes. "Yes. Helene was chosen as the other Aquinon councilor."

"That's wonderful!"

Helene and Isabel had arrived back in Aquinon over a month ago. Helene had been hard at work since, helping me and Aiden reform the People's Council, using Garyth's connections to find allies and root out any potential threats.

We'd also helped her rebuild her home, which she turned into an orphanage and rehabilitation center for former prisoners.

Melaena named the two councilors for Winspere and Pravara as well. "They all seem like lovely people. I'm excited for our first meeting next week. We have much to discuss."

"And we will be happy to hear it before our trip," I assured her with a smile.

Aiden had suggested a royal tour through the kingdom after we married. That way, we could meet with as many Rellmirans as possible to promise we'd wash away the decades of my father's influence.

We also planned a few destinations that had nothing to do with our royal duties. Such as stealing away to see where Aiden grew up in Twaryn. Perhaps climbing some trees and eating a few moonbloods as well. Going for another naked swim, but this time off the southern coast where the water wouldn't turn me blue, as Dagriel's had.

It sounded perfect.

Just as I was about to start pacing again, my door burst open.

"I'm here! I'm here!" Delysia cried as she bustled inside.

"Finally!" I leaped to my feet and embraced my little sister.

She returned the hug, then yanked away. "Your dress, Kiera!"

Melaena chuckled. "Don't bother. It'll be a miracle from the Four if she makes it to the Temple intact."

Delysia shook her head with a smile. "Some things never change. Now let's tidy up so we can get you married!"

I called my new maid—a young girl named Tessa—back into the room. She helped Delysia change into her wedding finery, a rose-colored silk dress. Then all three of them circled me, tucking, pinning, and smoothing until they declared me ready.

Tessa brought in a tall mirror so I could see myself.

The vision was stunning. My long brown hair was brushed to a shine, a few golden strands sparkling in the sunlight. I liked to think they were little gifts from Mother.

Melaena had accented my dark eyebrows and red lips in a way that still looked like me.

Gold earrings shaped like suns hung from my ears, and a

simple gold necklace looped around my neck. All of which had been Mother's.

My dress was a work of art. Sweeping lines of gold silk overlaid satin skirts of deep orange and crimson. The fabric shimmered with gold flecks whenever I shifted. I was a gilded flame, glowing with happiness.

My scarf—the one Aiden had made for me—was cinched around my waist, the dressmaker having incorporated it into her design.

I looked like every version of myself that I cherished.

The beautiful, hopeful princess, but with the scars from years of fighting and surviving.

Melaena had offered to further cover the scar on my cheek, but I'd refused. Nikella had never hid from her scars. She'd worn them as proof of how strong she was.

I wanted to do the same. I didn't want to hide anymore.

I was to be a queen, and I would live in the light.

"Mother would be so proud of you," Delysia whispered, blotting tears away from her cheeks. "And so am I."

My eyes burned, as did my heart. "Thank you, Lys. That means the world to me."

She sniffed, fanning her eyes. "Ugh, now my eyes will be all red and puffy. We'd better go put your beautiful betrothed out of his misery."

"You saw Aiden?" I asked eagerly.

"Yes, I left Henry with him, thinking maybe a few boring reports would get Aiden to stop pacing the Temple steps."

I grinned and hurried out the door with Delysia and Melaena on my heels.

A few guards escorted us across the partially constructed bridge to meet our carriage. I was eager to ride Ozlow again, but this dress wouldn't survive horseback. Besides, he seemed to enjoy his pampered life in the royal stables with Wicked.

We rolled through the city, many people waving as we passed, making their own way to the Temple for the wedding.

The Noble Quarter gate was open, as it had been for weeks. Guard still patrolled the quarters, but we no longer inhibited travel between them.

"Did your Dag friends arrive?" Delysia asked as we bumped along.

"Yes, about a week ago." I smiled, remembering the nights we'd spent with Maz and his sisters at *The Weary Traveler*. Maz had given the whole tavern quite the eyeful of his new tattoo—a black heart inked on his right ass cheek.

Their entire party was staying in the palace with us, filling the palace with their raunchy jokes and loud competitions. But Aiden was right—having friends, family, and love here had banished so many unhappy memories that I now struggled to remember what it was like before.

My heart beat harder and faster as we wove past the taverns. The Temple burst into view in a blaze of white marble and clanging bells.

The carriage slowed to a crawl due to the enormous crowd that spilled out of the Temple and filled the square to the brim.

Everyone waved and cheered, calling my name and Aiden's.

The enormity of what we'd done, of what we were going to do, crashed over me like a waterfall. But instead of fear, it brought clarity. Purpose.

This was my place in the world.

Guards cleared a path from the carriage to the Temple and helped me step out. Delysia and Melaena followed, adjusting my dress even as the mischievous breeze rumpled it.

I glanced at the sky. White clouds billowed across the endless blue. Perhaps Mynastra would send another storm. Perhaps not. But no storm could break me today.

I walked toward the open Temple doors, heart in my throat.

Once inside, the cool shadows breathed relief against my skin. The scent of lilies and sweet smoke soothed my mind while harmonious chanting stirred my soul.

A sea of people stood inside the Temple, packed around the soaring marble columns apart from one strip of floor. A walkway led to the middle of the Temple, bathed in a mix of torchlight and sunlight from windows out of sight in the dome.

A short journey surrounded by our allies that ended with the person I loved most in the world.

The moment I laid eyes on him, nothing else mattered.

I didn't wait for a signal. I forgot to acknowledge those who'd gathered to witness. I saw nothing but the man waiting for me.

I strode down the aisle.

Aiden's green eyes widened, and his lips parted as he drank me in.

His black hair was glossy and fell over his brow as it was wont to do. My fingers curled, desperate to dig into it. Even though he must've shaved, the shadow of his stubble still carved out his cheekbones and clenched jaw.

He wore a formal suit of deep violet, embroidered with gold. His father's ring glinted on his finger.

He descended the dais to meet me, stretching out his hand. I grasped it hard, my body trembling.

"You're more beautiful than the sun, Kiera," he murmured, his whole face glowing with admiration.

I smiled and, because I couldn't help myself, rose on my tiptoes and kissed his lips.

He returned the kiss as if he'd been starving for a taste of me all day.

I faintly heard a few chuckles and one whistle that had to be Maz.

We broke off.

"Marry me," I whispered.

"Forever," Aiden promised.

We climbed the dais to face Librius, who gave us a fond smile. Everett grinned at us from his place with his Teacher brothers and sisters in their long hoods. One girl wore Nikella's patched cloak—a gift we'd bestowed to a Teacher in need. Nikella would've appreciated that.

Librius lifted his hands and began a prayer to the Four, whose statues surrounded us.

I clung to Aiden's hand, barely hearing the prayer. Rather, I listened to my heart drum in anticipation, fancying I could hear Aiden's as well. Like the drums we'd danced to on Arduen's Night.

Finished praying, Librius nodded to us. "You may speak your vows now."

I took a deep breath and faced Aiden. "Aiden Falcryn," I began, trying to ensure my voice carried through the Temple. "I vow to be your wife for as long as my soul inhabits my body."

Aiden's hands tightened around mine as emotion flared through his gaze.

"I will be a light when you can't find your way in the shadows," I continued, my voice growing stronger as I shared the unscripted words. "I will fight at your side against every enemy. I will be your truest ally, your honest friend, and your most loyal counsel. I vow to trust you even when I'm afraid and to tell the truth, even when it hurts." I stared into Aiden's deep green eyes, finding all the love and acceptance I'd been looking for shining within.

"I love you," I whispered as a few tears escaped down my cheeks.

Aiden smiled softly and caught them with his thumbs, letting his own tears fall.

I swallowed hard and finished my vows. "We share our life as we share our breath. May the gods never find one without the other."

The crowd murmured in unison. "May the gods never find one without the other."

Aiden continued to hold my face in his hands. "Kiera Torvaine, I vow to be your husband as long as my soul inhabits my body."

The words rumbled through me like a storm, shaking me with their raw power. More tears ran down my cheeks.

"I vow to find you in my heart and in my world every day. I swear you will never be alone. I will endeavor to never cause you pain or worry, only to vanquish it. I will give you the life you deserve, with all the happiness freedom can bring." He rubbed his thumb over my cheek, his voice deepening further. "You will be mine, Kiera Falcryn, as I am yours."

I shuddered again. Gods, he was going to reduce me to a puddle of joy and desire in front of all these people.

His smile flashed. "We share our life as we share our breath. May the gods never find one without the other."

"May the gods never find one without the other," the crowd intoned.

Librius beamed. "By the grace of Viridana, the might of Terraum, the love of Arduen, and the mercy of Mynastra, you are now—"

I didn't hear the rest because Aiden stole my lips in a victorious kiss that rippled through my body like a glorious wave.

I flung my arms around him and kissed him back. My husband. *My husband!* The words kept echoing through my mind like the cheers of the crowd echoed through the Temple.

Aiden bent me over backward, kissing me like he had forever. Which we did.

When Librius cleared his throat, Aiden reluctantly pulled away from my lips.

"I hope you're not too attached to that dress, wife," he whispered in my ear. "I'll be tearing it off you the moment we get home."

Wife. Home. Those words were music to my ears.

Heat pooling in my core, I grinned. "That's the best plan you've ever had."

All of Melaena's and Delysia's fretting, and I simply hoped this dress would be ribbons by the end of the night.

Librius cleared his throat again. "We should get on with the coronation, if you please."

We faced him once more.

Librius said another prayer and beckoned my brother. They lifted the two crowns I hadn't noticed from a small table. Aiden's was the same as ever. He'd elected to keep the chips of sunstone as a reminder of a dark time our kingdom had survived.

Mine was beautiful as well. We'd designed it together. A gold sun crested in the middle, with waves of flames arcing away from it. Gold lilies twined around the band.

The sun was for Rellmira—and me, according to Aiden. The flames represented the battles we'd faced, but also the love that had never died. The lilies were for Mother. For me. And for all the women who had struggled for a place in this world. I hoped their example would guide me and every queen who came after me.

We spoke our vows to protect and cherish Rellmira. To guard its people and bring prosperity. Together.

Librius placed Aiden's crown on his head, and Everett nestled mine atop my hair. "Love you, little sister," he whispered.

I smiled through my tears.

"Very good. Now face the crowd," Librius murmured.

We obeyed, and he raised his voice to fill every corner of the vaulted Temple. "Hail King Aiden Falcryn and Queen Kiera Falcryn! Long may they reign!"

The crowd cheered and applauded, stomping their feet and whistling as they called out their allegiance and well wishes.

Aiden clasped my hand and raised it high.

I beamed and laughed, my heart welcoming every face in the crowd. Maz whooped and clapped his hands over his head, his blue eyes sparkling. Yarina, Sigrid, and Bruna shouted words I couldn't hear, waving. Ruru and Daire jumped up and down, their smiles bright enough to light the world.

Melaena and Delysia were a bit more dignified and much more teary-eyed. Behind them, Henry laid a fist over his High General's badge, a show of loyalty. Helene and Isabel waved—a green lizard perched on Isabel's shoulder.

Skelly and his bone-rattlers hollered their congratulations. Jek gave us a solemn nod, lifting Nikella's spear in salute.

And there were more. So many more. Soldiers, servants, and city folk that we'd come to know, who'd proven themselves allies. All cheering for us, for the life we promised, for the Rellmira we honored.

I glanced at Aiden to find him already looking at me with that heated look in his eyes that never failed to warm my soul.

Because, in the end, the greatest victory was love. And we would change the world with it.

BONUS EPILOGUE

Want to see *The Weary Traveler* scene where Maz shows off his new tattoo? Scan the code below to read it. You'll also be added to my newsletter where you'll get all kinds of perks!

- Access to my library of bonus content (a chapter from Renwell's POV, prequel chapters, and more!)
- First chance at ARC team signups
- Bookish news, sales, giveaways, and personal updates

READ MORE

FROM LEAH MARA

If you would like to read more of my books, please scan the code below:

Acknowledgments

Thank you so much for reading *Siege to the Throne*! I can't believe Aiden and Kiera's complete story is finally written and out in the world!

This was a joyful, yet painful, story to write. I was going through a very hard time in my life—grief, illness, and anxiety. I put a lot of my emotions into this story, and it helped heal me in a way. For that, I'm thankful.

I'm also extremely grateful to my husband for poring over every detail of this book with me and for being an unflagging supporter. You believed in me even when I didn't believe in myself.

And to my son, you are a light in the darkness.

To Eddie: I hope you're basking in the biggest puddle of sunshine <3

Thank you to Melissa, Jennifer, and Marilyn for all your edits.

Thank you to Bianca for the gorgeous covers.

And finally, to my readers, THANK YOU! It's one of the best feelings in the world to share my stories with you. Your love for my writing keeps me going!

ABOUT THE AUTHOR

Leah Mara loves to write stories where the romances are just as epic as the unique worlds they're set in.

She discovered the magic of reading at a young age, and once she learned she could create that magic with writing, she never looked back.

Leah also enjoys road trips, games of any kind, binge-watching TV shows, staying up way too late, and spending time with her family at home in Minnesota.

To learn more about Leah, scan the code below:

www.ingramcontent.com/pod-product-compliance
Lightning Source LLC
Chambersburg PA
CBHW031230310726
48971CB00004B/954